Praise for *Lady Jasmine*

"She's back! Jasmine has wreaked havoc in three VCM novels, including last year's *Too Little, Too Late*. In *Lady Jasmine* the schemer everyone loves to loathe breaks several commandments by the third chapter."

—*Essence*

"Jasmine is the kind of character who doesn't sit comfortably on a page. She's the kind who jumps inside a reader's head, runs around and stirs up trouble—the kind who stays with the reader long after the last page is turned."

—*The Huntsville Times* (Alabama)

Praise for *Too Little, Too Late*

"[In this book] there are so many hidden messages about love, life, faith, and forgiveness. Murray's vividness of faith is inspirational."

—*The Clarion-Ledger* (Jackson, Mississippi)

"An excellent entry in the Jasmine Larson Bush Christian Lit saga; perhaps the best so far. . . . Fans will appreciate this fine tale. . . . A well-written intense drama."

—*Midwest Book Review*

Praise for *The Ex Files*

"The engrossing transitions the women go through make compelling reading. . . . Murray's vivid portrait of how faith can move mountains and heal relationships should inspire."

—*Publishers Weekly*

"Reminds you of things that women will do if their hearts are broken. . . . Once you pick this book up, you will not put it down."

—UrbanReviews.com

Praise for *A Sin and a Shame*

"Riveting, emotionally charged, and spiritually deep. . . . What is admirable is the author's ability to hold the reader in suspense until the very last paragraph of the novel! *A Sin and a Shame* is a must read. . . . Truly a story to be enjoyed and pondered upon!"

—RomanceInColor.com

"*A Sin and a Shame* is Victoria Christopher Murray at her best. . . . A page-turner that I couldn't put down as I was too eager to see what scandalous thing Jasmine would do next. And to watch Jasmine's spiritual growth was a testament to Victoria's talents. An engrossing tale of how God's grace covers us all. I absolutely loved this book!"

—ReShonda Tate Billingsley,
Essence bestselling author of *I Know I've Been Changed*

Sins
of the
Mother

Victoria Christopher Murray

A Touchstone Book
Published by Simon & Schuster
New York   London   Toronto   Sydney

Touchstone
A Division of Simon & Schuster, Inc.
1230 Avenue of the Americas
New York, NY 10020

First Touchstone trade paperback edition June 2010

TOUCHSTONE and colophon are registered trademarks of Simon & Schuster, Inc.

For information about special discounts for bulk purchases, please contact Simon & Schuster Special Sales at 1-866-506-1949 or business@simonandschuster.com.

The Simon & Schuster Speakers Bureau can bring authors to your live event. For more information or to book an event contact the Simon & Schuster Speakers Bureau at 1-866-248-3049 or visit our website at www.simonspeakers.com.

Manufactured in the United States of America

10   9   8   7   6   5   4   3

Library of Congress Cataloging-in-Publication Data
Murray, Victoria Christopher.
    Sins of the mother : a novel / Victoria Christopher Murray.
        p. cm.
    "A Touchstone book."
1. African American women—Fiction. I. Title.
    PS3563.U795S57 2010
    813'.54—dc22
                                                        2009047706

ISBN 978-1-4165-8918-1
ISBN 978-1-4391-7228-5 (ebook)

Dedicated to E. Lynn Harris.

An amazing man, a wonderful mentor. Gone way too soon,
but you have left a legacy that fills all of us with pride.
Rest in peace, my friend.

One

"LOVE MAMA!"

Jasmine scooped her toddler into her arms. "You do love your mama, don't you?" She laughed.

Mae Frances rolled her eyes as Jasmine smothered her son's cheeks with kisses.

"Don't make no kind of sense, Jasmine Larson," her best friend said. "Teaching that baby to say that."

"What's wrong with him loving his mama?" But before Mae Frances could answer, Jasmine stood straight up and scanned the crowd that packed the new mall. In just seconds, her gaze locked on her daughter, crouched in front of the pet store window. "Jacqueline!"

The girl's brown curls bounced when she jumped up, startled, and skipped back to Jasmine and Mae Frances.

With a firm hand, Jasmine grasped her daughter's wrist. "I told you to stay where Nama and I could see you."

Jacqueline bowed her head. "But Mama," she sighed, "I could see you."

"Well, I couldn't see you, so why don't you sit down for a moment and cool off," Jasmine said as she wiped the thin line of perspiration that dampened her daughter's hairline.

"I'm not hot," Jacqueline protested. It was the look on her mother's face that made Jacqueline wiggle onto the bench next to Mae Frances. With her eyes on Jasmine, she buried her head on the shoulder of the woman who, years before, had been nothing more than a friend of the family, but was now so close to the Bushes that Jacqueline thought of her as her grandmother. When Mae Frances put her arms around Jacqueline, the girl glared at Jasmine as if she never planned to love her again.

Jasmine shook her head, then her eyes widened when her rambunctious daughter rolled her eyes.

No, she didn't.

Jacqueline had never done that before, and Jasmine opened her mouth to scold her, then just as quickly changed her mind. When her daughter peeked back at her, Jasmine rolled *her* eyes. Jacqueline giggled, and Jasmine laughed, too. But when Jacqueline moved to get up again, Jasmine stared her back down.

Jacqueline pouted and bounced hard against the back of the bench, but the silent tantrum didn't faze Jasmine. She planned to let her four-year-old (or fourteen-year-old, depending on the day) sit and think about how she'd run off.

"Are you ready to go home?" Mae Frances grumbled.

As Christmas Muzak piped through speakers above, Jasmine realized this trip to the mall wasn't the best idea she'd ever had. But how could she have missed this day? The new Harlem mall had been open for only two weeks, and this was the first big shopping day of the season; she had to make her own contribution to Black Friday.

Now as she looked at Mae Frances and Jacqueline—a set of ornery twins, with their arms folded and their lips poked out—she wished she had thought this all the way through. Because if she had, she would have come alone.

"I wanna go home, too!" Jacqueline exclaimed, as if she was in charge of something.

Looking at her son, Jasmine shook her head. "You don't want to go home, do you, Zaya?" she asked, calling him by the name that Jacqueline had given to him two years ago when he had been born. Hosea had been too difficult for her to say, and no one wanted to call him Junior.

"No, no, no!" Zaya followed his mother's lead before he toddled over to his sister. "Yaki, Yaki, Yaki!" He called her by his own made-up name.

Mae Frances sucked her teeth and tightened the collar of the thirty-five-year-old mink that she loved. "Don't make no kind of sense, the way you manipulate that boy."

"He's my baby. He's supposed to be manipulated."

"Get away from me, Zaya!" Jacqueline exclaimed, and pushed the toddler away.

"Don't do that to your brother," Jasmine scolded.

Jacqueline stood up, put one hand on her side as if she had hips, and, with the other, squeezed her nose. "He! Stinks!"

Jasmine sniffed, then hoisted her son up into her arms. "Your sister's right." She grabbed the diaper bag from the stroller and reached for Jacqueline's hand. "Come on, we've got to change Zaya's diaper."

Jacqueline folded her arms and sat back down next to Mae Frances. "I don't wanna go." With a pout, she pointed toward the pet store. "I wanna see the puppies."

"We'll see the puppies after," Jasmine said, still reaching for her daughter.

"Leave her with me." Mae Frances put her arms around Jacqueline. "No need for her to have to go with you when I'm here."

Jasmine's hesitation waned after just a moment. "Stay right there next to Nama," she demanded sternly. "And then we'll go see the puppies, okay?"

Jacqueline nodded as she scooted back on the bench. With wide eyes and an even wider smile, she blew Jasmine a kiss. "I love you, Mama."

Jasmine laughed. Her precious little girl—always the drama queen.

Inside the restroom, Jasmine twisted through the long line of waiting women, and as she made her way to the changing station, her cell phone rang. But just as she pulled her phone from her bag, it stopped.

She glanced at the screen. "That was your daddy," she told her son as she laid him on his back.

He giggled and reached for her cell.

"No," she said, taking it from his grasp.

His laughter stopped. His bottom lip trembled. His body began to shake. And before the first shriek came, the phone was back in Zaya's hands.

"Love Mama," Zaya cooed as he pushed buttons.

Jasmine laughed. God had blessed her with a drama queen and a drama king.

That thought made her pause in wonder. Who would have ever thought that she—Jasmine Cox Larson Bush—would end up in this place? She—the ex-stripper, ex–man stealer, ex-liar, cheater, thief. The jealous girl who'd done everything she could to sabotage the success of her best friend, Kyla. The unsatisfied wife who'd badgered her first husband until he'd finally left her.

The lonely woman who lived to tear husbands away from their wives. There was hardly a sin that she hadn't committed. But that life, those abominations, were far behind her.

Today, she was a proud wife and mother—the first lady of one of the most influential churches in the city. Today, her life was filled with leisure—it was difficult to call the work she did as first lady and the time she spent with the Young Adults Ministry a job. Today, each of her needs and every one of her desires were met. And she had a Central Park South apartment, a closet full of endless racks of designer clothes, and an upcoming New Year's family vacation in Cannes to prove it.

This life was God's reward for her having turned away from her transgressions. As she glanced at her reflection in the mirror, her lips spread into a slow smile. Bountiful blessings. All she could say was, "Thank you, Father."

Seconds later, Zaya was back on her hip, her cell was back in her bag, and she was back in the mall. But then, her steps became measured as she moved toward Mae Frances. Her friend's head was down as she pushed buttons on her cell.

Jasmine's voice was as deep as her frown as she yelled, "Mae Frances?"

She looked up. "Did you just call me?"

Jasmine let the diaper bag slip down her arm. "Where's Jacquie?"

Mae Frances waved her hands. "She's right over there. With the puppies. Did you just call me?"

Before Mae Frances had finished, Jasmine's eyes were searching the crowd. With Zaya still in her arms, she pushed through the mass of men and women, arms filled with packages, children close at their sides.

"Where's Jacquie?" The question trembled from her lips to a young boy in front of the pet store. "The little girl who was here—where is she?"

His face was pressed against the glass as he answered, "She's gone."

There was no time to question him further. A woman, two giant steps away, grabbed the boy's hand.

"Didn't I tell you not to talk to strangers?" the woman admonished as she dragged the boy from the window.

Jasmine's eyes were wide as she spun around, clutching Zaya to her chest, searching the space around her. It had been only a minute, but terror was already crawling up and down her skin.

"Jacquie!" she screamed through the holiday din.

She tried to keep herself in check as she gripped Zaya and barged through the pet store's doors. The stench of the animals did nothing to cover the fear that was already surging from her pores.

"Jacquie!" she shouted. She kept telling herself that this was nothing: Jacqueline had just wandered off.

Pressing up one aisle, then rushing down the next, she hunted through the crowd.

"Jacquie!" she yelled.

Jasmine grabbed a pink-apron-wearing teenager who was crouched down in front of the cages. "Please," she said to the young man, obviously one of the store's employees. "Have you seen my daughter?"

The blond spiked-hair boy glanced at Jasmine and then looked around the store, his expression telling Jasmine that her question didn't make much sense to him. "There've been a lot of kids here today," he answered before he returned to feeding the kittens.

"Jacquie!" she screamed one last time as she rushed back through the doors.

Outside, in the middle of the passing crowd, Jasmine turned slowly, exploring each face, searching every space.

"Jacquie!"

Her distress went unnoticed; the holiday shoppers were buried under their own cares.

"Jacquie!" Now her heart banged against her chest.

Both she and Zaya were crying by the time she hurried back to the bench. In the eyes of the woman she called her friend, Jasmine saw the same unadulterated horror that was in her heart.

"Where's Jacquie?" she screamed at Mae Frances.

Mae Frances shook her head. "She . . . she was . . . right there," she cried as she pointed back to the store.

But Jasmine didn't bother to turn around. She didn't need to look at the store or anywhere else in the mall. Because in the space inside of her where truth lay, she knew.

As "Joy to the World" squeaked out from the speakers above, Jasmine knew that her daughter was gone.

Two

PLEASE, GOD! PLEASE, GOD! PLEASE, God!

Jasmine clutched her now-sleeping son to her chest as she rocked back and forth on the bench.

"Mrs. Bush?"

Through eyes blurred with tears and terror, Jasmine glanced up and focused on the pair of blue-suited security guards.

"Your daughter is probably just lost," the black security guard told her again. "Children wander off every day. We have officers searching the stores, but like I told you, it would be best if you came with us to the office." His plea was the same as it had been just minutes ago. "It would be better to talk up there, away from this crowd."

But just like the last time he'd said that, her head was shaking before he finished. "No," Jasmine told him, her eyes still frantically scanning every passing face—as if the secret of her daughter's disappearance was hidden inside someone's expression. "I can't . . . because when Jacquie comes back . . . this is where . . . she'll look for me here." She glanced at the store straight in front of her. "She'll come back to see her mommy. And the puppies."

Jasmine and the guards exchanged glances, but she was the first to turn away. She had to—she couldn't bear to look into eyes that were filled with such sympathy.

A walkie-talkie crackled, and both of the guards turned away. Jasmine returned to her mantra, "Please, God! Please, God! Please, God!"

Over her shoulder, she heard soft sniffles, but she paid no attention to those cries. All she could think about were her babies—the one she held and the one that they had to find.

"Please, God. Please, God. Please, God."

"Okay, roger that." Looking at her with an even deeper sadness, the guard said, "Mrs. Bush . . ."

She squeezed her son tighter.

"It really would be best if we took you to the office."

"Maybe that's what we should do."

For the first time since the guards had joined them, Jasmine turned to Mae Frances.

Tears had left streaks through the makeup that shellacked Mae Frances's face. She said softly, "Let's go upstairs, Jasmine. We have to do everything we can to help them find . . ."

The venom in Jasmine's eyes pushed Mae Frances two steps back. But before Jasmine could spew the poison that was in her heart, she heard another voice.

"Jasmine!"

She whipped around and collapsed right into the thick arms of her husband.

"Hosea," she cried. "They took my baby!"

"I'm here now," he whispered as he pulled her down onto the bench and held her as tight as he could with their son in between them. "So, tell me . . ." he said to his wife, but his eyes blinked between Mae Frances and the guards.

He spoke with the calm that Jasmine was used to, but in his eyes, she saw something she'd never seen before—not even when his father had been in a coma. Now she saw a new fear, a new horror. And that made her tremble more.

Placing his hands square on her shoulders, he asked, "What happened?"

The images scattered through her mind: Jacqueline in front of the store, Jacqueline blowing her a kiss, Jacqueline gone—and hysteria rose within her. All she wanted to do was scream, cry, pass out, and stay unconscious until her baby came home. But she had to stay strong to find her child.

"I went to the bathroom to change Zaya," she began, giving Hosea more details now than when she'd called him twenty minutes before. "I left Jacquie with"—the name stuck in her throat—"Mae Frances. But when I came back—" Jasmine stopped. That was enough; he knew the rest.

"All right." Hosea jumped up from the bench. "What's being done to find my daughter?" he demanded of the guards.

"Everyone in security is on it, Mr. Bush." This time, it was the white guard who spoke. "What we want to do now is take Mrs. Bush and Mrs. Van Dorn upstairs to our offices. To get a formal statement. But I want to assure you that lost children are always found."

Hosea nodded. "What about tapes?" he asked. "The mall is filled with cameras, right? We'll be able to see if she just wandered off."

The guards nodded together. "The parking lots are covered, and we have a few throughout the mall. The stores are being contacted now, so that we can get their tapes."

"Okay." Hosea squared his shoulders and reached for Jasmine's hand. Helping her up from the bench, he said, "Go to the security office. Give them everything they need."

Again, she shook her head. "But suppose Jacquie comes back here?" she asked through fresh tears.

Hosea turned to the guards. "Can one of you stay?" It was a question that sounded more like a demand.

"Yeah, I can, but it doesn't matter. We have guards throughout the whole mall. We'll find her."

Hosea added, "Okay, then can you call for someone to escort my wife to the office." Before they responded, he explained, "I want to walk through the mall myself with one of you."

For the first time since this began, Jasmine felt hope. Her husband was here, taking charge. He was such a man of God. Surely he was praying. And surely God heard his prayers doubly.

Hosea directed, "Nama, go with Jasmine."

Jasmine opened her mouth to protest, but then she pressed her trembling lips together and willed herself not to say anything about cavorting with the enemy. She needed to help Hosea stay focused.

He lifted Zaya from her arms. The tears that came to her eyes were old and new as she watched her husband gently kiss their son's forehead before he handed the little boy back to her. As a third guard joined them, Hosea hugged Jasmine.

In his arms, she didn't notice the Christmas crowd, didn't hear the Christmas music. Just imagined that in a few minutes, Hosea would come rushing into the security office carrying Jacqueline with him.

Then he pulled away and urged, "Go ahead. I'll be back soon."

She nodded and followed the security officer, keeping her eyes away from Mae Frances, who was several paces behind.

She held on to good thoughts: she and Zaya waiting—Hosea bursting through the door holding Jacqueline—the four

Bushes reunited, never to think about these horrible minutes again.

Just before she stepped into the elevator, Jasmine looked over her shoulder to the place where she'd stood with Hosea just a minute ago. The last place where she'd seen her daughter.

He was gone.

Panic surged through her veins. But then she took a calming breath. Hosea was safe; he could take care of himself. And he would find Jacqueline.

As the elevator doors closed, she began her mantra again. This time, it was a duet. Because as she said, "Please, God. Please, God. Please, God," behind her, Mae Frances joined her in that same song.

Three

JASMINE GLANCED AT HER WATCH—an hour and seven minutes. That's how long it had been since she'd seen her daughter.

"You don't have any pictures?" the guard asked in a tone that let her know he was having a hard time believing that.

"I already told you," she sighed, feeling nothing but exhaustion, "I didn't carry my wallet because I was coming to the mall."

"That's when people carry their wallets," he said.

She couldn't believe she was having this conversation. What did this have to do with finding her daughter? "Look," she began, trying not to let her hysteria rise, "I carry as little as possible when I'm in a crowd. Just my license, a credit card, and a few dollars. That's it. Nothing else. No pictures."

The man nodded—now he understood, but his tone was still filled with frustration. "What about your cell? Everyone has pictures of their kids on their phone."

"I have a BlackBerry," she said, as if that was explanation enough.

"What? BlackBerrys don't have cameras?"

"Not the one I have," Jasmine said, her hands flailing in the air. "Look, what does any of this have to do with finding my daughter?"

"A picture will help, ma'am. We have to give something to the officers."

"I have a picture."

For the fifteen minutes Jasmine and Mae Frances had been in the Renaissance Mall security office, Jasmine had ignored Mae Frances. It was easy to do in the chaos that filled the small space. Besides her and Mae Frances, the office was packed with three other security guards and now two New York City police officers—a man and a woman—who had been dispatched to the mall. Everyone was talking—on walkie-talkies, on cell phones, to one another.

Mae Frances took cautious steps toward Jasmine. "I have pictures," she said to the guard. Then more steps. "I took pictures before . . . I think . . . I don't know how to use this phone." Her glance moved from the guard to Jasmine. "That's what I was doing when you were in the bathroom. The phone rang and it was your name, and I was trying to figure it out!"

Her explanation sounded like a plea for forgiveness, but Jasmine rolled her eyes and turned away. She heard Mae Frances's gasp, then a sob, but there was no care in her heart. There was nothing Mae Frances would ever be able to do. No way she could ever explain how she had let Jacqueline wander away.

Jasmine closed her eyes and began her mantra again. And she took herself back to that good place: Hosea and Jacqueline walking into the room—and this time, her daughter would be carrying a puppy.

The squeak of the room's door made Jasmine's eyes pop open. She jumped up. Her heart pumped faster. She prayed for the scene that played out in her mind to play out in her life.

Then . . . Reverend Bush walked in.

This man wasn't her husband. And Jacqueline wasn't with him. But there wasn't another soul on earth whom Jasmine wanted to see more.

In two steps, she was in her father-in-law's arms.

"Dad!" she sobbed into his shoulder.

"It's all right, baby," he said, his voice soft, soothing. "It's going to be all right."

She didn't move for a moment, needing to stay inside the comfort of his arms, his words. When she pulled back, she asked, "Hosea called you?"

Reverend Bush nodded as he looked around the room. For the first time, he noticed Mae Frances, and he rushed to her side.

Jasmine pressed her lips together as she watched her father-in-law give comfort to the woman who was the reason they were here. Her shaking stopped when Reverend Bush returned to her. "Mae Frances said that Hosea is searching the mall."

She nodded. "He said he's going to find Jacquie."

"He will," he said. "We will," he added.

She held his hand as he lowered himself into the chair next to her.

"So, what happened?" he asked.

She shook her head slightly, not wanting to go over this again. She would never survive if she had to continually dredge up the memory of coming out of that bathroom and instantly knowing that danger had made its way into their lives.

"If you don't want to talk about it . . . ," Reverend Bush said softly.

"It's just that . . ." And before she could finish, the door squeaked again. Jasmine jumped up—again. Her heart pumped faster—again. She prayed—again.

In walked Hosea . . . and he was alone.

The pittance of hope that she held in her heart vanished.

Hosea hugged his father before he pulled Jasmine into his arms.

"Hosea, what are we going to do?" she cried as she held him.

Even though his voice trembled just like hers, he spoke encouraging words. "We're going to pray. We're going to keep looking. We're going to find her."

She tried to believe him, but before she could find that kind of faith, the female officer said, "Mr. and Mrs. Bush, we need you to come down to the station. At the precinct, we can get a lot more going."

"But what about Jacquie?" Jasmine asked. "We can't leave without her."

"Officers will stay at the mall," the woman explained. "We just want to get the information out to the public as soon as we can. We need to get to the precinct," she reiterated.

This time, Jasmine nodded.

"I'll take Zaya home," Mae Frances said, her hands already on the stroller.

Jasmine whipped around. "Get away from my child!" Her scream silenced everyone. She ripped the stroller from Mae Frances's grasp, the force of it awakening Zaya.

"Don't you go anywhere near me or my children ever again," Jasmine yelled as Zaya's cries joined his mother's.

"Jasmine!" Hosea and Reverend Bush called her at the same time.

While Reverend Bush picked up his wiggling grandson from the stroller, Hosea eased Jasmine aside.

"Calm down, sweetheart."

Her mouth barely moved when she said, "I'll be calm as long as you keep Mae Frances away from me. Away from all of us."

Mae Frances's hand flew to her mouth to stifle her sobs. But her cries were clear as she grabbed her purse and scurried from the room.

Curious eyes were on her, but Jasmine didn't care. She didn't care what her husband or her father-in-law or any of these strangers thought. Mae Frances was the cause of her pain, and she would never be a part of their lives again.

Jasmine took a deep breath and reached for her son. She needed Zaya near. Once she quieted him down, she turned back to her husband.

"Okay," she started, composed once again, "let's go. We have to find Jacquie."

Four

THIS WAS THE DEFINITION OF insanity.

The detective jotted the same notes on the same pad, her responses to the same questions that he'd been asking over and over.

"Mrs. Bush, did you notice anyone in the mall?" "Mrs. Bush, was Jacqueline talking to anyone?" "Mrs. Bush, did you see anyone watching you and your children?"

"No! No! No!" was what she said, no matter how many times he asked her the same questions. Did he really think that, if she'd seen someone watching them, she'd have left Jacqueline alone with Mae Frances?

A short tap on the door interrupted the inquisition, and as the female officer who had been at the mall came in and whispered to the one who had been alone with Jasmine and Hosea for the last forty minutes, Jasmine pressed down the madness she felt rising inside. She wasn't sure how much longer she would be able to sit still inside this cold concrete room answering questions that did nothing to help find Jacqueline. She needed to be out there in the streets, in the hunt, searching.

Once they were alone again, the officer, whose name tag identified him as Detective Cohen, asked, "Now, Mr. and Mrs. Bush, do you know of anyone who would want to hurt Jacqueline?"

This time, Jasmine jumped out of her seat. "Of course not," she shouted, her impatience and hysteria winning. She pounded her hand on the rectangular table.

It was only Hosea's gentle squeeze of her arm that made her slowly return to her seat. But that didn't calm her. "No matter how many times you ask us the same questions or come up with new ones that are even more ridiculous, the answer's going to be the same. All you're doing is wasting time. We should be out there," she pointed to the closed door, "looking for my daughter."

The detective nodded, as if he had much experience with distraught mothers. "I assure you, Mrs. Bush, there is not an officer in this country who doesn't take the disappearance of a child seriously. We're doing all that we can. There are dozens of men assigned to this case already," he explained. "They're back at the mall, out on the streets, getting statements. It's just that we have to get all the information we can from you so that we can move forward."

When Hosea said, "We understand," Jasmine rolled her eyes. She wanted to tell her husband that she didn't understand a damn thing, but she pressed her lips together.

"Can you think of anything else, Mrs. Bush?" the detective asked in the same cool tone.

"No. Please. I've told you everything I know. You really need to be talking to Mae Frances. She's the one who was with Jacqueline."

"We're talking to her, too," he said, still cool, still collected, as if what she and Hosea were going through was normal. "Your friend is next door with one of the other officers."

"So what do you want with me?" Jasmine asked, folding her arms, intent on not answering any more questions.

Another tap on the door. Another interruption that made Jasmine want to scream—until Reverend Bush walked in with Detective Foxx, a police officer who was also a friend and a member of their church.

Detective Foxx shook hands with Hosea and then hugged Jasmine. "I just want you to know," he began, "that we're out there, full force."

"Thank you," Hosea said. "We've been talking to Detective Cohen," he glanced at the officer, "and he's been very helpful."

No, he hasn't! was what Jasmine was thinking. But then her eyes widened as she looked once again at her father-in-law. "Where's Zaya?" she screamed, and she pushed past her husband to get to the door.

"Calm down," Reverend Bush said, holding up his hands. "He's right outside with Sarai and Daniel," he said, referring to his assistant and his armor bearer. "Right outside this door."

"He's not with Mae Frances?"

Reverend Bush shot a quick glance to Hosea before he said, "No. Zaya's been with me the whole time, but I didn't want to bring him in here."

Jasmine nodded, but still she walked to the door and peeked outside. Sarai Whittingham sat in a chair across from the office, rocking Zaya in her arms, and Brother Daniel Hill stood next to her, her guard. Though for years, those two had considered Jasmine a gold-digging, trifling tramp because they thought she'd tricked Hosea into marrying her, Jasmine marveled for a small moment on how she now trusted them more than she trusted Mae Frances. She was sure that Zaya was safe, but she kept the door ajar as she turned back to the officer.

To Detective Cohen, she said, "I can't answer any more questions. I have to get my baby," she said, not knowing if she was referring to Jacqueline or Zaya.

"We're finished here," the officer told them. "I'll let you know if we have any more questions. We do need you to know that we're setting this up as a kidnapping case."

Jasmine's hand rose to her mouth. Of course that's what it was. But hearing that word aloud brought a pain to her heart that she'd never felt before.

"Now, it's still possible that she's just lost," Detective Foxx picked up, "hiding somewhere in the mall, but if that's not the case, we want to be on it early," he explained. "We're setting up a station at your apartment. I'm going to be there with another detective. We'll be waiting for a call."

Ransom. Jasmine didn't think it was possible to sink any further into the abyss, but she was falling, falling.

"Anything!" she cried. Tugging on Hosea's arm, she added, "We have to give them anything they want."

Detective Foxx said, "Jasmine, let's not get ahead—"

"But if we don't pay—"

"If anyone has Jacquie and they call, we're going to get them." Detective Foxx nodded. "Don't worry about that."

She took a breath and wondered how anyone could tell her not to worry.

Reverend Bush said, "In the meantime, I've set up a press conference. They're waiting for us outside."

"Pops," Hosea said, hugging his father, "thanks for that."

"Whatever we have to do." Reverend Bush looked straight at Jasmine. "We are going to find my granddaughter."

Jasmine held back as many tears as she could. She had to

face the cameras—it was the only way she could talk to her daughter.

Hosea turned to Detective Cohen and thanked him.

But Jasmine didn't have a single kind word for the man who'd wasted so much time. She grabbed her purse and stomped out of the room. Her mission: to get her son and then do everything in her power to find her daughter. Now!

Five

With Zaya gripped in her arms and Hosea by her side, Jasmine was set to go.

Taking rapid steps, the five adults marched down the long hallway toward the front doors of the 25th Precinct.

Over his shoulder, Hosea asked, "Pops, you're going to do this with us, right?"

Reverend Bush hesitated for a moment. "I'm not sure. I was thinking that maybe it should be just you and Jasmine. Jacquie's parents."

Hosea paused, making them all stop. "No, I think it would be better . . . it should be all of us." He looked at Brother Hill and Mrs. Whittingham, too. "If someone has Jacqueline . . ." He stopped as tears glazed his eyes. "If someone has Jacquie," he continued, "he needs to see that she has a family—so many who love her." Reverend Bush nodded, and Hosea added, "Brother Hill, Mrs. Whittingham, I want you there, too."

"Of course," they spoke softly, but Mrs. Whittingham looked straight at Jasmine.

In all the years that Jasmine had known the woman, this was the first time she had seen something other than contempt in her eyes. It was compassion, Jasmine was sure.

Mrs. Whittingham stepped closer to Jasmine, wrapped one arm around her shoulders, and said, "I know you want to hold your baby, but I'm here if your arms get tired . . . if you need me . . . for anything."

Her words, her expression, were so warm that Jasmine wanted to cry again. Why was it only tragedy that brought people together this way?

With the lineup decided, they all turned toward the front doors. Jasmine could see the awaiting faces of the press, lingering on the steps in the sub-twenty-degree temperatures. No matter the cold, they were hungry, Jasmine knew, for the details of a missing-child story. This was always a heartbreaking event, one that made great news.

How many times had she seen this scene play out on television? How many times had she cried with the parents as she sat in the haven of her home with Jacqueline tucked safely in bed? How many times had she thanked God that nothing like this would ever happen to them because they were under His grace and His mercy and His favor?

"Wait a minute." Reverend Bush stopped them right before they stepped through the precinct's doors. "Where's Mae Frances?"

"No!"

Hosea said, "Jasmine, we all need to stand together through this. We need one another."

"No!" she exclaimed again. "Aren't you listening to me? Don't you get it? This is all her fault!"

"Jasmine?"

Five pairs of eyes turned to face the voice. Mae Frances

stood just feet away, her mink wrapped around her, her hands trembling. It was clear that she'd heard every word.

"Jasmine, sweetheart." Mae Frances took two steps and paused. "I love you."

As if her son was in danger, Jasmine clutched Zaya closer to her chest, and with eyes as cold as her words, she said, "Just so we're clear—*you're* the reason Jacquie's gone . . . and I hate you."

Mae Frances shook her head from side to side. "Please, you can't blame me for this. I love her, too. She's my granddaughter."

"No, she's not." Her hate gave her courage to jump right into Mae Frances's face. "You're not related to us. You're just an old woman we pitied."

"Jasmine!" Hosea grabbed her arm, but that didn't stop her.

"We should have left you alone, left you to rot in that old apartment by yourself. Left you"—Jasmine sobbed—"the way you left Jacquie."

"That's enough," Hosea said, jumping in front of Jasmine as if he could block her words with his body. "Jasmine, please."

"I don't want her here," she cried.

"Okay," Reverend Bush said. He gave a slight nod to Brother Hill, and without words, his friend gently placed his hand on the edge of Mae Frances's elbow and, with little effort, led her back down the hall. Another nod, and Mrs. Whittingham followed Brother Hill and Mae Frances, leaving Reverend Bush alone with his son and daughter-in-law.

Six

Six cameras. From the three major networks, and from NY1, MSNBC, and CNN. Then there were the print reporters, a few holding microphones in their gloved hands.

There weren't as many newspeople as she expected—surely, she and her husband, with his award-winning television show and his position at one of the premier churches, should have garnered more attention. But then, she remembered that Reverend Bush had pulled this conference together quickly. In a few hours, there would probably be dozens of cameramen anxiously waiting outside of their apartment building, wanting to help get out the news of Jacqueline's disappearance.

Jacqueline's disappearance. Those two words made her shudder.

Standing in between her husband and father-in-law, Jasmine listened as Hosea cleared his throat.

"Thank you for coming today," he said, his voice strong as he began. "We just wanted to talk about our daughter, Jacqueline Bush, who was at the new Harlem mall this morning.

Jacquie disappeared around noon from in front of the Paws Pet Shop. She was wearing a pink velour suit . . ."

Jasmine leaned closer to Hosea and whispered, "With matching ribbons in her hair."

Hosea repeated what Jasmine told him, then continued, "And pink sneakers. She's about three and a half feet tall, and she weighs thirty-eight pounds."

Just hearing that description made Jasmine want to sit down right there on the steps and weep. This was surreal. This was ridiculous. This wasn't *her* life.

But with a might she didn't even know she had, Jasmine held back her tears. And then she wondered why. Maybe tears would be better. Maybe tears would be good for the person who had taken Jacqueline to see.

"We're asking for the public's help. Our daughter is only four, almost five. She's a gregarious, fun-loving little girl, who's as smart as a whip." Hosea paused, and when he continued, his voice wasn't as strong as it had been. "Jacquie knows her name, of course, and her address and telephone number. She knows the name of her school and her church and probably a dozen other things I can't think of right now. So if you see her, she will be able to identify herself."

As her husband continued, Jasmine peered into the faces of the journalists. The men and women wore the blank expressions of veterans—not a bit of sympathy, just professional curiosity.

"Here's a picture," he said.

The good parent, Jasmine thought, *the one who always carried photos of his lovely children.*

Then when he said, "Please," Jasmine heard his voice tremble, and she couldn't help it. She sobbed, and both Hosea and Reverend Bush put their arms around her.

"We just want our baby home," Hosea said quickly, as if he knew that his wife didn't have enough inside to continue standing there. "Please"—he held the picture higher—"if anyone has any information," and then he ran out of words.

Reverend Bush jumped in. "We want you to know that we're putting together a reward for Jacqueline Bush's safe return," he boomed in his pastor's voice. "We will be announcing that tomorrow. Thank you so much for your help in getting this story out. God bless you."

Hosea tried to nudge Jasmine away from the microphones, but at first, she wouldn't move.

Looking straight into the camera held by the CNN man, Jasmine squeaked, "Jacquie, if you can hear me, Mommy and Daddy love you so much. And so does Zaya and Papa." She gulped, but stayed steady. "We're going to bring you home, baby. Soon."

There was silence, at first, as if all were stunned by her words. This time, when Hosea took her arm, Jasmine moved. But they were just steps away from the podium when the questions, one over the other, rained down.

"Why hasn't an Amber Alert been issued?"

Hosea paused halfway down the steps to answer that one. "Because we don't have enough information or even a description . . . of anyone. Not yet."

He trotted down the steps, prodding Jasmine along a bit faster. But the reporters kept up, and their questions kept coming.

"Pastor Bush, do the police have any suspects?"

"Mrs. Bush, have you been contacted by anyone?"

The barrage followed them as they moved toward Reverend Bush's car, which was waiting at the curb. His driver had the doors already open for them.

Just before Jasmine slipped into the SUV, she was hit with one last question: "Mrs. Bush, with your history, do the police consider you a—"

She gasped, but Hosea closed the door before the word *suspect* came out of the reporter's mouth.

Seven

EMOTION AND EXHAUSTION MADE EVERY bone in Jasmine's body ache, but her eyes widened when she stepped into her apartment. The living room—the grand room—was filled with friends and members of the church. The chatter was soft, the mood solemn, the room heavy with the ambiance of a funeral.

Malik, her godbrother, hugged her first, and then Deborah Blue followed.

"I didn't even know you were in New York," Jasmine said before she handed Zaya to a teary-eyed Mrs. Sloss, the nanny who had been with the Bushes since Jacqueline was born. As Jasmine hugged Deborah, she thought about how glad she was to see her.

Deborah's husband, Triage Blue, was the other host and executive producer on Hosea's award-winning talk show, *Bring It On*. But Deborah was a star in her own right—a Grammy and Stellar Award–winning gospel singer, who'd just landed another number one hit with a duet with Yolanda Adams.

"I've only been here a couple of days. I'm supposed to leave tomorrow," Deborah explained. "But I'll stay, if you need me."

Jasmine's first thought was that of course Deborah would leave tomorrow; she wouldn't need her friend. Surely, Jacqueline would be home by morning. With all the people looking for her, with all the reports that would be on the news, Jacqueline would definitely be right back here tomorrow.

"Thank you," Jasmine said, this time squeezing Deborah's hand.

Deborah looked straight into Jasmine's eyes. "You do know that we're going to find Jacquie, right?" She didn't even wait for Jasmine to answer. "God is not going to let anything happen to that little girl."

Jasmine nodded but didn't get a chance to say anything because, in an instant, she was encircled by many more—Mrs. Whittingham, Brother Hill, other members of the church—all offering condolences, but at the same time telling her that God (and fervent prayer) was going to bring Jacqueline home.

"Do you want anything to eat?" Mrs. Whittingham asked. "There's plenty of food."

Over Mrs. Whittingham's shoulder, Jasmine eyed Mae Frances, far away from all of them. She stood in front of the mantel, staring at the photographs of Jacqueline and Zaya.

Just seeing that sight made Jasmine's fingers curl into a fist. How could that woman have the audacity to show up at their home?

But then her fingers relaxed. She couldn't afford to waste energy on Mae Frances—everything she had needed to be saved for Jacqueline.

"Jasmine," Mrs. Whittingham broke through her thoughts, "I'm going to fix you a plate."

She shook her head.

"You've got to eat something," the woman insisted, as if food would give her comfort.

"No!" Jasmine said, then softened when she added, "maybe later."

A voice made them all turn to the television.

It was Hosea's voice booming through the living room as his, Jasmine's, and Reverend Bush's high-definition images appeared on the forty-two-inch flat screen. Jasmine stood mesmerized as she watched a replay of their press conference. She stared at herself, and her own eyes stared back, filled with unadulterated fear. "I . . . I need a moment," she said, already moving toward her bedroom.

They all nodded, in unison, their sadness in accord.

Deborah reached for her hand. "Do you want me to come with you?"

"No. Just give me a couple of minutes." She paused and looked at everyone who'd come to bring her comfort. But she found no relief in their presence. They were a contradiction—speaking soothing words, while their faces were filled with their hopelessness. Their faces told their truth.

She closed her eyes, not able to look at anyone any longer. How could she, and still keep her faith?

Turning away, she took a step and bumped into Detective Foxx. She swayed, and he held her steady with his hands.

"Sorry," they said to each other.

Jasmine hadn't noticed the detective when she'd first come in, and now she saw the other man behind him, an officer she didn't know. The headphone-wearing man sat at the edge of the room, in front of a folding card table. His fingers danced across the keys of a laptop; he never looked up, not at all distracted by the bustle around him.

When Jasmine asked, "What's going on?" Detective Foxx reminded her that they were treating this case as a kidnapping.

"We're here just in case," he said.

Her legs wobbled, but his strong hands held on to her.

"This is a good thing, Jasmine," the detective assured her. "It puts more people on the case, including the FBI. Trust me, this is best."

"Yes," was all she could get out before she rushed to her bedroom. Slamming the door behind her, she leaned against it for a moment, trying to steady her breathing, steady her heart.

This was where she needed to be, this room, her refuge—her pristine, bright-white haven that had been purposefully designed to bring her peace.

She looked around at the tranquil space. Not that many hours had passed since she'd packed up Jacqueline and Zaya and they'd left for a normal outing. But she'd left with two children and returned home with only one.

Jasmine whispered, "Where are you, baby?" and tried to will her mind to connect with Jacqueline's. "Where are you?"

She glanced at the window and gasped when she saw that darkness had descended. The blackness brought new fears. Jacqueline was out there in the pitch-dark center of the night . . . alone. She wondered if her daughter was warm enough. Was she hurt? Was she scared? Was she calling for her?

Was she saying any of those prayers that the two of them said together every night? Was she singing her favorite song, about God having the whole world—and her—in His hands?

The questions were driving her mad. There was no way she could wait until morning for Jacqueline to come home. She wouldn't make it through another hour, another minute, another second without her child.

"Where are you, Jacquie?" she cried a bit louder. Louder. And then even louder. She screamed, "Hosea!"

Quick steps approached the bedroom, and in just moments Hosea was holding her in his arms.

"I'm here," he said, bringing her close to his chest.

But she fought to push him away. Comfort was not what she was seeking.

"We have to go out there; we have to find Jacquie," she cried.

"We have officers all over the city," Detective Foxx said, from the doorway behind them.

Jasmine looked up and saw the crowd standing at the edge of her bedroom, gaping at her as if she was the show. But she ignored them all and spoke only to her husband. "That's *our* daughter," she told him. "*We* have to go." She pounded her hand against her chest. "We have to go!"

"All right," Hosea finally agreed. "But you stay here. I'll go."

She shook her head. "No."

"Pops, Brother Hill, Malik, and I will go. You stay here with Zaya."

She paused. "Zaya?" Then a new panic rose—she hadn't seen her son in minutes. "Zaya!"

"He's in his room." Hosea tried to hold her again.

But still she cried, "Zaya!"

"Here he is." Deborah rushed into the bedroom, cradling Zaya in her arms.

Jasmine's cries didn't stop until she held him herself and settled onto her bed. She closed her eyes, rocked him in her arms, and imagined that Jacqueline was sitting right there. She imagined that the three of them were playing and laughing and singing just the way they'd done last night.

Her eyes were still shut when she heard the footsteps moving away from her, the gentle closing of the room's door. Then she felt someone next to her on the bed. She didn't have to open her eyes to know.

Hosea whispered, "There are a lot of police out there looking for Jacquie."

Her lips trembled as she fought to stay strong. "I know," her voice was as soft as his, "but no one loves her like we do."

Those were the words that made him agree. "Okay, I'll go. I'll take Pops, Brother Hill, and Malik with me."

She opened her eyes and thanked him.

He said, "Detective Foxx is going to be here, but I'm going to ask Mrs. Whittingham and," he paused, as if he knew Jasmine would need a moment, "Mae Frances—"

"No," she said, her agitation growing again. "She needs to go. She shouldn't be here anyway."

"Jasmine," he said, taking her hand, "she's part of our family. She's hurting, too."

"She needs to hurt." She spoke slowly, as if that would help Hosea understand. "She let Jacquie get away."

"Not on purpose."

"Like purpose matters."

He opened his mouth, as if he had a lot to say, but all that came out was, "All right." Leaning over, he kissed his son's forehead and then his wife's.

A new terror made her heart pound as she watched Hosea walk away from her until he disappeared from her sight. She wanted to call him back, tell him that she had changed her mind, that she wanted him to stay with her and Zaya.

But she took a breath and told herself that he would be safe; he would be back.

Jasmine laid her son on her bed, and then she rested next to him. But while Zaya slept, her eyes stayed wide open, even as she prayed.

And after she said prayer after prayer, she sang. Jacqueline's song. Softly, "He's got the whole world in His hands . . . He's got Jacquie Bush in His hands . . ."

Though she prayed, and though she sang, her fears stayed. She'd never been this afraid in her life.

Still, she kept praying. And singing. And hoping for tomorrow to come. Quickly.

Eight

"ARE YOU SURE YOU DON'T want me to go back home with you?" Reverend Bush asked his son.

Hosea shook his head before he leaned over and hugged his father tight. "No, Pops. I'll be fine. I just want you to be fine, too."

"Don't worry about him," Brother Hill said from the backseat. "I'll take care of your dad."

Reverend Bush said, "I'll stay with Daniel tonight, and tomorrow I'll go home and pick up some clothes. But I'm going to stay here, in the city, until Jacquie's home."

"Maybe . . . ," Hosea began, then paused. "Maybe you'll be able to go home tomorrow," he said with little confidence in his voice.

Reverend Bush patted his son on his back. "Even before then—that's my prayer," he said before he slipped out of the car.

Hosea watched as his father and godfather took weary steps to the front door of Brother Hill's Harlem brownstone, then he eased his car from the curb. When he glanced at the clock on the dashboard, he couldn't believe that it was just after ten. It felt more like days or even weeks had passed in the hours that he, his father, Malik, and Brother Hill had roamed through Harlem. At first, they had parked in front of the mall on 125th and wandered up and down the darkened side streets—stopping the few people who ventured out in the bitter cold night, showing Jacqueline's picture, talking to anyone who would talk to them.

But soon, their talking stopped, and they walked quietly together, sending up their own silent prayers. They walked and walked, prayed and prayed, until exhaustion and frostbite took over.

Pressing the Bluetooth button on his dashboard, Hosea dialed his home number; the phone rang once, then twice, then a third time. He knew that the police were just preparing—this could be the call.

"Hello," Mrs. Whittingham answered, sounding afraid.

"How's Jasmine?" he asked quickly, wanting to put her and the listening police at ease.

Mrs. Whittingham blew out a long breath before she said, "She's still resting. I've been checking on her, trying to get her to eat, but she won't move. Her sister called from Florida, but she wouldn't take the call. And now she won't even let Mrs. Sloss put Zaya in his bed."

"That's okay. Let him stay with her. She needs him tonight." *I need him tonight.* The emotions that he'd been pressing down all day began to rise. "I'll be there in a little while," he said, rushing off the phone, not wanting Mrs. Whittingham to hear his tears. He needed to be the strong one.

But how was he supposed to be when his mind was boggled with fear and rage? Someone had taken *his* daughter!

In his mind, he could see the culprit's neck. His hands

gripped the steering wheel, and even when he began to shake, he couldn't let go—the image of the faceless man wouldn't leave him. It took a mighty effort to edge the car back to the curb.

Long moments, deep breaths, and then his hands relaxed. Slowly, he opened his fingers and released the wheel. With his palms, he wiped away the tears that he'd been trying to hold captive, but the emotional water had escaped from his eyes anyway.

How could this have happened to his daughter? To his family? On his watch? He was the man, the head of his household, the provider, the protector. Yet he hadn't protected the most vulnerable among them.

He jerked the car back into traffic, causing the driver behind him to brake hard and blast his horn. Hosea could imagine the curses being thrown his way, but he didn't look in his rearview mirror—he just kept his eyes on the road.

There was no way he would be able to survive if his daughter didn't spend this night in her own bed.

Jacqueline had to be found now.

Nine

HOSEA PARKED, THEN DASHED ACROSS the street and up the same steps where he had stood with Jasmine and his father just hours before.

Inside, the station was bustling with police—male and female—moving about, taking calls, tapping on computers. The high energy was a contrast against the dark night—inside, it felt like the middle of the day.

At first, Hosea was just a figure, one among them until a female officer glanced across the desk.

"Mr. Bush," she called him.

Then every eye turned to him.

He hadn't come with a plan, and now he really didn't know what to say.

"Mr. Bush." This time, a man called out to him, from his right.

"Detective . . . Cohen."

The officer motioned for Hosea to follow, and in the room

where they'd talked before, the detective leaned against the table as Hosea sat.

"It's kind of late," the officer said.

Hosea nodded.

"Is there something you wanted to tell me?" the detective asked, as if he thought Hosea was about to make a confession.

"Nah, I just came by to check out what was going on."

The man closed his eyes, pinched the skin above his nose. "Right now, there are about sixty officers working this case— and that's just in this station. We're doing everything we can, but we don't have much—really nothing."

"I can't believe . . . nothing? What about the cameras at the mall? There has to be something by now."

The detective inhaled, then exhaled. "Seems like . . . well, you know the mall just opened, and it seems like the cameras weren't working . . . yet."

"What?" Hosea exclaimed.

The officer nodded, the ends of his lips turned down as if he was sorry. "They were scheduled to be checked out tomorrow." Hosea groaned, but Detective Cohen continued, "We don't have the cameras, but there've been lots of calls. Lots of leads."

That made Hosea sit up. "Anything?"

The policeman shook his head. "Like I said, nothing . . . yet. But we're following up on everything. Detective Foxx is still at your house, right?"

Hosea nodded. "My father and I were just searching the streets."

"That's not a good idea, Mr. Bush." The detective shook his head. "We're getting out photos, speaking to folks. We're doing our jobs."

"I know, and believe me, I appreciate all that you're doing.

But this is a job for you. For me . . . this is my life." He had to pause to keep the trembling from his voice. Then, "What am I supposed to do? How can I—" He stopped again. Calming down, he finished, "How can I go home to my wife?"

The officer nodded in understanding.

"I had to do something," Hosea felt the need to explain even more. "That's why I came by. But . . ."

"The best thing you can do right now is go home and get some rest. I'm going to want to talk to you and Mrs. Bush again tomorrow."

At first, Hosea nodded, and then he frowned. "Why? We've told you everything."

"Yeah, but sometimes after time has passed, people remember things." He put his hand on Hosea's shoulder. "Go home, Mr. Bush. We'll talk in the morning."

Hosea took steps toward the door, then stopped. Turned back to face Detective Cohen. Swallowed before he said, "Tell me the truth."

The officer frowned.

"What are the chances . . . that Jacquie will come home?"

In the second that it took for the detective to respond, Hosea had his answer. And the force of that fact knocked him against the wall.

The officer said, "If you want it, I'll give it to you straight." He paused, giving Hosea a chance to change his mind. Hosea nodded and Cohen continued, "There's a direct correlation between the number of hours missing and the chances of a child returning home. The more hours that pass, the less chance of the child being found." Inside his head, Hosea counted. In just a little while, Jacqueline would be missing for twelve hours. Detective Cohen continued, "And if it's a nonfamily abduction, well . . ." He stopped for a moment when Hosea held up his hand. After a second, the man continued, "But that doesn't mean that good things haven't happened. I'll give you a name . . . Elizabeth Smart."

Hosea inhaled as he remembered the young girl who had been abducted from her own home in 2002 but was found alive and well nine months later.

Detective Cohen said, "Elizabeth Smart went home."

Hosea nodded, grateful to the detective for that hope. This time, when he turned to the door, it was Cohen who stopped him.

"Mr. Bush, I have a question for you." The detective paused. "I asked you and your wife this earlier, but maybe now that she's not here—" He stopped again, as if he wanted to give Hosea time to think. "Do you know of anyone who would want to do this to your family?"

"No! Why do you keep asking me that?"

"Because like I said"—he looked straight into Hosea's eyes—"with time, people remember things . . . or decide to tell everything." His stare was still intense. "There're lots of reasons for child abductions; we need to explore them all."

Hosea said, "No one I know would do this."

The detective nodded, then shocked Hosea with, "What about you and your wife. Are things good?"

"Yeah." Hosea frowned.

"There's no affair that I need to know about, no disgruntled lover who may be trying to get back at you?"

"No!" Hosea shouted.

But Detective Cohen was unfazed. "What about your wife?" He kept the questions coming. "Is she happy, or are the kids too much for her?"

Quick steps took Hosea right up to the officer's face. "Get this, and get it right—no one that my wife or I know would do anything like this."

"Okay," Detective Cohen replied casually, totally unmoved.

"And neither would my wife or I. We love our children."

"Okay," Cohen said again, as if his questions and Hosea's responses were no big deal. The detective held up his hands, letting Hosea know that this was over, for now. "Like I said, I'm just doing my job."

Hosea stared the detective down. Still, he wanted to heave a table and toss it across the room. But the man leading Jacqueline's case was not the enemy. Even though Hosea was insulted by the insinuations, like the detective had said, this was his job.

Hosea marched out the door, out of the precinct. He was still furious when he clicked the remote to his SUV, but by the time he slammed the car door shut, his fury began to fade.

There're lots of reasons for child abductions.

As he twisted the steering wheel and moved away from the sidewalk, Hosea played the detective's words in his head again. And in the next instant, Natasia Redding jumped into his mind.

Natasia, his ex-fiancée who had come back in 2006 and wreaked all kinds of havoc in their lives—including the day she had disappeared with his daughter. At the time, Natasia had said that she'd just taken Jacqueline to the car to get some toys, but from that day forward, he'd never trusted her. And eventually, he'd had her removed as an executive producer from his show.

Then there was Brian Lewis, Jacqueline's biological father—although Hosea couldn't imagine Brian's being involved. He had given up all rights to Jacqueline—had told him and Jasmine that he wanted Hosea to raise his little girl. No, Brian would never do this.

Like he had told Detective Cohen, there was not a person in his life who would be involved in a kidnapping.

Still, Hosea swerved his car to the left, crossed over into the northbound lane, and headed back to the station. Maybe he and the detective needed to talk just a little bit more.

Ten

DETECTIVE COHEN HAD TOLD HIM he would handle the calls when Hosea gave him Natasia's and Brian's names. But there was no reason to wait.

He pulled his car to the front of the garage, but he didn't go inside. Not yet. He needed to check out some things before he went upstairs to Jasmine.

He made the first call; the phone hardly rang before it was answered.

"Mae Frances," he said.

"Have you heard anything?" Her voice quivered, as if she'd been crying. Hosea had no doubt that she had been.

"No news, yet. But I wanted to ask you, do you have Brian Lewis's telephone number?"

"No." He could hear her frown in her tone. "Why?"

"I want to give it to the police—they want to contact every-one."

"I don't have it, but Jasmine . . ." The mention of her name changed the subject. "How is she?" she whispered.

Hosea sighed. "Mrs. Whittingham says she's resting. I'm on my way home now."

"I cannot believe she won't let me stay with her," Mae Frances wailed, her voice louder now. "I love her as if I'd birthed her myself. And my granddaughter," Mae Frances sobbed, "I can't believe this has happened. You know I love all of you, don't you know that, Hosea?"

Hosea. He could count the number of times she'd called him by his name instead of by the nickname he wasn't too fond of—Preacher Man. But right now, he yearned to hear her say "Preacher Man." Because that would mean life was once again normal.

"I know you love us, Mae Frances. I know you love all of us. And I don't think this is your fault."

"But the baby was with me. And I looked down at the phone," she testified again, as if saying it over and over would make their lives better. "Jacquie was right there. And then she was gone," she cried.

"Mae Frances. Calm down."

"I don't know what I'm going to do."

"This is not your fault," he assured her. "Evil was going to find us no matter what."

"But why now?" she wailed. "And why the baby?"

Hosea closed his eyes as he asked, "Do you want me to come over there?"

"No, no, go home," Mae Frances sniffed, "Jasmine needs you. But please, call me . . ."

"Tomorrow, first thing. I'll let you know what's going on."

Then, with a sniff, Mae Frances added, "I'm going to find her, Hosea."

He frowned. "What are you going to do?"

"I know some people. And we'll find her."

He gave her the advice that he'd just been given. "Don't do anything, Mae Frances. Let the police do their job. If we interfere or get in the way . . . it could be bad."

She told him, "Okay," but he wasn't sure he really believed her. Not that she could really do anything. What was her plan—to roam the streets in her old mink, in near-zero-degree temperatures? No, there wasn't a thing that Mae Frances could do.

After another promise to call her in the morning, he hung up, scrolled through his PDA, and made the second call. He wasn't even sure if this number was good anymore, but he had to try. Glancing at the clock, he was glad that Chicago was one hour behind. Not that it mattered; he would have made this call at two in the morning if it would lead to Jacqueline.

As the phone rang, he pressed his cell closer to his ear, knowing that he would know the truth within seconds; he'd be able to hear it, if she answered.

And she did.

"Hello."

"Natasia, this is Hosea."

There was a pause, but then, "I'm surprised to be hearing from you. What's going on?"

The police were going to follow up on this lead, but he almost wanted to call Detective Cohen and tell him to save that time. Natasia Redding was a jilted lover, a disgruntled employee, a pissed-off friend. But she didn't have his daughter. He'd had Natasia's heart once—he knew her and would be able to hear any sign of guilt.

He said, "I . . . ah . . . just wanted to know how you were doing?"

She chuckled. "You mean you wanted to know if I picked myself up after you had me fired?"

Now he just wanted to get off the phone. "Maybe I shouldn't have called."

"You're right, you shouldn't have." And she hung up, saving him from having to do the same to her.

So Natasia wasn't responsible. And he still doubted Brian Lewis's involvement. So who had taken his daughter?

The image of the faceless man spun around in his mind again. And with that picture came his rage.

He peered through the car windows. Though taxis and other vehicles rolled down the streets, the sidewalks were deserted as the clock ticked toward eleven and the temperature plunged toward zero. With another glance to his left, then to his right, he bent over and fumbled beneath the seat until he felt the box.

As it rested in his lap, he fondled the gray leather exterior before he unhitched the flap. The nine millimeter gleamed under the overhead streetlight.

Hosea lifted the eight inches of steel from the pocket. He fingered the custom diamond-wood grip—the reason that he'd purchased *this* gun. The grip and the name.

It's called the Target, he remembered the dealer telling him.

That was what had moved him to spend over a thousand dollars on this weapon. He'd purchased and registered the gun right after his father had been released from the hospital almost three years ago. His father had spent months in a coma after being shot—caught between rival gangs . . . at least that's what the police still told them. There had never been an arrest, which was one of the reasons why Hosea had bought the revolver.

With a little girl (and now a son) he hated having a gun in his possession. But if the police couldn't protect his family, then he would do it.

But he had failed. He had the gun, and even more than

that, he had his name, his father's name, and one of the biggest churches in New York—and still his daughter had been abducted.

Feeling as useless as the gun had been, Hosea tucked the box back under his seat and worked to press his fury down. It did no good to think about what he'd failed to do. All he needed to focus on was doing everything right now.

That was all that mattered.

Eleven

JASMINE HEARD THE CRIES.

"Mama!"

They were faint, at first. Then louder. And louder.

"Mama!"

Jasmine's eyes fluttered open.

"Jacquie," she whispered as she shot up straight in the bed. "Jacquie!" She jumped up and stumbled through the dark.

"Jasmine?" Hosea called. "What's wrong?"

"Jacquie! She's home."

Rushing across the living room, Jasmine didn't notice the two policemen who slept—one on the sofa, the other on the love seat. She dashed past them, hurrying to her daughter's room.

Thank God! was all she could think.

Thank God this had all been a dream. A bad dream. But now her daughter was home. Safe.

Jasmine swung open the door to Jacqueline's bedroom and inhaled the scent of the fresh baby powder that lingered. She ran to the bed. Tossed back the covers. And stared at the pink sheets.

"Jacquie?" she called softly. "Jacquie?" she said a little louder now. She threw the cover on the floor, got on her knees, searched under the bed. "Jacquie?" Frantically, she stood and ran to the closet. "Jacquie?"

Behind her, she heard rushed footsteps. She twisted, looked into her husband's eyes, and she realized it hadn't been a dream.

The reality made her wail, "Jacquie!"

Her knees buckled, but Hosea caught her before she hit the floor. Slowly, he eased her down and held her as she screamed her daughter's name. Jasmine never saw Detective Foxx and the other detective as they ran into the room. She never saw Hosea wave them away.

She saw no one, saw nothing through her tears.

"My baby, my baby!"

"I know," Hosea said softly. "I know."

"Jacquie," she cried as he held her.

Soon he was calling their daughter's name with her. And as Jasmine cried, matching tears rolled down his cheeks. She raised her arms and held him, too.

And they cried.

Together.

On the floor.

For hours.

Together.

Twelve

TOMORROW HAD COME.

And Jacqueline was not home.

Jasmine rushed down the hallway of the NBC studios, Hosea's steps far behind hers. She stopped in front of the GUESTS sign and swung the door open. Her pounding heart slowed the moment she saw Reverend Bush and Mrs. Sloss standing guard over Zaya as he slept in his stroller.

Releasing a deep sigh, she pulled her son into her arms.

Reverend Bush said, "I told you, sweetheart, nothing's going to happen to him. I promise."

She had no idea how—after everything that had happened—anyone could make any kind of promise. But she said nothing as she rocked Zaya in her arms. He squirmed and whined, as if he didn't want to be disturbed, but Jasmine didn't care that she'd awakened him. She needed to feel his heartbeat against her own.

"Ssshhhh," she purred as she walked back and forth across

the room. "It's all right," she said, more to herself than to her son.

It had been torture to leave him for the minutes she and Hosea had been on camera, just as torturous as when they had stopped at ABC and CBS earlier.

She'd been so hopeful when Reverend Bush had called while darkness still owned the sky, and had told Hosea that he'd arranged for interviews on all three networks.

"The weekend shows don't have the audience that the weekday shows have," Hosea had repeated his father's words to her, "but I'm sure they'll replay it tomorrow, and on Monday, if Jacquie isn't home before then."

But a battle began when Jasmine jumped from the bed and began to dress Zaya to go with them.

"We can leave him here," Hosea had said. "We'll only be gone a couple of hours."

"Are you crazy?" she had asked her husband in a screaming fit. "I am not leaving my child!"

"He's not going to be alone, Jasmine. Mrs. Sloss, the detectives, they'll all be here to protect him."

"No!"

"If you want, I'll even have Pops come over, but Zaya will be safer here than anywhere."

Even as he'd given her reason on top of reason, Jasmine had ignored her husband and bundled up their sleeping son. She didn't care if Colin Powell was standing guard—her son would be safe only with her.

The second fight began when they arrived at the ABC studios. She and Hosea had settled into the Green Room with Reverend Bush and Mrs. Sloss when the producer came for them. Holding Zaya in her arms, Jasmine had stood to follow the headphone-wearing woman.

"Ah," the producer began, "you can leave your son in the Green Room. It's best if it's just you and your husband on camera, in case your son wakes up."

"He'll be fine," Jasmine said.

The producer's insistence made Jasmine give in, but only after she had Reverend Bush's assurance that his grandson would never leave his sight. She repeated her fight at CBS and then NBC; but at each network, she'd had to acquiesce. It was all over now, however. She could go home where she could safely watch over Zaya and pray for Jacqueline.

Exhaustion finally made her sit down. Hosea crouched in front of her, his face etched with the same exhaustion that she felt. She was certain that her eyes were as bloodshot as his, but she wasn't sure if the weary redness they shared came from the hours they'd spent crying, or from the restless hours that followed when they'd lain awake in bed, as Zaya slept between them.

"Are you okay?" he whispered.

She nodded. "I'm fine, just tired." She looked down at their son. "Ready to take my baby home."

He said, "We have to make another stop first." Her frown made him add, "We have to stop by the police station."

She searched his eyes, wanting to know if there was more to his words. "Is it about—"

"No!" He shook his head. "I mean, yes. They want to talk to us some more about Jacquie. But there's nothing new, not yet." He looked down at his cell phone. "I got a message from Detective Cohen; he saw us on the morning shows and has a few questions."

Laying Zaya back in his stroller, she said, "I've told him . . . you've told him everything."

"I know, but if it will help in any way, we can't answer enough questions."

She nodded. Of course she would go to the station. Anything. Whatever. Everything she could do.

As she slipped into her coat, she said, "Zaya is coming with us."

Hosea had no arguments left. He just nodded and glanced at his father before he reached for the stroller and followed Jasmine out the door.

Thirteen

They were back—in the same room, in the same chairs, where they had sat less than twenty-four hours ago. Like before, Detective Cohen was on one side of the rectangular table, across from Jasmine and Hosea—only this time, Zaya's stroller was right at Jasmine's side.

"Thank you for coming back down." Detective Cohen leaned forward, his arms resting flat on the table. "I know this is a lot—"

"Anything to find Jacqueline," Hosea interrupted, and reached for Jasmine's hand.

"I really don't know why we're here," Jasmine said. "If you don't have any news on Jacquie, and we've already told you—"

"I understand, Mrs. Bush," the detective interrupted. "This may seem redundant, but we're following up on every lead. And sometimes it helps to go over some of these leads with the people involved."

Hosea leaned forward. "Do you have—"

Before Hosea could finish, the door behind them opened.

They all turned to face another of the detectives Jasmine recognized from yesterday.

"Sorry to interrupt," he said to all of them. Then, to Hosea, he asked, "Can I get you out here for a moment? We have some . . . paperwork . . ." He stopped, as if that was enough.

Hosea frowned, and Detective Cohen nodded. "Go ahead. I can go over these things with your wife."

Before he could even ask, Jasmine waved him away. "I'm fine."

He kissed her cheek before he stood and left the room.

With a sigh, Jasmine leaned back in the chair.

The detective said, "I know this is difficult, Mrs. Bush."

Nodding, she looked down at her son, sleeping, as if their world was normal. Serenity was all over his face. Her heart ached as she stared at her son and saw her daughter. Not that her children looked too much alike—the brother and sister had each taken on the features of their respective fathers, and therefore they didn't look much like siblings at all. But the way they slept—that was the same. Eyes closed, mouths open, lips upturned just a bit. As if they saw angels in their dreams.

Even now, Jasmine imagined Jacqueline sleeping, and she prayed that at this very moment her daughter was just like her son. Resting. Filled with peace.

The detective drew her back into his world. "Is there anything you can think of, Mrs. Bush? Anything else that you want to tell me?"

"I don't know what you want from me." The words felt heavy as they left her mouth.

The detective glanced down at the piece of paper he held. "Mrs. Bush, do you mind if I read you something?"

Without taking her eyes from her son, she said, "Go 'head."

A beat passed, then, "This is an e-mail that came into the station this morning."

Still, she didn't look up.

"The woman who sent this said that she attends your church."

Jasmine pulled the blanket that covered Zaya up to his chin.

"She starts off by saying that she knows what happened to Jacqueline."

Jasmine jerked, her attention now on Detective Cohen. "Someone knows where—"

He held his hand up, stopping her. "She says . . . well, let me read this."

Jasmine leaned onto the table, trying to get closer to the detective, wanting to hear every word.

He focused on the paper he held, then slowly raised his eyes. Looked straight at her. "'Jacqueline was murdered.'"

Her tears—the shock—were instant. Her hand flew to her mouth, covering her cries.

Jasmine panted, but the detective kept going. "'Her mother killed her—'"

"What?" She squinted. His words—her thoughts—were confusing.

As if Jasmine hadn't spoken a word, the detective continued, "'Because Pastor Bush is not the girl's father.'"

"What?" she asked again, this time a bit louder. "What is this?"

His eyes didn't leave the paper; he kept reading, "'And now that they have their own child, Jasmine didn't want to live with the memory of what she had done.'"

The legs of the chair squeaked as Jasmine jerked back, jumped up, and reached across the table, ready to snatch those lies away from the detective. But with just a little shift, he was able to keep the paper beyond her grasp.

"Give that to me!" she yelled. "How could you read that?

How could you make me sit here and have to listen to those lies when my daughter—"

"Lies?" His eyebrows rose, though his voice stayed even. "Are you sure they're lies, Mrs. Bush?"

Now she wanted to reach across the table and grab him. Choke him until he stopped asking those stupid questions and spewing those lies.

But she stood frozen in her space, with trembling lips. "You . . . you couldn't possibly believe that I had anything to do—" It was hard for her to breathe. "No!" She shook her head.

"No what?"

"That letter—it's a lie. I would never hurt my daughter," she cried.

He leaned forward, his voice softer now. "Maybe you didn't want to. Maybe it was an accident."

Her head whipped from side to side. "No," she yelled, her cries now mixing with those of Zaya, who had been startled awake.

"I could understand it, Mrs. Bush." He stayed soft and gentle, as if he was her friend.

"No." She fell back and down onto the chair.

"It's happened before," he said. "An accident, the mother panics. Then she gets her friends involved, and they make it look like someone took her child."

She was crying as hard as her son.

"You know, if you have a temper, and you lost control—"

"I would never hurt my daughter," she whimpered. "I would never—"

The door behind her swung open. "Jasmine!"

She jumped up and into Hosea's arms.

"What's going on?" As he held his wife, his eyes searched the detective for answers.

Detective Cohen leaned back in his chair as if nothing had happened. "We were just talking."

Jasmine sobbed into Hosea's chest. "He said . . . the e-mail . . . that I . . . killed . . ." She couldn't say any more.

The officer leaned forward and offered Hosea the paper. "I was just sharing with your wife an e-mail we'd received."

As Jasmine's cries mixed with his son's, Hosea scanned the note.

He stiffened as he read the words, and then he hurled the e-mail back at the detective. For seconds, it floated like a paper airplane, and the three watched until it landed at Cohen's feet.

Hosea's eyes didn't leave the detective's. "Jasmine, get your coat," he whispered.

She was still gasping for breath as she tossed her coat over her arm. Behind her, Hosea quieted their son before he turned the stroller toward the door.

The detective said, "Mr. Bush, I would like to talk to you. I have some—"

Hosea was shaking his head before the officer could finish. "That's not gonna happen," he said. With a stare that was meant to intimidate, he growled, "The next time you want to talk to us, do it through our attorney."

Jasmine held the door open, and the Bushes marched out of the room.

Fourteen

HOSEA'S HANDS STILL SHOOK AS he strapped Zaya into the car seat. His son had calmed, but not his wife. And neither had he.

Slipping into the driver's side, he pointed the key toward the ignition, but then stopped. He had to take a deep breath, find a way to cool down before he took his family anywhere.

His family.

That thought made him glimpse into the rearview mirror. He half expected to smile, the way he always did when he glanced at his daughter. But the sight of her empty car seat behind him tugged hard at the strings that were barely holding his heart in one piece.

Quickly, he diverted his eyes. Swallowed hard. Tried to keep himself together.

"I can't believe what that man did," Jasmine gasped. "Who would do that, Hosea? Who would send that e-mail?"

He dropped the keys in his lap and took her hand. "I don't know." He spoke softly, trying to keep his own emotions hidden.

"I don't know what that was about. I don't even know if there was really an e-mail," he said, remembering that it had been a Yahoo account, so there would be no way to trace it.

"What do you mean?" she asked. "Do you think they just made that up? Printed up something to trick me?"

He shrugged. "It's been done before. But if that's the way the police want to play it, I guess we're gonna have to do this on our own."

"How? We can't find Jacquie by ourselves. The police have to help us."

Again, he swallowed, pushing back the helplessness he felt rising within. He couldn't lose it now—he was the head of the family, the protector.

His family.

This time, he kept his eyes away from the backseat as he unhooked his cell phone from its holster. He held the device to his ear, and not even two seconds passed before the phone was answered.

"Any news, son?" Reverend Bush asked without even saying hello.

Even though his father couldn't see him, Hosea shook his head. "Nah, but we've run into some trouble." With as few words as he could, he told his father about the confrontation. When he mentioned the e-mail, Jasmine sobbed, and he reached for her hand.

Reverend Bush said, "I received that e-mail, too."

What! Hosea screamed inside. But he only said, "Really?" thinking about his theory that the e-mail had been fake. If it had been sent to his father, then it was real.

"Yeah," Reverend Bush said. "I've gotten quite a few calls. It seems that whoever started it asked people to forward it. And apparently the folks who attend City of Lights don't think before they press Send because it's going all around the church."

The reverend sighed. "I can't believe Jasmine has to deal with this on top of—"

"I know," Hosea said, peeking at his wife once again. He didn't know what Jasmine would do once she found out that the e-mail was real—and circulating around the church and probably beyond. "Look, Pops," he began, his voice lower now, "I don't know what that was all about, but . . ." He stopped right there.

It was all the years that they'd been bonded as father and son that made Reverend Bush respond without Hosea needing to finish his thought. He said, "We need to get right on this. Where are you and Jasmine now?"

"We're heading home."

"No, come here first," his father said. "Dale's with me now; we were going over some ways to galvanize the community, but we need to talk about this."

Hosea closed his eyes. He was relieved and glad that he didn't have to say it. Glad that his father had brought up their lawyer, Dale, himself.

"We're on our way." He clicked off the phone, and when Jasmine's eyebrows bunched into a frown, he answered her un-asked question. "Pops wants us to drop by the church." He put the key into the ignition but paused before starting the engine. "Dale Brody's with him now, and Pops thinks it may be a good idea for us to talk to him."

They stared at each other, and without a word Hosea knew Jasmine's question: Did they really need a lawyer?

Then she asked, "No one is going to believe that e-mail, right?"

"Of course not," he said, but he couldn't look in her eyes when he told that lie. He breathed easier when Jasmine leaned back and closed her eyes. As he turned the key, then twisted the steering wheel and eased into traffic, he shook his head.

This was not the way all of this should be going down. They—the entire city—were supposed to be united behind finding Jacqueline. But instead, they were dealing with stupidity.

This is ridiculous! That anyone would even believe Jasmine would harm Jacqueline—it was the most absurd accusation that could be made.

But Hosea had seen situations like this before—had watched innocent people accused and tried without any evidence.

As he drove, he prayed. And he thanked God that Dale Brody, one of the premier attorneys in the city, was not only their friend but their legal protector as well.

Because he had a feeling that he and Jasmine were going to need every bit of legal protection they could get.

Fifteen

JASMINE WALKED BECAUSE SHE COULDN'T SIT. She paced the width of the church office—back and forth, in front of the oversize mahogany desk where Reverend Bush sat. Hosea leaned against the desk's edge, his arms crossed as he listened to the attorney.

"This is not unusual," Dale Brody said again, as if repeating those words would make them feel better about what they were going through.

Forming a triangle with the tips of his fingers, Dale explained, "The detective's questions are normal."

"That doesn't make a lot of sense, Dale," Reverend Bush said. "How could they have taken that e-mail seriously?" He shook his head. "Come on. As soon as they saw that the sender was named Jane Doe, and that it came from one of those free accounts, they should have thrown it away."

"Jane Doe?" Jasmine frowned.

The reverend nodded.

Hosea snapped, "You mean to tell me the e-mail that went

to the police was from a Jane Doe?" His eyes were wide as he looked at his father. "I didn't even look at the name; I was so mad." He turned to their attorney. "And that detective had the nerve to go after Jasmine with that?"

Those were her thoughts, too, but Jasmine said nothing, just kept walking. Back and forth. Just kept wondering how many other people in the church had received that e-mail and if any of them had noticed the name. Not that the name would matter. There weren't too many members of City of Lights who liked her, and she would bet that most would even love to see her demise. If that e-mail was circulating, most would believe the worst about her.

"Frankly, Jasmine hasn't been accused of anything," Dale said.

"I need to find out who sent that e-mail," Hosea growled.

Dale shrugged. "First of all, it's from one of those untraceable accounts. And what does it matter? We need to see this through the detective's eyes. Whether he received that e-mail or not, he was going to be looking at you two first. Any time a child is missing, the parents are the first suspects."

"Suspects? That's crazy," Jasmine cried. "How could anyone believe that I would hurt my child?" She pressed her hand over the center of her chest, feeling like that was the only way to keep her heart inside.

"Darlin', anyone who knows you knows that you didn't have anything to do with this."

"Tell that to whoever wrote that e-mail." She looked at the attorney. "How can someone just spread a lie like that?"

"The Internet's not governed." He shrugged. "It's used all the time to spread lies and hate. Look at what happened to Obama before he was elected. People were circulating amazing lies about him, and that stuff is still going on. So I guess if it could happen to the president, it can certainly happen to you."

Jasmine glanced over at the open office door, peeked out to where she'd positioned Zaya's stroller right outside. Behind the stroller, she saw Mrs. Whittingham standing guard over her baby. Satisfied that her son was safe, she slumped into the chair in front of Reverend Bush's desk.

Dale continued, "But here's the thing—once they look at you and Hosea, once they look at your family, everything will point to Jacqueline's having a happy home life."

"It's ridiculous that they're looking at Hosea and me at all," Jasmine whispered. "That man treated me like I was guilty."

"Standard stuff."

"He even asked me if I had a temper."

"A typical interview."

"Didn't feel typical to me," Jasmine snapped.

"Look, I'm just trying to explain it," Dale said. "The fact is that in sixty percent of these cases, the parents *are* responsible for the child's disappearance or murder."

Jasmine shook her head. "Jacquie is not dead," she said, her tone absolute.

Three pairs of eyes stared back at her. Three pairs of eyes that were filled with doubt. But she didn't care what they thought. She was Jacqueline's mother, and these men didn't know what she knew.

She explained, "I gave birth to her." Looking straight at Hosea, she added, "I know. I can feel it here." She pressed her hand against that place where she'd carried her daughter. How could she explain that a little piece of Jacqueline was still there? She said, "She's alive."

Reverend Bush looked away—for a moment. Dale looked down—for a moment.

Only Hosea kept his eyes on her; he walked to where she sat, crouched down, took her hand, then asked Dale, "So what do we do now?"

"We play offense." The attorney paused. "You're not going to like this," he added, moving his glance from Jasmine to Hosea to Reverend Bush, "but it's the only way to get the police back to where they need to be—focusing on finding Jacquie." He said, "Take a polygraph. Both of you."

The Bushes spoke at the same time.

Hosea said, "Okay."

Jasmine said, "No!" With wide eyes, she looked at her husband. "No! I haven't done anything. *We* didn't do anything. This is crazy! They just need to be out there looking for Jacquie."

"That's exactly why we have to do this." Hosea spoke with a calm that wasn't evident on his face. "We don't need to waste any more time."

"*This* is a waste of time," Jasmine said, her voice louder now, her hands flailing in the air. "We are locked up in this church talking about polygraphs, and no one is out there looking for our daughter," she cried.

"That's not true, Jasmine," Dale interjected. "You better believe the police are still searching; they haven't stopped. It's just that they're going to ask you to take a polygraph anyway, so we might as well do it now."

Dale snapped his briefcase shut as if the subject was closed. "Let me go down to the station, talk to the folks in charge, and I'll get back to you."

He shook Reverend Bush's hand before he turned to Hosea and Jasmine. He said, "This is really for the best."

She wasn't even sure where the tears were coming from; she had to be on empty by now. But before Dale was out the door, tears were making tracks down her cheeks.

Gently, Hosea pulled her into his arms, and Jasmine cried and asked over and over, "Why? Why?"

Reverend Bush stood and left his son and daughter-in-law alone.

Sixteen

THE MINUTES TICKED ON. THE hours rolled by.

Then Sunday came.

Jasmine was relieved when Hosea didn't jump out of bed at six declaring that it was time to go to church. Not that she expected that. After that hateful e-mail, her hope was that he—and she—would never go back there again.

But on this Sunday morning, Hosea lay on his back, just like she did, staring at the ceiling. She knew his thoughts were the same as hers: Where was their daughter?

Jasmine wanted to stay home, not only today but every day. Stay with Hosea by her side. With Zaya asleep between them. With the police camped out in the living room, waiting for that call about Jacqueline. Waiting for her hope and faith to be proven true.

Then Sunday went.

And though the phone had rung constantly throughout the day and night—calls from Malik and Deborah and other members of City of Lights who wanted to be the first to tell

Hosea about the e-mail that they'd received. There was no call from the man Jasmine saw in her dark dreams. No call from the one who had taken Jacqueline away.

Still Jasmine had hope, until Monday morning. When Detective Foxx announced that the police were packing up their surveillance equipment.

"Usually the ransom call comes in within twenty-four hours, forty-eight hours, tops," he explained as he, Jasmine, and Hosea sat in the living room.

"So what does that mean?" Jasmine asked.

"Just means that we need to regroup, and truthfully, I want to get out there and hit the streets myself." And then, as an afterthought, he added, "This is a good thing."

You're lying! Jasmine thought. This couldn't possibly be a good thing, especially not with the expression that was etched on his face. If Jacqueline's disappearance was no longer considered a kidnapping for ransom, then the motive was far more heinous.

"We're going to leave this behind," the detective said, holding up the black box that was attached to the telephone. "It's a recording device that's hooked up to a main board at the station. If you get a call, press this button"—he showed them—"and we'll be able to get a trace going from down there."

Jasmine and Hosea nodded.

Detective Foxx said, "Do you want me to show Mrs. Sloss?"

"That's a good idea," Hosea said.

But Jasmine said, "No, that's okay. I'm going to be here."

"But suppose you go out?" Detective Foxx asked. "It's best that everyone in the house know how to use this."

"I won't be going anywhere." Jasmine folded her arms. "Not until Jacquie comes home."

"Jasmine," Hosea began, but she didn't wait for him to say another word. She just turned, left the room, and imagined the men whispering behind her back.

She didn't care what any of them said; she was going to stay with her plan. With her hope waning, all she had left was her faith—and her desire to protect her son the way she hadn't protected her daughter. She would stay home and pray . . . and keep Zaya from harm.

For the rest of the day, Hosea tried to make their lives as normal as any other Monday. Except for the fact that he was home and not in his office at the church. Except for the fact that one quarter of their family was not with them.

Hosea stood shoulder to shoulder with Mrs. Sloss at the stove, cooking a hearty breakfast of pancakes, sausages, and scrambled eggs. Although Jasmine joined them at the table, she ate nothing, just picked up bits of eggs and pancakes that never made their way to Zaya's mouth as he fed himself. And she stared at the empty chair across the table.

Then, when Zaya pounded his fists on the table and chanted, "Yaki, Yaki, Yaki," Jasmine pushed back her chair.

She told Hosea, "I need to lie down."

He nodded, his eyes sad; he knew their son's call for his sister had slain her heart.

As she handed Zaya's fork to Hosea, her son said, "Bye-bye, Mama."

Inside their room, Jasmine crawled into bed and surrendered to her exhaustion. She submitted to the nightmares that met her on the other side every time she closed her eyes. But even with that darkness, sleep was better than consciousness.

Her rest was not deep. She could feel the passing of time, the warmth of the daylight heating the room, then cooling as the sun made its journey from east to west. Then there were the sounds: Zaya laughing with Hosea; whispers in the living room between Hosea and Malik, then Hosea and Mrs. Whittingham, then Hosea and Deborah; the voices from the television as Hosea and Mrs. Sloss flipped the channels from cartoons to the news, looking for the story of Jacqueline, which had all but disappeared from the news.

And then there was the telephone that kept on ringing. But the call was never from the one they wanted to hear from.

So Jasmine just kept on sleeping.

Time passed, and she finally awakened with a heavy head and heavier heart. Her eyes focused on the clock on the nightstand: 6:17.

Why wasn't Hosea awake?

Usually he was up before six, bustling through their room, preparing for work.

Behind her, she heard Hosea's soft snores, and when she rolled over, she almost smiled when she saw the way he held Zaya under his arm. But then the sight of her son reminded her of their daughter, and she became aware again of the heartache that swarmed around her.

She pushed herself up, then tiptoed into the bathroom. The mirror told her story—deep, dark crescents framed her swollen eyes, and she saw lines on her face that she'd never seen before, as if time felt the need to mark its passing on her.

Turning to the shower, she hoped to wash away some of the agony. But the water did nothing to take away the images. She leaned against the marble tile and pressed her hands against her head. For just one minute, she wanted to breathe, wanted to escape, wanted to be free.

But all she could do was imagine her daughter . . . with someone.

"Hold on, Jacquie," she whimpered, keeping her cries as low as she could. Her tears mixed with the shower's rain. "Hold on, baby," she said, praying that, somehow, Jacqueline could hear her inside her heart. "Hold on. Mama's coming."

After long minutes, Jasmine turned off the shower and her

tears at the same time. She had cried for almost three days, and that had done nothing to bring Jacqueline home. There would be no more tears. She had to remember who she was—Jasmine Cox Larson Bush—and somehow, she would find a way to bring her daughter home.

Jasmine grabbed the towel with a new resolve. Her fight would begin now—she would start with the polygraph exam.

Seventeen

THE BELL RANG, AND JASMINE wondered for a moment how anyone could reach their door without first being announced by the concierge. But then she remembered—they were expecting New York's finest. The police didn't announce themselves to anyone.

"Mrs. Sloss," Jasmine called out from her bedroom, "can you get that, please? It's either Detective Cohen or our attorney." Then she opened the bathroom door. "Hosea." Right away, the shower turned off. "They're here," she said.

"They're early," he said from behind the glass. "But I'll be right out."

As she waited, she paced in their bedroom. It was still unbelievable that she actually had to take this test. What an insult! But it was an insult that she could endure since Dale assured them that it would help.

She heard Mrs. Sloss's gentle knock on the door.

"Just tell them that we'll be right out," Jasmine said. There was no way she was going to face those men without Hosea.

"It's not the police, Ms. Jasmine," Mrs. Sloss said so quietly, Jasmine had to strain to hear.

With a frown, she asked, "Who is it?"

Mrs. Sloss bit her lip, hesitated before she answered, "You should come and see."

It was instant, the way her heart began to pound. The look in Mrs. Sloss's eyes let Jasmine know—this had something to do with Jacqueline. She rushed past her housekeeper and dashed into the living room.

Then she stopped.

"What are you doing here?" she asked through clenched teeth, controlling herself so that she wouldn't scream.

"Jasmine," Mae Frances said, holding the back of the couch to steady herself. "I . . . I had to talk to you."

Jasmine folded her arms. "There's nothing I want to hear," she began, her voice rising with each word, "and nothing I want to say." She paused. "Well, actually, there is."

Mae Frances's eyes brightened with a bit of hope.

Jasmine stepped forward. "I told you before," she began calmly, "but you obviously didn't understand. So let me break this down for you. If you know what's good for you, you'll stay away from my family."

Mae Frances shook her head. "That's what I wanted to talk to you about. Your family is my family. And I've been praying that you wouldn't still be this angry."

"Angry? Is that what you think I am?" She pointed her finger in Mae Frances's face. "Angry would be if you forgot to give me an important message. Or if you lost my keys. But this . . . this is not anger," Jasmine said, yelling now. "This is rage. This is hatred."

"But I never meant for this to happen."

Jasmine stomped to the door and pulled it open so hard that it slammed against the wall.

"Listen to me," Mae Frances pleaded. "Please, Jasmine."

Jasmine said nothing more. Just stared at Mae Frances with a look that told her to get out now.

But Mae Frances didn't move. "You have to know how much I love you. How much I love Jacquie."

Her daughter's name passing through Mae Frances's lips made Jasmine snap. She marched across the room until she was within an inch of the woman's face.

"Get out of my house," she screamed, spittle flying from her mouth. "Get out now if you value your life. Get out now, or I won't be responsible for what happens to you."

"Mrs. Bush?"

Jasmine turned and stared into the faces of Detective Cohen, Dale Brody, and another man she'd never seen. But it was Detective Cohen who had called her name, who stood in front of the others, looking at her most intently.

He stepped forward. His glance moved between Mae Frances and Jasmine. "Is everything all right in here?"

It took a moment for her to stop shaking. Then Jasmine said, "This woman was just leaving." If the man who'd asked her if she had a temper wasn't standing right there, Jasmine would have pushed Mae Frances to the door, then, with the tip of her boot, kicked her out. But she kept her hands and her feet to herself, and just watched as Mae Frances staggered away. The woman had barely stepped over the threshold before Jasmine slammed the door behind her.

When she turned around, Jasmine tried to face the men with some kind of smile. The three stared back, still shocked by her explosion.

As if nothing happened, Jasmine said, "I'm going to see if my husband is ready. Please have a seat." She walked away without looking back, and so she never saw the glance that passed between the men.

"Are you sure you're going to be able to do this?" Dale questioned as he huddled in the kitchen with Jasmine and Hosea.

Jasmine nodded. "I told you, I'm fine."

Hosea whispered, "What just happened . . . with Jasmine and Mae Frances. It won't affect the test, will it?"

Dale shook his head. "No, they ask baseline questions to get a steady read, but I always prefer if my clients are calm."

"I said I'm fine!" It came out louder than she wanted, but she didn't care. This was all too much: Mae Frances, a polygraph, a detective who looked at her now as if she really were guilty. Detective Cohen couldn't seem to keep his eyes away from her, staring as if he were about to take the handcuffs out and cart her away.

But she didn't care what the detective thought; this polygraph would prove that he was a fool and that she was innocent. Then, finally, they'd get back to the real business.

"Okay then, if you're ready, just remember," Dale spoke softly, a sign to Jasmine to do the same. "Be yourself. Answer all of the questions honestly."

Behind them, in the dining room, the examiner, a member of the police department staff, was setting up the equipment. Detective Cohen was there at the request of Dale. "I want complete transparency—we need them to see how cooperative you are."

After the scene they'd walked in on, Jasmine was sure Dale regretted that invitation now.

As they moved toward the dining room, Dale said, "Like I told you before, these tests are not one hundred percent accurate, but if you tell the truth . . ."

Crossing her arms, she wondered why he kept talking about the truth. It wasn't like she would lie.

She knew where his words came from, though. Dale Brody was a long-time friend of Reverend Bush, and he probably knew every single one of her transgressions, knew every lie she'd ever told.

But that was her past.

Looking over the rims of his spectacles, the examiner nodded at Dale.

"I'll go first." Jasmine marched toward the man with nothing but confidence. She sat, banged her arm down on the table, and stared straight ahead. She focused on the floor-to-ceiling windows that framed the fireplace. And then her eyes moved to the mantel as the examiner attached sensors to her skin.

The man began, "Is your name Jasmine Bush?"

The framed photos on the fireplace were in her sight; the pictorial history that told the story of the Bushes and their wonderful life. "Yes," she said evenly.

"Do you live in New York City?"

Now she looked at the picture of Jacqueline alone—her daughter with her bright smile, with her legs crossed, with her hands folded right above her knees.

"Yes," Jasmine responded again.

"Are you forty-five years old?"

Her eyes got bigger, for just a moment. Jasmine wanted to raise her hand and ask if she could have another question. Not that she was going to lie, but she had lied so much about her age, she wasn't completely sure of the real number. She did a quick calculation. "Yes," she answered, and hoped that was the truth.

"Were you in the bathroom when your daughter disappeared?" "Did you have anything to do with Jacqueline's disappearance?" "Do you know where Jacqueline is today?"

That last question made her close her eyes, and inside the blackness, behind her lids, images formed—of an unfamiliar man with her child.

"No," she answered as calmly as she could, just like she'd done with the other questions. It didn't do any good to be offended.

"Thank you, Mrs. Bush," the examiner said, sooner than she expected.

She looked up, and both Hosea and Dale were smiling, looking like they were about to clap—as if she'd done something major. All she'd done was tell the truth, but to them maybe that was special.

It was Hosea's turn. Just like with her questions, the time passed quickly. Could the examiner really determine their innocence that fast?

When Hosea stood, she hugged him as Dale and Detective Cohen chatted. Then a cell phone rang, and the officer excused himself.

"Well, that wasn't so bad, was it?" Dale asked.

But before Jasmine could tell him that of course it hadn't been bad for him, Detective Cohen said into his phone, "Okay, I'll let them know."

She broke away from Hosea's embrace and searched the detective's face. "Was that call about Jacquie?"

The detective hooked his phone back into its holster and nodded. "Yup, that was one of the FBI agents assigned to the case. We've made contact with Doctor Brian Lewis."

"Brian!" Jasmine exclaimed. "Brian has Jacqueline!"

Her head was spinning with questions. But even though she had no answers, she was drenched with relief. If Brian had Jacqueline, then her daughter was safe. He would never harm her.

"Thank God you've found her," she cried. "When can I see my daughter!"

Eighteen

Brian stared at his American Express bill. Eight hundred dollars—not bad compared to what he usually spent in a month's time on food, clothes, and entertainment.

Except on this bill, six hundred of those dollars had been spent in one place—Flowers For You. He took another sip of his wine and, in his mind, added up how much he'd given this flower shop since June 2008, the month his divorce had become final.

This is getting ridiculous.

Especially since it didn't seem like he was making any progress.

Yes, Alexis always called him. Yes, she always thanked him. But that's where her gratitude ended, with just a simple: "Hello . . . thank you, Brian, but you've really got to stop doing this . . . take care."

It seemed that, unlike him, his wife had moved on.

But how was he supposed to accept that? Just let her go? Giving up just wasn't in his DNA.

This drive for his ex-wife had his sex therapist more than a bit concerned.

"You've made Alexis your new obsession, and it's going on too long. Any reconciliation would never work if she's your new addiction."

But that was as ridiculous as the amount of money he'd been spending on flowers. How could Alexis ever be an addiction when she was the love of his life?

"Alexis." Just saying her name made him take another sip of wine. "Alexis." And then, after a moment, he put the glass down. Maybe it was time—it had been three years since they'd first separated. She'd moved on; he had to do the same.

The ringing doorbell stopped those thoughts. And Brian sighed. Since any guest had to be announced by the concierge, he knew who was standing on the other side of the door.

Misty.

His new neighbor had been living in the building for only thirty days, but from the moment they'd met in the elevator on her move-in day, Misty had found one reason to keep stopping by.

"Do you have any sugar?" she would ask him with a faint southern drawl.

What Misty lacked in creativity, she made up for in persistence. Though he'd never given her any grounds to believe he was interested, Misty needed sugar at least three times a week.

But even if he could find a way to give up on Alexis, he wouldn't be heading toward the blond ponytail-bopping twentysomething. That was not how he rolled.

The bell chimed once more, and he brought his wineglass

again to his lips. When the bell chimed a third time, Brian pushed himself from the sofa. If he was going to move on, maybe Misty could help him get back into the game.

Taking quick steps, he thought about what he would say. No doubt, Misty would be wearing her signature Daisy Duke shorts and some sort of cutoff shirt—even in the dead of Los Angeles's sixty-degree winter. Maybe he would tell her that he wanted to borrow some of *her* sugar.

That thought made him crack up with laughter, but then it all stopped when he swung open the door.

A couple of seconds passed before Alexis said, "Are you going to invite me in?" She didn't wait for his response, just stepped past him as he stood with his mouth wide open.

It was the whiff of the flowers she held that brought him out of his stupor.

"I just stopped by to see if you still had any furniture," she said, peering around the apartment that the two of them had shared for more than five years of marriage.

Brian frowned as he finally closed the door. "Any furniture?" he echoed like a parrot. That was all he could say as he stared at his ex-wife. She sure looked good, still wearing the short, curly haircut she'd gotten when they'd first divorced.

"Yeah." She unbuttoned the cashmere swing jacket that she wore. "'Cause you've been spending all of your money on these." Holding up the bouquet, she grinned, though it looked more like she felt sorry for him than anything else. "By now," she kept on, "I thought for sure you'd be broke and that you would've started selling your furniture."

He chuckled, getting his bearings, ready for their banter. "As you can see," he said, opening his arms wide, "I haven't changed a thing." Then, with a more somber look and tone, "I'm keeping everything the same so that when you come home . . ."

It was a slow fade—the way the edges of her lips eased

down and her smile went away. She shook her head. "Start selling the furniture."

So cold, yet so cute. But he wasn't fooled. She'd come straight to his apartment, straight to him. "If you're not coming home"—his steps closed the gap between them—"then what're you doing here?"

"I just came by to tell you to stop." She held up the flowers. "Save your money."

He shrugged. "It's my money."

"And you're wasting it."

Shaking his head, he said, "You're wrong. My plan's already working. You're here, aren't you?"

Her expression showed that she was more amused than stumped. "I told you why I'm here." She shrugged her coat from her shoulders and strutted by him. Pulling kitchen cabinets open as if she still lived there, she searched until she found the glass vase that had been one of their wedding gifts.

As she filled the vase with water, Brian leaned against the wall, folded his arms, and watched the scene that he'd dreamed of unfold. This was just how he imagined her—coming home from work, still wearing her burgundy tailored suit that showed just how much time she spent at the gym, and doing something totally mundane, like setting flowers in a vase.

He held back a sigh as she stuffed the elegant red, pink, and white design of roses, daisies, and lilies inside. Once done, she swept past him again and centered the floral arrangement on the living room table. He was still standing in the same place when she picked up her coat.

"Anyway, thanks again for the flowers. But I think I'll leave these with you. My apartment is filled with the ones you sent me three days ago." She tilted her head when she added, "You *really* need to stop." She frowned a little, waiting for him to speak. He didn't, and she just shrugged.

But when she made her move toward the door, he jumped in her path. "Have dinner with me."

"What?"

"Since you're here, have dinner with me. I'll cook. Or we can order in—whatever you want."

"I don't want anything." She frowned. "No!"

"What are you afraid of?"

"I'm not afraid, Brian." She wrapped her coat's belt around her waist. "I'm just smart enough not to go backward." She paused, then added, "I never put a comma where God's put a period."

He laughed. "You can come up with all the clichés you want, but I have one, too."

He could tell that she didn't want to ask, but it was her natural curiosity that made her say, "And your cliché is . . ."

"I always win."

She bowed her head just a bit as she stepped around him, but even though she tried to hide it, he didn't miss her smile.

The way she didn't say good-bye, the way she didn't even close the door behind her, made Brian laugh out loud. Oh, yeah—he was getting to her. Finally!

Back in the living room, he reached for his glass and turned it upside down, swallowing the little bit of wine that was left. Then he raised the empty wineglass into the air—a salute to himself.

"Yup," he said, "I always win."

Nineteen

ALEXIS SLAPPED HER HAND AGAINST the steering wheel.

Why did I do that?

Going to Brian's apartment had never been part of her plan. After a day filled with client presentations at the advertising agency she owned, her desire was to get to her town house before the evening news ended, strip down to the suit she'd been born with, and then soak away her pressures in her Jacuzzi tub.

But just as visions of her stress-free evening danced in her head, her assistant had popped into her office with the bouquet.

"You got some more!" Kennedy had exclaimed with a giggle.

Alexis hadn't even looked up; she knew what her assistant was talking about. Grudgingly, she had taken the flowers and wondered what to do with this bunch. Already there was a bouquet from Brian sitting on her credenza. And her home was also filled with the fragrance of her ex-husband's gifts.

Still, as she carried the bouquet to her car, her plan was . . . to stay with the plan. But then she got behind the steering wheel, and her BMW headed west instead of east; before she could figure it out, she was in front of the condominium where she'd spent four years of immense ecstasy and one year of total agony.

Now she was so mad at herself.

So why am I grinning?

She shook her head, but that didn't stop her mind from pressing Play again. And hearing Brian's last words: *I always win.*

Glancing at her image in the rearview mirror, she used her hand to wipe her smile away. "What am I doing?" She tried to talk herself down as she squeezed her car out of the circular driveway.

It was almost eight o'clock, and the traffic moved easily down Wilshire. She turned the radio's volume up, blasting Mary J through the car. But not even her girl singing about her life helped.

She needed to talk.

Turning down the radio, she pressed the Call button on her dashboard.

"What's up?" Kyla, her best friend, answered on the second ring.

"I just left Brian's," Alexis blurted out.

"Brian? As in your *husband,* Brian?"

Kyla was at least eight miles away, hanging out in her Ladera Heights home, but Alexis could see her friend now—suddenly sitting straight up and on the edge of her couch.

"My *ex*-husband Brian," she reminded her.

Kyla's screech reverberated through the car.

"Would you stop it?" Alexis said.

"I'm sorry; it's just that I'm happy." She could hear Kyla clapping. "My two best friends are getting back together."

"I didn't say anything like that. We're already divorced."

"So what? Simon and Sylvia Webb were divorced for a

year before they got back together. And do you know the Alstons at church? He sings in the choir. They've gotten remarried . . . twice! And then there's—"

"Dang!" Alexis said, stopping her friend. "Did you keep a list?"

"No, it's just that when people get back together, everyone talks about it. 'Cause it's just so exciting to do it the right way . . ."

Alexis rolled her eyes, knowing exactly what Kyla was going to say next.

Kyla finished, "Since God hates divorce."

Alexis sighed, almost sorry now that she had called Kyla. Not that her friend wasn't always there—Kyla was her two a.m. friend, the one you called at any time. The one who would come running anywhere. But Kyla was also her Christian friend, the one who would quote God's word to you right when you didn't want to hear it.

Not that she could hate on Kyla for that; back in the day, she'd given Kyla a million scriptures when she and her husband, Jefferson, had been going through their own marital challenges after he'd slept with Kyla's other best friend, Jasmine Larson.

"God hates divorce," Kyla repeated, as if Alexis needed to hear those words again.

"Would you stop saying that!"

"Why? Just because you don't want to hear it doesn't make it any less true. You know I never agreed with your leaving Brian. I supported you because I knew what happened was hard for you . . ."

Hard? Was Kyla kidding? Hard didn't even begin to describe what she'd been through. And she knew that Kyla, her mild-mannered Christian friend, would have never been able to handle the news of her husband being a sex addict, either.

"Plus," Kyla said, breaking through Alexis's thoughts, "Lord knows Brian still loves you or else he wouldn't have worked so hard to get that little sex-addiction thing under control."

"Little sex-addiction thing?"

"You know what I mean. But my real point is, *you* still love him."

Her back stiffened, her grip tightened. "I don't love him," she said, with indignation all through her tone.

"Ah." Kyla giggled. "I think you protest too much and—"

"You know what? I don't want to talk to you anymore." She pressed the Disconnect button without saying good-bye, but in the more than twenty years that the two had been friends, they'd done that to each other hundreds of times. So she knew Kyla wouldn't be mad. In fact, Kyla was probably thrilled to get off the telephone. That way, she could run to Jefferson and tell him that ridiculous happily-ever-after story that was in her head. Alexis could imagine it—Kyla clapping, jumping up and down, singing as if she were in elementary school, "Alexis and Brian sitting in a tree! K-I-S-S-I-N-G!"

Alexis glanced into the rearview mirror again, and her forehead was bunched together in a deep scowl, her smile long gone.

Why did Kyla have to take the conversation there? All she'd wanted was for her friend to listen, then tell her that going to Brian's condo wasn't the craziest thing she'd ever done. But no, Kyla had to turn her little fifteen-minute visit into some kind of grand reconciliation.

Well, Kyla . . . and Brian needed to get over it because that reunion was never going to happen. No matter how often she remembered their good times—the way Brian had proposed to her, coming to her apartment at midnight, dressed in a tuxedo with flowers and a ring. No matter how often she recalled every late-night stroll they'd taken on the beach, or the days when they'd snuck away from work for a picnic in the park.

No matter how often those images seeped past the little part of her heart that still hurt, those memories could never obliterate the fact that Brian had blown her world apart when he'd confessed that he was a sex addict and had bedded hundreds of women. Still, that wasn't what had killed their marriage. It was that in the middle of his addiction, he'd fathered a child with her archenemy, Jasmine Cox Larson Bush. *That* was the unforgivable sin!

Alexis shook her head. Oh, no! Whenever she was tempted to remember the good, all she had to do was think about the opposite—Jasmine.

She needed to do something—like dive back into dating, just like she'd done when her final divorce decree had been delivered. She'd had a dinner date that same night two years ago at Commotions, a trendy downtown club/bar/restaurant that was always filled with beautiful single (and secretly married) Los Angelenos. There, she'd hooked up with Cabot Adams, the wealthy attorney who was an acquaintance of Jefferson's. Her first date should have been wonderful, and it would have been—if the man had noticed that she was there.

While they stood at the bar, she'd counted how many times he glanced at himself in the mirror. And once they sat for dinner, she could've swore that he held up his knife, searching for his reflection in the metal.

She'd gone out with Cabot a couple of times, and after him there had been others. She'd dated all kinds: athletes and artists, policemen and politicians—an eclectic mix of men who'd been willing to spend lots of money wining and dining her. Some made her laugh. Others made her think. All helped her to put Brian behind her.

At least that's what she'd thought.

It was the gorgeous Wesley Brown who'd told her that wasn't true. About six months ago, Wesley, a top gun at the

LAPD, had driven her home, and as they had sat in the drive-way of her town house, he'd asked, "Have you ever thought about getting back with Brian?"

There were a couple of things about that question that had shocked her, but the most important was, how did he know her ex-husband's name?

She had twisted in her seat to face him when she said, "Of course not. Why would you even ask that?"

"Because," he began with a smirk, "you can't stop talking about him."

Her eyes were wide when she said, "That's not true."

Wesley had chuckled. "Ms. Alexis, I hate to break it to you, but you've got it bad." Then he'd jumped out of the car, walked to the passenger side, and helped her out. At her front door he said, "Look, if you decide to do it again with Brian, I know a couple of judges who might be able to hook you two up and speed up the process." Then he'd kissed her forehead, trotted down the driveway, and got back into his car, not even looking back.

She hadn't been on a date since.

It was because of Wesley that she'd stopped. He'd made her wonder if what he'd said was true. She couldn't imagine that—she was clearly moving on, having fun, living her life.

So why was Brian always in her head?

Because he still has your heart!

There it was again—the voice that came from deep inside. The one that prodded her in the midst of her hectic days and reared its head in the middle of her quiet nights. It was prob-ably that voice that had made her drive to Brian's tonight.

"Don't listen," she told herself, as if she could really block out the voice of God.

She had to set up some kind of barricade. Because even though she was grateful that God had answered her prayers, had healed her pain, and had given her peace, she was shocked to discover that once the ice had melted from her heart, there was still a little bit of love there. It was only a remnant, but she was grown enough to know that sometimes leftovers made the best meals.

And that's what made her mad: at herself for even thinking she could love Brian again, and at God for telling her that she did. Her heart and God obviously didn't know what she knew—that time didn't heal all wounds.

Her tires screeched as she made a sharp turn into her driveway. But even though she was home, she didn't gather her things. Instead, she reached for her cell, scrolled through her contact list, found the name Cabot Adams, then pressed Call. She was pretty sure he was still single, since he'd left a message on her voice mail about six weeks ago.

"This is Cabot," the deep voice rang out.

Just hearing him made her want to hang up, but she pressed the phone to her ear. "Cabot," she said in a singsong voice she didn't even recognize, "it's Alexis Lewis."

"Alexis, sweetheart. It's been a long time. How are you?"

She exhaled. At least he was glad to hear from her. "Fine. Look, I'm sorry I didn't return any of your calls . . ."

"You should be. A beautiful woman like you could give a man like me a complex." He laughed.

Alexis rolled her eyes. There wasn't a woman alive who could give the mirror-loving Cabot Adams any kind of complex. But she half laughed with him.

She said, "I've just been busy. But I was wondering if you'd let me make it up to you."

"So you're saying you want to hook up?"

No! "Yes," she squeezed the word through her throat. If anyone could make her forget Brian, it was the bigger-than-life Cabot Adams. "How about tomorrow?" she asked, knowing she had to do this quickly or she would change her mind.

"How about tonight? You can come over here, we can share a bottle of champagne, and . . ." He stopped as if she could fill in the blanks.

Was it her imagination, or had his already sonorous voice become deeper? She glanced at the clock on her dashboard. It wasn't all that late, but it was late enough for someone like Cabot to think it was a booty call.

"Tomorrow would be better," she responded in a tone that said she would shut this whole thing down if he didn't step correctly.

"Well," he sighed, as if her suggestion was painful, "I guess I can wait."

She forced herself to stay on the phone a bit longer and listen as Cabot talked about a new teen group he'd just signed—the Divine Divas. She said "Uh-huh" where she was supposed to, half chuckled when she was supposed to, and rolled her eyes the entire time.

What am I doing?

After almost twenty minutes, she hung up and leaned back against the headrest. Did she really want to go out with Cabot Adams again?

No!

Yes!

Because she had to. Of all the men she knew, Cabot Adams was the only one who could set a bomb and blow Brian right out of her mind . . . and out of her heart, too.

She just prayed that this time it would work.

Twenty

"I'm telling you, Doctor Perkins," Brian said, "I'm the man." He leaned back on the leather couch, crossed his legs, and grinned at his therapist.

But although Brian was smiling so wide that the doctor could see all thirty-two of his pearly whites, her face was as stiff as her white-blond bouffant hair.

Shaking her head, the thin-lipped, Cinderella-looking therapist warned, "Be careful. I told you before, don't make Alexis your new addiction."

Brian had to resist jumping up and marching right out of there. But even though he glared, letting her see his disapproval, the doctor continued, "You know the danger of replacing one addiction with another," she said.

"I don't get it." Moving to the edge of the couch, he cupped his hands together. "That's what this therapy has been about. Making sure I didn't use sex as a stress reliever—and finding something else to replace that urge."

She pointed her pen at him. "The key word is *something*,

not *someone*. Your relationship with Alexis—or anyone else—
has to be based on love, not on the chase."

He bowed his head, shook it from side to side. "You just
don't know, Doctor. You don't know how much I love my
wife."

"Ex-wife," she corrected.

He was a second away from cursing her out. Then, "The
courts might say that she's my ex, but I told you, that's not
what's in my heart."

She was not impressed with his declaration of love. "I'm
just saying, Brian, that you've made so much progress. I'm concerned about where this obsession will lead. If you and Alexis
were to get back together, I'm afraid it wouldn't be real."

"I don't know how you could say that."

"It's my *professional* opinion."

"And my *personal* opinion is that I'm fine. The fact is, Doctor, I never give up. And I have never given up on Alexis and
me."

There was triumph in her eyes—as if he'd just proven her
point. "Those words alone are indicative of your addictive behavior."

He stared her down.

She stared right back.

He looked away first. Since she wasn't hearing him, there
was nothing else to say.

He'd been in enough of these sessions to know that there
was about ten minutes left, but he glanced at his watch anyway. "Doctor Perkins," he began as he rose from the sofa, "I
forgot to tell you that I couldn't stay for the whole session
today." He paused. "Ah . . . I have . . . a surgery."

Her eyes thinned, and her lips did the same. He could tell
that she knew he was lying. But what was she going to do—tell
a grown man who was paying the bill that he had to stay?

"All right." Glancing down at her calendar, she asked, "So I'll see you next week, same time?" Their appointment had been a standing one for more than three years. Yet every week, she said those same words. Only today, there was no certainty in her tone.

He nodded, but that was all he gave her. Usually, he spoke aloud, told her that he would definitely be here. But as they looked at each other, both of them knew that this was probably the end.

By the time Brian walked out the door, he knew he wouldn't be back. There was no need; his time in therapy had done what it was supposed to do. All those years and he'd never fallen off. He had stayed the course of a faithful husband.

It was true that he wasn't married, so he couldn't really be called any kind of husband. But that was such a small, soon-to-be-changed technicality. All that mattered was that he was cured.

Trotting down the steps, he aimed his remote toward his car, and the engine revved. Jumping inside, he paused for a moment to savor the glove-soft leather of his Lamborghini.

A Lamborghini. He still couldn't believe that he'd spent this much money on a machine that didn't fly. But this had been his consolation prize on the day the divorce papers had arrived. He hadn't planned to buy a new car, but as he had sat behind his desk and stared at the papers that severed his marriage, he'd needed something to put his heart back together.

He'd driven aimlessly home that night, not paying any attention to the passing streets, until he was on Wilshire. And he passed all those Beverly Hills dealerships. Before he could think about it, he was signing on a dotted line for the shiny red car.

Though he enjoyed the car and it certainly was a chick magnet, it had never served its purpose. It did nothing to mend his heart.

He glanced one last time at Dr. Taylor Perkins's gray stucco home. The Hancock Park house was such a small structure, so nondescript that the first time he'd driven right by.

Today, Brian saluted as he eased his car from the curb. He would take control of his addiction from here. Now that he knew what he was up against, he had no doubt that he would never fall again.

By the time he rounded the corner, he'd left thoughts of his sex therapist behind. All that was on his mind was his ex-wife and how he could finally push her over the edge and right back into his arms.

Twenty-one

THERE WAS NO CHANCE THAT Brian was going to come up in any conversation, no chance at all, since Alexis had barely had a chance to say more than two words after hello.

They were sitting shoulder to shoulder in Chantilly's, the chic French restaurant that was so exclusive, reservations had to be made three weeks in advance. Unless you were Cabot Adams, who had scored a spot at one of the twelve white-clothed tables for tonight. With its brick walls, dim lighting, and fresh-cut lilies, Chantilly's was as elegant as it was intimate. Romantic, really, which was why Alexis wondered why she hadn't suggested another place when Cabot had called her this morning.

Sitting so close that she could feel the gentle press of his knee against hers, Alexis marveled at the way Cabot's lips never stopped moving. Wearing a blue suit (that was, no doubt, designer) and a white tailored shirt (that was so starch stiff it could have stood on its own), and with a face that was made for the movies, Cabot looked like a man who had a role in every woman's dreams.

Except he never stopped talking.

Cabot's head tilted back and he laughed, but Alexis wasn't sure what he was laughing about. He'd said so much, it was hard to keep up. So instead of laughing with him, she took a final sip of her wine. Before she could place the wineglass down on the table, the waiter was right there, refilling it.

Vive la France!

Cabot picked up his knife and sliced away a small piece of his duck à l'orange. "So enough about me . . . tell me what's been going on in your life, Alexis."

It startled her, at first. He actually expected a response. Taking a moment, she glanced down at the braised lamb that sat practically untouched on her plate. "Not much has been happening," she said. She inhaled, and the fragrance of the lilies took her away for a moment—to her living room. There had been lilies in the last bouquet from Brian, and that memory made her smile.

But then she cleared her throat and expunged that thought. Turned back to Cabot, and said, "I'm just working hard, keeping my agency afloat."

With the tip of his napkin, he wiped the corner of his lips and leaned in closer, though the way the chairs were situated at each table—side by side—he couldn't get too much closer without sitting in her lap.

"Oh, come on," he whispered. His eyes were intense, as if he was truly interested. "You're doing more than that; I've been reading up on you. Read that Ward and Associates acquired the Addicts Anonymous and then the Hunter Transportation accounts. That's big-league stuff." He paused as if he wanted her to be impressed that he'd probably Googled her. "So you've been doing more than *just* working. You've been making it happen, Ms. Ward." And then, under the table, she could feel him pressing his knee just a bit harder against hers.

Without turning her head too much, Alexis peeked at the couples around them, heads close, conversation hushed. Smiles on the women's faces, lust in the men's eyes.

Then she glanced at Cabot and had to take another sip of wine.

"That's one of the things I love about you," he said. "You're successful." As he sliced away another piece of duck, she noticed the shine of his fingertips, his manicure far better than hers. He chewed for a moment, then chuckled as if he suddenly had a thought. "You're the kind of woman who would make a wonderful wife."

Another sip.

Then he frowned and looked down at her plate. "You're not hungry?"

She nodded, but held up her glass. "Yes, but the wine is so good."

"Ah, yes." He lifted his own glass and clicked it against hers. "There's nothing like the French!" Then, lowering his glass and his voice, he whispered, "So, Ms. Ward, would you be a wonderful wife?"

She leaned away, trying to get back her personal space. "I wasn't good at it the first time," she said, shaking her head.

"You just had the wrong husband. See, if you had been with me . . ." He stopped, as if she was supposed to know what he had been going to say.

Alexis couldn't remember how many times she'd gone out with Cabot. It was more than five, fewer than ten. But every single time he brought up marriage. At least the man was consistent—he never stopped talking about himself, and he made it clear that he wanted a wife.

But what woman would be able to stand him? Even at the altar, he probably wouldn't stop talking long enough for his wife to say "I do."

"I want to walk in the destiny God has for me," he'd told her about fifteen minutes after they'd first met. Standing at the edge of the bar in Commotions, surrounded by the beautiful people, he'd added, "I'm supposed to be married."

He'd gone on to say that his first marriage, straight out of college, had ended before their first wedding anniversary.

"She wasn't ready for me," he had told Alexis, even though she hadn't asked. It wasn't like she was trying to get into this man's business—she certainly didn't want him in hers.

But he had kept on anyway, "The end of my marriage was not my fault. I was moving up; she wasn't." He had gazed straight into her eyes when he'd said, "I need a woman who's winning her own game."

On that first date, Alexis had just stared back at him, saying nothing—just like she was doing now.

Not that Cabot wasn't a great catch—from the entertainment agency he'd built to his home in Bel Air, from his debonair aura to the fact that he attended Sunday services at West Angeles, one of the largest churches in the city.

Women should have been falling at his feet.

As if reading her mind, Cabot said, "I know that I'm the perfect man, and the woman I choose has to be bringing it, too."

Alexis had that thought again: no matter who he was or how much money he made, who could stand him?

He paused, as if she was supposed to say something—maybe he expected her to agree. But when all she did was sip more wine, he put his fork down and took her hand. "I brought you here because I want us to really get to know each other. So," he gently squeezed her hand, "I wanna know what *you've* been doing since the last time I saw you."

His gray eyes were suddenly filled with a sincerity that she hadn't seen before. Now she put down her glass. "Well, I have been kind of busy . . ."

She paused to see if he was going to start talking. But he only smiled, like he was eager to hear.

For the first time, she smiled back. "I worked quite a bit on the Obama campaign."

"Really?"

His eyes were wide and clear. Focused, as if he cared. So she rested her arms on the table, tilted her head. "Yeah, I'd never really gotten involved in a campaign before. I mean, I gave a little bit of money to Jesse when he ran the second time in eighty-eight, but this was the first time that I really got in there and worked to make a difference." She told him about the thousands of phone calls she'd made, the hundreds of doors she'd knocked on, the scheduling she'd done to keep the local office organized.

He listened. He nodded. He laughed.

"So, you're an Obama gal?"

"Is there anything else?"

He chuckled. "I guess not. Why didn't I know this?" Before she could respond, he said, "Because I'm an Obama guy! I was on his National Finance Committee." He stuffed his mouth with more of his duck before he added, "I knew I wouldn't have time to work in one of those little neighborhood offices like you did." He waved his hand as if those volunteers—like Alexis—didn't count. Then his head rose a bit more when he said, "I joined his team as a bundler."

Alexis blinked and wondered what had happened to the man who had been there a moment ago. As Cabot shut her and took over the conversation, she put down her fork and picked up her glass once again. She tried not to roll her eyes when he spoke of the two star-studded fund-raisers he'd held at his home.

"Now that I think about it, I wish that I'd invited you. You would have made a great date. Much better than—" He stopped himself, cleared his throat. "Well, anyway, I wish you'd been there with me. I could've introduced you to Magic and Cookie, and then Denzel and Pauletta were there. Samuel and LaTanya . . ."

Alexis wanted to lean over and bang her head on the table as he named just about every celebrity who lived in Los Angeles.

But when he said, "And you know, this way I was able to give more than the twenty-three-hundred-dollar limit," her eyes got wide.

"What?"

"You know . . . those stupid rules limiting how much you can contribute to a campaign. Well, just by pulling a couple of names from a phone book," he lowered his voice even more, "I was able to get around that." Pride was all up in his grin. "I learned how to do that after I attended a Republican fund-raiser years ago. Now those cats, they know how to make the money work."

Alexis couldn't believe it. Cabot Adams had just confessed to committing a crime, and if there'd been a policeman nearby, she would've had him arrested. Not for his confession, but for impersonating a man on a date.

"And then," he continued his soliloquy, "Page Six . . ." He paused. "You're familiar with them, right?" Even though she nodded, he went on to say, "They're the gossip page in the *New York Post.* Well anyway, my last fund-raiser was even mentioned in their column." He flicked invisible lint from the sleeve of his jacket. "I couldn't believe it."

That makes two of us, Alexis thought. She couldn't believe it either—couldn't believe that she was still here.

It took more than thirty minutes for him to finish his Obama stories—and for the waiter to clear the table.

Then the young man was back, saying, "Can I tempt you with dessert? A chocolate soufflé, perhaps?"

"No," she said.

"Yes," Cabot said, and looked at her. "Come on, this is a special night. Shouldn't we share something?"

Yeah, conversation! That's what she wanted to say. But then she remembered her pastor's sermon from last Sunday.

"Only a fool says everything on their mind," was what Pastor Ford had said. *"I bring that to you straight from Proverbs."*

So instead of telling Cabot off like she wanted to do, Alexis leaned back and pressed her hand against the purple silk of her dress. Rubbing her stomach, she said, "I'm watching my weight," hoping that would convince him to end the evening.

But all he did was put his arm around her shoulders and say, "Can I watch it with you?"

When he laughed, she did the same, hoping that would fast-forward them to the part where they said good night. But after his laugh, he said, "Well then, you'll just have a spoonful."

He nodded to the waiter, but Alexis stopped him. "Actually," she began, looking at her watch, "it's getting late, and I have to work tomorrow."

He glanced at his watch, as if his expensive timepiece was more accurate than hers. "It's only eight. You can't be tired already."

"I am," she said lightly, and shook her head like she couldn't believe it.

It still took more than twenty minutes for him to pay the bill, brag a bit to the waiter about his latest client, then promise the maître d' that he would get him tickets the next time Beyonce came to Los Angeles.

She wanted to faint with gratitude when she saw her car right in front when they stepped outside. She dove inside before Cabot could say a word.

Fastening her seat belt, she wished that she could ignore his tap on the window, but she hit the button and lowered the glass.

"I had a great time," he said.

"Thanks for dinner," she said. Because she had been raised right, she added a smile as she curled her fingers into a wave.

"Wait!" he shouted as she put the car into drive. "Give me a call in the morning; let's hook up this weekend."

Alexis wasn't even going to tell that lie. But she didn't want to tell the truth either—that when she got home, she was going to lose his number.

So she rolled up her window. She couldn't say anything through the thick glass. Pressing her foot to the accelerator, she gained speed when she hit Santa Monica Boulevard.

"You deserved that," she scolded herself. Using one man to forget another was obviously not the way. But she would find something else to do, because there were two things she knew for sure. One, she was never going to call Cabot Adams again. And two, she was going to get Brian out of her heart. That was a promise—no matter what she had to do.

Twenty-two

I AM A MAN! A man on a mission! A man with a plan!

That was Brian's mantra as he took the turn on the second level of the underground garage. His tires screamed as he swerved, but then he slowed down and eyed the assigned parking spaces.

"There she is," he whispered when he got a glimpse of Alexis's BMW. Not that he'd had any apprehensions; he'd already checked in with her assistant and had sworn Kennedy to secrecy.

Pulling into a space three spots away from hers, Brian took a final peek in the rearview mirror. He didn't need to do a thing. He looked good!

He pressed the elevator button and glanced at his watch at the same time. Knowing Alexis, she had been at work for hours, even though it was not yet noon. But he was going to get her to have lunch with him; of that, he was sure. Because he was a man on a mission. A man with a plan.

Glancing at the EXIT sign that led to the stairwell, Brian was just about ready to run up the twelve flights when the elevator doors finally parted. He stepped into the chamber with a quickness, then paced the small space as he ascended.

It was amazing that he was here—less than a minute away from seeing Alexis, from spending some real time with her. Just two days ago he'd been prepared to give up, throw in the bouquet. But then with that last bunch of flowers, Alexis had done what he'd expected her to do months ago—she had come to him.

That was the plan—for her to open the door, and he would walk right through it.

He took a cleansing breath as he stepped off the elevator and pushed through the double glass doors stenciled with gold letters: WARD AND ASSOCIATES.

Kennedy's grin greeted him the moment he stepped inside. "It's good to—"

Brian smiled back but put his forefinger against his lips. Kennedy giggled, and pointed toward Alexis's office.

Even though there was a ruckus of activity behind Kennedy's desk as account executives chatted on calls, prepared for meetings, or mulled over sales projections, Brian took soft steps toward Alexis's door. He raised his hand to knock, but then he eyed her through the small space where the door was ajar.

What he'd expected was for Alexis to be in front of her computer, feverishly tapping on the keys. Or sitting with her head down, studying some report. But she wasn't anywhere near her desk.

Instead, she stood at the window, staring out as if her focus was far beyond her office. He could see only her profile, but it was enough to know that she was smiling. She was so deep in thought that he could almost feel what was going through her mind.

What he saw made his stomach turn over. Who was she thinking about? Who had her head, her heart, so much that she had stopped to fantasize about him in the middle of her day?

He felt like an intruder, stealing in on her private moment. He needed to back away.

But he couldn't; it wasn't part of his DNA.

He cleared his throat; she turned around and pressed her hand against her chest, startled. "Brian!"

"Hey," he said softly.

"I didn't hear you come in." She moved away from the window, the lines in her forehead deep. "What . . . are you doing here?"

He held up his hands. "Nothing's wrong."

The worry lines in her forehead faded fast. But still, she said, "So . . . ," leaving the rest of her question unspoken.

"I hope I'm not disturbing you."

The corners of her lips twitched, as if she was trying to hold back a smile. "No." With a motion toward the chair across from her desk, she invited him to sit down.

It was then that he breathed, and forgot all about whoever was in her mind. His swagger returned as he strutted across her expansive office, which was decorated like a grand living room with a desk in the middle. The glint in her eyes let him know that this part of his plan—to wear the black blazer, black shirt, and jeans—had worked.

He didn't sit until she squirmed a bit in her chair; then he took his seat.

Before he spoke, Alexis raised one finger as she buzzed her assistant. "Could you bring me a cup of coffee?"

Brian grinned. Sat back, unbuttoned his jacket, crossed his legs. He said, "I wanted to come by—"

"Please don't tell me that you brought more flowers?" she joked, as Kennedy placed a mug on her desk.

Chuckling with her, he said, "No, sorry. This time, all you get is me." Then he paused, giving her a chance to say words he dreamed about. Something like, *That's fine 'cause all I want is you.* But all Alexis did was bring the coffee mug to her lips. He continued, "I have some news."

Another sip. "Good, I hope."

He nodded. "I wanted you to be the first to know, 'cause you stood by me."

She held on to her mug.

"Doctor Perkins . . ." As soon as he mentioned his sex therapist, her smile slipped away. But Brian kept on, "I had my last meeting with her yesterday. She said that I'm cured." Another pause. More silence. Until Brian added, "It seems that I've made so much progress, there's no reason for me to continue."

With just a bit of a frown, Alexis finally placed her mug down. "I didn't know there was such a thing as a cure."

"Maybe *cure* is not the word. It's just that I've learned all that I can. I mean, look how long it's been . . . so now, it's up to me." He leaned forward. "And believe me, all of that is in the past."

Her head bobbed up and down. "I'm really glad for you, Brian."

"I figured that since this is what destroyed our marriage, I had to tell you. And I think . . ." He stopped.

"What?"

"I think you should go to lunch with me."

She was already shaking her head.

He said, "Sort of a lunch date."

More shaking. "I've passed my date quota for the week," she said with a little chuckle that made him frown.

But he had no intention of being denied. Brian pushed, "I just want someone to celebrate with."

Although her head kept shaking, this time she didn't say no out loud.

"Come on," he urged. He lowered his head. "Look, I don't want anything from you. It's just that . . . this is pretty big, and there's no one else I want to share it with. It's important to me, Alex."

It was hard to believe, but it didn't look like any of his words had moved her. She stayed quiet, just looking at him. He was ready with more, and he moved to the edge of his chair. "I'm sorry. I guess I was just excited and—"

"I can't have lunch with you today," she interrupted.

Okay, he thought. *That's not a total no.* And he had to remember what had happened with the flowers.

She said, "I'm swamped, so how about dinner?"

It took a moment, then, "Dinner? Oh, okay. Dinner."

"It's just a meal, shared between friends, Brian." She paused and then added words in a tone that was meant to be a warning, *"Nothing else."*

"Of course not." He kept his expression solemn. "I don't know what you're thinking."

"Well, I know what *you're* thinking," she said.

He held up his hands. "It'll just be a great evening, two friends, talking. Celebrating."

She nodded. "That's all." And then she buzzed Kennedy for another cup of coffee.

He wanted to jump up and kiss her. But all he did was rise from the chair and strut toward the door. Over his shoulder, he told her that he'd call her in an hour. By the time he looked back, her head was down; she was back at work.

Inside the elevator, he would've given himself a high five if he could have. By the time he got to his car, he was laughing full out. Reality was so much better than the plan—he hadn't had a single hope for dinner.

But really, how could she resist? He'd gone to her with all guns drawn. He had dressed the part. Spoken the part. There was nothing else she could do.

Looking in the rearview mirror, he bobbed his head as if he heard music, even though the radio wasn't on. "Yeah, that's what's up!"

He guided his car from the garage and headed toward home. It had been a long time since he'd had this feeling—like he was the champion of the world.

Twenty-three

BRIAN WAS NOT PLAYING FAIR.

He was forging forward, a full-court press. And to Alexis, he was committing every foul in the book.

It had started this afternoon, when he'd shown up at her office wearing all black on the top and blue jeans on the bottom.

Foul!

She remembered even now, the way her eyes had roamed over him. And then she'd committed her own foul—she had undressed him with her eyes. That's when she'd called Kennedy for her first cup of coffee.

As if he had no idea what he was doing to her, Brian had leaned back in the chair and stroked her with his voice, caressed her with his smile, made her insides swoon with his eyes.

Foul!

Finally, blessedly, he'd left her alone, but then an hour later, he'd moved into flagrant foul territory when he'd called and said so casually, "Let's go to Heroes for dinner."

She'd just taken a sip of coffee and a long stream exploded

from her mouth, landing right on top of the computerized storyboards for Addicts Anonymous that sat on her desk.

"No," she'd told him after she'd gotten herself together.

"Why not?"

"'Cause that's where we've had all of our good times," she said, as if her logic showed just how illogical he was.

He'd laughed. "Well, I want to have a good time tonight, don't you?"

No! "I guess."

"And anyway," he'd added, "where else can we go?"

As if there weren't a million restaurants in Los Angeles. As if there wasn't one in a million that wasn't filled with their memories.

But then he said, "What about if we do it early. Then it won't feel so much like . . . a date."

She agreed. That did feel better. Four o'clock was much more innocent than eight.

So now they were at Heroes, where Brian was committing his final foul. Where Brian was just being Brian.

Without her saying a word, he'd ordered all of her favorite Heroes dishes: Barbecue Salmon, Shrimp Mousse, and Pecan-Crusted Chicken sat in the middle of their table, as if they were in a Chinese restaurant, rather than this upscale Continental eatery.

Then, of course, there was her favorite wine—Sauvignon Blanc—that seemed to be filling her glass much faster than his.

Their conversation flowed with ease; their banter was effortless. He was as attentive tonight as he'd been on their first date all those years ago when they'd sat at the edge of the Pacific Ocean from noon until the moment the sun settled in the west. Tonight, just like then, Brian was making their time together all about her.

"Jefferson told me you worked on the Obama campaign. What did you do?" he asked.

It was a déjà vu question; but unlike last night, when she'd been given little time to answer, tonight she talked leisurely, and proudly, without interruption.

"Wow, that's impressive," Brian said. "You make me feel a little guilty. I didn't do half as much."

Then their chatter turned easily to the books they were reading, to the movies they'd seen, to the songs they loved.

"By the way, I saw this great article about the rise of all things Christian—literature, music," he said. "I'll get the magazine and bring it to you tomorrow."

She didn't miss the way he said *tomorrow*, as if it was just an extension of tonight.

"So, any surgeries this week?" she asked, then froze. Both were taken back to the days when they were married and she'd asked him that same question. Every Sunday.

Brian broke the quiet and told her of an upcoming surgery on a six-month-old girl whose parents were bringing her to Los Angeles from Texas. Alexis sipped and listened with the same fascination she always held when he discussed his responsibilities as an ophthalmologist.

The moments moved along, and they kept right on talking. About everything. Then, anything. Sometimes, nothing.

When Brian said, "I think we should share a dessert," she frowned. Was it time for dessert? She glanced at her watch and wondered who'd stolen their time. It couldn't be almost eight.

"So do you want some?"

She looked up and into his eyes. His lips were so close. Lover's lips. In the old days, she would have just leaned forward two inches and pressed her lips against his. But today, she stared and wondered if he still tasted like chocolate.

Foul!

She backed up and took a final sip of wine. "No dessert for me," she said.

With a chuckle, he raised his hand for the waiter and settled their check.

"Thanks so much for dinner, Brian," Alexis said, and then she stood. "Whoa." She wobbled just a bit, then steadied herself against the table. In an instant and without a word, Brian was at her side. He scooped the palm of his hand underneath her elbow and led her through the maze of tables.

At the entrance, Alexis dug in her purse for the valet ticket, and when she found it, Brian took it from her. She frowned a little when he pulled the attendant aside and whispered to him. The man glanced at Alexis and nodded before Brian returned to her side.

"What's going on?" she asked.

He said, "I'm going to drive you home," just as his Lamborghini came to a stop in front of them.

She was already shaking her head. "I can drive." She closed her eyes, licked her lips, tried to get the fuzziness behind her eyelids to go away.

But he acted like she hadn't spoken when he took her arm and led her around to the passenger's side. It was hard to put up a fight when it took so much effort to walk.

Inside, she sank into soft leather and thought, *This is embarrassing*, as Brian trotted to the other side.

Getting drunk at Heroes was becoming too much of a habit. This had happened before—a couple of years ago when she'd had dinner with Jasmine's husband. She'd had too much wine then, too; that night she had been building courage to sleep with Jasmine's husband. But what did she need courage for tonight?

Brian shifted into drive. "We'll pick up your car tomorrow."

There was that *tomorrow* word again. But she wasn't going to argue. She'd let him take her home, then she'd catch a cab in the morning. And after that, she was never going to have another glass of wine. Ever.

As Brian twisted the car through the streets, Alexis wondered what had happened to their words? They'd had so many before, but now there was total silence between them. Only the low, soft bedroom voice of the radio DJ streamed through the car.

"Back to the Quiet Storm," he crooned. "We're going to continue with our celebration of the best love songs. Here's Mr. Luther Vandross."

Foul!

Anything by Luther wasn't good right now. Especially not this song. When Alexis heard the first three chords of "Here and Now," she wondered if Brian was going to change the station. When he didn't, she wondered if she should, because surely they didn't need to be listening to this.

But Brian just stared ahead, focused on the road and totally unfazed by the music. So she did the only thing she could— she settled back, closed her eyes, snuggled into the soft seat, and pretended that she wasn't in a car with her ex-husband listening to the song that had played at their wedding—their first dance.

Then Luther passed the baton to Kem. And Kem to Robin Thicke.

Four more songs played before Alexis felt the car slow to a stop, and then there was just the gentle purr of the car's engine before it shut off completely.

Slowly, she opened her eyes. "Thank—" she began to say. But Brian was already out, on his way to opening her door.

The cool air and the lover's concert that had played in the car had sobered her.

"Thank you for dinner," she said, when he took her hand and helped her from the low seat. Then she wondered, what was the proper good-night etiquette with an ex? Did you shake hands? Give a peck on the cheek? Or do one of those Sunday church hugs where you made sure your pelvis was two feet away from his?

Since she wasn't sure, she just turned toward her home. But she could hear Brian's footsteps on the asphalt behind her, following.

As she inserted her key, he stood so close that his heat negated the cool of the November night. She pushed her door open, then turned around. "Well . . ." she said, hoping that was enough of a good-bye.

"Well," he repeated. "Can I come in?"

She sighed, shook her head.

"Come on, I've never seen your place." He held up his hands. "Just a little tour. Quick in and out."

She had so many reasons to tell him no, but instead she said yes, then led him through the two-thousand-square-foot, two-level, two-bedroom town home as if she was just his tour guide.

"This is nice," Brian said after he trotted down the steps behind her. He sat on the couch and unbuttoned his jacket. "It's strange that I've never been here before."

"What's strange about that?" she asked, still standing. She looked down at him sitting on her couch. Didn't he remember his promise—a quick in and out?

"'Cause we were . . ." He pointed back and forth between them. "We are friends, right?"

Now she sat on the other end of her eight-foot-long sofa. As far away from him as she could get. "Yeah, but not the kind who get together like this."

He spread his arms wide along the back of the couch,

seemingly so comfortable in her space. He did that thing with his eyes again . . . looked right through her. Made her twist and turn and try to get away from his gaze.

"Well, after tonight," he said, leaning toward her, "I hope you'll invite me over again."

She leaned deeper into the cushions, giving herself more space since he'd moved closer.

He asked, "Aren't you going to offer a friend a drink?"

What she wanted to do was pull him up and push him out the door. Tell him good night and good luck. But she stood and strolled, as if having him here—with his heat and his lips and his eyes—was no big deal.

His brows rose when she handed him a bottle. "Just water?" She shrugged, and he said, "I was hoping for something a little more . . . adult."

"Well, water is all I got. So if you want anything else, you need to do what Jesus did when they gave Him water."

Brian laughed as he took a swig.

Still standing, she spread her arms wide and yawned. "Oh, my goodness." She put her hand over her mouth. "Excuse me. I guess I'm just tired."

Her hint hit its target.

Brian said, "I guess I need to get going." Then, suddenly somber, he added, "Thank you, Alex, really, for celebrating with me tonight."

His tone made her stop pretending. Made her sidle onto the couch next to him.

He continued, "It meant a lot that you were there." He paused, as if he'd gone deep into his own thoughts, memories. "You were with me from the beginning," he said softly. "And now you're here . . . at the end." A pause before, "I know I hurt you, and I'll never be able to tell you how—"

She held up her hand. "You've said sorry so many times,

Brian, and I really do believe you." His eyes were filled with doubt, so she added, "I forgave you a long time ago."

He held her gaze for a moment longer before he said, "I never wanted a divorce."

She kept her lips pressed together, not knowing what to say. His words weren't new; she'd forced him into the divorce. But after what he'd taken her through, his wants didn't matter.

He placed the water bottle on the table, then stood, buttoned his coat, and moved toward the door before she had the chance to blink. But the confident swagger that he'd come in with was gone. He faced her with glassy eyes, as if tears weren't far away but would never come because he was such a man.

It was his eyes that made her arms move before her brain did, and she held him in an embrace. She held him the way she used to, when he would stagger home exhausted, filled with stress from his important work.

The longest minute passed before he pulled away. "Thank you," he whispered.

She was looking down when she nodded, but when she raised her head, his lips were right there. Again. So close.

Then time. Took over.

Before Alexis had another thought, his lips were pressed against hers. Or maybe her lips were against his—Alexis wasn't sure. Not that it mattered—they were connected. By their lips only.

She wanted to scream, *Foul!* But she didn't. Because if she screamed, he would stop. And she didn't want this to end, not yet. She just needed a couple more moments. Then it would be enough. Then it would be over.

But then it was more than just his lips. When his arms wrapped around her, she didn't resist. When he pressed in closer, she didn't push him away. When she felt his desire, she showed him hers.

With a deep moan, he swept her up off her feet, and into his arms. And she did nothing to defend herself. Just wrapped her arms around what was familiar and let him lead as their tongues danced. For a second, she took her mind from their kiss and wondered if he'd be able to carry her through her home, without stumbling and bringing this moment to an end and bringing them to their senses.

But it was as if he knew that precision was vital. He stepped through the living room and to the stairs as if he'd been here before tonight. At the top of the landing, Alexis counted the steps in her head—one, two, three, four, five—and they were right outside her bedroom. He turned; he knew.

He never broke their embrace as he laid her on her bed and stretched out on top of her. Now their bodies danced—a horizontal waltz. Their moans were their music. She was the melody. He was the harmony.

Finally, he tore his lips away from hers. Directed his tongue to her neck, where his kisses made her moan more. She groaned when he ripped her blouse away, buttons scattering across the room.

She did the same to his shirt, his pants, his boxers until she felt nothing but his flesh. Her flesh.

Then the two became one.

After three years.

It was done.

Twenty-four

ALEXIS COULD HEAR IT AS much as she could feel it.

The pounding of her heart. Still.

She lay on top of Brian, amazed at their rhythm. Each breath they took—in and out—they took together.

Just like it used to be.

That was exactly why Alexis rolled over. But Brian didn't let her get away. He held her and pressed against her—his front to her back. A spoon made of skin.

And they sighed, together.

She had wanted this, had yearned to have him. And at the same time she was sickened by the thought of being this close to him.

It was the memory of their last time that made her almost physically ill. It was while they were in bed, with Brian's hands and lips all over her, that she had known she had to get a divorce. Because of his affair with Jasmine. On that last night, Jasmine had been right there in the bed with them.

Of course the feel of Jasmine, the smell of Jasmine, the

voice of Jasmine had been only in her mind that night. But it was real enough to make her jump from their bed and walk away. Never turning back and promising never to give her heart to a man again.

So what am I doing here?

Then . . . the sound. She frowned. Was he snoring?

She shot up in the bed, turned on the light. And nudged him until his eyes were wide.

"Huh!" Brian's face was scrunched with confusion as he glanced around. Then his memory came back, and he opened his arms, reaching for her.

Alexis tugged at the sheet and wrapped the sateen around her nakedness. "You have to leave," she demanded.

He frowned.

She jumped from the bed, leaving Brian exposed. But he didn't seem to mind. With his eyes boring into her, he stretched as if he wanted to give her more of himself to see.

She sighed and remembered when she'd called all of that hers. She had to look away. "You need to get up. You need to go."

"No, that's all right. I'll just go home in the morning."

"No!" She shook her head wildly. "I want you to go home now."

He laughed. "Are you kidding?" When he saw that she wasn't laughing, he rolled to his side. "What's wrong?"

"I want you to leave."

He paused for a moment. "There's nothing wrong with what happened here, Alexis," he said, with the patience of an adult explaining a situation to a child. "I love you. We've waited a long time . . . for each other."

That declaration made no difference, and she repeated her request for him to go.

He stayed quiet, even though his eyes were still on her. The way his brows bunched together, then relaxed, then bunched together again—Alexis could tell that he was thinking, measuring, deciding. After a while, he rolled to the other side of the bed.

When he pushed himself up, she tried not to stare at the muscles that kept his back broad and his behind taut.

"I'll be . . . downstairs." She rushed past him, into the hall. It wasn't until she was in the middle of the living room that she remembered she was swathed only in a sheet. But this would have to do; she wasn't going back up there.

She waited. She paced. She thought.

How had this happened?

Before she had formed the question completely in her mind, she knew the answer. She had let it happen, had wanted it to happen. This had been building from the moment they first separated.

Well, she'd had her taste, and it had been enough. It wouldn't happen again.

Behind her, she heard his soft steps on the stairs, and when she turned, she inhaled. That was the thing about her ex—he looked as good with his clothes on as he did with them off.

She shuddered and prayed for strength as he strutted toward her.

He didn't stop moving until there wasn't more than an inch of air between them. When he leaned forward, she held her breath, then exhaled when his lips landed only on her forehead.

His eyes shined when he stepped away. "I'll call you tomorrow."

"No." She shook her head. "There's no need for all of that."

"I know I don't need to." She opened her mouth to protest more, but the tips of his fingers pressed against her lips, silenced her. "Just go with it, sweetheart. I told you the day I agreed to the divorce that I would be back."

"You're not—"

This time it was his lips that kept her quiet. And took her breath away, too.

He opened the door, and the cool air swept inside. But he didn't look back as he rushed to his car.

It was only the wind and her pride that kept Alexis from standing there, watching him. She closed the door but stayed in place until she heard his engine fire up. Then, still wrapped in nothing but the sheet, she ran up the stairs two steps at a time.

Inside her bedroom, the evidence was right before her—the comforter was balled up on the floor, the pillows were tossed to the side, the sheets were undone.

But she ignored all of that as she scurried across the room and grabbed the telephone. She glanced at the clock as she dialed. Just a bit after midnight. She made calls this late only when it was an emergency.

This certainly was an emergency.

And it was a Friday. Maybe that would help.

Even so, Jefferson's voice was filled with sleep when he answered.

She said, "Sorry to be calling so late, Jefferson—"

"Alex, what's wrong?"

"Nothing, I just needed to speak to Kyla. Is she asleep?"

Even though she could tell that he'd cupped his hand over the phone, she could still hear him whispering. And then her best friend (who sounded much more alert) came onto the phone. "What's up, girl?"

"I have to tell you something," she began, wondering why she sounded so giddy, "but you can't tell Jefferson."

"Hold on." Long seconds later, Kyla was back. "Okay, I'm in the den. What's up?"

"I don't know how it happened," Alexis said, getting right to the point, "but . . . I slept with Brian."

"Oh, my goodness! You didn't!"

"Ssshhh," Alexis said, trying to quiet her friend. "Remember, I don't want Jefferson to know."

"Why not? There's nothing wrong with what you did."

"What? I thought you'd be the first one quoting scriptures about how I shouldn't be fornicating and you'd rush right over to soak me in some holy oil."

"First of all, quoting scriptures is your thing. And second, it's not fornicating if you're sleeping with your husband."

"Ex-husband."

"Your soon-to-be next husband." Kyla laughed.

She didn't want to, but Alexis smiled. "You're crazy. I called you to—" She stopped.

"To what? To get me to say that you shouldn't have done it?"

"Yeah, isn't that what a Sister in Christ is supposed to do?"

"I'm supposed to tell you the truth, and the truth is that this is a good thing. Just go with it, Alex. Don't think. Just see where this takes you."

"I don't want to be taken anywhere. This was a mistake, and I just needed to talk to my best friend about it."

"Uh-huh."

"It's never going to happen again."

"Never say never."

"That's all you have for me? Some tired cliché?"

"Tell the truth, shame the devil."

"Okay, now see, you're getting on my nerves."

Kyla laughed. "And you're getting on my nerves acting all silly."

"I wouldn't call having my heart broken being silly." Alexis pouted.

The change in Kyla's tone was instant. "I know, sweetie, but all I'm sayin' is that that's behind you."

"It may be, but I'll never give my heart a chance to hurt like that again."

There was a pause before Kyla spoke, softer this time. "Don't close the door, Alex. Especially not if God wants it open."

As soon as Kyla brought up God, Alexis said a quick good night. She didn't agree with Kyla, but she did feel better. Talking it out had helped, and now she could say with conviction that it would never happen again.

She'd just needed this one time; now Brian Lewis was completely out of her system.

Thank God for that.

Twenty-five

MY VIBE IS RIGHT!

That was his thought as Brian rolled over and glanced at the clock. It was Saturday, so it wasn't like he had to be up. But he just couldn't sleep.

He turned onto his back, clasped his hands behind his head, and stared at the ceiling, just as he'd been doing since he'd slipped into bed way past midnight. But last night, it wasn't restless, regret-filled thoughts that had kept him awake. Last night, he couldn't rein in his exhilaration. The memories of being with Alexis were still so fresh, he could reach out and touch them. He could still see her, smell her, taste her, as if it had all happened just a minute ago.

For what had to be the thousandth time, he replayed the fantasy. The way Alexis had leaned in and kissed him with such passion, he hadn't been able to breathe. But then he'd recovered from his shock and had taken over, making sure that she didn't change her mind.

He played the moments in slow motion—their lips locking,

Alexis weightless in his arms, his tearing her clothes from her body.

Her body.

He took deep breaths and fought to keep his nature at bay. No need to go there now. There would be plenty of time to make up for what they'd missed over the years.

He still couldn't believe that it'd been that long since he'd been with a woman. It was a good thing none of his friends knew the truth. He could hear them now, especially Stanley . . .

"Man, there isn't a male on the face of this planet who would wait that long for any woman. Please, it would never happen!"

Yeah, he could hear Stanley talking that mess, as if he knew every man on earth. Well, he had something for Stanley and anyone else who thought he was a fool . . . he was a fool in love who'd won.

Cool air tickled his skin the moment he tossed back his comforter. The sun exploded into the bedroom when he drew back the drapes, but he stayed in front of the window, not concerned about his nakedness—no one could see him through the tinted glass.

He raised his hands above his head and stretched, then chuckled as he remembered doing that in Alexis's bed last night. He'd been pleased with her reaction—the way her eyes had soaked in his body. The way she'd sighed. But then she'd kicked him out of her bed and out of her house. As if that was going to help her. As if that was going to keep him away.

Alexis just didn't know; she didn't stand a chance. Because his vibe was better than right—it was tight! It was a fact now: he was going to get his wife back.

Then he wondered, would she still be considered his second wife or his third? Maybe she would be his second wife and this would be his third marriage. He laughed out loud at that mind twister. The only thing that mattered was that she would be his wife—second, third, fourth, whatever. It just needed to happen. Now.

He paused in front of the dresser and picked up the photo of Alexis and him that had been taken at the bed-and-breakfast in Oceanside where they had renewed their wedding vows just months before they'd separated. The photo made his smile dip. That was the last time they'd been really happy. It was before he had broken her heart into what he imagined were a million little pieces. Before she'd found out about Jasmine. And Jacqueline.

Jasmine. He hadn't thought of her too often. Really, hardly at all. But Jacqueline—she was different. His daughter often came to his mind.

There were times when he'd actually thought about calling Jasmine and asking her for a photo of his little girl. Not that he needed it. He'd seen Jacqueline for only a couple of minutes, but her face had been permanently etched in his mind. How could he forget when she looked so much like him? From her eyes to her lips to the cinnamon tint of her skin, she'd taken every bit of his DNA.

But though she wore her paternity on the outside, he'd still given up his rights. It was far better for Jasmine and her husband to raise her without his interference.

That fact didn't stop him from thinking about Jacqueline, though. No matter how much he tried to keep her away, hardly a day passed when her image didn't dance through his mind. And there was that small corner of his heart that yearned for her, too.

He didn't really understand that; he had two sons that he hardly ever saw. Maybe it was regret that made him wish it could be different with Jacqueline. Or maybe it was because she was a girl—he wasn't sure. But it didn't matter because a relationship with her would never be possible. There was no plan he could devise that would include Jacqueline and Alexis—the two could never coexist, and that meant he had to make a choice.

And he chose Alexis.

He sighed. Why was he even thinking about this? His focus needed to be singular—Alexis only.

Returning the picture to its place, he rushed into the bathroom. And beneath the warmth of the shower's spray, he vowed never to think about the past again.

Twenty-six

"So . . . explain this to me . . . again," Kyla puffed as she stopped running. Bending over, she rested her hands on her knees and inhaled deeply. "Why . . . are we out here . . . running in . . . twenty-degree weather?"

"Stop exaggerating," Alexis yelled over her shoulder. "This is L.A. It's against the law for the temperature to drop below fifty."

"Then someone needs to arrest the weatherman because it's sure 'nuff cold out here!"

Still jogging, Alexis glanced back, then sighed as she turned around and ran to where Kyla stood.

Kyla whined, "Let's just go to the gym."

Alexis shook her head. "I need to talk to you without a whole bunch of people around."

Kyla glanced up the beach. It was shocking that they weren't alone at the edge of the ocean. Other diehards were scattered along this part of the Pacific that was just a bit away from the Santa Monica pier. Behind them, at the top of the ridge, dog lovers strolled in the cold with their pets, and there was even a group of four women doing yoga together as they faced the blue brine.

Kyla tucked her gloved hands underneath her arms. "Just tell me what you wanna talk about so that I can get someplace warm."

Alexis rolled her eyes. "Don't be a punk," she said, turning away. "A little cold scares you?" But now she didn't jog, just walked.

She didn't have to turn around to know that Kyla was following her, waiting to hear the big news that had dragged them both out of their beds before seven on this November morning.

It should have been easy to talk to the woman who had been her best friend for more than twenty years. Since their days at Hampton University, there hadn't been a topic they hadn't discussed. But this was different because she knew what her friend's reaction would be—not good.

Alexis didn't face Kyla; instead, she spoke to the ocean. "I'm going to give Cabot a call," she said as the mist kissed her. "I'm going to ask him if he wants to go out again."

"What!" Kyla grabbed Alexis's arm and spun her around.

Standing nose to nose, Alexis repeated what she'd said.

And Kyla did the same. "What!" she exclaimed, as if Alexis was speaking a different language. "But you just slept with Brian."

"Don't remind me."

"How can you call Cabot? And why would you want to? You told me that he was a bore. That you had nothing in common. That if he was the last man on earth—"

Alexis held up her hand. "I know what I said."

Kyla continued her rant. "So why are you doing something as dumb as this?"

"Because I'm desperate." Alexis wasn't sure if Kyla was scrunching her face out of disgust or confusion. But she didn't ask. She just turned and trudged forward on the soft sand.

Suddenly, Kyla was able to keep up. "You're not desperate."

"Yeah, I am," Alexis said, catching breaths in between her words. "I'm desperate to get Brian out of my head, out of my mind, out of my heart. And this is the only way I know how to do it."

Kyla was out of breath, too, but she marched, matching Alexis step for step. "It's not going to work, Alex. 'Cause he's *in* your head and your mind and your heart."

"It's going to work," Alexis said, as if the force of her words could make it so. "And you're going to help me."

Kyla stopped moving, folded her arms again. Stared her friend down as if she hoped that gave her some sense.

But Alexis was not daunted. "Set up a dinner. Not this week because I'm sure he has plans for Thanksgiving, but first thing next week. Maybe Monday. You, Jefferson, Cabot, and me."

Kyla sighed. "This whole thing is ridiculous, but if you have to go out with someone, why Cabot? You hate him."

"I don't hate him, I just don't like him."

Kyla's eyes widened.

Alexis continued, "But I think I might be able to like him one day. There's something about Cabot—he's bigger than life. He's bigger than Brian."

"Are you talking about his money?"

"No! You know I'm not like that. It's just that Cabot takes up so much space, there's no room for Brian. He's the only man I know who can overpower my past and help me leave Brian in the dust."

Kyla exhaled a deep breath.

Alexis said, "I know it doesn't make sense to you, and

maybe it's a long shot, but I'm hoping that Cabot will look better and sound better and be better when we're among friends."

Kyla shook her head. "This is just plain stupid."

"Do stupid with me this one time. And if it doesn't work, I'll give up and try something else."

"Here's a thought: try making it work with your husband."

Alexis rolled her eyes. "Just tell me, are you going to help me or not?" She looked out to where the ocean met the earth, knowing that Kyla was trying to figure this out. If she had more words, she would've explained it better. But all she knew was that she'd just been delivered from that place of pain, and she didn't want to go back there. Cabot was her ticket out.

As if Kyla heard what was going on in Alexis's head, she said softly, "Okay."

With relief, Alexis looked up. "Thank you," she said before she hugged her friend. When she pulled back, Alexis shivered and looked back at the ocean behind them. "Do you know how cold it is?"

"Ah . . . yeah. That's what I—"

"I cannot believe you have me out here like this," Alexis said with a frown. Shaking her head, she plodded through the sand. "You need to take me somewhere and buy me a cup of coffee," she yelled out to Kyla. "Having me out here like this . . . what kind of friend are you?"

Behind her, she heard Kyla cracking up. She didn't turn around, but she could imagine her friend, bent over, her hands resting on her knees. Laughing.

Alexis smiled. She was so grateful that Kyla was willing to stand next to her through all of this craziness. But soon, if Cabot could get it together, maybe this madness would be over.

Twenty-seven

"DOCTOR LEWIS, ARE YOU ALL right?"

Brian paused and glanced up at the receptionist as he took the stack of messages that she held out to him.

"Yeah, what's up?" he asked the young woman, an intern from one of the local colleges.

Her braids swung from side to side when she shook her head. "I don't know." She frowned. "You just seem kind of different."

Brian grinned as he slowed his strut and tried not to cha-cha down the hall. He guessed he did look a little different. That's the way love goes.

He paused in front of his office but didn't go inside. Instead, he crossed one leg in front of the other and spun around, trying to get his old-school Temptations groove on. But 180 degrees into his turn, he bumped right into Jefferson.

"Whoa," his friend said as he bent down and picked up the folder that Brian had knocked out of his hand.

"Sorry, man." Brian slapped Jefferson on his back before he stepped into his office.

"No harm, no foul." Jefferson followed Brian inside. "Wow, you look happy. So what's going down?"

"Nothing," Brian said, sifting through the message slips he'd been given.

"Yeah, right." Jefferson dropped into the chair in front of Brian's desk. "I think you're finally getting into the single life. Who's got you dancing in the halls?"

Brian settled into his seat. Looked straight at his friend and leaned forward, ready to tell his news. But before he started, he stopped.

For the four decades that the two had known each other, he'd shared just about everything with his best friend. But now he hesitated. Should he tell what was going on with Alexis? Because if he told Jefferson, Jefferson would tell Kyla, who would tell Alexis. And his plan was that his soon-to-be wife had to be kept off guard, not knowing what was coming next, which was why he had called her only once since Friday night, and he'd sent her only one bouquet.

But he was going to call her tonight and invite her to spend Thanksgiving with him. He was going to tell her that they would eat out, even though he was sure that they would end up at his place (or hers) again.

When Brian didn't say a word, Jefferson added, "So are you going to share? Is that grin that you're sportin' because of anyone I know?"

Brian chuckled. "I'm not ready to talk about it," he said. "Don't want to jinx it."

Jefferson waved his hand in the air. "Man, I don't believe in that kind of stuff. But I hear you." He paused. "Maybe you'll introduce her to Kyla and me soon."

Brian nodded slowly. "Maybe."

Jefferson's smile was wide. "Well, I guess I don't have to worry about you anymore."

Brian basked in his happiness.

Jefferson was a bit more somber when he said, "You know, there was a time when I held out hope that you and Alexis would get back together." He paused, and when Brian just shrugged, he continued, "But I'm so glad you've both found a way to move on."

Brian's smiled dipped a little. Had Alexis said anything to Kyla? If she had, then he could go ahead and tell Jefferson.

But before he could say anything, Jefferson added, "I guess I can tell you this now. I was worried about saying something before—"

"What?" Brian frowned.

Jefferson shifted. "On Monday, Kyla and I are going out with Alexis . . . and Cabot Adams. I think the two of them have been going out for a while."

"Cabot?" Brian's frown deepened.

Jefferson nodded. "Yeah, remember my friend, he used to be my attorney before he went into entertainment."

Brian nodded but didn't say a word.

Jefferson continued, "I wanted you to know because I don't want you to think that I'm cooking up something behind your back. Getting together with Alexis and Cabot wasn't my idea, man."

It was a struggle, but Brian kept his face straight.

Jefferson continued, "This is something that Kyla and Alexis planned." He paused and frowned when Brian said nothing. "I'm sorry. I just thought I should tell you, and this seemed the perfect time—"

Brian held up his hands. "No harm, no foul," he said, pushing strength into his voice. "I'm fine. I was just a little surprised, that's all." He had to take a deep breath to say, "I'm glad you guys are helping Alexis."

Jefferson stared as if he was trying to figure out if his

friend's words were the truth. Finally, "You're a good man, B,"
he said, nodding his head. "I know it had to be tough to let
Alex go, but this shows how much you really did love her."

"Yeah, well . . ." Those were the only words Brian had.

Jefferson glanced at his watch. "I have to get going."
He strolled out of the office, not looking back to see Brian
slumped in his chair.

Alexis was going out with Cabot? That didn't make any
sense. They might be divorced, but he knew his wife. She
would've never gone to bed with him if she were dating someone else. Plus, the other night, he could tell that she hadn't
been with another man. He knew that surely, just as surely as
he knew that he hadn't been with another woman.

But Jefferson had said it—Alexis *was* going out with Cabot.
She had played him, was probably just getting back at him for
all that he'd done to her.

He chuckled, but there was no joy in the sound. Looked
like his plan was over before it started.

Time passed, but Brian just sat behind his desk. Thinking.
About his life and the women who had been part of it. He'd
chased many of them—for sex. But Alexis was the only one
he'd chased for love. She was the only woman who was worthy
of that pursuit.

But the longer he sat, the more he thought. And then the
revelation came to him—maybe not even Alexis was worth this
kind of effort.

Twenty-eight

It wasn't as bad as it could've been.

But even with Kyla and Jefferson at the table, Cabot still talked. And talked. But this time, it felt a little more normal, because occasionally Jefferson got the chance to say something, too.

And truly, it was good to at least have her best friend there with her, except for the assaults. The first time Alexis felt the kick, she was sure that someone had hit her accidentally. But then the kick came again. A little harder, this time. The third time, the kick almost made her cry out.

Pissed, Alexis turned to Kyla, who just rolled her eyes. The question was all over Kyla's face: Are you happy now?

Okay, so maybe this had not been the best idea. At least it had taken her thoughts away from Brian for an hour or two.

"Would anyone like another glass of wine?" The waiter held up a bottle as he smiled at Cabot.

Jefferson looked at each of them. "No, I think we'll just wait for our dinner."

When the waiter walked away, Jefferson said, "Alex, you'd better watch out. That guy has eyes for Cabot."

Cabot shook his head. "No way! Now I'm politically correct and all that good stuff, but that's not how I roll. No! Way!"

Jefferson and Kyla laughed, but Alexis wanted to call the waiter back and say, Take him!

Alexis picked up her glass, took a sip of water . . . and choked.

"Are you all right?" Jefferson asked right before Brian stepped to the table.

"Hey, guys."

Jefferson pushed back his chair so hard it almost fell over. He looked at Alexis, then at Cabot. Finally, he turned to his friend. "Hey," he said, his tone filled with confusion. "What're you doing here?"

Brian answered Jefferson, but his eyes were on Alexis. "We just came in for a drink."

Alexis's hand trembled as she lifted her glass again; she paused to steady it before she brought the rim to her lips. Now, she wished that *she* could do that water-wine-Jesus-miracle thing.

Brian said, "Oh, everybody, this is Misty." His grin was wide; his voice was full of cheer. "Misty, this is . . . everybody." He paused and focused on the only person at the table who wore a smile. "I don't believe we've met," he said to Cabot. He held out his hand. "Brian Lewis."

"Cabot Adams." He shook Brian's hand.

From the corner of her eye, Alexis could see Kyla staring Brian down, just like she was doing.

Brian said, "Well, I'll let you guys get to your dinner. Have a good night."

Before Brian and Misty stepped away, Cabot asked, "Would you like to join us?" Alexis gasped, but Cabot didn't seem to notice. He continued, "I'm sure we can fit two more—"

Kyla said, "I'm sure Brian and his . . . friend would like to be alone."

Brian's smile never wavered. "Yeah, actually, Misty and I have some . . . business to discuss."

Alexis and Kyla rolled their eyes in unison.

"Have a good one," he said, taking a final look at Alexis.

Brian and Misty had barely moved when Cabot said, "Seems like a nice man. Are those two married?"

Alexis wanted to slap him. Hadn't he heard Kyla call that girl Brian's friend? And even if he hadn't, did Cabot really think that a twenty-five-year-old (twenty-six, tops!) surfer girl would be Brian's wife?

But she said nothing, just lifted her eyes, made contact with the waiter, and raised her glass—a signal that more wine would be appreciated right about now.

For the first time since she'd met him, Alexis was glad that Cabot never shut up. He kept on and on, bragging about his business, about his contacts, about things that didn't matter to anyone except him. And she prayed that he would never stop, because if he did, she might have to talk to Kyla or Jefferson about Brian.

By the time their dinners arrived, Alexis was ready for another glass of wine. But she switched to sparkling water tonight, remembering what had happened the last time she'd tried to find courage in a glass—Brian had ended up in her bed.

It took a gargantuan effort to keep her eyes away from the bar. But she lost the battle and glanced over, promising herself that it would be quick. But her eyes stayed right there, right where Brian stood with Misty. Right where the two chatted and laughed and drank.

Alexis watched Misty take sip after sip of a golden liquid. Was the girl trying to find the same courage she'd found? Would she end up in Brian's bed tonight?

She shook her head, not wanting that image. And why should she care anyway?

Turning her attention back to her plate, she forced forks filled with lobster salad into her mouth, then rested her chin in her palm and pretended to hear and care about what Cabot was saying.

But her eyes kept going back until she watched Brian walk with Misty toward the door, without a good-bye or even a glance toward their table. Clearly, he wasn't as curious about her as she was about him.

He'd made a fool out of her . . . again.

The clanking of her fork on the china echoed throughout the restaurant. She wasn't sure if the utensil had fallen from her hands or if she had thrown it, wishing her plate was the middle of Brian's chest.

"Sorry," she said, when she looked up to find three pairs of eyes on her.

Her apology didn't stop their stares.

Kyla said, "Are you all right?"

No, she wasn't. She didn't want to play this game anymore. She shook her head. "I don't feel well." She pushed her chair back slowly.

"Do you think it's something you ate?" Cabot asked.

"No. I'm just . . . it's just . . ." She stopped. "Look, I don't want to interrupt this dinner. Please," she said, putting on her jacket, "you guys stay, enjoy, but I need to go."

Cabot tossed his napkin onto the table. "I'll take you."

"No," she said. "That's not necessary. I'm well enough to drive, and I'll feel bad if I ruin tonight for everyone."

This time, it was Jefferson who was shaking his head. "No, Alex." He turned to Cabot. "We'll make sure that she gets home."

But before he could stand, Kyla rested her hand on her husband's. "Baby, I think Alex is okay enough to get home." Looking up, Kyla said, "Just make sure you call me."

Only a best friend could do that, could instantly have your back. Alexis had no doubt that Kyla had figured out what was going on.

"At least let me walk you to your car." Cabot told Kyla and Jefferson that he would be back. In silence, he escorted Alexis to the valet stand.

"I'm really sorry about this," she said.

"No problem." He handed her ticket to the attendant. "I was glad that you wanted to get together again," he said in a way that made Alexis think he didn't get many chances at second or third dates.

They stood in silence until her car pulled up. Cabot tipped the young man, then helped Alexis inside. Before he closed the door, he leaned over and gently kissed her forehead. "I really like you, Alexis. And I hope we'll get another chance," he said, like he knew those were words she needed to hear. "We can do this dance slowly, but let's let the whole song play. Let's see where this goes."

She nodded, so surprised.

"I'll call you tomorrow," he said, then closed the door.

She waved good-bye before she sped away, still taken aback. Maybe this plan of hers *had* worked. Yes, Cabot was still a big bore, but he sounded as if he knew that and wanted to do better. Maybe she could talk to him, let him know what would work best for him, for them. Maybe she could give him exactly what he asked for—a chance.

Right there she decided: she'd take Cabot's call tomorrow and tell him that she agreed that they should pursue this . . . slowly. She definitely needed slowly.

Yes, she'd do that tomorrow. But there was something that she had to take care of tonight.

Twenty-nine

THIS WAS GOING TO END—right here, right now.

Alexis jumped from her car, ignoring the words that screamed at her from the left side of her brain. *Do not do this.*

"Can I leave my car here for a couple of minutes?" she asked Steven, the concierge who had worked in the building from the time she'd moved in years ago.

"Sure, Mrs. Ward-Lewis."

She cringed. That was another thing that had to stop. When they'd divorced, she'd kept her name hyphenated with Brian's—it was just easier. But after tonight, she didn't want any part of him. First thing tomorrow she was going to begin the process of getting herself back totally—she would be Alexis Ward from now on.

In front of the elevator door, Alexis paced as she planned her words. Her left brain was still screaming, now about humiliation. But she refused to listen to reason; she'd listened to reason for far too long.

She'd listened to reason when Brian had announced that he

was addicted to sex. She'd listened to reason when she'd found out that he'd slept with hundreds of women. And reason was still there when she accidentally stumbled upon the fact that he'd fathered a child with Jasmine.

So she had no reason left. It was time for her to go off, and tonight Brian was going to hear every bit of her mind. She was going to tell him how he needed to stop sending her flowers. How he needed to lose her number. And how he needed to truly understand that she didn't love him and would never love him again.

As she moved to his door, she thought about the keys she still had tucked inside her purse. It would serve him right if she just let herself in and broke up his . . . tryst with his surfer girl.

It had been, what, two days since his therapist had said he was cured? And he was right back in bed with strange women, after declaring his great love for her and his greater hope that they would once again be together.

Yeah, right!

Well, she wouldn't believe his lies anymore.

With a deep breath, she raised her hand, pressed her knuckles against the door in a not-so-soft tap. It was only then that she noticed how her heart raced.

It was reason that made her mind say, *Maybe this isn't the brightest thing I've ever done.*

What made her think that he'd be here anyway? He was probably sharing his woman's bed, just like he'd shared hers. That thought made her knock again, harder this time.

She had no doubt that if he was here, he'd answer. He always answered—the beeper, the telephone, the door—he was a doctor, after all.

But still, no answer.

Until she turned away. Then the door swung open.

"Alexis!" Brian exclaimed, as if he was happy to see her.

She noticed the glass he held—half empty. She noticed that he was dressed—fully.

I guess they haven't gotten started yet.

"So . . . ," he said, as if he expected her to finish the sentence.

She opened her mouth, then stopped. She hadn't really thought this all the way through. Was she supposed to curse him out while she was standing in the middle of this hallway with gilded mirrors and crystal chandeliers? Or was she supposed to walk in and air their business in front of his woman of the night?

She opted for the latter and marched past him, half expecting to see a naked woman leisurely lying on the couch that they had shopped for together all those years ago. But the living room was empty.

With just the slightest bend of her head, she peeked outside, checking the balcony. Nothing. Turning around, she frowned at the way the edges of Brian's lips twitched. As if he was holding back a huge laugh.

She said, "I know you're busy, but I need to talk to you."

"I'm not busy at all. Just surprised that you're here." He took a sip of whatever was in his glass, his amusement apparent. "So . . . what brings you by? I thought you'd still be on your date."

"I thought you'd still be on yours."

He put his glass down, shook his head. "I wasn't on a date." He stepped closer to her. "But you—"

Taking a breath, she interrupted him. "Brian, I came by to tell you that this is—"

She didn't even have a chance to finish before his lips were on hers, his arms around her waist pulling her so close. It was quick, deep, filled with too much passion. And too many seconds went by before she used both hands to push him away.

She wanted to smack him the way those starlets did in all of those old movies. But instead, she panted, "I'm not doing this with you. Not anymore."

"Why not?"

"Because . . . because," her voice rose with each word, "you're obviously not cured. You're still addicted to sex, and I'm not going to be an enabler, or a victim, or whatever."

He frowned, as if he didn't know what she was talking about. "Addicted to sex?" He chuckled. "Sweetheart, I haven't made love with anyone . . . except for you."

She twisted her mouth, letting him know that she was no longer going to believe his lies. "What about that woman? Bitsy or Ditzy or . . ."

"Misty. She's a neighbor; her parents just bought her an apartment in this building, and she wanted some advice about becoming a surgeon."

Alexis laughed, remembering the chick in the too-tight top and too-short skirt. "You expect me to believe that?"

He didn't share her laugh, just shrugged. "I don't really care what you believe, but I'm telling you the truth. She wanted information, and I thought tonight would be the perfect time to take her out and talk. And I decided that the Haven would be the perfect place, especially since I knew you would be there."

She blinked, confused. "What . . . what . . . you *knew* I was having dinner?"

He chuckled. "Of course I did, Alexis. Please, don't you think that was too much of a coincidence?"

She absorbed his words. Was this nothing but a game to him? The emotions that had been simmering inside her exploded! The love, the hate, the jealousy. But before she could even think about raising her hand and slapping him, he grabbed her wrists, held her tight, stared her down.

Just like before, his lips were right there. So close, too close.

And she just couldn't help herself—she leaned in and kissed him.

It was a repeat performance—the way she wrapped her arms around him and let him carry her away, fighting all the thoughts that came from the left *and* right sides of her brain.

Not a minute passed before they were in the bedroom; then, only seconds after that, he was stretched, once again, on top of her. This time, they were filled with so much passion that they couldn't wait. A shift of her skirt, a zip of his pants—it took barely two minutes.

And they were done.

But there was no rest in between, no time to think about what they'd done. His lips found hers, and now they tore at each other until they were naked.

And then they did the same thing all over again.

Her question broke through the quiet.

She asked, "What are we doing?" and her voice trembled.

The way Brian held her before he spoke let Alexis know that he'd heard her fear. He lightly kissed her cheek before he said, "We're finding our way back to each other."

Only a bit of light from the living room illuminated their space, but Alexis could still see the ceiling. She stayed on her back, staring at the cracks and crevices in the stucco that were so well known to her. For a moment, this felt like home, but there was no way that she could come back to the familiar.

"I love you, Alexis," he whispered.

Her mind tried to close her ears, but her heart heard him and told her that his words were true. But what was she supposed to do with that?

She told him her own truth, "You loved me before, and it wasn't enough."

"I had a problem then, but I don't anymore. And I want the chance to prove this to you."

A chance. Just a couple of hours before, Cabot had asked for a chance.

She stayed silent, stared more at the ceiling. Connected the dots to see the old formations she'd created over the years whenever worries kept her awake and looking up.

"I promise," he began as he tightened his arms around her, "I will never lie to you again. You will never have to worry about other women . . . or anything."

She stared more at the crevices and wondered if there were new formations since the last time she'd lain in this bed.

His lips moved gently against her ear when he whispered, "I will spend the rest of my life making it all up to you. Give me . . . give us this chance."

She said nothing.

"We'll do it any way you want . . . we'll take it slow, or we'll go down to City Hall tomorrow."

With those words, she rolled onto her side. Leaned back against him—her back to his front. A spoon made of skin.

She turned her head slightly to look at the ceiling again. There did seem to be new formations, but it was still familiar.

This was home.

Thirty

I AM THE MAN!

This time, though, the words inside him were not boisterous. Instead, they were soft, sweet, almost too sweet. Made him lean over and kiss Alexis's lips.

She stirred but didn't awaken, and he was glad. He wanted her to stay just like this, asleep in their bed. So that he could look at her and not have to pinch himself. So that he could thank God for this blessing.

Everything he'd had to do—including waiting—had been worth it for this moment. Silently, he told God that he was never going to mess up again.

"There will never be another secret. Never another lie, sweetheart," he whispered, and hoped his words would somehow go deep into her soul so that when she awakened, she would know that his commitment, his love, was true.

She already had to know that he would do anything for her. Like last night, with Misty. It was a shame that he'd had to use the young woman like that. But she'd been up for it. When he asked her out for drinks, he'd told her up front that he was interested in getting his wife back. Misty had been surprised at first, but then agreed because he'd been "such a good neighbor." Turned out the young woman, who was engaging and intelligent and truly interested in being a surgeon someday, was studying now at UCLA.

Alexis moaned, stretched, then opened her eyes, looking straight into his.

"You're my Sleeping Beauty," he said.

"That is so corny."

"That's what happens when you're in love." He kissed her forehead. "I love you, Alexis." He waited for her to say the same.

But she didn't. Just raised herself up a bit and glanced over his shoulder. "It's almost nine! Why did you let me sleep so late?" She fell back onto the bed. "I have to get to work."

"I thought it would be good if we spent the day together." He leaned over her. "Preferably in bed."

She smiled.

"And then we can get up and run down to City Hall to get married, right before we go to your town house and pack up everything—"

She laughed. "I thought you said we were going to take this slow."

"Okay," he said, feigning disappointment that wasn't too much of a stretch. Not that he really thought she'd marry him today. But there was nothing wrong with hoping.

When she pulled him close and kissed him, his hopes rose.

The phone rang, and he ignored it at first. But by the third ring, he remembered he was a doctor, rolled over, and glanced at the caller ID. It was the New York City number that made him grab the receiver before the call went to voice mail.

"May I speak to Doctor Brian Lewis?" the male voice asked.

"Speaking," he said, still leaning over Alexis.

"This is Agent Ruffin from the FBI. Do you have a moment?"

He frowned. "What is this regarding?"

"I'm working with the NYPD regarding Jacqueline Bush."

Just the mention of his daughter's name made his heart skip a couple of beats. "Ja—" Stopping himself before he repeated her name, he rolled away from Alexis and planted his feet on the floor. Why would the FBI be calling him about his . . . about Jasmine and Hosea's daughter? "Could you hold on a moment?" he said into the phone, then, to Alexis, "Sweetheart, this is a . . . consultation." He cringed as the first lie slipped so easily between his lips. "I'm gonna take this in the living room so you can go back to sleep."

"I don't want to sleep," she said with a gaze that he hoped meant she'd soon say she loved him, too. He wanted to kiss her so badly, but it was the man on the other end of the phone who really had his heart pounding.

He walked quickly toward the door, then partially closed it behind him. In the living room, he moved to the far end of the sofa before he brought the phone back to his ear. He whispered, "How can I help you, Mr. Ruffin?"

"I'll get right to the point," the agent said. "I understand you're the"—there was a pause and then the ruffling sound of paper—"father of Jacqueline Bush?"

Brian nodded and then remembered that the man was three thousand miles away. "Yes, her biological father." He kept his voice low.

"Well, I'm sorry to tell you this . . . the minor, Jacqueline Bush, is missing." The words took Brian's breath away, but he didn't have any time to recover before he was asked, "Were you aware of this?"

"No," he said, louder than he wanted to. Then softer,

"No." Glancing over his shoulder, he asked, "What do you mean, she's missing?"

The agent told Brian about the trip to the mall, then he began to ask questions: When was the last time he saw his daughter? What was his relationship with her, and with Hosea and Jasmine? And did he know of anyone who would want to hurt the child? But it was the last question that made Brian raise his voice a bit.

The agent asked, "The mother, Jasmine Bush, do you think she's involved?"

"With her daughter being kidnapped? No!" And then he lowered his voice once more. "Definitely not."

"Okay, Doctor Lewis. Well, that's all the questions I have for you right now."

Now he had questions of his own. "So what's being done to find her?" He was surprised at the emotion in his voice.

"Everything we can. The detectives from New York may be in touch with you. They may have a few more questions."

"Yes, yes, of course. Anything I can do." He assured the agent that he would be available. Finally, he clicked off the phone, shaking.

The FBI! Well, obviously, he wasn't any kind of suspect or else they would've shown up at his door. But still . . . he took a deep breath.

Jacqueline is missing!

The touch of her hands on his shoulders made Brian jump inches into the air.

"Sorry," Alexis said, moving from behind him. "I didn't mean to scare—"

He held up his hands. "No, I'm sorry."

She came around to the front of the couch, and his eyes began at the tips of her pumpkin-colored toes and slowly rose. He paused at her calves and remembered the way her legs had been wrapped around him last night. Right above her knees, the cloth began—one of his starched white shirts that covered her but somehow made her look as sexy as when she was nude.

But though all he wanted to do was take her into his arms, he couldn't. He couldn't touch her at all, not with the news he'd just heard. Because if he touched her, he would tell her. And if he told her, he'd lose her. He was sure that the mention of Jasmine's name, even in the middle of this, would drive Alexis far away.

"Are you okay?" she asked before she sat next to him.

He nodded. "I'm fine." *My second lie.*

She hesitated for a moment before she wrapped her arms around his neck and kissed his ear. "You know, I was thinking," she said between nibbles, "you're right. Let's stay in bed today."

Brian closed his eyes. He was in the moment, the one that he'd been praying for, waiting for. And as slowly as it had come, it was quickly slipping away.

He faced his ex-wife and forced his lips to spread. "I'm so sorry, sweetheart, but I can't."

She leaned back. "Ooookay . . ."

"I just found out . . . ." He paused and prepared lie number three. "I have to go into the office." He watched the suspicion rise behind Alexis's eyes, and he wanted to hold her, assure her. But his hands stayed in his lap. After too many silent moments, he said, "Let's make plans . . . to get together . . . later . . . maybe."

"Ooookay," she said again, jumping up from the sofa.

Moments later, he heard her inside the bedroom, moving quickly, trying to make a fast getaway.

"Please, God," he said under his breath, though he didn't know if he was praying for Alexis or Jacqueline.

It didn't take Alexis even five minutes to dress and return to the living room looking the way she had when she'd come into his apartment. From the clothes she wore to the expression on her face, she was back to the woman who'd walked in last night. She was brewing with hurt and anger.

His heart ached already.

He walked her to the door and kissed her before he opened it. Said, "I'll call you later," but he didn't answer the questions that were in her eyes. When she stepped outside, he hated that he felt relieved. He hated that he didn't wait for her to get on the elevator before he closed the door. But he needed to be alone.

He trudged back to the bedroom and lay in the same space where they'd made beautiful love. But his thoughts were not on Alexis.

There were so many questions; he needed so many answers. But there was one thing that he did know—he had to help his daughter.

It didn't make a lot of sense to him—the way he wanted to do something. It wasn't like he had a relationship with Jacqueline . . . she had no idea who he was.

"She's my daughter," he said, as if he was in a debate with himself.

For long minutes he thought about what he had to do. He thought about how this decision would affect the rest of his life. It was the latter thoughts that sickened him; that made his head throb, his stomach rumble; and that gave him the biggest pain in his heart.

Still, he had to do this. Even though he knew that it was going to cost him.

Thirty-one

ALEXIS HAD A SINKING FEELING. It had begun the moment she'd seen Brian's face when he'd answered the phone. It continued even now, hours later. If it didn't stop, it would drag her heart back into the abyss she had just climbed out of.

How had this happened again?

She was back in this place—the dark side of Brian, with his secrets and his lies.

Though it wasn't like he had actually told her a lie. He hadn't told her anything. But he definitely had a secret.

She slammed the budget report onto her desk. "This is what I get for going backward," she said.

The thought that she'd gotten caught up this way with Brian sickened her. It was ridiculous to think that she and Brian could do this again, and even more ridiculous to believe that Brian had changed. He just came with secrets. And lies. And plenty of drama.

Springing up, she stepped to the window, the events of the last hours as clear as the glass in front of her.

Most of their time together had been beyond wonderful. The way he'd taken her to that fantastic, familiar place as they made love. The way he'd held her all through the night. The way he'd whispered promises of undying love and complete truth when he thought she was asleep. She'd fallen for it all.

Then.

This morning.

The phone rang.

Alexis thought about each moment again, trying to catch a clue as to what had happened. Who was that call from? What had been said that wiped away every effort Brian had made over the weeks, the months?

She had no idea why she was asking herself that. She knew who it was—a woman. It was *always* a woman. And truth— she was almost sure what that call had been about. Something she'd feared since she'd found out about Jasmine and Jacqueline. This was another woman stepping up, telling Brian that he had fathered *her* child.

She sighed, acknowledging the fear. There had to be more children lurking out there. There had to be. With the hundreds of women he'd slept with, he couldn't have been lucky enough to father only one.

She shook her head. She'd been crazy to think that she could handle this. She wasn't woman enough. Or maybe she was too much of a woman.

The ringing phone interrupted her confusion, and she took two giant steps and grabbed the receiver.

"Hello," she answered, mad at herself for being so eager.

"Hey, I just wanted to make sure that you're okay. You didn't call last night."

At the sound of Kyla's voice, Alexis shrank into her chair; her hope that it would be Brian professing his love for her was gone. "I'm sorry," she said. "Last night . . . I . . . just fell right into bed," she said, leaving out the part that it was Brian's bed she'd fallen into.

"Really?" Kyla sounded disappointed. "I thought . . . now, don't get mad at me, Alex, but I thought you'd gone to Brian. At least, that's what I was hoping." She paused when Alexis didn't respond. Then continued, "I know you were upset about his showing up with that girl, but you've got to know that he was just trying to make you jealous. Jefferson told me that he'd told Brian . . ."

Alexis massaged her closed eyes and wondered if she should tell Kyla that she'd been a fool, that she'd slept with Brian and he'd gone right back to his lying, cheating ways.

"Are you listening to me?" Kyla asked.

"Yeah, I'm just . . . tired. Still not feeling that great."

"You know, there's a mean flu going around."

"Yeah, that's what it is—the flu," Alexis said, feeling more of an urge now to tell her friend. She had to tell someone about the hurt that had come back to her heart. Pressing the phone closer to her ear, Alexis said, "Something did happen last night—"

Then her office door opened. And Brian walked in.

They stared at each other for a moment before Alexis simply said, "Gotta go, Kyla." She added, "Business," so that Kyla wouldn't call her back.

Even after she hung up, Alexis didn't move. She stayed in place, studying Brian.

The look on his face forced her to ask, "What's wrong?"

There was nothing close to a swagger in his steps as he moved slowly toward her. Taking her hand, he pulled her up from the chair and into his arms.

Alexis went along with him. She stayed within his embrace, feeling that their time for holding each other like this was coming to an end. That was why she didn't pull back right away.

But when he did, his voice was soft. "I'm sorry about . . . this morning. It was just . . . I got . . ."

"That call," she finished for him.

He nodded. "I didn't want to tell you, but I promised myself, there would be no more lies, no more secrets between us."

She breathed, a bit relieved, though she was still nervous about what he had to say.

"The call," Brian continued, "was from New York. The FBI."

Her deepening frown made him tell the story quickly. She could feel the changing expressions on her face—from shock to horror and then suddenly to suspicion. When he finished, she asked, "Brian, you don't think . . ." She paused, not even able to imagine what she was about to say. But this was Jasmine's daughter, after all. So she asked, "You don't think Jasmine had anything to do with this, do you?"

Now it was his expression that metamorphosed from confusion to shock and then to something Alexis couldn't decipher—disappointment, maybe.

He frowned. "No! She didn't . . . how could you . . . why would you even think that?"

She shook her head, not wanting to go through the long list of reasons, beginning with Jasmine's being a liar and a cheat. She held up her hands. "I'm sorry." She paused and directed the conversation back to the child. "How long has Jacqueline been missing?"

"Since Friday."

"Wow!" Alexis tried to imagine what that would be like, not having your child for four days. In that moment, she felt compassion for her enemy.

He said, "I'm just afraid the longer . . ." He stopped, but in her mind Alexis finished the sentence for him.

The longer she's gone, the less of a chance of her coming home.

She turned toward the couch. "So what are they doing to find her?"

Brian shrugged as he lowered himself next to her. He sat close, so close that their knees touched. She wanted to back away but didn't.

"I don't know exactly," Brian said. "I didn't get to ask a lot of questions."

The sadness in his voice made her take his hand. "I wish you had told me this morning."

He looked down to where their fingers were entwined. Kept his gaze there as he said, "I wanted to, but I was shocked. I needed some time to think it through." He looked up and into her eyes. "And truthfully, I was afraid. Not just for Jacquie. I was thinking about us."

She frowned.

"Alex, I don't know. I don't understand the draw. I don't have any kind of a relationship with her, but"—he sucked in air—"I have to go. To New York. I have to see what I can do."

It took Alexis a moment to understand what he had said, what he meant. Then, slowly, she slipped her hand away from his and inched away, putting space between them. She found the right words to say. "Of course. You have to go. Definitely." A big breath before the finale. "She's your daughter."

His eyes searched her face as if he wanted to see if her words were the truth. "I don't know what I can do," Brian explained. "But . . ."

She nodded and inhaled before she asked, "Have you . . . spoken to . . . Jasmine?"

He shook his head. "No, I didn't call her or Hosea," he said, as if he wanted to remind Alexis that Jasmine had a husband. "I'm not even sure if I'll contact them when I get to New York. I'm not sure what I'll do. It's not like I think I'll really be able to help." He paused. "I just have to be there," he said, before he took Alexis's hand back into his. "I'll be gone for only a couple of days, Alex. I'll go, find out what's happening. And really, prayerfully, maybe she'll be home before my plane even lands in New York."

"That would be wonderful," she said, even though she drew away from him again.

He watched her slide across the couch. She'd moved only inches, but it felt like miles. "I don't want to lose you again, Alexis."

She stood, walked to the window, putting even more distance between them.

He said, "Can you . . . can we just put what we started on hold until I come back?"

It took an effort to face him, but she did. She knew that there was only one word he wanted to hear, but she didn't have "yes" anywhere inside of her. What she did have was, "You shouldn't even be thinking about us right now. Just go to New York." She lowered her eyes; she had to before she added, "Go to Jasmine."

Time moved on, and when she lifted her eyes, they were already filled with tears. Brian moved across the office toward her, slowly, as if he knew he had to savor these last moments. He held her, and she hugged him back, knowing this time would be their last.

She closed her eyes when he kissed her forehead. Nodded when he said, "I'll call you," and just stayed in place, even minutes after he'd left her alone.

At least, this time, there would be no temptation to follow him. No risk of falling into bed again. No chance of rekindling their love. Because if Jasmine was in his life, in any capacity, there was no room for her.

This time, Alexis was sure. This time, it was over.

Thirty-two

It was the same dream.

Jasmine snuggled deeper into her pillow as the blurred edges of the vision faded and the image became clear.

Brian.

At first, she saw only his face, wearing the smile that had lured her all those years ago. Slowly, he stepped closer, and as he did, she could see more: his neck, his chest, and, finally, his hand holding on to their daughter.

"Here she is, Jasmine," he said. "I brought our little girl home."

She ran in slow motion, her arms propelling her forward until she reached them. First, she grabbed Jacqueline. Lifted her and swung her around before she drowned her in kisses. And then, she turned to Brian. "Thank you," she whispered, before their lips met in a soft and gentle bond. The kiss of everlasting lovers.

Her moan was long and deep, and in her sleep, Jasmine stretched. Her eyes fluttered, then slowly opened. And the first thing she saw was the picture of Jacqueline. She'd moved her school photo from the living room into the bedroom.

It had been a dream, the same one she'd had over and over for the last forty-eight hours, ever since Detective Cohen had told them about Brian.

She'd been so sure when the detective had said Brian's name that Jacqueline was safe. But when she'd asked, "When can I see my daughter?" the detective had shaken his head and held up his hands.

"I'm sorry, Mrs. Bush, but according to the agents, Doctor Lewis doesn't know where your daughter is."

It felt like she'd been punched in the gut, the way the hope (that had been there for only a moment) was sucked right out of her. She'd collapsed, feeling like she'd lost Jacqueline all over again.

Then things got worse. The next day, Dale told them that while Hosea had passed the polygraph, Jasmine's results were not as clear.

"It's a bit confusing," Dale had said, his eyebrows bunched together. "They found deception in even your baseline questions. But like I said, these things are not one hundred percent."

"So what does that mean?" Hosea had asked.

"Of course they're out there full force looking for Jacquie, but since Jasmine can't be ruled out, they'll probably have more questions for the two of you."

He spoke to both of them, but Jasmine knew this nightmare was all about her. How could the polygraph not show her complete innocence? It felt like the world was spinning against her; nothing was the way it was supposed to be.

At least she had Hosea and Zaya. Hosea kept her strong; Zaya kept her sane. Without the two of them, she would have already given up.

Jasmine lifted her head a bit to peek at her son in the crib just a few feet away. Yesterday, Hosea had said that he needed sleep and that he couldn't get it with the toddler in their bed. But Jasmine had no intention of letting Zaya too far from her sight. So she'd rolled his crib into their bedroom and hadn't closed her eyes for more than fifteen minutes at a time since.

Jasmine pushed herself up, trying to see Zaya. She sprang up, dashed to his bed, drew back the blanket, and released a toe-curling scream.

"Zaya!"

A new someone—or maybe it was the same someone—had snuck into their bedroom and taken her son, too!

"Zaya!" she cried again.

"Ms. Jasmine, Ms. Jasmine." Mrs. Sloss rushed into the bedroom. "What's wrong?" she asked, her voice as frantic as Jasmine's.

"Zaya! My baby. He's gone!"

"No, Ms. Jasmine." The nanny shook her head wildly. "He woke up." She spoke so quickly, her English sounded more like Spanish. "And I took him. Didn't want to disturb you."

Distress had deafened her. Jasmine cried, "Zaya," as she leaned on the crib for strength. She closed her eyes and trembled; there was no way she could live now.

Then she heard his giggles.

"See, Ms. Jasmine." Mrs. Sloss rocked Zaya in her arms. "He's fine. He was—"

Before she could finish, Jasmine snatched her son from the woman's arms. "Don't you ever take him away from me again!"

Jasmine screamed, not noticing that Zaya's giggles had stopped or that her son now looked at her with wide eyes and a trembling lower lip.

"Love Mama," he whispered.

But neither Mrs. Sloss nor Jasmine heard him.

The nanny said, "Ms. Jasmine, I was only trying to—"

"I don't care what you were trying to do. Never take him out of this room! Not unless I tell you to."

Now Zaya was screaming as loud as his mother.

"What's going on?" Hosea rushed into the bedroom.

Jasmine pointed an accusing finger toward Mrs. Sloss. "She took my baby!"

"No, no," was all Mrs. Sloss said.

"Yes, you did." Jasmine's voice had quieted a bit, but not Zaya's.

Hosea coaxed Mrs. Sloss out of the room before he turned to his wife. "Calm down, sweetheart." He placed his hands on Jasmine's shoulders. "You're upsetting Zaya."

"I don't care! I'm keeping him safe," she screamed.

"Jasmine," Hosea whispered. "Jasmine," he kept saying over and over, softly and soothingly, until her cries—and Zaya's—began to subside.

When she finally sat down on the bed, Hosea said, "Let me take him."

It still took a bit more persuading for Jasmine to open her arms and hand her son to his father. Her eyes stayed with the pair as Hosea backed away from her. At the door, he said, "I'm just going to take him to his room." Before she could protest, he added, "He's going to be right down the hall. I'm here, you're here, Mrs. Sloss is here. He's safe."

Then they were gone.

The only way she could stay and not run after Hosea was by taking deep breaths—in and out. But really, how did she know that Zaya would be safe? Hadn't she thought Jacqueline was safe when she had been taken?

Her tears began all over again.

Hosea returned and held her as she cried. "What are we going to do?" Jasmine asked her husband. "I can't go on like this. I can't go on without Jacquie."

"I know," Hosea said, pulling her closer. "But we have to keep it together. We have to take care of Zaya while we look for Jacquie."

"What do you think I'm doing?" Jasmine shrugged away from his hold. "That's why I didn't want him to leave—"

Hosea shook his head. "No, sweetheart. We have to take care of him, not make him a prisoner. You haven't let him out of this house in a week."

"You say that like it's a bad thing. I'm just doing what I have to do. What do you want from me?"

"I want Zaya's life to be as normal as possible. He has to sense the tension, but I want him to feel safe and loved like he felt before . . . before this happened."

"That's impossible," Jasmine said, anger replacing her sadness for the moment. "None of us will ever be normal again. Not until we find Jacquie."

"I understand what you're saying—for you and me. But for Zaya . . . come on, Jasmine. He's going to be fine, but not if we don't find a way to give him his life back."

She understood what Hosea meant, but she didn't know how to make things normal with her son when life was so abnormal without her daughter.

She paced in front of him. "I'm scared, Hosea," she said. "Tomorrow will be a week, and . . ." Her head bowed with fresh tears. She had no idea how she'd survived these days, but she was certain that she wouldn't be able to survive many more.

He said, "We have to think about Zaya."

"And forget about Jacquie?" she asked, amazed at his words.

"Of course not. It's just that we're responsible for Zaya, too."

Jasmine shook her head. Hosea may have been listening, but he wasn't hearing her. Didn't he realize that everything she was doing now, she was doing for Zaya?

Hosea said, "I need you to do something for me." Her eyes questioned him. "Get dressed. I want to show you something I've been working on."

Days had passed since she had last left the apartment, and her intention, really, was never to again leave.

But then Hosea added, "This is about Jacquie," and she couldn't get dressed fast enough. She would go anywhere, do anything, at just the mention of Jacqueline's name.

It was hard enough thinking about Jacqueline. Wondering if she was scared, if she was cold, if she was calling for her mama and her dad.

Now Jasmine had to worry about Zaya, too. She couldn't believe that she'd let Hosea convince her to leave their son at home. He kept saying that Zaya would be safe inside the secure building, behind the locked apartment door, with Mrs. Sloss watching him every second.

But *safe* was not a word she could really comprehend anymore.

Even so, Hosea had convinced her with the promise that this outing would be worth it. And then, she'd agreed only after he'd assured her that she'd be home within an hour.

Her thoughts had her so far away that Jasmine didn't notice the passing streets as Hosea zoomed uptown. She didn't see that he had turned onto 125th and had eased the SUV to a stop in front of the Renaissance Mall.

The sight made her gasp for breath. Why were they back here—at the place where she'd lost Jacqueline?

Her eyes never left Hosea as he walked from the driver's side to her. When he opened the door and took her hand, he said, "I want you to see how many people love Jacquie."

Even though it was the first week in December, officially the holiday season, the mall was Thursday afternoon quiet; there was just a sprinkling of customers passing through.

Jasmine's eyes locked in first on the pet store. Then she glanced at the bench where she and Mae Frances had sat—the last place where she had seen her daughter. She inhaled, feeling the past as if it were the present. She could see and hear it all—how Jacqueline had waved, had said "I love you," then had blown that kiss. She remembered how she'd waved back, not knowing that would be the last time . . .

She shuddered and turned her head away. Hosea squeezed her hand as if he was having the same thoughts.

Yuletide music wafted from the speakers above—just like last week—and she had to hold Hosea's hand tighter as they ascended on the escalator. At the top, Jasmine followed Hosea down a long hall. When they neared the end, she heard the chatter. They stepped inside what looked like a conference room, the perimeter filled with computers and telephones atop long tables.

Inside, there were about thirty people: some tapping on computers, others talking on the telephones, some folding papers. Everyone was absorbed in a task.

No one seemed to notice Jasmine and Hosea standing at the edge until Reverend Bush looked up.

He smiled and rushed over. "Jasmine, sweetheart."

As he kissed her on the cheek, others turned. And that's when the applause began.

Jasmine didn't know why they were clapping; surely, it

couldn't be for her. She hadn't done anything, except lose her child.

Reverend Bush took her hand and guided her into the room. "We've been working with the police and the mall on this," he explained. "But it was all Hosea's idea."

Hosea nodded. "I worked it out with the folks from the National Center for Missing and Exploited Children. They told me exactly how to set this up."

Her eyes were wide as she looked at her husband, then moved alongside her father-in-law. As they passed, the volunteers wished her well.

"We're going to find her," and "We're all still praying," and "You know God's got this."

Some—the ones she knew, like Mrs. Whittingham and Brother Hill—hugged her. The way those two had treated her over the last week still made Jasmine marvel at the irony of tragedy . . . bad times plus old enemies equaled new friends.

Reverend Bush spoke through her musing. "We have a smaller unit like this set up at the church, but Hosea thought it would be good to set up this one closer to . . . where it happened."

"And this is a good thing, Jasmine." That came from Detective Foxx. "Because it's always good to have a unit like this where the crime first occurred."

"We have people downstairs all the time"—now it was Malik explaining—"talking to everyone coming into the mall. We're asking people if they were here last Friday. And if they were, then one of the officers interviews them. The police tell us that these people are still our best shot. Someone had to have seen something; they just don't realize it yet."

They all nodded, as if this pep talk had been rehearsed.

"The key is, baby," Hosea said, bringing up the rear, "that

we're all working on this. We've got a real shot at finding our daughter."

They were at the back of the room now, and when Jasmine turned around, the people who had clapped and hugged her had all returned to their tasks. From where she stood, she recognized more of the faces. So many were from the church—some were even among those who had rolled their eyes or snickered when she passed by the pews on any given Sunday. Now they were standing by her side.

"I want to help," Jasmine said, surprising them all.

"Are you sure?" Hosea asked. "I just wanted you to see this, and then I was going to take you right back home."

She pulled out a chair at a desk in the back of the room. "No, I wanna stay. Just call Mrs. Sloss and make sure that Zaya's fine." She nodded at Hosea, knowing he needed her reassurance. She really did want to stay. Here, she felt close to Jacqueline; she needed to be a part of this center.

But then she picked up one of the papers from the stack that was piled on the desk. The top half was a picture of Jacqueline—the same photo that was in the frame on her nightstand. Below the image were her daughter's vital statistics: her age, weight, what she'd been wearing, and when she'd last been seen.

Before the first tear crawled down her cheek, Hosea was by her side, pulling her up into his arms.

"Let's go home," he whispered as he held her.

She squeezed her eyes shut and nodded. She thought she'd be able to handle this; she wanted to. But it was too much, too soon.

Jasmine backed away from Hosea's embrace, opened her eyes, and gasped.

There she was! The image of her daughter. Right here. Right in the front of the room.

Jasmine tore away from Hosea and ran. She was sobbing by the time she reached Brian and fell into his arms. Holding him as tightly as she could, she released her grief as his arms wrapped around her.

With her head bowed and her tears flowing, Jasmine never saw the shock that was frozen on Brian's face.

And she didn't see how stunned Hosea was either.

Thirty-three

BRIAN WAS GLAD THAT THEY were away from curious eyes.

In the hallway, there was no one to stare him down the way the volunteers in the center had just minutes before when Jasmine had rushed him and held him as if they were lovers. He had been beyond surprised, but he had to comfort her as she wept. What else was he supposed to do? Inside their embrace, the press of her body against his was uncomfortably familiar, but still, he stayed—until Hosea peeled his wife from his arms.

Now the three of them sat together right outside the conference room, where the volunteers had returned to work but surely had not forgotten what had just gone down.

"So when I finally talked to Detective Cohen," Brian continued his story, "he told me about the center, and I wanted to come and help." Then he added, "I'll be here only a couple of days," more to Hosea than Jasmine.

The way the Bushes stared at him—Jasmine with a smile and Hosea with a look that was contrary to his wife's—made Brian feel like there was more to explain. "I'm sure you probably have enough volunteers, but I had to do something . . . to help."

"And we appreciate it," Hosea said, though his tone didn't sound as if he felt any gratitude.

Brian didn't miss the way they held hands—or rather the way Hosea held on to Jasmine. It was a message directed at him, and Brian wanted to make sure that Hosea knew he'd received it. He said, "Alexis sends her best," hoping that Hosea understood *his* message—that he had his own woman, his own love; that he wasn't there to do anything to mess up what he—or Hosea—had. He added, "She's praying . . . for both of you."

Hosea and Jasmine nodded together as if they were one. But even though they moved as a matching pair, Jasmine kept her eyes on Brian, staring as if she never planned to let him go.

The heat of her stare made Brian shift and focus his attention on Hosea. But it was hard to keep his eyes away from Jasmine. Not that he was attracted to her in any way—it was her pain that pulled him in. Her heartache was palpable—it seeped through her pores and filled their space with the stench of tragedy.

Hosea said, "I'm sorry you came all this way; if you'd called, I would've been glad to keep you up to date." He paused and added, "I wish you had called."

His words made Brian raise his hand to loosen his tie, and then he remembered he wasn't wearing one. "I didn't want to bother you. With all . . . of this." He looked straight into the other man's eyes. "I hope you don't mind my being here, but if it's a problem, I'll leave."

"No!" Jasmine exclaimed, her first word, shocking both of them. "We're glad you're here." She turned to her husband. "Right, Hosea?"

Hosea's smile was as stiff as the rest of him. "Of course." Then, as if he had second and third thoughts, Brian watched

Hosea settle, saw his face and shoulders relax. "Everyone can help. This is all about Jacquie." Hosea stood up and glanced down at Jasmine. "We should show Brian around."

"Definitely."

Brian released a soft stream of air as Hosea led Jasmine into the room. He followed, though now his head was filled with questions. Had he made the right decision to come to New York? Maybe he was more of a distraction than a help—and that was not at all what he wanted to be.

Inside the conference room that Hosea called the command center, Hosea introduced Brian to his father; to Keith, a full-time volunteer; and to a host of friends. They were all polite enough, but behind their eyes, Brian saw their suspicion, even their disdain for Jacqueline's biological father. Did any of these people think that he had come back to usurp Hosea's position?

More doubt rose inside. *Maybe this isn't my place.*

But then when Malik, whom he'd met several times before, shook his hand and said, "Glad you're here, man," Brian settled his thoughts. He was Jacqueline's father, and he was here to do a good thing.

As Hosea explained how they were using the Internet to get Jacqueline's story out and how they were working with police departments in every city in the tristate area and beyond, Brian was aware of Jasmine standing close, moving by his side, as if he were her partner rather than Hosea.

Brian asked, "What about the media? Are they working with you on this?"

Hosea said, "That's been the hard part. The first day or two, they were all over it; but after that, we were dropped. Guess it wasn't interesting enough for them."

"What?"

"You know how it is," Malik joined in. "No matter that

Jacquie is the granddaughter of a prominent pastor, she's still a black girl. So the media . . . not interested."

Brian shook his head. "Well, I have some contacts. Let me work on a few things."

When Jasmine exclaimed, "Brian! That would be great," he took two steps back, making sure that she didn't wrap herself around him again.

Hosea handed Brian one of the flyers. "One thing that we're working on here is remembering the basics." He paused as Brian's eyes perused the paper. "Our goal is to get these into a million hands. And we're mailing them to doctor and dentist offices as well. You never know who's going to see one of those."

Brian couldn't stop staring at the photo of Jacqueline. Her face—his face—stared right back.

The eyes of his little girl seared through him, instantly deepening his pain. And he sensed other eyes, Jasmine's eyes, watching him. He had to turn, had to face her now, and when he did, he shared every ache that she felt. Now he was the one who couldn't turn away, and he looked at Jasmine with a new heart. She was the mother of his child. Never had he really thought of her that way.

The flyer slipped from his hands. "I'm sorry," he said, catching the paper before it floated all the way to the floor. Then as he stood straight, he added, "I've got to go."

Jasmine frowned. "No."

"I have to," he said, not looking at her, not looking at Hosea.

Hosea asked, "Is there anything wrong?"

Brian kept his glance away from both of them as his hand rose once again to loosen the nonexistent tie. Shaking his head, he said, "I'm fine. I just need . . . to check into the hotel."

"Can't you do that later?" Jasmine asked, her question sounding more like a plea for him to stay forever.

"I'll be back . . . tomorrow morning." Before anyone could say another word, he dashed out of the room, feeling the curious, suspicious, disdainful eyes once again.

It wasn't until he was outside, in the New York December air, that he breathed. He jumped into the town car that had driven him into Harlem from the airport. "I'm going downtown," he said to the black-suited driver, "to the Plaza."

The man only acknowledged him with a nod, and Brian was glad that this would be a silent ride.

As the car pushed from the curb, he sank into the leather seat. But even behind his closed eyelids, the image of his daughter remained. He could see her eyes staring, her lips smiling.

Is she smiling now? he wondered. That was his hope. He couldn't bear to imagine the alternative. He shook his head so that he wouldn't go there—he couldn't think that way.

But now another image came to his mind. Jasmine, with all of her sorrow and all of her pain. Then in the next instant, Alexis.

It was the image of Alexis that made him sigh. All he wanted to do was to go back to Los Angeles. But he couldn't. He had to do what he came to New York to do.

He wouldn't be here too long. Especially once he got the media involved; Jacqueline would be home within a couple of days, and then he could return to his life. He could go home to Alexis.

Yes, it would be only a little while. At least, that's what he kept telling himself.

Thirty-four

KYLA'S EYES WERE ALMOST AS wide as her mouth, but Alexis wasn't sure which part of the story had her friend's face stretched with shock. Was it the part about Jacqueline being missing, or was it the part about Brian and her doing the horizontal rumba when the call had come in?

"I cannot believe that," Kyla whispered when Alexis finished talking. "As much as I . . . can't stand Jasmine, I wouldn't wish this on anyone!" Then she paused, asked, "You don't think—" She shook her head. "Nah, not even Jasmine."

Alexis nodded. "I wondered the same thing. If this was one of Jasmine's tricks, but with the police and the FBI involved . . . I don't think so." She sighed and repeated what Kyla had just said, "Not even Jasmine."

Kyla said, "So Brian went to New York to help?"

Alexis didn't say a word as she looked down at her paper plate. Even though they'd been talking for almost an hour, she'd taken only a single bite. She pushed her plate aside and the plastic legs of the chair scraped against the concrete as she shifted.

It was one of those eighty-degree December days when Los Angelenos came outside in droves while the rest of the country was under winter lockdown. But the high temperatures did little to warm Alexis, and as she thought of Brian and Jasmine and Jacqueline, she shivered. Finally, she said, "Yeah, that's what he said. That he went to New York to help."

Kyla leaned in close. "I know you're not thinking that something's up with Jasmine and Brian."

Alexis shook her head. "No, not in *that* way."

"Not in *any* way." Kyla paused, waiting for Alexis to agree, but when she didn't, Kyla continued. "I don't get you sometimes. Brian loves you, and you love him. Why are you making everything so complicated?"

"I never said that I loved him."

"You don't have to." Kyla waved her hand in the air, dismissing Alexis's words. "It's in what you do. You wouldn't keep jumping into bed with him if you didn't love the man."

"Love has nothing to do with sex."

"Maybe for other people, but we're talking about you. And anyway, it's not just the sex part. It's all the other stuff that counts. Like what's in your eyes whenever you talk about him."

"You don't see love," Alexis insisted.

"You're right, I see more than love. I see every emotion that ever existed when you talk about Brian. I see more than love— I see passion."

"When did you become a romance novelist?" Alexis chuckled, but then she looked down, and then away, and then at the next table. If what Kyla said was true, if her emotions shined in her eyes, she didn't want her friend seeing into her soul right now. Because then Kyla would be able to see her sorrow. And she didn't want anyone—not even her best friend—to see her weakness.

Kyla asked, "So why aren't you in New York with Brian?"

"Because there's no reason for me to be."

"There's no reason for you to support Brian?"

"No, there's not. I'm not part of his life, especially not when it comes to this."

Kyla's eyes became slits, like she was deep in thought. "Are you staying away because of Jasmine?"

Alexis didn't move. How could she tell Kyla that, yes, it was because of Jasmine? She could never say that aloud because it was ridiculous. It wasn't like Jasmine had called Brian and said, Let's get together. This was a heartbreaking situation that should have drawn everyone together.

But Alexis couldn't help it—it bugged the mess out of her. No matter the reason, Brian had stopped his life, had made that cross-country trip . . . to be with Jasmine. It was absurd to be thinking this way; she knew that. But that's what just the mention of Jasmine's name did to her—it made her crazy.

As long as that woman was any part of any equation, it would never add up for her and Brian. She had worked hard to forgive Brian. But forgiving Brian *and* Jasmine? She didn't have enough forgiveness inside of her for both of them.

"Don't do this, Alex." Kyla's face was scrunched into a frown, as if she'd been studying her and had heard every word she'd thought. "Don't let this situation destroy two families. Don't let what's happened to Jasmine and Hosea mess up your chances with Brian. If anything, he needs you way more now than before."

Alexis was sure that God had put those words into Kyla's

mouth; He had to have because those were the same sentiments He'd tried to engrave onto her heart every hour of last night. But she was about to tell Kyla what she'd told the Lord: there was no reason for her to be in New York with Brian because that would only make them look and feel like a couple. That would only give them hope, when there was no hope at all.

When Alexis stayed quiet, Kyla shook her head. "This makes me sad. All of it. That baby without her mother." She raised her hand to her mouth, as if she was holding back a sob.

Alexis knew that Kyla was thinking about her own daughter, Nicole, who was a teenager now. And because Alexis knew the pain the mere thought caused Kyla, she could imagine Jasmine living this truth. Even though there wasn't even a tiny part of her that liked Jasmine, Alexis couldn't stop thinking about the little girl with Brian's face. It made her heart ache.

Kyla said, "I just hope and pray that they find her." She sighed. "This world . . . what is it coming to? God bless us all." She locked her eyes on Alexis. "You really need to think about this," she said, as if it was a command. "Brian needs you."

"And he has me. Just like you, I'll be praying for him."

Kyla pressed her lips together like there was so much more she wanted to say, but instead she just rolled her eyes. Swinging her purse over her shoulder, she pushed back her chair. "Are you ready to go?" she asked, sounding like Alexis had gotten on every single nerve she had.

Alexis shrugged and followed Kyla through the maze of plastic white tables and chairs filled with lingering lunch patrons. She was not moved as Kyla stomped in front of her. Her friend would get over it. After all, Kyla should know that she was going to do the Christian thing—she was going to pray. It was prayers that Brian and Jacqueline needed now.

After she hugged Kyla good-bye, Alexis got into her car,

eased into the traffic, and said a prayer for Jacqueline, pleading with God to bring her home and to keep her safe in the meantime. As she turned onto Wilshire, she added Brian to the mix and prayed that God would give him peace with whatever happened.

When God placed Jasmine on her heart, Alexis didn't say a word at first. But God wouldn't go away. So she pulled her car to the curb. Turned off the engine, closed her eyes, and pondered the scripture that said we should love our enemies.

And once she let Matthew 5:44 settle on her heart, Alexis sent up a little prayer for Jasmine, too.

Thirty-five

A WEEK. AND THIS WAS the first morning that the water wasn't seasoned with Jasmine's tears. She tilted her head beneath the shower's spray and then did something that always brought pain—she closed her eyes.

Though today, she wasn't afraid of the images that waited behind her lids. She knew for sure that all she would see would be happiness and glee. She'd see Jacqueline playing, laughing. And when Jasmine inhaled, her nostrils even filled with the slight scent of baby powder.

Despair was still with her; it was the marrow inside her bones. But now her misery was wrapped inside hope.

Hope.

Because of Brian.

Leisurely, she replayed every second of that part of yesterday, just as she'd been doing all night. In the video inside her mind, she again watched Brian stride into the room, saw him stand tall, felt the hope he brought right in with him.

A rush of cool air assaulted her, disrupting her daydream, making her eyes open wide.

"You scared me," she said to Hosea, who was standing at the open door. She turned off the shower and then stepped into the towel that he held up for her.

"I was just checking on you," he said.

She felt him watching as she moved toward the sink and grabbed her toothbrush.

He said, "I was surprised . . . I didn't expect you to be up."

She nodded but said nothing as she looked at her husband through the mirror. She understood his words—in the last week, she'd spent more hours in bed than out. She'd lain in her bed with Zaya, waiting for the good news to come.

But after yesterday, she realized there was no need to lie and wait; she needed to become part of the solution. She needed to be active in Jacqueline's rescue.

After she rinsed her mouth she glanced up, and in the mirror's reflection she saw Hosea, still there, looking at her with a smile. On his face, she saw *his* hope, but it wasn't the kind of hope that she needed. His hope was all about her—getting up, getting better, getting ready to take care of Zaya. His hope had nothing to do with Jacqueline.

She said, "I'm going to ride with you to the center. I wanna do something to help."

"Are you sure?" His frown was slight. "After yesterday . . ."

She wanted to tell him that yesterday wasn't today. At the beginning of yesterday, there was no Brian. But she said, "It was just a shock to see that flyer, but I'm fine now. I don't want to just sit around and wait anymore."

When he wrapped his arms around her from behind, she

almost smiled. Especially when she thought about the other arms that had held her. The arms of the man who looked so much like Jacqueline.

Hosea said, "I'll take you over. I've got to stop at the precinct . . ."

Jasmine knew what that was about—her husband was keeping Detective Cohen away from her by going to see the man himself just about every day.

He continued, "And then I'll head to work at the church after that."

Work? How could he do anything except look for Jacqueline? How could he go on as if life was normal? Even Brian had given up everything for her and Jacqueline.

"You don't have to take me," she said, ducking from his embrace. "I don't mind catching a cab."

"No, I want to," he said as he shrugged off his bathrobe. "What about Zaya?"

His question made her pause. Should she take Zaya with her?

She said, "He can stay here. With Mrs. Sloss. But I don't want her to take him out. Not anywhere."

"Okay." He nodded with a smile, as if she had taken the first step in a twelve-step program. "He'll stay here, inside, with Mrs. Sloss . . . today." Before he stepped into the shower, he added, "I'm glad you're getting out."

She didn't bother to tell him that she was glad, too. Because if she said a word, she was sure that her husband would be able to see the real reason behind the little bit of joy that she'd found.

Instead, she rushed to her closet and stood in the middle of the walk-in space. She had to pick the right outfit for her first day at the center.

• • •

Jasmine's hand trembled as she held the doorknob. She didn't move for a moment, just said a quick prayer before she pushed the door open. Her eyes scanned the room, searching, then settling. Her heavenly request had been answered.

Brian was there. In the back . . . just waiting for her.

Well, maybe not waiting. But he was there, sitting at the same desk where she'd been sitting yesterday.

That was a sign.

For the first time since Jacqueline had disappeared, Jasmine's lips spread into an easy smile. All she wanted to do was dash across the room, but eyes were watching. So she edged inside, into the middle of the chatter, and forced herself to take slow steps.

"It's good to see you," Malik said.

"You just saw me yesterday."

"What? I can't be glad two days in a row?" He kissed her cheek. "I've gotta run, but you'll be cool here with Keith, right?"

She nodded, her eyes on Brian. Malik followed her gaze, and when he turned back to her, he had a slight frown. "Be careful," was all that he said before he kissed her again and walked out the door.

She didn't know what her godbrother was warning her about, but she didn't care. All she wanted to do was get to Brian. But first, she had to get past Mrs. Whittingham.

"We've received quite a few calls this morning," the woman said, speaking as if they were friends. "I have so much hope."

Next it was Keith who blocked her path. "Hosea didn't tell me you were coming," he said. "I would've met you downstairs."

"I wanted to come by, help a little." She snuck a quick glance toward Brian. "I was thinking I could do something—like stuff envelopes."

"Well, here," Keith said as he led her back to exactly where she wanted to be. "That's what Brian's doing."

At the mention of his name, Brian turned around. She held her breath as he gazed at her—his eyes moved up, then down, and she was ready for his perusal. Her outfit was casual—just skinny black jeans and an oversize winter-white turtleneck. But it was the knee-high stiletto boots that took the outfit to chic, and Jasmine knew she looked good. A nanosecond later, when Brian smiled, she knew she looked good to him, too.

"Jasmine's going to stuff some envelopes with you," Keith said. Then, to Jasmine, he asked, "Do you need anything? Do you want me to sit back here with you?"

Brian spoke up, "I'll take care of her, Keith."

It was just the tips of Brian's fingers that touched Jasmine's elbow as he guided her to a chair, but the earth shook from the electrical bolt that shot through her at the moment of contact. It took focus now for Jasmine to place one foot in front of the other until she settled into her seat.

She was still smiling, but then she looked at the flyers stacked in front of her, and every good thing she was feeling went away with the image of her smiling daughter under the word MISSING.

Like before, sadness overwhelmed her. But right next to her sorrow, she now had hope.

After a deep breath, she turned to Brian. "So all we're doing is stuffing these flyers into envelopes?"

He nodded. "Like Hosea said, we're using lots of technology"—with his thumb, he pointed over his shoulder to the computers—"but I decided to hang here with the old-fashioned stuff."

"Okay." But her hands rested like stone in her lap. She couldn't move. Not with Jacqueline's picture staring right into her eyes.

Brian scooted his chair a bit closer. "I have an idea," he said casually, though he snatched the stack of flyers away from her view. "I'll fold and all you have to do is stuff." He grinned. "Deal?"

With a release of breath that sounded like a sob, she nodded. She so wanted to be here, doing something for Jacqueline. She so needed to be here, sitting next to the man who had shaped Jacqueline. But she wasn't sure how long she would last if she had to keep looking at that photo . . . under that word.

Then Brian gave her the first sheet, folded so that she couldn't see the picture. She knew she'd be okay.

For minutes, Brian folded, and she stuffed. They worked without words, giving Jasmine space to think. There had never been a time when she and Brian had been together like this. For all the years she'd known Brian Lewis, their relationship had been about battles—from the day they'd first met at Jefferson Blake's birthday party, where he'd chosen Alexis over her, to the day she'd had to tell him the truth about their child. Even the hours they'd spent in bed had felt like combat—wonderful wars full of lust and desire and . . .

Those memories made her sigh.

"What's wrong?"

"What?" she asked, trying to focus on his eyes and not his lips.

He said, "This isn't too much for you, is it?"

Maybe. "No, I'm fine. I was just thinking . . . about something."

"About Jacqueline?"

She nodded.

He picked up another flyer, made two creases, and handed the paper to her. "Tell me about her."

"Jacquie?"

He nodded. "If you can. If you want to."

Now she really looked at him, all of him . . . and all she could do was stare. His face was Jacqueline's, and it truly took every bit of her breath away.

"She's wonderful," she said, trying to keep the quivers from her voice. "She's smart and gregarious and delightful and independent and mature." The tears had been in her voice, but now they rose to her eyes. "Did I say smart?" she asked, trying to lighten the burden of grief that suddenly hovered over them.

He scooted closer. "I'm sorry."

"No, I want to talk about her." She looked into his eyes, Jacqueline's eyes. "I want you to know . . . her."

Brian glanced down at the flyer. "I don't know what it is," his voice was low, "but I feel like part of me does . . . know her. That's why I wanted to be here." He paused. "I hope you understand this, but I feel . . . I know . . . she's a part of me. She's mine."

She wanted to smile and she wanted to cry at his words. "Do you think we're going to find her?"

"Definitely," he assured her quickly, confidently, as if it was a fact.

"Thank you."

"For what?"

"For saying that. No one else is as sure as you are."

"That's the only way I know how to be."

She nodded. "That's what I need, because I don't know what I'll do if she doesn't come back." The tears eased out now.

"You don't have to worry about that; she'll come home." Brian paused and took her hand. "I'm here to support you and Hosea. I'm never going to give up on finding . . . our daughter. Believe that."

His words, his touch, made her sob more. Then, with the

arms of a lover, he gently pulled her toward him and rested her head on his shoulder.

All Jasmine could do was close her eyes and sob. Even though she felt others watching, she didn't care. She needed to be held by Jacqueline's father.

But she could feel the heat of the stares, and though she didn't want to, she opened her eyes. And looked straight into Hosea's.

His face was taut, stretched so tight that not a wrinkle creased his skin. Only a single muscle in his temple throbbed.

Quickly, Jasmine released Brian. Backed away, praying that Hosea would understand. But as she looked into her husband's eyes, there was no anger there. "Hosea," she said, and slowly she rose from her chair, "what's wrong?"

She watched his Adam's apple shift as he searched for his voice. "I have some news."

Her hand jerked upward, covering her mouth. But that didn't hold her cries inside.

He shook his head before she could even ask. "I don't know . . . if it's Jacquie. But they found a little girl."

"Oh, no," she moaned. Her knees bowed, but before she could fall, Brian eased her down into the chair.

Hosea knelt next to her, held her hand. "Baby, we don't know anything yet. So don't think . . . not like that. Not yet." He hugged her before he stood, before he explained. "I got a call from Detective Cohen. A young girl, about five, was found. They don't know if it's Jacquie or not." He paused and swallowed his own sob. "He asked me if Jacquie had any identifying marks. Any way to recognize her so that I wouldn't have to go to the morgue."

Jasmine groaned, and he leaned over to hold her again.

"We could wait for tests, for dental records, but I don't

want to." He stopped. "I'm gonna take you home," he said, reaching for her hand. "You can wait for me there."

"No!" She shot up from her seat. "I'm going with you."

This time, it was Hosea who shouted, "No! You don't have to do this, Jasmine."

"I don't care . . . what you say." Her sobs made her words sound like Morse code. "I'm . . . going."

Brian said, "I'm going with you, too."

The Bushes both turned, as if they'd forgotten that Brian was there.

"Yes," Jasmine said in a voice that sounded like she wasn't breathing. "Let's go."

But she turned away from Brian and held Hosea's hand. With unsteady steps, Jasmine hobbled toward the door. The eyes that had been filled with curiosity now overflowed with sympathy. Hosea hadn't said a word to anyone else, but they could see that whatever the news, it wasn't good.

She said nothing to anyone. She had only a few words inside, and she had to save them all. She needed every single word for the prayer she had to send up to God.

Thirty-six

Waiting. That's all she'd been doing for a week, and now the coroner had her waiting some more.

"How long are they going to keep us out here?" Jasmine asked Hosea.

He shifted his hand so that he could glance at his watch and still hold on to her. "It hasn't been that long, darlin'." Hosea looked up at Brian pacing across the thin gray carpet. "The coroner will be out here soon." He spoke to her, but his eyes were on Brian. Finally, Brian looked down at them, and Jasmine watched the men exchange a glance.

She frowned. *What was that about?*

Hosea turned back to her. "Jasmine, before the coroner comes out here—"

She didn't even let him finish. She shook her head. "Don't even think about it; I'm going in there with you."

"But you don't need to. You're here. That's enough."

"No."

"I don't want you in there," he said, more sternly this time.

"Just let me do this. I can . . . check . . . and see." His eyes pleaded with her before his words did. "Please, Jasmine. Let me take care of this."

Her head was still shaking, but before she could tell him no again, Brian stopped in front of them. "Hosea's right. Stay out here, and I'll stay with you." Then, to Hosea, he said, "You go in."

As if it had been planned and choreographed, the two men moved and, in an instant, exchanged positions. Now Hosea stood above her, and Brian sat, holding her hand. Then, in the next moment, Hosea disappeared behind the thick concrete-gray doors.

Jasmine found her voice. "I should be in there."

"You're going to be fine out here."

Her lips trembled. "Fine? If that's Jacquie," she breathed, "I'll never be fine again." She tore her hand away from his. Stood, then paced the same path that he had walked just moments before. She tried to still her heart that pounded so hard her chest ached. But there was nothing she could do to stop her heart from hammering or stop the images that were already in her head. She could see her—a little girl, lying stiffly still, inside an oblong-shaped, refrigerated box.

Jasmine shivered.

She imagined a man with white gloves slowly pulling the sheet back, showing Hosea the face.

Jasmine groaned.

Brian leapt from the chair and held Jasmine by her waist, steadying her. "You should sit down."

But she grabbed the lapels on his coat and cried, "What am I going to do?"

"We don't know anything yet."

"If that's Jacquie," she said, as if she hadn't heard him, "I'm going to die right here."

He pulled her close, held her tight, tried to give her comfort.

"God, please," she cried into Brian. "God, please. God, please . . ." She squeezed her arms around him, feeling the muscles that she'd once loved and hated at the same time.

Then the doors behind them swung open.

Jasmine's eyes widened. Hosea walked out. His steps were slow.

She had been holding Brian, but now she pushed him aside. For another moment, she stared into her husband's glassy eyes. That was all she had to do. It was their years of marriage, their connection; he didn't have to utter a word.

She knew.

She cried, "Thank God," as she fell into Hosea's arms.

Hosea held his wife as he said to Brian, "It wasn't Jacquie."

Even though her face was pressed into Hosea's chest, Jasmine could hear Brian's relief.

"Okay," Brian said, sounding as if he was taking his first breath after emerging from underwater. "So let's get back to work."

Hosea said, "I'll drop you off back there, but I want to take Jasmine home."

This time, she didn't protest.

Brian said, "No, no. I can catch a cab."

"Thanks, man," Hosea said, still holding Jasmine. He helped her walk past Brian. Then together, they stumbled out of the New York City morgue.

Thirty-seven

It wasn't yet noon, but today Hosea understood Jasmine's wanting to do nothing more than crawl into their bed.

"Are you sure you don't want anything?" he asked as he drew the duvet up to her chin.

"No," she said, her eyes already closed. "I'm just going to rest for a little while. Will you check on Zaya?"

He nodded. "I'm going to call Detective Cohen, and then I'll give Zaya his lunch."

Hosea was sure that she was already asleep when he kissed her forehead. In unconsciousness, she wouldn't have to think about what they'd just been through. Slumber—the great escape.

He treaded softly from their bedroom, and once inside the study, Hosea sank into the oversize chair. The December sun warmed the room to a summerlike heat, but still he shivered. Exhaustion made him want to lean back and close his eyes, but there was no way that he could. Because behind his lids was the image . . . of that little girl.

The little girl with brown curls . . . just like Jacqueline. Wearing a pink jogging suit . . . just like Jacqueline.

It had taken only seconds for Hosea to tell the coroner that the girl lying on that gurney, covered by that white sheet, in the center of that windowless room, was not his daughter. He hadn't given the unknown girl more than two seconds before he left the coroner alone with all of that death.

But outside in the hallway, he had leaned against the wall, and minutes had passed before he had been able to take a single step. All he could do was stand there and cry.

He wasn't sure if his tears were ones of joy or pain. Joy, that there was still hope for Jacqueline. Or pain, because that little girl was someone else's daughter.

A soft groan passed through his lips. What he needed was to be with his son. To hold Zaya, and kiss him, and love him. Hosea pushed himself up, but then he remembered why he'd come into the study.

Just as he reached for the telephone on the desk, his cell rang. Glancing at the screen, he took a deep breath and put a smile in his voice.

"Nama," he said to Mae Frances.

"Hosea, I just found out . . . about the little girl . . . in the morgue."

He frowned. "How did you know about that?"

"Some people I know . . . but it's not Jacquie, right? They told me it wasn't my granddaughter."

"No," he rushed to say. "It was another . . . little girl." But he wondered, how did Mae Frances know? Besides himself and the police, only Jasmine and Brian had known.

Mae Frances asked, "How's Jasmine?"

"She's resting."

"That was too much for her to go through."

"It was." Then before she could ask, he said, "It wouldn't be good for you to come over. Especially after what happened the other day."

"I know," she said, sounding like she wanted to cry. "But maybe you can tell Jasmine that I love her."

"I'll do that," he lied. His wife wasn't ready to have a calm discussion about Mae Frances. He wasn't sure if she would ever be ready. "I'll call you if we hear anything."

"Yes, please. And, I'm still working from my end," she said before hanging up.

Those were her words, every time they spoke—though he was never able to figure out what she was talking about.

He picked up the phone again and made the call he intended.

"Detective Cohen," he began, the moment he was put through. "I guess you've heard by now."

"Yeah. It wasn't your daughter. So we'll keep working on it."

The detective sounded just a bit too casual. "Will you?" Hosea asked.

"Of course. This is my job."

Even though the man couldn't see him, Hosea nodded. He wasn't a fool, though; he knew that with each day the number of officers assigned to this case decreased.

Hosea said, "Detective, let me ask you something. You don't believe that my wife or I had anything to do with this, do you?" He knew that Dale would have a fit if he found out about this conversation. But Hosea didn't care about protocol; he wanted to make sure that the detective's focus was where it should be—and not on him or Jasmine.

The detective said, "No, Mr. Bush. From everything we've seen, it doesn't look like you, or your wife, were involved."

"Doesn't look?"

"You can't fault me for asking the extra questions . . . about your wife."

"Just because of that ridiculous e-mail," Hosea mumbled.

"And the polygraph exam. We have to take every lead, every bit of information, seriously."

Hosea didn't have an explanation for the lie detector test, but the e-mail—he was still pissed about that. "I don't know how you can give any credibility to some anonymous note that comes across the Internet. That could have been written by anyone."

"We have to consider every lead."

Hosea said, "You call that a lead? An e-mail that's untraceable?"

"Mr. Bush, that e-mail is past us now."

It may be past you.

The detective said, "It doesn't matter, because as I said, we've ruled out you . . . and your wife. We're working this case as if it is a stranger abduction."

He and Jasmine were cleared, but the detective's words provided no real relief.

"We're concentrating now on sex offenders in the area . . ."

Sex offenders? He couldn't listen to any more. After a quick good-bye, Hosea hung up, not giving Detective Cohen time to pull his hope down any lower.

Hosea pressed his hands against his temple and tried to massage the fear and the anger away. He closed his eyes for just a moment of rest, but this time, it wasn't the little girl from the morgue who waited behind his lids. It was that faceless man. With hands. With his daughter.

Sex offenders.

It was instant. It was automatic.

He felt his fury rise.

This had happened so often that he knew what to do: slowly, he uncurled his fingers, which had clenched into fists. Opened his mouth wide and inhaled oxygen. Let two seconds pass.

Exhaled carbon dioxide. Again and again. Then he counted from ten to one.

But still, his heart raced.

So he started at twenty and counted backward again. Slower, this time.

Finally, he was back to normal.

There had never been a time in his life when he'd felt such rage. It had been close to this when his father was shot. But then, at least he'd had his father with him—he could see him, touch him, protect him, and pray over him.

But he couldn't do any of that for Jacqueline. And that's what filled him with a fury that bubbled over, more each time.

And now he had to listen to Detective Cohen talk about child molesters . . . the scream was building up inside of him, but he couldn't release it. It felt as if he were on the brink of crazy.

He grabbed the telephone and felt a bit of the peace that he was seeking when he heard, "Son!" But then he heard his father's anxiety.

Reverend Bush said, "I was getting ready to call you. I just spoke with Mae Frances." His father kept on, not taking a breath, not giving Hosea a chance to say a word. "Why didn't you reach out to me? I would've gone down there with you. That's not something you should have done alone."

Then, when there was a pause, Hosea said, "Jasmine went with me, and it was something we had to do, because we can't keep making this about everyone else."

His father exhaled a long stream of air into the telephone. "We're a family; we're in this together. But okay, at least we know that Jacquie's still out there."

How do we know that? Hosea wondered. Right now, his little girl could be . . . he had to squeeze his eyes tight as the image of his daughter and that man was back.

"Son?"

His father's voice sounded like an echo through the pounding in his head. Finally, Hosea answered, "Yeah?"

"What's wrong?" his father asked.

"I . . . I . . ." He panted and counted: *Ten, nine, eight . . .*

Reverend Bush said, "I know you're not getting weary."

His breathing was back. "It's not that, Pops, it's . . ." He pressed his lips together, not sure that he wanted his thoughts to turn into words. "It's my head. All the things that I see. Everything that I imagine happening to my baby girl. I can't stand it."

"I know," his father said softly. "We can't get weary."

"But how can I not when I can see her hurting? Hear her crying. She's so afraid, Pops."

"Hosea—"

"I can't take it. And sometimes I wish . . . I almost hope . . ." Even though his eyes were shut tight, tears still squeezed through. "Pops, a part of me wishes that girl in the morgue . . . I almost wished it were Jacquie, because the thought of her being abused and tortured . . . Pops," he sobbed, "sometimes I pray that she's dead—"

A gasp. Then a scream. And Hosea's eyes popped open.

In front of him, Jasmine stood, horror all over her face.

"Pops, I gotta go," he said.

"What was—"

He hung up on his father's words; his eyes were glued to his wife. "Jasmine," he said as he wiped away his tears.

Her eyes were huge. She stared at him as if she didn't know him. "You want Jacquie to be dead?" she whispered.

"No." He stood slowly. "That's not what I meant. I wish to God that she was here."

Jasmine shook her head. "That's not what you said," she cried. "I heard you. You said you wish she was dead."

"I only meant that I can't stand the thought of what may be happening to her. I don't want her to suffer; I don't want her to have any pain. I don't want her to be afraid. And since I can't be there to protect her . . . then I . . . I . . . if that's what's happening to her, then I'd rather give her to God."

"How can you say that?" Jasmine cried. "How can you give up on her like that when she's out there?"

"I'm not giving up!" Hosea said. "Never. I was just talking to my father about what's in my heart."

"And your heart wants our daughter *dead*?"

"No. My heart wants her safe. My heart wants her happy. My heart wants no harm to ever come to her. But with every day that goes by, with each hour that passes, I know that our chances of finding her—"

He couldn't finish that thought, not the way Jasmine barreled toward him, her hands already raised, her fingers coiled into fists. He grabbed her wrists before she could take a swing.

"Let go of me," she growled as she fought to escape his grasp.

After a moment, he released his grip, but then stepped away from her reach. "Jasmine," he began.

"Don't say anything else to me, Hosea." She shook her head as tears tracked down her face. "I can't believe you," she sobbed. "I can't believe you would give up like this." Only the walnut desk that she leaned on kept her from dropping to her knees.

"I'm not giving up," his voice quivered as he tried to convince her. He let a few silent moments pass before he took a step forward. He needed to hold her and make her understand.

But when he moved, she did, too. She glared as she backed up. Looked at him as if she would never be able to love him again.

"I understand," she whispered.

He wanted to believe that she did, but the way she spoke, he knew that she didn't.

She said, "I understand your lack of faith. I understand why you want to forget Jacquie. I understand your horrible words. Because she's . . . not . . . your . . . daughter."

Her words were so sharp, they went beyond his heart. She slashed straight through to his soul. "No!"

She continued as if he hadn't spoken. "She's not yours," she repeated, deepening his wound. "So you couldn't possibly love her the way Brian and I do!"

"No!" But even though he yelled, he knew her heart had hardened; she couldn't hear him.

Jasmine stomped out of the office and slammed the door behind her.

You couldn't possibly love her the way Brian and I do!

For the next hour, Hosea sat and heard those words over and over again.

Thirty-eight

REGRET! THAT'S WHAT BRIAN WAS living with. Like a chronic disease, his regret was ever present, ever growing.

He couldn't pinpoint the exact date when he first noticed the symptoms, though he was sure the first prickling probably came when he'd allowed Hosea to raise his child. But the doubts hadn't disturbed him much then—they'd just lingered in a corner of his mind, simmering. After all, wasn't he doing the right thing for everyone?

But then he'd received the call from the FBI and had made the trip across the country. He'd sat with Jasmine and shared her grief. And his regret had begun to bubble.

Then there was yesterday. The fear he'd felt when Hosea had walked into that room and said that a girl had been found made every bone inside of him tremble. While he'd waited on the other side of those heavy doors at the morgue and wondered if the dead little girl was his, his bubbling regret began to boil.

By the time he'd stumbled into his hotel room last night, his regret was volcanic. Full blown. Chronic.

Brian was sure that was why Jacqueline had come to his dreams last night, crying out for him to save her. And that was why before the New York sun even began its rise, he was already out of bed, on his knees, praying like he never had before—for forgiveness for what he'd done and for God's mercy to bring Jacqueline home.

Then after he'd eaten and dressed, he made a list of friends and contacts who could hook him up with media. He'd make those calls tonight.

Now at the mall, Brian rattled the doorknob of the center, but the room was locked. So he waited. And paced as he waited. And thought as he paced. And his thoughts became a strategy.

"Hey, you're here early."

The voice startled him from his deep thoughts.

As Keith unlocked the door, he said, "Maybe I should give you the keys and let you open up in the morning." He chuckled.

"Whatever it takes," Brian said, trying to keep the impatience from his voice. He wasn't interested in any kind of chit-chat; he was ready to work his plan. First, he would stuff one thousand envelopes, then he'd hit the computers. After that, the phones. Then he would go to the police and the FBI and anyone else who was involved.

"So . . . you're from California, right?" Keith asked as he clicked on the lights.

"Yeah." Brian was already heading to the back of the room where he'd sat with Jasmine yesterday.

"So . . . how long are you going to be here?" Keith asked.

Brian pivoted and faced the young man. Twenty-four hours ago, his answer would have been just a day or two. He would have explained that he'd come just to give his support, but there wasn't really anything that he could do. Then last night, he'd slept with all that regret.

After a moment of thought, he said, "I'm gonna stay for as long as it takes."

The light-brown-eyed young man nodded. "Yeah, 'cause she's your daughter, right?"

From the moment he'd walked into this room two days ago, Brian had known he was the topic of many hushed conversations. He'd said nothing, not wanting to be any kind of distraction.

But this, he wasn't going to take. This, he had to set straight.

"Hosea's her father," he said with more baritone than was naturally in his voice. "And you need to understand that. I'm just here to help Jasmine and Hosea find *their* daughter." His stare was hard. "Just like you are."

Keith held up his hands, began to back away. "Hey, sorry. Didn't mean to offend."

"No offense taken," Brian responded, though they both knew he was clearly disturbed. "I just want to make sure that everyone knows the real deal."

Keith said, "I know now."

"Yes, you do." Though he was finished, Brian didn't make a move. Just glared at the man as if his message could be sealed with a stare.

The air was thick with tension, with silence. Then their release as the door behind them swung open.

Keith turned first, as if he was looking for any reason to back away even farther from Brian. "Hey, Hosea, Jasmine. I didn't expect you guys here so early."

Hosea glanced at his wife before he said, "Uh, I have to get to the church, but I wanted to make sure Jasmine was fine."

Standing behind her, Hosea couldn't see the way Jasmine crossed her arms, rolled her eyes.

But Brian saw.

"I have a conference call," Hosea began, "and I'll be back right after."

Brian frowned just a bit, his glance moving back and forth from Jasmine to Hosea. He was sure Hosea's words were meant for his wife, but she said nothing.

Only Keith responded, "Okay, I'll take care of Jasmine till you get back."

Hosea hesitated, waiting for an acknowledgment from his wife. But when Jasmine moved toward the back of the room without a word or a glance, Hosea shook his head and walked out the door.

Brian said to Keith, "I'm going to finish up those envelopes that I was working on yesterday."

"Sure," Keith said with more than a bit of relief in his tone. "Let me know if you need anything."

Brian had already moved away—his eyes, his thoughts, on Jasmine. She'd returned to the chair where she'd been sitting yesterday.

It must be the strain, Brian thought as he looked at Jasmine, so different than when he'd seen her the day before.

He sat next to her and lifted a flyer from the stack. "Should we just pick up where we were?"

Jasmine didn't look at him when she nodded. She stared at the envelopes on the table until Brian handed her a folded flyer.

Silently, the two moved together. Their own assembly line: a flyer, then an envelope. A flyer, then an envelope.

Brian kept up with her, but with a sideways glance he studied her slumped shoulders, slackened face, and dreary eyes. He could tell that she hadn't taken the care to get dressed the way she had yesterday. He was used to seeing Jasmine in only high-end clothes and perfectly applied makeup, no matter what she was going through. But not today.

The faded black jogging suit she wore with its frazzled sleeves looked just about ready to be thrown away. Her hair was pulled back in a simple ponytail, though there was more hair outside of the elastic band than there was being held back. And without makeup, Brian could see the worry lines and the circles under her eyes.

He let some time pass, then, "Are you okay?"

Tears were already making paths by the time she raised her eyes. Brian didn't wait for an answer, just grabbed her hand, lifted her from her seat, and led her toward the door.

Keith frowned as they passed; he opened his mouth, took another look at Brian, and then shut his mouth hard.

Jasmine and Brian kept moving until they bumped into Mrs. Whittingham.

She took one look at the two holding hands, and she said, "Where . . ."

But they were already down the hall at the escalator by the time Mrs. Whittingham finished her question. Only then did Brian release Jasmine's hand.

Jasmine sniffed and asked, "Where *are* we going?"

"I don't know." He shrugged. "We can grab a cup of coffee. Or we can just walk. Whatever you want."

She didn't respond, at least not with words. At the bottom of the escalator, she simply strolled past the shops sprinkled with early-Saturday-morning shoppers. And Brian followed. They walked in rhythm to "Hark the Herald" that rang from the ceiling speakers.

As they wandered, he studied Jasmine and thought about what had gone down between her and Hosea upstairs. It was just stress, he was sure. He knew the feelings in his heart, and he couldn't imagine what Jasmine and Hosea were going through.

Suddenly, she stopped.

"What?" he asked.

At first, he thought she was falling, but when he tried to grab her, she pushed his hand away. She crouched down in front of the glass window, pressed her face against the pane, and stared at the yipping puppies.

It took him a moment to get it, and his eyes widened. He hadn't thought this through. This was the mall where Jacqueline had disappeared. Though he didn't know specifics, this store must've had something to do with it.

"Come on, Jasmine," he said, taking her arm.

She shook her head, stayed in place. She pushed in even closer to the window, as if she were trying to get through the glass.

Brian looked to his left, then to his right, before he squatted down next to her.

"Jacquie loved these puppies," she whispered, her hand flat against the window.

As he put the scenario together, he lifted his hand and covered hers. They stayed that way, staring at the barking puppies, until Brian's knees began to ache. He pushed himself up before he took her hand and helped her to stand, too. She was already sobbing when he pulled her close.

They stood that way, connected beyond the physical. They were oblivious—oblivious to the crowds, to the music, to the yelping puppies.

And they were oblivious to Hosea . . . who stood across from the pet store, watching his wife in Brian's arms. Watching his wife turn to Brian in her grief.

They never saw Hosea. Never felt his stare. Never saw him turn around and walk out of the mall.

Thirty-nine

Hosea held his head in his hands.

What am I going to do?

The light tap on the door startled him.

"What are you doing here?" Reverend Bush asked as he walked into the office. Before Hosea could answer, his father sank into the chair in front of his desk.

With all that was on his mind, Hosea smiled. He couldn't help it. In fact, every time he looked at his father, he thought of God . . . and he smiled.

Sometimes he felt as if he was living in the middle of his father's miracle. It was a wonder how, after being caught in the middle of gang-related gunfire, being shot in the head, and being in a coma for months, his father had awakened one day and never looked back.

After a year of physical therapy—from a wheelchair to a walker and then to a cane—and speech therapy, there were few signs of what he'd been through. It was because of his father's miracle that Hosea held on to the belief that he and Jasmine could have their own.

"I thought you were going back to the mall," Reverend Bush said.

"I did." By the way his father's smile washed away, Hosea knew that he saw and felt his pain.

Now Reverend Bush leaned forward. "You heard something about Jacquie?" he whispered.

Hosea shook his head quickly. "No, I spoke to Detective Cohen this morning, but there's nothing new."

The reverend released a breath before he reached for his son's hand. "Don't get weary. We're gonna find her."

Hosea sighed and wondered if his father really believed that or if it was just what he was used to saying—just like everyone else.

Those words of comfort had worked for the first few hours last Friday. Then he'd been sure himself that Jacqueline would be found playing hide-and-seek behind some closed door. But that was seven days ago, and now those words were no longer reassuring. Now they felt like an empty promise.

It was the statistics that made him crazy, that had his hope fading. He was trying to hold on, but . . .

It sounded as if everything inside of him ached when he moaned.

"Son," his father began.

Hosea held up his hand. "It's not just Jacquie," he breathed. "I'm not giving up; I never will. But I feel like I'm losing everything. Jacquie and Jasmine . . ."

Reverend Bush frowned. "Jasmine?"

"Jasmine and I got into a bad fight yesterday."

"Oh." Reverend Bush waved his hand as if Hosea's words were no big deal. "That's to be expected. Both of you are under a lot of pressure."

Hosea pushed away from the desk and wandered to the window that looked out onto the parking lot where Reverend Bush had been shot. When he turned back, one glance at his father made him remember again that miracles were possible.

He said, "Jasmine and I didn't have any ordinary argument." He shook his head. "Yesterday, when you and I were talking, and I said that I wished . . . the little girl . . ." He had to pause, because in his head he heard Jasmine's cry, remembered her look. "Jasmine heard me say that I wished Jacquie was dead."

Reverend Bush let out a long whistle before he walked over to his son. "She had to know what you meant."

He shrugged. "I tried to explain, but she wouldn't listen. All she heard were those words . . . and she lost it. Now she thinks that I don't want—"

"No." Reverend Bush didn't let him finish. "She knows that you love Jacqueline."

"I'm not sure that she does." He slumped back into his seat and told his father what Jasmine had said about Jacqueline being loved only by her and Brian.

Reverend Bush leaned against the desk, moving as close as he could to his son. "I'll admit that was tough for Jasmine to hear, and okay, maybe you're in for a fight, but I have no doubt that you'll win this. Keeping relationships on track is never easy and this . . . this kind of thing is tough. But you'll be able to do it for two reasons: first, you're holding on to the hand of God, and second, you and Jasmine love each other."

"I thought we did."

"Thought? Man," Reverend Bush began, waving his hand in the air, "you and Jasmine have been through so much, you can't help but make it through this. You need each other."

Hosea nodded at his father's words. That's what he wanted to believe. He and Jasmine had survived so many lies, the worst had been revealed when he discovered he wasn't Jacqueline's biological father. And then there were the lies she told about her age, about not having been married before, about forgetting that she'd been a stripper while she attended college.

They'd survived loads of lies.

But Brian was bigger than all of that.

He didn't even have to close his eyes to see Jasmine in that man's arms. It was like a montage that played through his mind—every time Brian was around, he was holding Jasmine. From the day he arrived. Yesterday. Today. It never stopped. Jasmine kept turning to him. As if he was the man that she loved.

Reverend Bush said, "Trust me, Jasmine will be fine. It was just a shocker for her to hear those words like that."

"And then there's Brian."

Reverend Bush folded his arms. "He's not a part of this," he advised.

"It feels like he is. It feels like there are three of us in this now."

The reverend shook his head. "Don't give him credence; he's not a part of your relationship."

Hosea shrugged, like he wanted to believe his father's words but didn't.

Reverend Bush leaned forward, his face close to his son's. "Listen to me. This is about you and Jasmine, only. Stay in that lane."

Hosea nodded.

The reverend continued, "Now Jasmine may not have enough inside of her to fight, but you do." He paused and stared into his son's eyes. "Your faith is deeper. You know how to really hold on to God's hand; you know how to talk to Him. So tell Him! Tell Him to carry you and Jasmine through this. Fight this with all you got. The fight might be all yours, but you have enough of Him inside for both of you." His father stood. "Go back to Jasmine. I've got it all under control here; go take care of your wife, because she needs you."

Alone, Hosea replayed his father's words, then picked up the phone and speed-dialed Jasmine's cell. It rang five times before it hit her voice mail. He hung up and tried again, sure that she was still angry and was just ignoring his calls. She'd answer the second time for sure.

She didn't.

He called the center. "Hey, Mrs. Whittingham," he said when the woman answered. "I was checking on Jasmine. I'm on my way back and—"

"She's not here. She left a while ago . . . with Brian," she said, whispering the last two words.

He fought to keep the image—of Jasmine and Brian— away.

"Ah, they probably just went to get some coffee . . . or something." That's what he had to believe. Their lives didn't need any more drama.

Mrs. Whittingham huffed, "That's what I thought, but they've been gone a couple of hours." Her voice got even softer. "Why don't you try her cell?"

"I'll do that." He hung up the phone and, with the tips of his fingers, massaged his head. He wasn't trying to get rid of his ever-present headache, but he was trying to rub away his thoughts, because right now, Jasmine was with Brian . . . somewhere.

He released an audible sigh. His focus had been on fighting for Jacqueline, but now he'd have to fight for Jasmine, too. His father was right, though—his wife, his family, were worth fighting for. He could do it, and he would.

It would just be a lot easier if Brian wasn't in New York.

Forty

"THANK YOU," JASMINE WHISPERED AS the taxi jerked a bit, then rolled to a stop. "I really needed this."

Brian's smile was without any sign of cheer as he looked down to where his hand held hers. They'd been connected that way most of the day after they left the mall, then roamed through the streets of Harlem. As they'd walked across 125th Street, then back, across Lenox Avenue and then Eighth, they'd hardly exchanged a word. But Brian knew their thoughts were the same as Jasmine's eyes scanned each building, searched each window, as if she hoped to uncover a clue about where their daughter might be.

But though they'd found nothing, it seemed the walk had been therapeutic for her; her tears had been gone for hours and she'd spent an easy afternoon away from the burden of sadness that was a part of her now.

She said, "I really appreciate your getting me out of there."

"I'm glad you had some time . . . away."

The way she stared, Brian could tell that she wanted to say more.

"Would you like to come up?" The way his face spread in surprise made her add, "Well, maybe not up to my apartment, but there are lots of places around here," while looking out the window.

His eyes followed hers to the line of stoic, century-old buildings that lined Central Park South.

She said, "Maybe we can grab something to eat."

Her question reminded his stomach that he hadn't had a thing since breakfast, and his insides growled so loudly that even the cabdriver glanced at him through the rearview mirror.

Still, he said, "I'm not hungry."

"Are you sure?" she asked with hope. "We could grab something at . . . the Plaza. It's right down the street."

When he shook his head, he didn't bother to mention that the Plaza was where he was staying. She didn't need to know he was that close.

He reached across her lap and squeezed the door handle, opening the door for her. "I'll see you tomorrow," he said.

He didn't look back as the cab pulled away from the curb, but he knew that she was still standing in front of her apartment building, watching him. He didn't have far to go; her building was on one end of Central Park South, and the Plaza was on the other.

As memories of the day tracked through his mind, he wondered, *What is going on?* This day was not one that he'd planned, even though, he had to admit, it had been enjoyable—at least as enjoyable as it could be in the middle of all this grief.

For hours he and Jasmine had walked hand in hand, as if they were a pair. And for some of those hours it had felt as if they were.

Brian sighed. He couldn't deny that there had always been chemistry between the two of them, though *chemistry* wasn't really the word. It was more like lust. Jasmine had been part of his addiction. Nothing more.

Except now, it felt like so much more. Every time he saw Jasmine, he wanted to hold her. Not as if he loved her, but as if he cared. He couldn't help but care.

It was because of her face.

To him, she'd always been an attractive woman; he'd just never noticed before how much emotion was in her expressions. Every feeling she had was right there. The pain, the grief, the torment. It was the torment that made him care the most, the torment that made him want to hold her all the time, the torment that made him want to stay.

But what did that mean? Was he willing to give up his life in Los Angeles?

No! It certainly wouldn't come to that. He would be here only until Jacqueline was found. A week, two at the top. By then, his daughter would be home and he would return to L.A. At least that was his constant prayer.

In the morning, he'd call Jefferson and have him explain to their other partners. No one at the clinic would fault him for being a devoted father.

But if he was going to stay, there would have to be a few changes. He couldn't be around Jasmine so much—at least not in the way they'd been today. It was Hosea's hand that she needed to hold. Just like he needed to be holding Alexis.

Alexis.

There was a big part of his heart that wasn't even in New York—the part of him that Alexis owned. Not an hour passed when he didn't think of her. But he never allowed her image to linger long. He couldn't, because if he did, he'd have to acknowledge that he hadn't heard a single word from her. He'd have to acknowledge what that meant.

He knew that Alexis had decided as long as Jasmine—and Jacqueline—were in the picture, there was no place for her. Her rules, not his. Because if he'd had his way, she'd be here right now, holding him, comforting him, encouraging him.

Brian shook thoughts of Alexis away as the cab stopped in front of the hotel. He tossed a twenty to the driver, signaled that he didn't want change, and jumped out of the car. There was no use pining away for Alexis; he'd put her on hold until this mission was accomplished.

As he moved toward the hotel, his plan began to take form: he'd start with this evening—order room service, call his friends about media contacts, go to bed early, sleep without regret. Then tomorrow, he would be at the center, first thing, and would begin this all over.

His head was down as he headed toward the elevator, his thoughts already on the room service menu.

And then he heard, "Brian."

His first thought was that Jasmine had followed him; she'd caught a cab and trailed him, determined to have her way. The only thing—that wasn't her voice. But it was a tone that he knew so well—the sound of an angel.

He turned around, not hoping, yet full of expectation. And every wish he'd ever made stood right in front of him.

He looked into the eyes of Alexis.

Three years of celibacy made them efficient, but still, this had to be some kind of record. For how quickly Brian and Alexis had stepped into the elevator, locked lips as the chamber ascended, stumbled through the eleventh-floor hallway, tripped over unfamiliar furniture inside the suite, and then finally made their way into the bedroom. By the time they hit the sheets, they were naked, their clothes blazing a trail from the door to the bed.

It didn't take more than four minutes.

Now they rested beneath the dampened sheets, holding hands in the dark.

"The truth is, Brian"—Alexis whispered, as if they were not alone and she didn't want to be overheard—"I fought it all the way. I really didn't want to come, but . . ." She paused and rolled over, still holding his hand, now facing him. "I had to be here."

He kissed the tip of her nose. "So you tracked me down because you love me so much." He chuckled.

"It wasn't hard to track you down," she said, ignoring the love part of his statement. "I made one call to your favorite hotel."

Now he dropped her hand and wrapped his arms around her, holding her tight. He closed his eyes . . . and then shuddered.

She looked up at him. Even in the dark, he could see her frown. "What's wrong?"

"Nothing," he said, pushing aside thoughts of Jasmine that didn't belong in his mind. "I'm just glad that you're here. I need you, Alexis."

They stayed that way, connected, just holding each other. Each with separate thoughts of what her trip to New York would mean.

And then his insides growled.

Alexis pushed herself up. "What was that?" she asked, feigning horror.

He clicked on the light and shrugged. "I guess I need to order room service."

She laughed and jumped from the bed, not bothering to cover herself. "Order something for me. And call down to the bellman. Tell them to bring up my bag."

His heart filled with love . . . and lust as his eyes followed her traipsing uninhibited toward the bathroom. Once she closed the door, he grabbed the phone. He needed to eat quick; he needed as much nourishment as he could get. Because he'd need his strength—to jump right back into the bed with the woman he loved.

Forty-one

IT HAD BEEN A HARD night.

Hosea had been pacing when Jasmine finally came home with Brian still in every part of her mind.

"Where've you been?" he'd asked.

She had stared for a second before she pushed past him and moved toward their bedroom.

"What? You're just going to walk by without answering me?" he bellowed. "Where are you going now?"

She spun around and gave him her first words. "You have a lot of questions."

The way he looked at her—with eyes packed with the same sorrow that was in hers—made her want to soften. But how could she when she knew what was really in his heart? When she knew that he wished her daughter was dead.

He released a soft sigh. "Jasmine, please don't do this."

"I'm not doing anything," she said, crossing her arms and tapping her foot as if she was already bored with their exchange. "I'm going to check on Zaya."

"He's fine," Hosea said. "Mrs. Sloss called me when she couldn't find you."

Her arms dropped. "Why? What happened?" She turned toward the bedroom. "Is my baby okay?"

"Yes!" His shout stopped her. "Mrs. Sloss wanted to check on her daughter, and I told her to go on. She'll be back in the morning."

She exhaled, not even realizing that she'd been holding her breath.

Hosea said, "You don't have to worry. I've been with him since she left. But I was worried about you."

Jasmine rolled her eyes.

He said, "I called the center."

She wondered if that's what this was about. Had someone told him that she'd left with Brian?

He asked again, "So where were you?" His tone told her he desperately wanted to know.

Now she was sure—this *was* about Brian. It wasn't like he had anything to worry about; it wasn't Brian who had kept her out past dark.

After Brian had left her standing on the curb, she'd spent hours walking the streets of their neighborhood. Not that she had anywhere to go—she just hadn't wanted to go home. She had no desire to be in the apartment if Jacqueline wasn't there. All she really wanted to do was take Zaya and go away. Somewhere. Anywhere.

But since she was sure that Hosea was probably home, she'd just rambled through the streets, from one block to the next. First, across Central Park South past the Plaza Hotel and then up Fifth Avenue. From there, she made her way across Sixty-fifth and then down Madison. She walked and walked the same path, passing the same holiday-decorated stores, unfazed by the biting December wind.

Then darkness descended, and the wind bit *and* scratched. So she'd done what she had to do—she'd come home.

"I just want to know," Hosea said, breaking through her thoughts, "where you were."

It was anger that fueled her glare and her words, "I was out looking for *my* daughter." Then she'd stomped into their bedroom.

She'd stood at the side of Zaya's crib, staring at her sleeping son. When her legs tired, she perched on the edge of their bed and watched him from there. She sat in the dark until Hosea came into their bedroom.

"Jasmine, if we can't talk to each other," he said, sitting next to her, "then we definitely need to pray together."

With just a slight twist of her body, she dismissed him. Without words, without a glance, she let him know that she had no intention of praying with him—and after the week she'd just had, she wasn't even sure that she would pray without him.

Still, he stayed, until he realized that she wasn't going to move. Then he'd stood and left her alone. After a time she'd gotten up and stripped, leaving her jogging suit in a pile right at the foot of the bed.

It wasn't even nine o'clock when she'd closed her eyes and, after a slow mental review of the day, drifted to sleep.

But now she felt soft kisses on her cheek, and she snuggled deeper into the sheets.

Butterfly kisses, she thought inside her dream. That's what Jacqueline called them, when she would kiss and kiss Jasmine until she awakened.

Jacqueline. Butterfly kisses.

She wanted to keep her eyes closed, stay in that place, feel the kisses and her daughter so near.

She sighed, reveling in the realism; she could actually feel lips against her skin.

Her lids fluttered open.

And she looked into the eyes of her son. And her husband.

"Love Mama," Zaya giggled as he leaned to kiss her again.

She fought to keep the smile on her face; she fought to keep her disappointment away.

"I love you, too, baby." She lifted him from Hosea's arms.

"Good morning." Hosea spoke with a smile, as if he'd forgotten all the anger she'd hurled at him last night.

"Good morning." She hugged and kissed Zaya, then wondered if she should do the same with Hosea. It was clear that he wasn't holding a grudge, and she didn't want to either . . . all she wanted was for Hosea to fight and not give up on their daughter.

Maybe he hasn't, she thought . . . she hoped.

That consideration made her look at him, smile, tell him with her eyes that she wasn't as mad anymore.

Hosea slid his arm around her shoulders and pulled her to him; together, they sat with Zaya between them. They watched their son pretend to read his book, pointing to each picture.

"Dog! Cat! El-phant!"

For a while, Jasmine smiled. Laughed even, as Zaya continued to read.

"Bear! Pig! Ga-raff!"

Then she remembered other Sundays. Mornings when Zaya and Jacqueline had joined them in bed, and the four Bushes had hung out before they prepared for church.

She wanted to cry, but the place where her tears came from had been sapped dry. So she just tucked herself back under the covers and rolled away from her husband and son.

"I'm going to take Zaya into Mrs. Sloss," Hosea said after a few minutes. "I heard her come in about an hour ago."

She closed her eyes and nodded.

Then, "I was thinking that we should go to both services today."

Her eyes popped open, and she sat up just as quickly. "I'm not going to church!"

His stare showed every bit of his disapproval, but with a giggling, wiggling Zaya in his arms, he left the bedroom.

Jasmine stayed in place, pulling the duvet up high to her chin. She shook her head, almost amazed at his words. How could he think she would go to church? After that e-mail?

And what was she supposed to do once she got there? Pray? It wasn't like her prayers—or Hosea's—were being answered.

But the way Hosea walked back into the room let her know that he was ready for a fight.

"We need to go to church, Jasmine," he said, sounding like the pastor talking to one of his parishioners.

The cover dropped from in front of her when she crossed her arms. "You need to go, but that church doesn't have a single thing to do with me."

"Since when?"

"Since someone snatched my daughter. Since those witches started sending around that e-mail."

"That e-mail was started by one person, and how can we let anyone drive us away from where we're supposed to be?"

She leaned back against the headboard, her stance stiff, suggesting she planned to stay that way for the long haul.

"Jasmine," he began softly and slowly, "don't turn your back on God; He didn't have a thing to do with Jacqueline's being abducted."

"You know what? That's what I wanted to believe. But if I listen to you and all the things you've ever said, then God has *everything* to do with this."

"What?"

"You're the one who's always saying that God is sovereign, that He's in charge of it all. Well, if that's the case . . ." She held up her hands to indicate she'd just made *her* case.

"It's not like that. God didn't cause this; He allowed it to happen, but this isn't because of Him, and it's not what He wanted."

"Well, I don't know how you explain it, but let me tell you what I know . . . Jacqueline is missing . . . I want her back . . . I asked God to bring her back." She stopped, tilted her head. "Is Jacquie in her bedroom?"

Hosea sat down next to her and lowered his head as if he was about to pray. "This is hard to explain if you're dead set against hearing it, but don't let your desire to understand what's going on make you question God. You're gonna have to figure out a way to trust Him. Whether you like or understand this, He's in control. No matter what the reason or what the outcome, God's got this, and He'll win."

Jasmine jumped up, needing to get far away from Hosea's words. "Don't preach to me! I'm not interested in understanding outcomes. And you can't give me a single reason for a child to be taken from her mother."

He nodded, agreeing. "You're right—there is no *earthly* reason for this to happen."

"Damn straight. And that's why *I'm* going to keep fighting for *my* daughter. Because I love her! And the truth—I'm not going to depend on anyone . . . not you, and if God isn't going to answer my prayers, then I don't need Him either."

He flinched, and a new sorrow glazed his eyes. For an instant, Jasmine was sorry that her words had hurt him so much. But she couldn't help how she felt; she just had to speak the truth.

After a moment, "No matter what you think," Hosea began so softly, she had to lean to hear him, "I love Jacqueline with a love that began before she was born. With a love"—he stopped, as if the thought of what he was about to say choked him—"with a love . . . as if she was mine. To me, she is. To me, she came from me." He looked right into her eyes. "So don't you dare question my love for Jacquie. I'm going to keep fighting until she comes home. No matter what you think, no matter what you say."

Jasmine blinked back tears.

Then Hosea added, "But no matter how long we look for Jacquie, we can't forget that we have a son, and we have a life with our church and our family and friends. Even as we look for Jacquie, we have to keep living."

Jasmine had softened, but now she was right back to being angry. "And how am I supposed to keep living when I can hardly breathe?" she wailed. "I'm not like you; I can't be sad for two days and then—poof!—my sadness is gone. I can't just move on."

"But we can't stop the rest of our lives either. We have to live beyond our grief."

"So you want me to stop grieving?" she asked incredulously.

"I didn't say that—"

She talked over him, "Because I didn't know there was an expiration date on grief. It's still right here," she said, banging her fist against her chest. "Missing Jacquie, being scared for her, has settled right in the middle of me."

He held out his hand to her; she cringed at first, not wanting any part of his touch. But then she let him take her hand and pull her down next to him.

He said, "I'm not saying not to grieve. I would never do that; everyone has to grieve in their own way, in their own time. But what I am saying is, let the grief fuel you. Let it move you to do everything to find Jacquie, but let it also move you to love your family more. Let it move you to love life more. Let it bring you up, not tear you down."

His words and his tone were soothing, and she looked down to where he held her hand. She watched his long fingers caress her skin, and she yearned for more. It felt as if years had passed since he'd held her like this, and all she wanted now was for him to lean back and hold her for hours.

And right when she thought that's what he wanted, too, he kissed her forehead. "We don't have to stay for both services if you don't want to."

It was a reflex, the way her hand jerked away from his. "I told you, I'm not going."

Behind his eyes, she could see his battle, but he'd stopped this fight. He rose and, with heavy steps, moved away from her. Right before he stepped into the bathroom, he said, "I'm sure Mrs. Sloss has already bathed him, but do you want to dress Zaya, or should I ask her to do it?"

She glared at him. "I told you I'm not going to church."

"I'm not talking about you. I'm talking about Zaya."

Her eyes widened; she couldn't believe his audacity. "*My* son is not going anywhere."

He almost moonwalked as he backtracked to her. "*Our* son is going to church."

"No." She shook her head before she tucked the pillow underneath her head and turned away from him. "He's not leaving. Not without me."

"Then you need to get up." He grabbed his bathrobe and stomped from the bedroom.

Jasmine jumped from the bed, snatched her own robe, and paced the width of the room. There was no way she was going to let Zaya leave this house.

Not even a minute later, Hosea was talking before he even reentered the bedroom. With his hands raised, he said, "I'm not having this argument with you." His tone told her that he was weary, but he looked straight into her face. "He's going to church; he needs to get out of this apartment. You have him on lockdown like he's done something wrong." It must have been the steam seeping from her that made Hosea soften. "Look, he'll be safe. I'll make sure of it."

"So you're going to take my son out of this apartment without my permission?"

After a long stare, he said, "I don't need your permission, boo," before he went into the bathroom and closed the door.

Jasmine sat on the edge of the bed and trembled. What was she going to do? She couldn't let Zaya go; her plan was never to let him out of her sight whenever he was beyond the front door.

But she wasn't going back to that church . . . ever.

She dashed into her closet. It wasn't a full-fledged plan yet, but she and Zaya would be gone before Hosea even came out of the bathroom. After jumping into her jeans and a T-shirt, she rushed out and right into Hosea.

His eyes wandered over her jeans. Still, he said, "Looks like you changed your mind," with sarcasm all in his tone and his eyes.

The jig was up; she knew that. Now Hosea would watch every move she made. She'd never get Zaya safely away.

"Please, don't take him from me," she pleaded, since begging was all she had left.

"That's not what I'm doing." Without looking back, he moved into his closet, dismissing her and the conversation.

In the minutes that it took him to get dressed, Jasmine couldn't come up with another plan. By the time Hosea came out of his closet, Zaya, dressed in a navy suit that matched the one his father wore, toddled into their bedroom with Mrs. Sloss behind him.

"Miss Jasmine, you're not ready?" Mrs. Sloss asked.

She shook her head, knowing if she said a word, she'd burst into tears.

"Kiss Mama bye-bye," Hosea said as he lifted Zaya.

Her son reached for her. "Bye-bye, Mama," he squealed.

A single sob escaped through her lips. "I love you, baby." She hugged and kissed him until Hosea gently pulled him from her arms.

He paused, giving her a last chance, but when she didn't move, he did, and Jasmine watched her husband take her son away. The front door had barely closed before her knees buckled, dropping her to the bed.

How could he have done this to her? Didn't he understand? No! Couldn't he tell what she'd been going through? No! And how could he? Why would he? He could never love her children the way she did.

The way Brian did.

Brian.

She crawled up the bed and grabbed the phone. Brian would understand. Brian would help her make this right.

Forty-two

THE TIPS OF HIS FINGERS formed a steeple as Hosea sat behind his desk, his chin resting on his hands, his eyes closed.

"Son."

It was so soft, it couldn't even count as a whisper. But Hosea opened his eyes.

Standing at the door, his father said, "Are you sure you want to preach today? You know, you don't have to."

Hosea nodded. "I've got to stand up there today, Pops, and talk about this. I've got to say out loud everything that I'm thinking. It'll help me . . ."

Reverend Bush nodded. He didn't need to hear any more. He understood exactly what his son was saying; he'd used the pulpit many times to work his way through challenges, too. "I'm proud of you."

For the first time in a long time, Hosea's lips spread into a grin. "This, I know."

His words surprised his father, and Reverend Bush chuckled. Playfully, he punched his son's arm. "Well, even though you know this, I can still say it, Hawke!"

Hosea's eyebrows rose with surprise. It had been a long time since his father had called him that. Actually, Hawke was short for the nickname—Hawkeye—that his mother had given him when he'd graduated from high school, barely seventeen, and signed up for the Marines. Not that Hosea had any real desire to serve his country in that way. It was just the only way he knew to get out of following in his father's holy footsteps. He'd been a preacher's kid and had no intentions of becoming a preacher. So he'd enlisted, ignoring his mother's cries and his father's chagrin. But four years later, both of his parents had been proud when he was discharged honorably, an expert marksman, with enough money to pay half his tuition at NYU. He'd still tried to stay far away from the ministry, but the calling on his life eventually became too strong.

"You haven't called me Hawke in years, Pops." He laughed, then stopped suddenly. Even though they were alone, his eyes darted around the room to make sure that no one saw them.

With a frown, Reverend Bush watched his son for a moment. "It's okay to laugh." He paused. "You know that, right?"

Hosea's nod was slight, without conviction.

His father continued, "Laughing, having this moment, has nothing to do with Jacquie."

"But maybe that's the point, maybe that's what's wrong with me. Maybe every moment needs to be about Jacquie."

"Son, you don't have to prove to anyone how much you love your daughter. You have to keep on living, even as we keep on searching."

The words were so similar to the ones he'd said to Jasmine.

Reverend Bush pressed as if he knew his son needed to hear more. "I cannot imagine a more devastating tragedy than what's happened to you and Jasmine, to all of us. But you're walking through this with your heart on God and your head held high. You can't do any better than that."

Hosea was thoughtful for a moment. "I can't? I mean, maybe I can do better by not being here. Maybe I'm supposed to be home with Jasmine—waiting to hear, focused just on our daughter. Maybe being out, going on like life is normal—maybe that takes away from Jacquie."

His father nodded and contemplated his son's words. "So you think settling behind closed doors, staying away from those who love you, leaving the work of finding Jacquie to others is the way to . . ." He stopped, waiting for Hosea to finish the thought.

Hosea sighed. It sounded ridiculous when his father summed it up that way. "I don't know, Pops. I just think about Jasmine . . . My wife is grieving, and her pain is so palpable—you can see it, feel it, touch it, taste it. She can't do anything except think about Jacquie. But me . . . I'm just . . . going on. I go to work, I go to church, I live."

"So living means you don't care?"

"It may seem that way to other people."

"And how does it seem to you?"

Hosea shook his head. "Pops, I can't tell you. I tried to tell you the other day, but . . ." Slowly, his fingers curled. "Each minute that passes . . . every hour that my little girl's out there." Now his fingers were fists. "She depended on me to take care of her, protect her. And I didn't." His breathing was rapid now. "I don't know who has her or where she is"—he inhaled and tried to keep the image of the man away—"and there's not a thing I can do to help her! But if I ever got the chance . . ." He banged his fist against the desk so hard it startled his father. "I keep moving, I keep working because if I stop . . ."

Reverend Bush let many silent seconds pass. "Then there's

no way anyone can say that you don't care." His words were soft. "Son, I told you before not to judge Jasmine and her grief. Maybe I should have reminded you not to judge yours either. You're more action oriented—you take charge and do something. Jasmine is more introspective. She's probably trying to figure out what's happening to Jacquie every moment of every day. Neither of you is wrong; neither of you is right. Both of you are human. And in terrible pain."

After he exhaled, Hosea said, "So, it's okay—my being here, bringing Zaya to church, going to work and doing everything else; it's okay." It was a statement; it was a question. Words that his father didn't even have to respond to.

All Reverend Bush did was point to his watch.

Hosea braced his hands on the desk and pushed himself up. He followed behind his father, but after two steps he turned around.

"Son?" Reverend Bush said, a question in his eyes.

Without a word, Hosea moved back to the closet and slipped the long, flowing burgundy robe that belonged to his father off its hanger. Reverend Bush wore the robe only on special occasions—like weddings and funerals. But Hosea had found his own use for the religious garb—he wore the robe when he felt he needed to have a special word with God, as if going before the Lord wearing this made God sit up and take notice.

Not that Hosea really believed that—or maybe he did.

He slid his arms through the billowed sleeves, clasped the thirty-two gold buttons that adorned the front, then faced his father. Reverend Bush nodded his approval, and then the two men walked shoulder to shoulder into the sanctuary.

City of Lights at Riverside Church had been one of the premier churches in the city for years, and there hadn't been a

Sunday—even after Reverend Bush had been shot and Hosea had taken his father's place—when the sanctuary hadn't been filled.

But today, not only was every seat taken, the perimeter was lined with standing worshippers. Hosea wondered what was the draw—had they come to hear the Word, or were they just curious? Were the people here to pray with him, or was one among them the kidnapper?

He shook that thought away as he approached the pulpit.

"Saints, it's happened again," he began. "Another tragedy, where I have been brought straight to my knees." His voice boomed through the congregation, and he'd expected someone to shout by now. An "Amen" or something. But he'd never heard so many, so quiet.

"When my mother died," he continued, "I gave up on God." Now he heard it—faint murmurs. They were with him. "But He never gave up on me! And from that situation, I learned about the true love of my Lord. So this time, there's no giving up for me. I don't give up anymore. All I do is look up."

The first "Amen" and "Hallelujah" rang through the sanctuary.

Hosea's hand caressed his Bible, as if he drew his strength from it. "You all know my story. You all know what's happened to my daughter. And I'm sure there are some of you who are wondering if the Bushes are so faithful, if the Bushes have such favor from God, then why would this happen to them?

"No one would ask that question aloud, at least not to my face . . ." He paused for the uncomfortable chuckles to cease. "But you know you've wondered: Are they being punished because of some sin in their lives? Is it because they didn't please God? Is it because they were never Christians in the first place?"

The murmurs were back.

"I know those are the thoughts of many. I know the things that have been said about me and my wife. I even know about the e-mail that's been circulating throughout City of Lights."

Now the murmurs sounded like a hum. He hadn't planned to go there; the words had just come out. Not that he was sorry. He needed to tell it all today.

He said, "But those thoughts, those words, don't matter. This is about me and *my* God. This is about my relationship with Him." He pointed toward the heavens.

"Amen!"

He said, "Now, there's not a lot I can tell you about what's going on, because I just don't know. But let me tell you what I do know. Our daughter being abducted is not a punishment from God. God didn't cause this. God didn't want this. God isn't about this. God's not happy with this!"

He had to stop now . . . because the parishioners were on their feet, waving their handkerchiefs, shouting words of encouragement.

"You better preach!"

Hosea waved his own handkerchief, then wiped his brow. He settled down, and the people in the sanctuary did also. He said, "But there *is* a question that needs to be answered. There is a question that, as a Christian, I must address. And that question is this: Why do bad things happen to good people?

"That's a question that's as old as time. A question that many have tried to answer. That's what the first book of the Bible is about—no, not Genesis. I'm talking about what many believe to have been the first book written . . . the Book of Job.

"You know that story, but I have to talk about the part where Job lost not just one child, but ten. All gone in an instant. What happened to him didn't make any sense. Everyone in the land knew how good Job was. Why would God allow Job or even one of his children to suffer that way? And I have to tell you, Saints, I have asked God the same thing about me and my wife. Why did this happen to us?" He pointed his finger at his chest. "But you know what's inherent in that 'Why me' question? What I'm really asking is, Why couldn't this have happened to someone else? Why couldn't it have happened to you?" He pointed out into the congregation, then twisted to the left side of the room. "Or you?" He pointed again before he turned. "Or you?"

The peopled shifted, his words, his actions, disturbing them—exactly the way he'd wanted.

He continued, "This burden shouldn't have happened to me; it should be carried by someone else. That's what I'm really saying when I ask, 'Why me?' And that's what you're saying when you ask that question." He paused to let the people twist some more.

"Here's the thing, Saints. We live in a fallen world where good *and* evil people will suffer. That's a fact, period. It's something we don't understand. It doesn't seem fair. It doesn't seem right. But what is right is that the good—those who have promised to follow God—have His promises. Oh, yes!"

He had to stop again because this time the shouts were louder, the stomping made the floor vibrate, the waving sea of white handkerchiefs was blinding.

When it was quiet enough for most to hear, he continued. "Just because we're following God doesn't mean our hardships are going to be eliminated—that's a lie that comes straight from the devil. Because if he can get you to believe that, he'll get you to forget about God's goodness when bad times do come. But let me tell you—I'm not going to let this situation or any circumstance in my life be the measure of God's goodness! What He's done for me already is beyond measure."

The shouts were back. They were on their feet again, stomping, waving.

He said, "Y'all might as well keep standing 'cause I'm just getting started!"

"Hallelujah!"

He said, "I've been trusting God in all of the good times, so am I just supposed to drop Him now? Am I just supposed to live and love God for the good, and then during the bad times, it's something else? No!" He banged his hand on the podium. "This is when my faith is tested, and I'm telling you, Saints, I'm gonna pass this test, this time."

"Amen!"

"You see, the test of our faith is not in the suffering alone, but in the *not knowing* what's going to happen . . . and trusting God anyway. Look at Job again—if he'd known what was going to happen, what would have been the test? If he'd known the outcome, how could you call that trust?" he bellowed.

"You know you right!"

"You better come on!"

"Preach!"

Hosea let them shout. He motioned for the Minister of Music to hit the keyboard, and they danced as they shouted. They sang—not words to a familiar song; they sang a new song. The words were personal, from their hearts, thanking and praising God even in the midst. And Hosea sang and danced with them.

He didn't know how much time had passed before they'd worn themselves out, before they sat from pure exhaustion.

Hosea was out of breath, but he continued, "And as I close, Saints, I want to leave you with this . . . the greatest test is to trust God's goodness where we see no goodness in life." They were contemplative now, silently listening. "That is what I'm doing. I cry—" He stopped abruptly.

"Take your time," rang out before some stood to their feet and clapped.

He lowered his head; he didn't deserve any applause—he hadn't brought his daughter home yet. He motioned for them to sit. "I cry," his voice cracked, "when I wonder about Jacqueline. I cry when I pray for her, but I still have joy," he said, though his eyes were filled with tears. "Because joy is based on His presence in us. And my joy is based on the fact that though I don't know what the future holds, I know who holds the future.

"At the end of this story—whether here on earth or whether in heaven—God will be the victor. And that means that I, and Jasmine, and most importantly, Jacqueline, will be victorious, too. Amen and Amen!"

Though they were weary, the parishioners were back on their feet.

And Hosea was just as worn out as he backed away from the pulpit. This was the part of the service where his father took over. As Reverend Bush gave the altar call, Hosea slouched in his chair. With his eyes closed, he prayed a silent prayer of thanksgiving. It was a message to the people, but he'd been preaching to himself. He had to remember his joy. And as long as he had joy, he could have hope.

"Come on down if you need prayer now," he heard his father say. "Come now to the throne of grace. Come now to the mercy seat."

Hosea raised his head, and his eyes widened as he saw the two who led the way. Brian, holding Alexis's hand, stopped in front of Reverend Bush.

It shocked him, at first, but it didn't take two seconds for Hosea to stand. He eased down the three steps that separated the altar from the rest of the sanctuary, and Alexis fell into his arms.

"I'm so sorry," she cried as he held her. "My heart aches for you."

He hugged her tight, tried to soothe her cries. He wanted to give her the strength that he'd just gained. Then, after another moment, he released her and embraced Brian. The two men held each other, recognizing, for the first time, their commonality. No matter how they had gotten here, the Bushes and the Lewises were in this together.

When Hosea and Brian separated, he was surprised to see the many who stood behind them at the altar—Mae Frances, who was falling out from her tears, was standing only because Malik held her up. Mrs. Whittingham stood next to them, cradling a sleeping Zaya. Then there was Brother Hill, and Detective Foxx, and even Triage Blue and his wife, Deborah. And volunteers from the center who hadn't been a part of their church, until now.

All were standing with them. All were crying for them.

"Reach your hands toward my family," Reverend Bush said, shedding his own tears.

Hosea stood in between Brian and Alexis and held their hands. And as the dozens surrounded them at the altar and the thousands sat in the seats, every head bowed, every eye closed. And the congregation sent up a united prayer for God's grace, His mercy, and their hope that Jacqueline Bush would finally come home.

Forty-three

BRIAN CLASPED ALEXIS'S HAND AND helped her ease out of the taxi. "Are you sure about this?"

She nodded. "Of course, I told you I'm with you." She hooked her arm through his, as if that would seal her words. "I want to see what's been set up for Jacquie."

He led her into the mall, and as they ascended on the escalator to the second level, he filled her in on the command center. The enthusiasm in her eyes encouraged him, and he shared the thought that rested in his heart. "I'm going to find her, Alex. I'm going to be the one to do it."

She squeezed his arm and told him that she had no doubt—if it was possible, he'd make it happen.

He smiled and thanked God that she was with him here, with him now. He was sure that a great deal of Alexis's eagerness to see the center was due to the fact that Jasmine wouldn't be anywhere near this place. The truth was, he was glad about that, too. Not that he was happy that Jasmine wasn't feeling well—that's what Hosea had told him after church when he and Alexis had joined him and his father in their private offices. But he was glad that now that Alexis was here, there would be real separation between Jasmine and him. Separation was what they needed.

Jasmine had a husband. And he had Alexis.

"This is it," Brian said before he pushed the door to the conference room open.

But before he could even cross the threshold, Jasmine rushed into his arms.

"Where have you been?" she asked, breathless. "I've been calling you; I've been . . ." She paused, frowned, then blinked as if she were having a hallucination. "Alexis?"

Oh, no! Brian thought. But then he watched Alexis plaster on a smile that didn't seem too fake as she stepped into the room.

"Hi." Her greeting was tentative, but then with more strength, Alexis said, "I hope you don't mind my being here," and she moved closer. "I want to help." Reaching for Jasmine's hand, she added, "I'm so sorry."

Jasmine flinched when Alexis touched her, as if she expected the contact to be much more than just a gentle stroke of sympathy. "Thank you," Jasmine replied, her words wooden. Jasmine looked at Brian, awaiting an explanation.

He said, "When we didn't see you at church—"

"You went to City of Lights?"

He nodded. "We thought you were sick. I didn't think you'd be here."

With a slight tilt of her head, Jasmine's eyes thinned, like she was trying to figure out exactly what his words meant.

She said, "I didn't have any reason to go to church, but I have lots of reasons to be here." Turning to Alexis, she asked, "So how long are you going to be in New York?"

Alexis paused before she responded. "I'm . . . not . . . sure yet. A couple of days, I guess."

"Well, thank you for coming," Jasmine said, her words softer this time.

Then she turned and marched to the other side of the room. Alexis began to follow, but Brian held her back.

"Do you want to leave?" he whispered.

"No!" Alexis glanced around at the stacks of posters and leaflets and envelopes. She smiled as the five volunteers who'd come out on this Sunday afternoon to help looked her way. "There's a lot of work to do."

Before Brian could say another word, Alexis strolled through the center, stopping to introduce herself to the others. Brian moved beside her, his eyes on Jasmine the whole time. Jasmine and Alexis were a combustible combination, and he didn't know what would be left standing if they had to share the same space for more than a couple of minutes.

He held his breath as Alexis approached Jasmine and asked, "How can I help?"

He didn't give Jasmine a chance to respond, "Well, Jasmine and I have been focused on these flyers." He passed one to Alexis, and she gazed at Jacqueline's photo. He added, "We've been stuffing these envelopes—the flyers are being sent all across the country to doctor and dentist offices."

Alexis pulled out a chair on the other side of Jasmine. "I'll help you stuff, if you want."

Brian wanted to keep talking for Jasmine, but now, he didn't know what to say.

Jasmine shrugged a little, as if she was as unsure as he was. She said, "This isn't very hard; you don't have to think much as you're doing this." She paused. "And for me, it's easiest when I don't have to think." Then Jasmine looked up, and the expectation was all over her face. She was waiting for one of Alexis's infamous put-downs—a one-line zinger like the others that Alexis had thrown Jasmine's way over the years.

Alexis said, "Then this is what I want to do, too." She shrugged off her coat. "I want to work with you."

The ends of Jasmine's lips spread into the smallest of smiles as Alexis slipped into the chair next to her. For a minute, Brian watched the two—who'd always considered each other more than a mortal enemy—work side by side.

Then he squeezed into the chair on the other side of Jasmine and began folding flyers so that he could keep up. The women didn't say a word—not to each other, not to him. But silence was probably best.

To Brian, this time was bittersweet. A child had been taken from them, but what they'd found in the midst was a way to behave as adults. He wondered if this would last, but then he just as quickly tossed that thought aside. There was no need to worry about tomorrow. He was going to focus on the quiet blessings of today.

Forty-four

THIS WAS HARDER THAN ALEXIS thought it was going to be, harder than it was supposed to be.

When Jasmine leaned over and whispered to Brian for what had to be the one hundredth time in fifteen minutes, Alexis jumped up so fast her chair fell backward onto the floor.

In a second, Brian was behind her. "Honey," he said, returning the chair to its upright position, "is something wrong?"

"No"—she shook her head—"I just need a moment."

"Okay," he said slowly. "Let's walk outside."

"You stay here," she said, waving her hand in Jasmine's direction. She waited for Jasmine to look up, but she didn't move. As if she knew what this was about. As if she knew that she had pissed Alexis off, and there was nothing Alexis could do about it. She said, "I'm just going to the restroom."

Brian hugged her before she walked away. "It's hard now, but it gets better," he whispered. "Each day you'll be able to look at that flyer, and even though you'll still be sad, it won't be as bad."

Alexis nodded, indicating that he was correct to interpret her mood that way, that this was all about Jacqueline. But once she was outside, she wanted to turn back and scream that he was wrong—it was Jasmine who had made her behave like a madwoman. She stifled a scream before she punched open the door to the ladies' room.

It had seemed so right, her coming to New York last night. So what had happened?

Jasmine!

As much as she tried, Alexis just couldn't like that woman, not even in the middle of this tragedy. She leaned against the sink, glanced into the mirror, and once again asked herself if Jasmine had anything to do with her daughter's disappearance. Not that she could imagine any mother—not even Jasmine—doing this. But that woman just seemed to be getting too much out of this situation.

She was getting Brian—he was so attentive, so concerned. And Jasmine was milking it; every other minute she was having another breakdown and Brian was right there, her refuge. Then in the minutes in between breakdowns, Jasmine just had to lean close to Brian and ask him this . . . or ask him that.

Putting her fist up to her mouth, Alexis released a muffled scream.

Where is Hosea?

She wished Jasmine's husband was here so that he could see what was going on. But Alexis knew Hosea wasn't going to help. Even if he was here, he probably wouldn't see what she saw. He would see only a grieving mother, which in fact was all there really was to see.

"Stop it, Alexis," she said to herself. She twisted the faucet, releasing the water full blast. Her thoughts were ridiculous, she knew that. Brian . . . loved . . . her! And there was nothing that Jasmine could do about it.

So why did she feel that, at any moment, Jasmine and Brian could very well run away together?

Leaning over the sink, Alexis flung cool water onto her skin and waited for the calm to come. She dabbed at her face with a paper towel, and when she tossed that paper into the trash, she threw away her absurd thoughts with it.

She marched back toward the conference room with a new resolve. She wasn't the whiny, jealous type. Never had been, never would be. She just needed to quit it. Get in there and suck it up. If anyone could do it, she could.

Then she walked into the room. And stopped. And stood. And watched. Yet again, Brian had his arms around Jasmine, and Jasmine was weeping into his shoulder. Milking it!

It was enough. It was too much.

She whipped around and bumped right into Hosea. With just a quick glance at his face, she could see that he'd just observed the same scene. Taking her hand, he led her into the hallway to a bench that she'd passed a moment ago, supposedly with a new attitude.

She sat next to Hosea, silent for a moment, until she asked, "How do you take it?"

He gave her a small sigh and a slight shrug. "Jasmine and Brian are just sharing a common pain."

That's all he said, but Alexis heard much more: that Jasmine and Brian had a common pain and now a bond that neither she nor Hosea would ever be able to share with them.

She said, "You know, Brian and I just got back together."

Hosea's eyebrows rose. "Really? I didn't know that you two had broken up."

"It was more than broken; it was done. Brian and I are divorced."

"Wow."

"But recently we've been trying to work it out." She paused. "I really think he's the man God wants for me."

Hosea took her hand and squeezed it. "Well, if that's the case, you'll find your way back to each other."

"I don't know," she said, shaking her head. "I don't know if we'll be able to make it . . . now."

There was more quiet between them until Hosea said, "This shouldn't tear you apart." A pause. "It should bring you closer together."

Her head tilted. Again she heard it—more behind his words. This time, she wondered if he was even talking to her.

He said, "We should get in there."

She nodded, but neither of them moved.

"Don't give up," Hosea said. "There's nothing going on with Jasmine and Brian." He paused, stared at the blank wall in front of them. "Nothing. Nothing." It sounded kind of like the words he'd used at the end of his sermon this morning, "Amen and Amen."

"Nothing?" Alexis hated the way she sounded. Like a whiny, jealous woman.

He turned toward her. Took her hand again. And with water in his eyes and not a bit of conviction in his voice, he whispered, "Nothing."

And that made Alexis lower her head, close her eyes, and say inside, *God, help us all!*

Forty-five

MOMMY, I'M HOME!

Jasmine heard those words, that voice, and she allowed them to play in her dreams over and over. Jacqueline was home, but it was who brought her that made this dream so special.

The pictures in her mind played again: Brian carrying Jacqueline. Brian saying, *I brought our little girl home.* And then Jacqueline's voice followed.

Close to consciousness, Jasmine knew that this was not reality. But she kept her eyes closed and let the scene repeat.

Stretching, she slowly opened her eyes. But even fully awake, she wanted to stay right there in that dream.

She heard Hosea say, "I'm going to get you," in a voice that she knew was supposed to be a scary monster, but sounded more like the Cookie Monster.

Then she heard Zaya's giggles and the patter of his feet as he ran from his father.

Jasmine couldn't help but smile as she snuggled back into

her pillow. This time, when she closed her eyes, all four of them were together: she, Jacqueline, Zaya . . . and Brian.

With a sigh, she pushed herself up and wiggled back against the headboard. She needed to get Brian out of her head. But when he was around, she always felt so good, always felt such hope. Brian's talk was all about finding Jacqueline. He wasn't preparing for, wasn't thinking about, any kind of future without her. Statistics didn't matter to him. The number of days that had passed didn't count. All Brian could see was that, one day, their daughter would be back.

Why couldn't we have been like this before?

Jasmine still remembered the days when there had not been a pleasant word exchanged between the two of them. Only the sex had been civil. But it was different now—there was nothing but kindness and caring and . . . love.

There. She admitted it. This felt like love to her. And she had no doubt that Brian felt the same way. She could tell by the way he was by her side—always, with a special word, with so much encouragement, and with his shoulder on which she could lean or cry. Yes, he had to be feeling the same way. He had to be feeling the love.

Actually, if she thought about it, they had probably always been in love. That's why they couldn't stay away from each other. That's why they always ended up in bed. That's why they'd kissed even after she and Hosea were married—when they were in L.A. and Brian found out about Jacqueline's paternity. Jasmine sighed now as she remembered that day. If her ex–best friend Kyla Blake hadn't walked into Brian's office, Jasmine had no doubt that she and Brian would've been on the floor, or on the desk, or leaning out the window making a sibling for Jacqueline.

So it had never been about just lust, and it was a relief to know that now.

But there was a problem—Alexis!

Jasmine couldn't believe that she hadn't thought a moment about Alexis until two days ago when she'd walked into that center. She'd almost had a heart attack when she'd looked up and into the eyes of her nemesis—the woman she'd hated for more than twenty years.

But even with Alexis there, Brian hadn't changed, and it made Jasmine wonder, *What was Alexis's game?* She said she wanted to help, but Jasmine wasn't fooled. Alexis couldn't stand her and had proven it yesterday. Sunday, she'd been civil, even on the verge of kind. But when she and Brian had walked into the center on Monday, after Alexis said, "Hello," Jasmine could have counted the number of words she'd spoken to her on one hand and had fingers left over.

No, Alexis may have said she was there to help, but she was there for another reason. And after thinking about it all night, Jasmine knew what it was—Alexis was there to get Brian.

Jasmine had figured it out when she peeped that neither one of them was wearing a wedding band. They must've broken up, maybe even divorced. Yeah, divorce!

And Alexis must've chased Brian all the way to the East Coast with the goal of getting him back. Well, that wasn't going to happen, not right now. Just like Hosea had to understand, Alexis would have to chill, too. This situation was all about her and Brian and their daughter. Everything and everyone would have to wait until Jacqueline was home. And even after that, it was up for grabs . . . if Brian loved her . . .

"Love Mama!" Zaya rushed into her bedroom, scattering her thoughts. He jumped onto the bed and wrapped his arms around Jasmine's neck.

"I love you, too, baby. Good morning."

"Yaki?"

Jasmine looked up and saw Hosea standing in the door, his

arms folded, his eyes sad at their son's question. Zaya didn't mention Jacqueline much, but in recent days, he'd asked about his sister more and more.

With her eyes on her husband, she hugged Zaya. "Jacquie's away."

"Away?"

Still she looked at Hosea, and he nodded, telling her to continue. She said, "Yes, but Jacquie's coming home soon."

"Comin' home?"

Hosea was still nodding, still looking at her. "Yes, soon," she said to her son.

Now Zaya giggled. "Love Mama."

From where he stood, Hosea said, "Son, that's something that you and I have in common." As he strolled into their bedroom, he added, "I love Mama, too." Hosea held Jasmine in his arms and squeezed her as if he planned never to let go.

His touch could always do this—make blood rush from her toes to her head. And she felt it now—the rush! And truth—she wanted it, she wanted him.

The problem was . . . she wanted Brian even more.

Jasmine busted into the center as if she were the police. With a quick scope of the place, she saw that Brian wasn't there.

Where is he?

He had to come soon because in two hours she'd be leaving to take Zaya to his pediatrician's appointment. In the past, this was something Mrs. Sloss would have done. But not anymore.

She'd had to let Zaya go to church with Hosea because she didn't have a way to stop him. But besides that, no one else was ever going to be responsible for her children.

So that meant Brian needed to come quickly. With everything that had been on her mind, she had to see him. Had to talk to him. Had to make sure that he felt what she felt.

"Have you seen Brian?" Jasmine asked Keith.

"Nah, I was hoping that he and *his wife* would be here."

The way Keith said "his wife" and grinned made Jasmine roll her eyes. Why did every man react that way to Alexis? She'd never been able to figure out what was so special about that woman.

He said, "I was hoping Brian and Alexis could help us with these. We could use the extra hands." Keith held up the over-size poster board.

It was the same photo of Jacqueline, under the same MISS-ING banner, and with the same telephone number beneath the picture. But now the background was bright red.

"These just came in, and we're going out in teams, put-ting a bunch up here in Harlem and all through the city. And Hosea even wants us mailing some out."

She nodded but turned away. Every time she saw that photo, her constant ache intensified.

She grabbed her cell phone and punched in Brian's number as fast as she could. When he answered, she breathed. "Brian, are you on your way to the center?"

"Ah, not yet. Why? Did something—"

"No," she said quickly. "There's nothing new, it's just that," she lowered her voice, "I really need to see you."

"What's up?"

She frowned. She didn't want to talk about this on the phone. She needed him—right here, right now. "There are new posters for Jacquie."

"Yeah, I know. I helped Keith design them."

That surprised her—Brian was working on things that she didn't even know about, all to find their daughter. "Well, seeing them . . . it just brings back everything. Brian, I miss her so much. Do you think she's safe?"

His voice got softer. "Yes, she's safe, Jasmine. And we're going to find her."

Jasmine nodded, repeating his words in her mind. "So when are you going to get here?"

"I'm in the middle of something right now."

She clutched the phone tighter; she could just imagine what that middle was all about. Still she pressed, "I need to see you, and I have to take Zaya to the doctor and . . ." She stopped, waited for him to say, Okay, I'll be right there.

Instead, he said, "Well, I'm not sure of my schedule. If I can, I'll call you back later."

Then he hung up. As if there was something more important than being with her.

She held the phone in her hand, just staring. What she wanted to do was throw it across the room, watch it crash into a million pieces. But with just a few deep breaths, she calmed down.

Don't get upset. He's coming.

Of course, he would be there; he'd never let her down. He just couldn't say it because Alexis was there, probably staring down his throat, listening to every word.

Or maybe she *wasn't* there. Maybe they'd had an argument. Maybe he'd told Alexis his true feelings and sent her home.

Yes, that made more sense—he'd probably told Alexis that she had no place in his life, at least not right now. Maybe he was just making sure that she got on that plane. And right after that, he'd be on his way to the center to see her.

With that scenario in her mind, Jasmine settled down in the chair that had become hers. Now that she didn't have to worry about Alexis, she could get to work. She would fold more flyers, stuff more envelopes. Maybe she and Brian would even go out together and hang some of those posters. She wouldn't have even thought about doing that twenty minutes ago. But with Brian by her side, she could do anything.

She glanced at her watch and at the same time said a prayer to God that Brian would get there soon.

Forty-six

ALEXIS BURIED HERSELF DEEP INSIDE the pages of the *New York Times*. But her eyes weren't focused. Instead, her ears stood at attention, concentrating completely on Brian's words.

When his phone had rung just a few minutes before, Alexis had presumed the call was from Jasmine. It was barely nine, so no one from Los Angeles would be calling this early. And the way Brian had glanced at the screen on his cell, then pushed himself away from the breakfast table that room service had rolled in, confirmed her guess.

Now, listening to just one side of the conversation, she knew what this call was about.

I need you, Brian! Help!

That's what she imagined Jasmine was saying in her best mother-in-distress voice. Hearing Brian having to explain that he was in the middle of something confirmed for Alexis that what she'd decided to do was the right thing.

It had come to her yesterday while they were at the center, during one of those moments when Jasmine was all over

Brian once again, crying as if her tears sprang from an ever-flowing faucet. It wasn't that Alexis couldn't empathize and sympathize—it was just that she hated Brian always being the prince. Where? Was? Hosea?

That was when she knew she didn't have enough heart to stand this, to do this, and she'd planned to tell Brian that last night. But they'd returned to the hotel, both emotionally exhausted: Brian, exhausted from Jasmine; and Alexis, from the calls she'd taken—many from sick fools who took pleasure in others' tragedies.

So they'd fallen asleep, so tired that they hadn't even had dinner. And now, as she listened to Jasmine through Brian's responses, she knew that not only had she made the right decision, but she needed to act today, before she fell into this relationship any deeper.

When Brian hung up, she stayed still, not turning to look at him. But with just a slight twist, she said over her shoulder, "I'm going home."

Even though she couldn't see him, she could almost feel the distress she was sure was on his face.

"Jasmine was just calling about the posters. Remember, I told you about those color—"

Now she turned to him and held up her hand. "It wasn't the phone call that made me decide to do this." She put down the newspaper. "I hadn't planned to stay too long anyway."

"I know, but I thought you'd stay at least for the rest of the week, through the weekend."

She looked down at her hands. "I have to get back to my business."

He nodded but said, "I need you."

Inside, she moaned and told herself that she had to go. She didn't have the fortitude to be one-third of any kind of threesome. So she said nothing.

When he sighed and tossed his cell phone onto the bed, Alexis spoke up. "I'm sorry; when I got here on Saturday, I should have told you that I was going to be here for . . . just a few days."

With slow steps, Brian closed the gap between them. "I understand."

She nodded and then had a thought—maybe this didn't have to be over. She asked, "Are you . . . going to stay?"

In the silence that followed, she had plenty of seconds to think. Was she really that selfish? Did she truly want him to leave behind New York . . . and his daughter?

Yes, she admitted . . . and also admitted that she hated that part of herself. But she didn't know how to live a life that included Jasmine.

While Brian stood in front of her silent, pondering, she had hope.

Until, "Yes, I'm staying. I have to."

She exhaled and blew away all of her optimism.

When he took her in his arms and said, "It won't be for much longer; we're going to find Jacquie soon," she had to press back tears. There was no reason to cry—this wasn't about her.

She stepped away from him and, without acknowledging his words, said, "I need to get dressed, and then I'll catch a cab . . ."

His eyes and mouth widened with surprise. "You're leaving now?"

She nodded. "It's best," her voice quivered. "I already called. There's a flight at two."

This time, his embrace was tighter, and Alexis squeezed him back before she gently pushed him away and turned toward the bathroom. But she'd barely taken a step when he grabbed her arm, swung her around, and kissed her with the passion of a man who'd known only one true love. Within seconds, he'd freed the belt of her bathrobe and she stood naked inside his arms. By the time they fell back onto the bed, Brian's bathrobe had fallen away, too.

Now they were connected by more than their lips, but unlike the night when she'd arrived, this morning their lovemaking was slow. And sweet. And Alexis wondered if Brian knew what she knew—that this moment in time would soon be a memory that would have to last forever.

Forty-seven

Even when Brian walked into the center alone, Jasmine didn't dare hope that every single one of those wishes she'd made in the last twenty-four hours had come true. Even when Brian shook hands with Keith, then moseyed back to where she sat, she still didn't really breathe.

"Hey," he said as he sat down.

She returned his greeting, and then with wide, innocent eyes, she looked around. "Where's Alexis?"

The smile that he wore faded slowly as he folded a flyer. "She went back to L.A. last night." Then, as if it was an afterthought, he added, "She said to tell you she's still praying . . . she just had to get home."

"Oh," was all Jasmine said, because if she'd said any more, she would have been on her feet doing the Electric Slide. She'd been right! Brian had sent Alexis away, and it was all because of her.

But while her heart was having its own celebration, on the outside she remained calm. "We missed you yesterday," she said. When Brian kept his head down, she added, "Keith was setting up teams to go out and put up posters, and I was hoping that you and I could have gone together."

Now he looked at her. "Are you sure you're up to that?"

She nodded. "If I can do it with you."

His head tilted a bit to the side. "What about doing it with Hosea?"

That question shocked her. "Ah . . . he's . . . working . . . at church. He can't just pick up and go out like that."

He looked as if he didn't believe her.

"I mean, he cares about Jacquie," she further explained, "but he knows that the people here will do whatever's necessary. And he has a life. So I want to go with you."

It took Brian a moment to say, "Let's finish up with these flyers. Then there are some follow-up calls I have to make, and I need to speak to Keith—"

"Anything you can talk about with me?"

He shook his head. "I don't want to upset you. You didn't sound good when I spoke to you yesterday."

Because you weren't here.

She wanted to tell him that she could talk to him about anything, especially Jacqueline. But she backed off.

Brian seemed a bit different today, not as easygoing and open as he'd been when he'd arrived a week ago. But it was just because of Alexis. It had to be tough on him, the way he'd probably thrown her out. After all, she couldn't deny that Brian did care for Alexis. She could see it every time he jumped when Alexis said something or had a question. Even though Jasmine knew what was up with Alexis, Brian didn't seem to know that he was being played. Alexis was just acting like a needy woman to get his attention. Jasmine had always hated females who used tricks . . . Alexis was proof that those tactics never worked.

Still, Jasmine knew she had work to do with Brian. Alexis was gone, but it would take a little bit of time for Brian to forget about her. And while he worked to get Alexis out of his system, she would be the shoulder he could cry on. She would be there for him, the way he was there for her.

From the corner of her eye, she peeked at Brian. Even now she had to inhale as his thick eyebrows bunched together like he was in deep thought—just like Jacqueline did when she was writing her name, or studying her numbers, or trying to color within the lines. And his profile—the small hook to his nose, his square jaw—and the rest of him, from the cinnamon tint of his skin to the walnut-brown color of his eyes, he'd given it all to Jacqueline.

Jasmine loved looking at him, and being close to him, and touching him. All she wanted to do right now was rest her head on his shoulder. Because when she was with him, they were both closer to Jacqueline.

She wanted to cry—fake tears so that he would hold her. But there would be plenty of time for that. Just as she waited for Jacqueline, she would wait for Brian.

And she had a feeling that she wouldn't have to wait too long.

Forty-eight

HOSEA DRAGGED INTO THE APARTMENT and rested for a moment at the front door. Every light in the front room was out, but he easily made his way through the dark.

He hadn't planned to be out this late, but there were a lot of storefronts, and bus stops, and tree trunks between here and Long Island. And since yesterday, Hosea was sure that he'd seen every one of them.

Sinking onto the couch, he kicked off his shoes and massaged his feet. It had been the longest two days.

Mae Frances—and a friend of hers—had joined him on his journey to put up the new posters all over Brooklyn. Though he'd been focused on the posters, he'd spent many of those hours trying to figure out Mae Frances's friend.

It had been a surprise when he'd gone to pick up Mae Frances and the man had walked out of the building with her. They were an odd couple: Mae Frances, so tall (almost six feet) and bundled inside her old mink; and the man, a good foot shorter, wearing an Indiana Jones–style fedora and a trench coat that hung down to his ankles.

"This is my friend, Sonny," Mae Frances had said simply when she stepped up to the car. "He's going to help us."

That was all she'd said. Hosea had wanted to ask a bunch of questions, but what did he need to know? Sonny was a friend who wanted to help. Lots of volunteers had come out.

But Sonny had a lot of questions for him. He sounded like the police, the way he interrogated him in his heavy Brooklyn accent: "So you don't know anyone who would do this?" "Did you or your wife ever feel like you were being followed?" "Have you ever been threatened?"

After a while, Hosea had glanced at the man through the rearview mirror. "What's up with all the questions?"

The man had stared right back at him. "I'm just curious. What . . . you don't want to find your daughter?"

That tone, his attitude, had made Hosea want to stop his car and tell the man to walk back to Manhattan. But then he'd remembered—Sonny had come to help. He was, after all, a friend of Mae Frances. Maybe Sonny was just as eccentric—and crazy—as she was.

So they'd driven through Brooklyn, and it didn't take long for Hosea to be glad that he had Mae Frances *and* Sonny with him.

But by the end of the day, Mae Frances had said that her legs ached; all the walking had been too much for her.

This morning, she'd told him, "I can't do it again, but Sonny wants you to call him and let him know what time to be ready."

Hosea never made that call.

Now he wondered if he should have taken Sonny up on his offer. Today, Hosea had worked alone, walking the streets of the eastern part of Queens and some of Long Island. But he'd put up all three hundred of the signs that had been in his car.

He shook his head and wondered if any of this was even doing any good. Was Jacqueline still in New York? Was Jacqueline still . . .

He had to do it again: Unclench. Breathe in. Breathe out. Count.

Now he was fine.

He whispered, "Where are you, Jacquie?"

Often, he released that question into the atmosphere, hoping for some kind of cosmic connection, some supernatural force that would allow him to feel his daughter, see her thoughts, find her, and bring her home. It just had to happen, and soon—because each day that passed without her took a piece of him away. A piece that he wasn't sure would ever grow back.

That thought of defeat made him roll off the couch, onto his knees. In the dark of his living room, he leaned against the couch and prayed, "Lord, I've never been a weak man, though that's how the world may see me because I follow you. But I feel helplessly weak now. I know that You're in charge and that this is part of Your divine plan, but Father, please bring our girl home. And in the meantime, hold her in Your arms. Protect her mind, protect her heart, protect every single part of her body." The last words were barely out before a sob rose from his throat, and he paused to hold back the others building inside. He was a man; he was not supposed to cry. And what were tears going to do anyway?

Pain made its way to his brain, and he released a soft, "Argh!" Looking down, he saw his hands—clutched into tight fists, his fingernails tearing into his skin. With more words to God, he relaxed and stood.

Moving into Zaya's room, he clicked on the light, and for

a nanosecond, panic rose in him at the sight of the empty space where Zaya's crib had stood. But in the next instant, he remembered that Zaya's crib was in their bedroom. When he entered his bedroom, he saw that he was right.

Only the soft glow from the moon that shined through sheer curtains illuminated the room. But the light shined right on Jasmine's face as she held their son. Both were asleep, though only Zaya snored. Hosea stood still and cherished the moment.

It was only during these times, when Jasmine was with Zaya, that he saw any signs of happiness in her. As she slept she smiled, and Hosea wondered if she was dreaming about Jacqueline. Did she imagine their daughter home?

I'm going to bring her home, Jasmine, he said to himself. *If she's still alive, I will find her.*

With a gentle tug, he pulled Zaya from Jasmine's arms, and both sighed in their sleep. He tiptoed to the crib and put Zaya to rest. Jasmine remained on top of the covers, leaning back against the headboard. Shrugging from his jacket, he flung it across the chaise then crawled onto the bed. Sitting next to his wife, he put his arm around her shoulders and pulled her to his chest. She opened her eyes for just a moment before she snuggled against him, her soft sounds of sleep resuming instantly.

He sighed with contentment as he held her and thought about the number of days that had passed when they'd hardly talked, and definitely hadn't touched. He had to stop that now. There was no way he could allow this to destroy his family, especially since there was the chance that Jacqueline was . . .

No! He wouldn't allow himself to finish that thought. At least not tonight. Tonight's thoughts would be about love, not loss. Tonight, he would remember all the ways that God had answered his prayers in the past—and the way God would answer him now.

"Hmmmm," Jasmine moaned in her sleep.

Hosea closed his eyes and squeezed her tighter.

"Hmmmm," she moaned again, and stroked his chest.

He smiled.

And then she whispered, "Brian!" wiping away every good thought that Hosea had.

Forty-nine

"I'M HER MOTHER," JASMINE EXCLAIMED as if that should be explanation enough. "Keith, I can do more than just stuff a flyer inside an envelope. We can get kids to do that."

"Yeah, but the phones?" He shook his head. "I don't know."

Jasmine sighed and looked around the center for someone to agree with her. Surely, if Brian had been there, he would have told Keith that she could handle the phones and much more. But Brian hadn't arrived yet, and there was no need for her to wait when she wanted to take action.

"Keith," she began, another strategy already in her mind. But before she could plead her case, Mrs. Whittingham waddled across the room to her rescue.

"Jasmine, Keith's just concerned because most of the calls we get are from some really strange people." Then Mrs. Whittingham turned to Keith. "But if Jasmine knows this, I'm sure she'll be fine."

Keith raised his hands in the air, surrendering, and motioned for Jasmine to take a seat at one of the tables with a phone.

"Now remember," he said, standing over her as if he was her protector. "If a call comes in that you can't—"

"Would you stop?" she interrupted him. "I'm okay." She turned her back and dismissed him.

She understood Keith's concerns. When she'd walked into the center on that first day, she'd been so fragile. Then Brian had arrived, and he made her believe. Since then, she'd been here every day. Yes, this was the place where she would see Brian, but it was also where she could help in the hunt. And today, she was ready to do more.

Because of Brian.

For the last two days, she and Brian had been a team, hanging signs through Harlem and talking to street vendors and store owners. Together, they were making people aware, and with every person who sent them on their way with a "God bless you," Jasmine's hope kept rising. So today, she was ready to move to the next level here at the center, too.

The ringing phone startled her, but she grabbed it before Keith could say, See, I told you!

"Hello, this is the center to find Jacqueline Bush; how may I help you?" she asked, breathless with anticipation. Would this be the call, the one that would finally bring her daughter home?

"I . . . have . . . her!" The voice sounded mechanical.

"What?"

"I . . . have . . . her! Do you want to know what we're doing right now?"

First, confusion.

"Do you want to know what the little girl is doing to me?"

Jasmine frowned.

"Ah . . . it feels so good."

Then, understanding.

"We're making love."

Finally, horror!

"And I'm planting my seed. She's going to have my baby!"

Jasmine screamed, "Oh, my God!" She stood up. "You sick bas—" Before she could finish the word, Keith pried the phone from her fingers.

He put it to his ear. "Hello . . . hello!" Then he hung up.

"No!" she yelled.

Keith frowned.

"You hung up!" she cried.

"We hang up on all of those calls," Keith explained.

"But he has Jacquie!" Every part of her trembled. "And you hung up on him! Are you crazy? Now we'll never find her!"

"What the . . ." Brian rushed into the room and pulled Jasmine into his arms. "What happened?"

Keith and Mrs. Whittingham told him about the call, and within minutes Brian had calmed Jasmine, got her to sit down.

Brian told her, "That man doesn't have Jacquie."

"But you didn't hear him," she exclaimed. "He said he had her."

"We get a million calls like that," Brian explained, keeping his voice soft, gentle. "And the police know which ones are legit and which are from . . . well, I don't even know what to call them. But I can tell you this, the man you spoke to doesn't have Jacquie." He stroked her hands.

Jasmine inhaled. "Okay," she said. "Okay, okay, okay," she repeated so that she would finally believe it. But the voice was stuck in her mind. The words played again and again. "I've got to get out of here," she said softly.

Brian nodded. He whispered something to Keith, and then as he helped her stand, Mrs. Whittingham hugged her.

"I should've never let you take the phones," the woman said. "But don't worry. We're going to find that baby."

Right now, that was exactly what Jasmine needed to hear,

and when she embraced the woman, every bit of disgust that she once carried for Mrs. Whittingham was gone.

Once outside the mall, Brian asked, "Where do you want to go?"

"To your hotel," she said.

He looked at her, his eyebrows raised.

She said, "I just need some time away from all of this. I don't want to see anyone; I don't want to talk to anyone . . ."

He said, "Let's go somewhere . . . grab a bite to eat."

She nodded. "That's what I was talking about—the restaurant in your hotel. It'll be better there, trust me, because Hosea and I know so many people in New York. We're always running into someone, and right now I just couldn't take it . . ."

"Okay," he said. Even as he hailed a cab and they slid inside, Jasmine could tell that Brian wasn't feeling this trip to his hotel. But she didn't care. She needed to get as far away from the mall, and Harlem, and that voice, as she possibly could.

Just before he told the driver their destination, her cell phone rang, and she glanced at the screen—Hosea. She knew what this was about. Keith or Mrs. Whittingham had contacted him. He was checking up on her, and he'd have a million questions. What had happened? Was she all right? Where was she right now?

She glanced at Brian, who was staring straight ahead—his eyebrows bunched—just like Jacqueline. Quickly, she pressed Ignore on her cell phone, then turned it off before it could ring again.

When the cab stopped in front of the Fifty-ninth Street entrance to the Plaza, Jasmine's face stretched with surprise. "I can't believe you've been this close to me all this time."

Brian didn't respond, just helped her from the car and led her into the hotel. Within minutes, they were settled inside the

Palm Court, which sat in the center of the legendary hotel's lobby.

When the server came by, Brian ordered iced tea for both of them.

Jasmine waited until the man stepped away before she said, "I should've ordered a drink. That's what I really need." With her elbows on the table, she dropped her face into her hands. "I still can't believe what happened," she whispered.

"Why were you answering the phones?"

"I wanted to." She looked up at him. "I wanted to help. I wanted to do more."

"I understand." He took her hand and squeezed it.

"That man . . . what if he really does—"

Brian shook his head. "Trust me, he doesn't have her." Her eyes were so wide with sadness, he asked, "You do trust me, don't you?"

She glanced down to where he held her. Stared at their hands, which looked like they were meant to be together.

He said, "I promise you, Jasmine. We are going to find her."

Every time he uttered a word, she felt better. She nodded, needing to believe every syllable he spoke.

Still holding on to him, she said, "When we get her back, when she comes home, I really want you to meet her. Not like before in L.A. I really want you to get to know her."

He smiled.

"You're going to love her," she said. "She's so smart."

"Ah," he leaned back, "you told me that before. I bet she got that from my side of the family."

She laughed and hit his arm. "What do you mean? I'm pretty smart, too, you know."

"Go on," he said, "tell me more."

"Well . . ." For the first time today, Jasmine's eyes were bright. "Jacquie is such a drama queen."

"I wonder where she gets *that* from."

She laughed again, but this time kept going. "Though she doesn't want to be an actress. She wants to be an astronaut."

"Really?" he asked, before they gave their orders to the waiter who'd been standing discreetly to the side of their table. "So, an astronaut. Where did she get that?"

"She loves to fly. And she says that she wants to get in a rocket so that she can take off and see God in heaven."

He nodded, and their chatter continued as Jasmine filled Brian in on everything she could think of about their daughter. Over their lunch salads, she told him how Jacqueline loved to sing and dance, but that what she loved most was reading. "She has a whole library in her room."

Jasmine told him how Jacqueline had given her brother the name Zaya, and how she had loved him to pieces when he was born, but soon found him to be a pest—her word—once he learned to crawl and take her toys.

Brian laughed and asked all kinds of questions. Jasmine told him about Jacqueline's favorite movie: *The Prince of Egypt.* Her favorite song: "He's Got the Whole World in His Hands." Her favorite color: Pink, pink, pink!

"Her world is all about pink. She even asked me if she could change her name to Pink!"

They laughed and chatted easily for more than an hour and a half, and when the waiter came to clear the table, Jasmine wanted to send him away, to tell him not to return until she was ready. But Brian called for the check, and Jasmine sighed. It was time for them to leave. It was time for her to go home. To Hosea. To a home without her daughter.

When Brian took her hand and helped her from the chair, she hugged him. "Thank you," she said after she finally stepped away from their embrace.

Then he mesmerized her. Held her captive with his eyes.

And when he pulled her back into his arms, electrical currents shot right through her.

The heat that surged between them brought tears to her eyes. And when strong fingers caressed her back, she did cry.

She'd been right—he did want her.

After a bit of time, he backed up and, with his fingertips, gently lifted her chin. "Stay strong," he said, his voice sounding husky to her. "We're going to find our daughter."

His words were like a blanket of warmth; his tone was filled with love. And his lips . . . were right there. She could tell he wanted her.

But she had too much class to stand in the middle of one of New York's most elegant restaurants and make out. It was hard, but she would wait. How much time could it possibly take to get to his room?

"Okay," she breathed. "I'm ready," she told him.

He held his hand against the small of her back and guided her through the restaurant to the front. When they stepped over the threshold, she paused, glancing to the left, then the right, searching for the elevators.

Brian frowned and bent over close. "What's wrong?" he asked, his face mere inches from hers.

Again . . . his lips . . . right there. And now she couldn't wait. She pressed her mouth against his, and in the millisecond that it took for him to respond, she parted her lips and invited him in.

There in the lobby, in front of patrons who'd paid six hundred dollars a night for a room, they kissed with the passion they'd always had.

Jasmine moaned and yearned for more.

Brian moaned, then grasped her shoulders and pushed her away. "I'm sorry," he panted.

She frowned, wondering why he was apologizing. "No, it's

fine." And then she realized they were standing in the middle of the lobby. She giggled nervously. "I guess we got carried away. Come on."

While he moved to his left, she moved to the right. They each took two steps, looked back, and frowned.

"Where . . . ," Jasmine started.

But Brian said, "I need to get you out of here. A cab . . ." He pointed to the front of the hotel.

"No!" she said, loudly enough to make the designer-clad men and women, who just seconds before had glanced away with embarrassment, turn to them again. "Brian, what are you doing? I don't want to go."

"Jasmine, please."

"I want you," she said. "And I know you want me."

He shook his head, then tentatively reached for her arm, as if he was afraid to touch her.

"No," she said as he guided her to the front. "No," she repeated as Brian, with just the smallest nod of his head, signaled the uniformed doorman.

Think, Jasmine. Think!

But seconds later, Brian was stuffing her into a cab, giving the driver a twenty because he was going only a couple of blocks.

"No!" she said again. "Brian, I want you!" She couldn't believe she was actually begging a man. And not just any man—this man. The one who had brought her nothing but grief, but who had also given her the greatest joy of her life—their daughter.

She was still mouthing no when the cabdriver edged into the heavy afternoon traffic. Twisting, she looked through the window, her face and her palms pressed against the glass until she couldn't see him anymore.

Defeated, she bounced against the seat. In her mind, she

turned over every hour, dissected every minute. Was it something she'd said? Something he'd said?

"Okay," she whispered. "Calm down."

She had to think. At least now she knew where he was staying. By morning, she'd figure this out. By morning, it would all be fine again.

And it had to be. Because without Jacqueline, all she had was Brian.

Fifty

BRIAN HELD HIS HANDS OUT in front of him, waist high, and watched as his fingers still shook. More than an hour had passed, and nothing he did stopped his trembling.

He grabbed the glass, half filled with the gin and tonic he'd made from the minibar. Tilting the tumbler back, he downed what was left, then slammed the glass onto the dresser.

How could this have happened?

It was the million-dollar question that he'd asked a million times. But he already knew the answer—he never should have brought Jasmine back to his hotel. Even the lobby restaurant was more private than public, and by definition, with their history, that was trouble.

But Jasmine had been so distraught, he'd had to get her away from the center. And this lunch was supposed to be just a meeting between friends; after all, they'd been spending a lot of time together, with only the most innocent of contact between them . . .

Brian shook his head. He'd been a fool. Acting like a man walking in the dark. Because really, he should've seen this thing coming.

So what did that mean? That this was something he'd wanted to happen?

He sighed out loud as he remembered the kiss. First, in slow motion. Then, in fast-forward time. Over and over. A loud groan of regret pushed through his lips.

There had always been this sick connection between the two of them—some kind of crazy lust that wouldn't go away. She was a major part of his addiction.

But the truth? Brian knew that he could blame it on his illness all he wanted, but that kiss didn't have a thing to do with his addiction. And it wasn't just lust either, because when he held Jasmine in his arms, he'd wanted her there.

It was love.

But it wasn't the kind of love that consumed every bit of his heart—it wasn't the kind of love that he had for Alexis. No, this was more like the love he had for Regina, the mother of his sons. A concern. A deep caring. A love for a woman who'd given birth to his child.

But however he tried to shape it, it *was* love. And that was dangerous. A dangerous love at a dangerous time.

Brian, I want you.

Those were Jasmine's words.

Brian, I want you.

That was what he couldn't get out of his head.

Brian, I want you.

How did that happen? He lay back on the bed, closed his eyes, and remembered. After he paid for their lunch, she'd hugged him and thanked him. It was the tears in her eyes that made him hold her again . . . just for an extra second, just to let her know that he heard her and that he cared.

He'd told her to stay strong. She'd said okay. And the next thing . . .

The kiss. She'd kissed him first, there was no doubt about that; but the lethal mistake was that he'd kissed her back.

And that was why he had to leave New York.

But how could he do that? Quit right in the middle? Give up before Jacqueline came home?

He'd made promises to himself and Jasmine that he was going to find Jacqueline. He didn't know why, but he still believed that she was alive, and because of that hope, he just couldn't leave—not before the job was done.

Then he thought about Dr. Taylor Perkins, with her white-blond bouffant hair and her stern, disapproving glare.

Be aware of the triggers! he could hear his therapist saying. *Never forget the stress.*

Brian took a deep breath and then nodded as if Dr. Perkins was there in the room. Right now, he was in the most perilous of places. With Jacqueline's abduction, with Jasmine's heartache, he was under more stress than at any other time in his life.

He had to go.

Brian pushed himself up, strolled across the carpet, and took in the music of the metropolis from his sixth-floor window. The Big Apple pulsed with residents and tourists bundled up and bustling through the streets. Car brakes screamed and drivers honked horns, creating a melody that belonged only to this city. Though he could hear little through the solid glass panes, the energy was thick; New York's power was contagious.

Brian inhaled, sucked in a portion of the city's vivacity . . . and thought about Los Angeles. His home. Where he belonged. Especially now.

He could do it; he could still help—work and strategize—all from L.A. His major contribution was working on securing media. He'd already spoken to the people at *America's Most Wanted* and *Crime Stoppers*. And this morning, he'd been late getting to the center because he'd been on the phone with Steve Harvey's and Tom Joyner's people. He was close to getting what he needed; he could finish it from the left side of the country.

His mental debate continued: with cell phones and e-mail and five-hour flights, he was easily reachable and could be back in almost an instant if he was needed.

But it wasn't until his thoughts turned to Alexis that the decision was final. He'd worked hard to preserve himself for her. His fidelity—through his illness—was a battle that he'd won and was a gift for Alexis.

Brian snatched his cell from the nightstand and paced while he spoke. It only took seven minutes; he had his return flight to L.A.

He would be leaving on the first thing smokin' in the morning.

Fifty-one

JASMINE'S HEART WAS STILL POUNDING, even after she'd walked into her apartment. Even after she'd greeted Mrs. Sloss and Zaya had run into her arms. Even after her son screeched, "Love Mama!" in a pitch so high and so loud, she worried that he wouldn't be able to talk for days.

"I love you, too." She squeezed him tight. But though she held her son, and then rocked him as she read from his favorite picture book, Brian stayed right on her mind. As she thought, and read, and played, she figured it out.

Brian had apologized—that meant he thought she didn't want to be with him. But she did, and she needed to let him know that. All they had to do was talk.

She wasn't sure if the conversation should be face-to-face or over the phone. Either way, by the time they finished, Jasmine had no doubt that they would be together again.

The sound of the front door closing interrupted Jasmine's thoughts and a moment later Hosea walked into Zaya's bedroom.

"Dada!" their son exclaimed as he jumped from Jasmine's lap and into his father's arms.

"Hey, son! What's good?"

"Me!" Zaya giggled as Hosea lifted him.

"You've been good?"

"Yeessss!" Zaya sang.

"Well, I've been good, too." Hosea turned to Jasmine, but he wasn't wearing a smile. Not that he looked angry—his eyes were filled with a sadness that she totally understood. "Let's ask Mama, Zaya. Let's ask Mama if she's been good."

Jasmine almost choked on the air that she inhaled. She coughed. And coughed. Looked up at Hosea. Now he was smiling.

"So, Mama," he asked as he held their son. "Have you been good?"

"Good, Mama?" Zaya added his own inquiry.

She nodded, because she couldn't get any words out. Did Hosea know something?

"Great!" Hosea exclaimed, as he turned Zaya upside down.

Her son's squeals gave Jasmine a moment—to sit up straight, wipe the tense smile from her face, act as if all was normal.

When Hosea turned back, she was breathing again. "So how was your day?"

It was a question he asked just about every night, but today it rang with new meaning.

"Fine."

He paused, looked at her some more. Tilted his head. "Are you sure?"

He knows! That I kissed Brian.

Jasmine crossed, then uncrossed, her legs. Crossed, then uncrossed, her arms. She didn't have time to figure out how he knew. All she could do was come up with some story, a tremendous lie. Or she could deny, deny, deny. Then twist it around somehow, put this whole thing on him.

"Keith told me about the phone call."

She blinked. And blinked. Then remembered. The call—had that happened today? With all that had gone down afterward, that phone call seemed so long ago.

He said, "I tried to call you." Moving closer, he asked, "Are you all right?"

"Yes." Her voice trembled, but he would attribute that to what she'd been through, she was sure. "I'm fine now." Her time with Brian had made her forget, but now because of Hosea, the memory was back.

The voice. Those words.

The recollection tackled her so fast, so rough, that she had to close her eyes. "You should have heard that man," she whispered, her voice filled with tears.

He called for Mrs. Sloss to take Zaya from the room, then he turned back to Jasmine. As he hugged her, he said, "Don't think about it."

"How can I not?" She pushed herself up from the chair and away from his arms. Pacing the length of the room, she said, "This whole thing—Jacquie, that man, everything—is driving me crazy. I don't know whether to live or just try to die. I don't know if I should stay home with Zaya or start pounding the streets myself. I don't know if I love . . ." She completed the thought in her head: *you . . . or Brian.*

"Go ahead." Hosea stood up straight. "Finish what you were saying."

She folded her arms, but she couldn't look at him. So with her head down, she said, "I'm just saying that it's all too much, and I don't know how much longer I can take this."

"You're stronger than you think," he said. "I promise, you're going to be all right."

But his assurances weren't anything like Brian's. Hosea's assurances were never about Jacqueline, and that brought new tears to her eyes.

She rewound the past hours and remembered how she had laughed with Brian. Now, here at home with Hosea, all she wanted to do was cry.

"Jasmine, I'm going to make sure that our family is okay."

Didn't he know that wasn't what she wanted to hear? To her, there was never a way that their family could be okay without Jacqueline.

Gently, he kissed her forehead. "I'm going to check on Zaya," he said, as if his son was his only concern. He had walked away without a single clue of how he could help her, what she needed.

They used to know each other's thoughts, could finish each other's sentences. They used to move as if they were one. But their connection was lost—the abductor had taken more than Jacqueline from them.

Jasmine shook her head as she returned to the rocking chair. She wondered what was going to happen to her marriage.

And then she turned all thoughts to Brian.

Fifty-two

LOS ANGELES, CALIFORNIA
DECEMBER 2009

THERE WAS A CERTAIN EXCITEMENT that Brian always felt whenever he landed at LAX. Even though it was still an hour before noon, the airport was bustling with Los Angelenos, strolling past Christmas decorations, dressed in shorts and T-shirts and flip-flops.

There was no place like home.

Except this time, Brian didn't wear the smile that always came to him when he headed out to the curb to wait for the car service. This time, his mind was still in New York.

Every minute of the five-hour-and-thirty-minute flight, Brian wondered if he'd made the right decision. Now that he finally had a chance to make a difference, was he deserting his daughter? But like all the other times he'd asked that question, he told himself that it didn't matter where he was—he would still do what he had to do.

Brian waved at a slowly approaching town car the moment he saw his name on the placard tucked in the window. Two minutes after that, he was inside, speeding down Century Boulevard. The moment the car turned left onto LaCienega, Brian pressed the Power button on his cell phone and pushed the first icon for his messages.

"You have thirteen new messages. First message . . ." Brian hit End before the voice could begin.

Thirteen messages. He didn't even have to check. He knew who the calls were from, and he needed to handle this now.

Scrolling through his contact list, he clicked on Hosea's name and was relieved when he answered right away.

"What's up, Brian?"

"Nothing. Listen, I just wanted to let you know that I'm back in L.A."

He could sense Hosea's frown in the silence that followed. Finally, Hosea said, "I didn't know you were leaving. I mean . . . I got the impression that you were going to stay longer." Then, when he asked, "What happened?" the gentle manner of the man was gone.

Brian replied, "Nothing, I just figured that I could do as much from here as I was doing in New York." More silence, so he added a lie, "See . . . ah . . . there was a surgery . . . that I'd forgotten. I had to . . . really, you know . . . get back for that." If his addiction had been gambling, he would've bet and probably won lots of money that Hosea didn't believe a word he'd said. But Brian kept on anyway. "It's tomorrow . . . yeah . . . and I wanted to get a head start, to get rested . . . you know . . ."

"Yeah, I know," Hosea said, in the tone of a suspicious husband.

Brian said, "Listen, I'm not giving up, man!"

"No, I know that." The loving father, the caring pastor, was back. "And neither are we."

"I'm going to keep working on those contacts. We're gonna score some major media somehow, someway."

"That would be great, since there hasn't been much in the last two weeks."

"Yeah, and I really want to stay in touch."

"Do that. Call me anytime, and check in with Keith, too."

Brian released a long breath of air. "Done deal."

"And, I'll call you if . . . when there's news."

"Thanks."

Then another pause before, "Does Jasmine know that you—"

Brian answered before Hosea finished, "No. This came up suddenly. Last night . . . I didn't have a chance . . . you know . . . to tell anyone. But . . . would you mind . . . you know, saying something to her for me." A moment of silence. "Please." He closed his eyes and wondered why guilt always made him sound like an idiot.

"Yeah, I'll tell her."

"Thanks, and Hosea, I'm gonna keep praying. I'll be in touch."

After his good-bye, Brian clicked off the phone. With the way he sounded, Hosea had to know that something was up.

But what was real was that there was nothing for Hosea to figure. Nothing was up. Nothing had happened. Nothing was going to happen.

Well, at least that part was done.

He leaned forward and said to the driver, "Change of plans. I need to make a detour. Can you take me to Ninety-five hundred Wilshire, please?"

Brian wasn't sure that he liked the look on Alexis's face. Shock, yes. But what he'd been hoping for was more of a look of wonderment. A look that said she loved him, that she was glad he was home.

But her eyebrows were furrowed so close together they almost looked like one. "What are you doing here?"

"I came to see you."

"I mean, what are you doing here in L.A.? On Tuesday, you said you were gonna stay until . . ." Her eyes widened.

"No," he shook his head, "Jacquie's not back . . . not yet."

"Then?"

His strut was back as he moved around her desk, pulled her up, and wrapped his arms around her. He noticed that it took a moment for her to hug him back, but he refused to be denied. "I missed you," he whispered in her ear.

She pulled away from him. "So you came home because you missed me?"

In that second, the image of Jasmine and their kiss flashed through his mind. He blinked it away, stepped back, and said, "Yeah . . . I came because . . . you know, I couldn't wait to see you . . . and because . . . well, there wasn't anything left for me . . ." He stopped, knowing that if he kept on talking he'd give himself away.

Alexis tilted her head and stared at him as if she knew he had a secret. "So, no news?" she asked.

Leaning against the edge of her desk, he folded his arms and shook his head. "Still getting lots of those weird calls, though." His words made him think of Jasmine and the call she'd taken that had led to the kiss. He couldn't believe it had all happened only yesterday.

Alexis's sigh dragged Brian out of New York, back to L.A. "I know about those calls, took too many while I was there." Shaking her head, she asked, "Why do people call up like that?"

Brian shrugged. "I've never been able to figure out crazy."

Alexis shook her head. "I don't know how Hosea and Jasmine are doing it. How are . . . they?"

Another shrug, and this time he worked to keep the guilt away. "They're just like when you left, still hanging."

"Being in New York with them was tough." She shuddered and crossed her arms, as if suddenly chilled. "I just pray for them. Hosea's such a good man, you know?"

He wanted to tell her that Jasmine was good, too. She was a good mother who loved her daughter and was suffering tremendously, too. But he wasn't about to defend Jasmine. Not to Alexis. Not right now.

"Well, I'm just glad to be home."

She said, "You should have stayed in New York."

His head reared back a bit at her words, her tone.

"I mean," she began, trying to warm it up, "Jacqueline needs you. And," a deep breath, "Jasmine does, too."

He frowned. Why would she say that?

"Jasmine doesn't need me; she has her husband." He leaned forward. "And anyway, the only woman I want to need me . . . is you."

She shook her head. "Your attention needs to be on Jacqueline right now."

"And it is."

"You need to be focused, without distractions."

"You're not a distraction. You're the woman I love."

She leaned back to put some space between them, then waved her hand like his words didn't matter. "There can't be any 'us' right now."

"Give me one good reason why, Alexis." Frustration was all in his tone.

"Because you don't know what's going to happen. You don't know if Jacqueline will ever be found . . ."

"She will be," he said, as if he was sure of it. "But what does that have to do with us? No matter what happens, there's still you and me."

"I'm just saying, let's keep everything the way it is and . . ." Her voice trailed off.

He shook his head; all signs of the cheer he'd walked in with were gone. "You're determined to fight us, aren't you?"

"I'm determined to do what's right."

He leaned so close that he inhaled the faint scent of her minty toothpaste. He wanted to take her right then, right there. On top of her desk, on the floor, on the sofa—just love her anywhere. And then maybe he'd be able to tear down this wall that she was determined to keep between them. "Let me tell you what's right . . . you and me," he said, with his face still right in front of hers. "Nothing's going to change that."

"Brian—"

When he pressed the tips of his fingers against her lips stopping her words, she closed her eyes and sighed.

Inside, he smiled. *Gotcha!*

But he didn't say another word. Just pushed himself up, strolled toward her door, and left her alone.

He didn't even bother to look back.

Fifty-three

HOSEA TUCKED THE BIBLE BACK onto the shelf, then, with a sigh, sat behind his desk. His plan had been to get an early start on Sunday's sermon so that he could spend more time at the center. But since Brian's call, he hadn't been able to concentrate.

He wasn't a fool. He was sure that Brian's quick decision to get out of New York had something to do with Jasmine. In his heart, he believed what he'd told Alexis—that Jasmine and Brian were connected only through this tragedy. But his head had him believing something else.

The doubt had started when he'd been holding Jasmine and she'd uttered Brian's name. For the rest of that night, straight through till dawn, he had not shut his eyes. All he wanted to do was snatch Jasmine from her sleep and demand an explanation.

But what was he supposed to say? "You called out Brian's name in your sleep!"

And what would have been her answer? "No, I didn't!"

Knowing Jasmine, she would have argued him down, come up with ten thousand words that sounded like "Brian." Or maybe she would have admitted it and said something like, I don't know what I said in my sleep, and I don't know why I said it. I've been spending a lot of time with Brian—maybe that's why. But whatever, it didn't mean anything . . .

And if that had been her explanation, she would have been correct. Just because they'd been spending a lot of time together, and just because he was always holding her, and just because she called out his name—none of that meant that she was sleeping with Brian.

Still, she called out his name.

And it didn't mean that she *wanted* to sleep with him. And even if she did, could he convict her on what was inside her head? Could he condemn her for something she might do?

But still, she called out his name.

He'd endured a lot with Jasmine, but since their vows, he'd never questioned her fidelity. He was the one who'd come close to having an affair. So why did he doubt her? Why couldn't he just understand the strain they were under?

He closed his eyes and thought about that truth—they *were* stressed. They were wallowing in their stress . . . and their de-spair . . . and their grief. They were drowning . . .

His eyes popped open. *Oh, my God!*

It was true—they were going through *all* of that. But now, Hosea wondered if Jasmine felt what he felt—like he was going through all of this *alone*.

He didn't feel like he had a spouse, and it had to be the same for Jasmine. Really, he had been absent; he'd been so busy trying to make it right—putting together the center, working at church, keeping life normal for Zaya. Where was Jasmine in all of this?

Hosea tried to remember the last time they'd talked, really talked. He wasn't thinking about one of their debates, when she'd told him that she didn't know how to go on living. And he certainly wasn't thinking about when he'd told her that he was taking Zaya to church no matter what she thought.

Hosea moaned as he remembered that argument. He hadn't thought it all the way through last Sunday—Jasmine must have felt so alone.

He grabbed the telephone, called Jasmine on her cell, then hung up when it went straight to voice mail. Next, he called home.

"Ms. Jasmine's not here," Mrs. Sloss told him. "She went out a while ago."

"Did she say where she was going?"

"No, Mr. Hosea."

He hung up, tried her cell again, then called the center, even though he was certain that she wouldn't have gone back there after yesterday.

"She's not here," Keith said once Hosea got him on the phone. Then he added, "She did come in this morning, but she wasn't here for five seconds. She didn't say anything, just took one look around and left. I think what happened yesterday really got to her."

Hosea frowned. *Then why would she go back there?* "She didn't say where she was going?"

"Nope, she didn't say a word. But with the way she looked, kind of crazed"—and then, as if he realized what he'd said, Keith added—"I mean, she looked like she was really sad. I bet you she went home."

Hosea's thoughts were deep as he hung up. In the past, if Jasmine was upset, she would have come straight to him, her husband, her comforter. But now they were living on separate islands.

Well, their healing would begin tonight; he would be there for her. He would comfort her, protect her. He would hold her, and they would talk, really talk. They would pray and work through this distance that had come between them. Tonight, they'd be one again; he'd make sure of that.

Now the call from Brian was no longer a distraction. He was glad Brian had called, glad that he was out of the way.

Hosea reached for his Bible again and tucked the Holy Book under his arm. It was time to get back to his sermon. But he would go home and work from there. Then he'd be home when Jasmine arrived. This way, he'd truly be there for his wife.

Fifty-four

AGAIN, JASMINE TURNED OVER EVERYTHING in her mind. Second by second, minute by minute, she reviewed every word she and Brian had exchanged. But nothing explained what was happening today.

She had already left so many messages, Brian's voice mail was full. When he didn't call back, she'd rushed over to the center, sure that he would be there. But just a glance told her that he was not, and that was when she'd made the first call to the hotel. But after three attempts, the woman at the front desk still said the same thing: Dr. Lewis had checked out.

The first time the woman had told her that, Jasmine had screamed into the phone, "That's impossible!"

"I'm sorry," the woman said, maintaining her decorum. "But Doctor Lewis checked out this morning."

Jasmine hung up, redialed, and asked the hotel operator to connect her to the front desk again. When the same woman answered, Jasmine asked for her name.

"This is Shawn."

Jasmine put on the sweetest voice she could. "Shawn, I'm calling about Doctor Lewis."

"Yes, ma'am, I recognize your voice."

"Can you please connect me to his room?" Her tone was still sugary.

After a pause, Shawn said, "Ma'am, as I already told you, Doctor Lewis checked out."

The sweetness was gone. "He did not!"

"I don't know what else to tell you."

Jasmine hung up; she couldn't stand service people who didn't do their jobs. It was not *possible* that Brian had checked out. She didn't believe that, because if she did, she'd have to consider that he'd left New York. Left her. Left their daughter. And that was the part that was impossible.

Standing in the middle of 125th Street, Jasmine hailed a cab, told the driver that she was going to the Plaza, then leaned back and planned her words as the taxi sped south.

In less than ten minutes, Jasmine walked through the doors (held open by the white-gloved doorman) of the legendary hotel. Like yesterday, her heels clicked against the marble tiles, and she paused for a moment in the spot where she and Brian had shared that kiss. She remembered and shuddered; she had to find him.

Moving toward the front desk, she took a deep breath, determined to stay calm by any means necessary.

She eyed the young woman, a twentysomething African American who, with a gold jacket and her hair pulled back into a severe bun, fit right into the elegance and opulence of the six-star hotel.

Straightening her coat's collar, Jasmine stepped forward and noticed the name on the golden tag pinned right above her heart: Shawn.

Just great. There was no way Jasmine wanted to talk to this woman, but the man behind the counter was engrossed with two guests.

Jasmine had no choice when the woman smiled and asked, "How may I help you?" showing perfect teeth.

"I'm here to see one of your guests," Jasmine said, with a bit of a southern twang so the woman wouldn't recognize her right away.

"Yes, ma'am." She pointed to a bank of gilded rotary phones lined up against the wall. "You can use one of the guest phones."

"Ah, I'm not sure of his room number. Can you just connect me?"

"Of course. What is the guest's name?"

Another deep breath. "Doctor Brian Lewis."

The edges of the woman's lips lost their curve. She squinted at Jasmine when she asked, "Did you just call here?"

Jasmine didn't respond.

Shawn said, "Doctor Lewis checked out this morning," in a tone that underscored, *I already told you this.*

"That can't be right."

She said, "Well, I don't know what to tell you," her decorum now gone.

"Why don't you check again?"

"I've already checked three times. Why don't you accept the fact that he's not here?"

"Because he would have told me if he was leaving."

"Maybe he didn't want you to know," Shawn said, snaking her neck just a bit.

Jasmine's mouth opened wide. "Let me speak with your supervisor."

Shawn's good manners came right back. "I'm sorry I said that. But you keep asking the same question, and I already told you—"

"Your supervisor," Jasmine said, holding up the palm of her hand, stopping the young woman's words.

The woman pushed her shoulders back and held her head high, but still, Jasmine saw her fear. A minute later, she knew why when she returned behind a lanky white-haired woman who looked like she spit fire and was just waiting for a reason to terminate someone on the spot.

"Hello, Miss." She paused, waiting for Jasmine to give her name.

"Jasmine Bush, and I want to file a complaint."

The woman folded her hands together, bowed her head a bit, and said, "I'm so sorry." She glanced over her shoulder at Shawn, who stood behind her almost trembling. "Our goal here at the Plaza is to make sure that all of our guests are completely satisfied—"

"But she's not a guest," Shawn said. "She's—"

In the most genteel manner, the woman held up her forefinger. That small motion made Shawn shut her mouth and made Jasmine smile.

Jasmine said, "I'm looking for a dear friend who's staying at this hotel." She lowered her voice. "He's been here for a week, and we even had lunch here yesterday. But Shawn refuses to let me speak with him."

The woman frowned. "Is he accepting calls?" She glanced at Shawn.

"He was . . . when he was here," Shawn said in a tone that suggested she'd forgotten to whom she was talking. "He checked out this morning."

"He did not," Jasmine countered.

The woman said, "Let me check that for you."

Again, Jasmine gave Brian's name. Again, his name was typed into the computer.

And the white-haired woman said, "I'm sorry, Mrs. Bush,

but it seems that Shawn is correct. Doctor Lewis has checked out."

"But—"

"I'm very sorry," the woman said, cutting her off. "But he's not here." In her tone, Jasmine heard the same implication that Shawn had made—he left and he didn't want you to know.

Jasmine started to protest, to tell the supervisor to check again. But it was Shawn who stopped her. Shawn, who stood behind the white-haired woman with her arms crossed. Shawn, who was no longer trembling. Shawn, with her smug smile. It was Shawn who made Jasmine just walk away.

Now it was Jasmine who pushed her shoulders back and lifted her head. But as she moved toward the door, all she could manage was a stagger that made her look intoxicated. And she was drunk, drunk with the realization that Brian *had* left her.

Maybe he just went to a different hotel.

But no matter what her head said, her heart knew the truth.

What was she supposed to do now? How was she going to make it through without him? He was the only person who understood her, the only one who gave her hope, the only one who helped her to see Jacqueline every day. She needed him. Without Brian, there was no way she could go on.

But the truth was, Brian was gone.

Fifty-five

JASMINE WALKED AND WALKED. TEARS streamed down her face. Her sobs were silent, but still she cried. Yet not one New Yorker noticed her.

And then she looked up. Stood still. She had walked dozens and dozens of blocks to come right back to where she'd started. She was across the street from the Plaza, in front of F.A.O. Schwarz—Jacqueline's favorite place.

Jasmine couldn't count the times that she'd brought Jacqueline to this famous toy store just blocks from their apartment. It was how they spent their special days. When Hosea took Zaya, she and Jacqueline would go shopping.

Mama, let's go!

She could almost hear her daughter as she pushed through the front door. The throng of tourists—with only thirteen shopping days till Christmas—slowed her down, but soon, Jasmine found her stride. She wandered through the aisles, retracing steps that she and Jacqueline had taken the last time they were here, just days before the abduction.

Her tears were still streaming, but the holiday crowd was too distracted to notice. Jasmine drifted from one colorful section of the store to another. She stumbled past stuffed animals, past Barbies, past rows and rows of LEGOs. On the up escalator, she held her breath until she got to Jacqueline's favorite part—the Book Monster.

That was when she heard her.

Mama, I want this! And this! And that!

Jasmine stopped. Looked around. That was a voice that she knew. She could hardly breathe as she listened.

"Mama, I want this!"

Now she tried to follow the voice. She had to find her.

"Jacquie!" Jasmine called out. But her voice faded amid the chatter and the laughter and the music.

No one heard her, but she could hear the little girl. "Mama, can I have this?"

Jasmine rushed past the larger-than-life stuffed animals and made her way around the store's famous teddy bear.

"Jacquie!"

Her steps were quicker now, but she didn't know where to go. She heard the voice of the little girl all around her, coming from every direction.

Her head was pounding as she stopped. She stood in the middle of the second floor and twirled in place.

"Jacquie," she cried, again and again.

"Excuse me, miss."

She stopped and wobbled a bit, dizzy now.

The man held her arm gently, holding her up. "Are you all right?" he asked.

For a moment, she stared at the man in the blue uniform. "My daughter," she whispered.

"Your daughter? Have you lost your daughter?"

She squeezed her eyes shut. She could still hear the voice in her head, but once she opened her eyes, she heard the voices of many little girls all around her.

She moaned and whipped past the security guard, then pushed through the crowd on the escalator. She rushed from the store and out onto the street.

Every part of her—her head, her heart, her feet—was aching. She fought through the Fifth Avenue crowd, bumping and dodging bodies until she got to the edge of the street. There she grabbed a lightpost, desperate to hold on. The steel against her hands felt frozen. But she couldn't let go. How else would she keep standing?

"Help me," she whimpered as she looked up at the sky that was more white than blue, with the cumulus clouds that looked like the welcome gates to heaven. "Help me," she cried.

She had lost Jacqueline. She had lost Brian. And now, she was sure, she was losing her mind.

Fifty-six

His toes were tingling and his fingers felt frozen stiff. But once Hosea pushed through the revolving doors (still huffing from the blocks he'd just jogged), he was greeted by the din of holiday happiness.

Above him, the three-story clock sang a welcoming song about the wonderful world of toys, and around him F.A.O. Schwarz was still thick with shoppers, even though the darkness of night had descended.

"Pastor Bush?" An African American man who looked as if he was a grandfather many times over called out to Hosea even though several feet separated them.

Still out of breath, Hosea blinked when the elderly uniformed man reached out his hand. "I recognized you from your TV show," the security guard explained as they shook hands. "You can come with me."

Hosea took off his gloves, blew on his hands, then followed the man through the children's wonderland.

"Your wife was outside the store," the man repeated what he'd already told Hosea when he called.

"Is she all right?" It was a question that Hosea hadn't had a chance to ask. Once the manager of security from F.A.O. Schwarz had called him and said that his wife needed him, Hosea had dashed from the apartment. There was no need to wait for a cab; the store was so close, though it had seemed much farther on foot, at night, in the cold.

"She seems to be good now, but she wasn't earlier." The man explained how he'd found Jasmine spinning in the middle of the store and then how he'd raced outside after her when she ran away from him. "It took me a couple of minutes to get her away from that pole," the guard said after he told Hosea how Jasmine had been clasped to the streetlight. "She was wrapped around that thing like it was some kind of lifeline." He paused when they stopped in front of an office. "Mrs. Bush is in here with the manager."

Hosea nodded and then stepped inside, his eyes wide with expectation.

With the stuffed animals, plastic dolls, pint-size cars, and shelves loaded with books, the room looked more like a children's playroom than an office. Jasmine sat in an oversize upholstered chair in the corner, shoulders slumped, her eyes focused on the paper coffee cup she held.

"Mr. Bush."

The woman standing behind the desk looked like any other Fortune 500 executive.

She shook Hosea's hand. "I'm Marley Morrison," she said, her voice low. "We spoke earlier." With kindly and caring eyes, she glanced at an unmoving Jasmine before she slipped from behind her desk. "Feel free to use my office for as long as you need it."

He nodded, then stayed in place when he was left alone with his wife.

On the phone, Marley Morrison had said that Jasmine seemed confused, but when he looked at her now, she seemed fine—except for the fact that she hadn't taken her eyes off the cup, not even to look at him.

She looked well, though, dressed in the emerald designer pants suit that he'd bought for her last Christmas. Her hair was upswept in a style that she reserved for the most formal of occasions. Whom had she dressed for today?

When he decided that he didn't need to know the answer to that question, he took steps toward his wife. Kneeling by her side, he whispered, "Darlin', are you all right?"

It took a moment, but then Jasmine slowly lifted her head, brought her eyes to his.

It took restraint for Hosea to hold back his gasp. She had looked fine to him, until then.

The foundation that she had undoubtedly carefully applied earlier was now streaked where her huge tears had left their tracks. Mascara was caked around her lids, and her lips were dry and chapped, as if she'd spent many hours in the cold without any protection.

But it was her eyes that disturbed him the most, her eyes that let him know that there was something majorly wrong. Her eyes were dull, unfocused, as if she had gone somewhere deep inside of herself.

I need to get her to the hospital.

But then in the next instant, she blinked and brightened just a bit.

"Hosea!" she said, as if she was just now seeing him.

He swallowed. "Yeah." His voice was shaky. "It's me. Are you all right?"

"I want to go home, but they . . ." She stopped, took a

glance around the room, and frowned. Confusion was written all over her face. She shook her head. "There were people here, and they wouldn't let me go . . . ?" It was supposed to be a statement, but it came out like a question.

"We can go home now." He took her hand and lifted her from the chair.

She adjusted the purse on her shoulder, and with the cup still in her hand, she stepped in front of him.

Hosea waited for a moment, to make sure that she was steady. But when she got to the door and looked back at him, he followed.

The store was still crowded with customers as the two moved through the masses, and while he didn't see Marley Morrison, Hosea did see the guard who greeted him when he'd first arrived.

The man smiled. "You take care, Mrs. Bush," he said to Jasmine as they approached the front door.

Jasmine paused for a moment, stared at the man, then dumped the cup she held into his hands.

Both Hosea and the guard frowned, but all Hosea said was, "Thank you," before he followed Jasmine onto the sidewalk.

Still, he wasn't sure if he should take his wife home or to a hospital. But looking at her now, standing at the curb, with her hand raised for a taxi, she seemed like any other New Yorker.

Even though it was Friday night, it took less than a minute to catch a cab. As the car pulled from the curb, Jasmine leaned her head on Hosea's shoulder, and he sighed. Maybe she was fine.

In just minutes, they were in the elevator of their apartment building. Hosea waited for Jasmine to speak, but all she did was take his hand. For the moment, that was enough.

Inside their apartment, Jasmine paused in the foyer and stared at the grand space of their living room.

One second passed, then another, and then another before Jasmine let her hand slip from his.

With quick steps and without a word, she moved toward their bedroom, leaving Hosea with his brows bunched into a frown.

"Jasmine, are you all right? Do you need anything?"

She paused and took a moment before she turned to him. Her dull eyes were back. She looked as if she'd lost a piece of herself just by walking into their home.

She shook her head. "I don't need anything."

"Have you eaten?"

"No, but I don't want anything." Before he could protest, she said, "Look, I'm just tired. I'm trying to figure all of this out." She must've seen the doubt in his eyes because she added, "I'm fine, Hosea. I don't even know why those people called you."

"They said you were confused."

It was her turn to frown. "Confused?" She spoke as if she'd never heard that word. "I wasn't . . . It wasn't that. I was in the store, and I heard Jacquie."

His eyes widened.

She pressed her fingertips against her temples. "Not Jacquie. I mean, I thought I heard Jacquie." She rotated her fingers as if she had a headache. "And then I was looking for Brian."

This didn't seem to be the best of times to tell her about Brian's phone call.

But then her eyes brightened, and she exclaimed, "Brian!" as if just the mention of his name brought her joy. She added, "I've got to call him."

Hosea knew he needed to tell her the truth. "Brian's not here," he said slowly, carefully. "He went home . . . to Los Angeles. He asked me to let you know."

There was no more confusion, no more dullness.

Jasmine kept her eyes on his, even as a single tear rolled

down her cheek. Hosea tried to keep himself straight, even as he watched his wife cry for another man.

"He didn't tell me that he was leaving," she said, seemingly cognizant now.

"It's fine that he's gone. I'm here."

She shook her head slowly from side to side. "You're not him."

He took a breath and worked hard not to be hurt by her words. He remembered that this was the woman whom God had chosen for him, the woman he'd promised the Lord he'd honor and cherish, for better or for worse. The woman who was so sick with grief that she couldn't possibly know what she was saying. Because of that, he was able to say, "You're right, I'm not Brian. I'm me. And for you, that's better."

She pressed her hand against her lips, but that didn't keep the sob inside.

"But if he's gone, then Jacquie's gone, too."

"No," Hosea said, taking a step closer. "He's still going to help us."

"I mean, if he's gone, then Jacquie's gone, because *he's* Jacquie."

He knew it now for sure—she needed help.

"No, he's not," Hosea said. Now, right in front of her, he spoke softly. "Listen to what you're saying, Jasmine. Brian's not Jacquie."

He could tell that she was replaying her words inside, trying to make sense out of her nonsense.

"But . . . but I know that. But the way he looks—"

"Yes, Jacquie looks like him."

"And so . . . that makes him . . ." Then she stopped. And right in front of him, Hosea watched the dullness return. He could see the way she retreated, then crawled inside herself.

Only this time, her eyes closed, and before she could drop to the floor, he caught her.

Fifty-seven

THIS IS JUST ABOUT BEING a friend. Alexis turned over those words in her mind. *Nothing more, nothing less.* She repeated that so much, it became her mantra.

She maneuvered into the circular driveway, then stopped in front of the building where she used to live.

"How ya doing, Mrs. Ward-Lewis." The concierge grinned as he opened the door. "You want me to park the car for you?"

She reached for the bags from Panda's that rested on the passenger seat; the aroma of the sausages inside the package filled the car. Balancing the two bags in one hand, she said, "No, Steven, don't park it. I'm just going to be a minute or two." *This is just about being a friend.* "Can I leave it right here since this is going to be quick?" *Nothing more, nothing less.*

"You got it," the doorman said, though Alexis never heard him. The mantra in her head was louder than his voice.

It had taken a lot for her to come here. She'd gone to bed last night determined to stay far away from Brian. She was no longer going to deny her deep feelings—she probably even loved him. But what pleased the heart wasn't always good for the soul, and she wasn't going to let her heart drag her backward.

But this morning, she'd awakened with new compassion. Just because she didn't want to be Brian's wife didn't mean she couldn't be his friend. And friends looked out for friends. He needed support now, with all that he was going through. It had to be hard to leave New York. That's why she decided to come by and help out a friend.

The elevator doors parted; Alexis stepped out, then paused.

"Good morning," Brian said, leaning against his front-door frame as if he was waiting for her. Dressed in jeans and a V-neck undershirt, he added, "Steven called. Told me you were on your way. He just wanted to make sure that I was up so that I could greet my wife properly."

Her eyes roamed over his body, and she had to take a breath to stay steady. *This is just about being a friend.* She moved past him—as if she didn't care—and said, "I'm sure Steven didn't say anything about my being your wife."

Brian stuffed his hands inside his jeans pockets and grinned.

"Anyway," Alexis turned away as she placed the bags with the takeout boxes on the kitchen table, "I was thinking that you probably didn't have anything in your refrigerator. And I know you're going to be busy catching up on everything—"

"Nope, I'm not busy at all," he said. "I'm gonna just relax today and tomorrow so that I can hit the floor on Monday."

As he talked, she stared. And took another cleansing breath. "Well, anyway," she said, "I brought you breakfast."

"Wow. Gee." He peeked inside the bags. "Thanks."

Then there was nothing. So after long moments of silence,

Alexis added, "I just wanted to make sure that you had some-thing to eat. There're pancakes and eggs and sausage."

"My favorites."

"And a couple of doughnuts."

"Thanks."

When that was all he said, she added, "About three or four."

"Three or four?"

"Doughnuts." Then, "Glazed." *My favorites.*

"Oh. Okay." He nodded.

She waited, sure that he was going to invite her to join him, since it was Saturday and she'd brought *extra glazed* doughnuts. She stood firm, ready to tell him no, that she couldn't stay.

But he didn't say another word, so she did. "I don't want you to think that this is anything more than just me being a good friend."

"Okay," he said.

Her eyebrows pinched together, just a bit. "Because all we can be right now, Brian, all that I can handle, is friendship." She shook her head. "I can't go backward and—"

He held up his hands, stopping her. "You've said that over and over, Alex, and, finally, I got you. I hear you. I'm done. I'm just going to accept that this is what you want. So no more flowers, no more phone calls, no more dates. No more harass-ment. Just friends." The smile he had greeted her with was gone.

"But . . ." She stopped, not sure what she wanted to say. She'd been ready for a fight—between friends—but here he was giving in, giving up on them. She pressed back her shoul-ders, raised her chin. "Okay. Great."

"Yes, definitely, great!" he said.

She waited.

Nothing.

Surely, he wasn't going to let them end this way.

Still . . . nothing.

Then, "Okay. Well. Let me get going so that you can start your day," she said, though she didn't move.

But he did. Toward the front door. He opened it as if he couldn't wait to get rid of her.

She glanced once again at the bags—one filled with her favorite doughnuts—that she'd left on the table. "Enjoy," she said, though there was no joy in her voice.

"I will."

When she paused at the door, he hugged her with a light pat on her back, then stepped back so that she could walk out. He closed the door the moment she was in the hallway.

She had been dismissed, just like a friend.

Exactly the way she'd wanted it.

But if this was what she wanted, then why did being a friend make her feel so bad?

Fifty-eight

THERE WERE VOICES. AND THIS time, when Jasmine's lids fluttered slightly, she saw blue. Azure really, the color of the sea. She tried to sink into the blue—this was so much prettier than the yellow she'd seen last time. And it was much better than the pink that had made her cry the first time she tried to wake up.

"I'm really worried."

Hosea!

She could hear him but couldn't see him. The voice was behind her. So she twisted to turn over. But her body felt like a block of solid stone, impossible to move.

"There's no need to be worried."

Who's that?

A woman spoke now. In a familiar voice. "It's really just exhaustion. Exhaustion on top of depression. With this stress, it's a wonder that you're not both down. She just needs rest."

And then there was a pause, as if they had stopped to look at her.

"I can't help worrying," Hosea said in a voice that was like the color pink, a tone that made her want to cry. "She's been asleep for more than twenty-four hours. That can't be normal."

"Trust me, Pastor Bush, nothing that you and Lady Jasmine have been through in the past two weeks is normal."

Someone from church.

"And," the woman continued, "the very best thing that she can get now is rest."

"What about eating? I'm worried that she hasn't had a thing." He sighed. "Maybe I should . . ."

What?

"No! For now, she's much better off here at home," the woman said as if she knew what Hosea had been thinking. "And I don't mind stopping by. She'll probably be awake in the morning, and I'll come by then. But call me if she wakes up before. We may have to give her something for depression."

"Thank you, Doctor Howard."

Tracy Howard. A psychiatrist. From City of Lights.

Then Jasmine felt them move away from her, until there was nothing but her and silence in the room. She wanted to tell Hosea so badly that she was all right. That, surely, she didn't need a psychiatrist.

She would have told him that, except her legs, her arms, her head, her eyes, were all so heavy, made her feel so tired. There was nothing more that she could do except lay there and listen.

But now she didn't even want to listen. Now even her ears were weary.

So she succumbed again, to the peace of slumber where she didn't have to think about anything that would make her cry. All she had to wonder was what color she would see the next time she opened her eyes.

Fifty-nine

BRIAN GLANCED AT THE CALLER ID and laughed out loud. All day long at the office, he'd been so concerned that it had been hard to concentrate. But the green digital numbers on the screen let him know that he had no worries and he'd been absolutely right.

He answered the phone, casualness was all in his tone. "What's up?" he asked, as if he was speaking to one of his buddies.

"Ah . . . nothing," Alexis said. "Just checking on you. You never called me back on Saturday."

He grinned, but kept his tone serious. "I didn't know you expected me to call."

"Well, I just thought after you ate the breakfast I brought, you would've said something."

"Oh. Okay. Sorry 'bout that. It was great," he said. "Thanks again." Then he said nothing. Waited for her.

It worked.

She said, "Okay, then . . ." Another pause. "Brian, are you sure you're okay?"

He grinned. *Why? Because I'm not all over you?* "Yeah, I'm fine." And then he threw her a bone. "I mean, I'm still worried about Jacquie."

"Oh!" she said, as if that explained his distance. "Definitely."

He gave and then took away. "But as far as everything else, I'm cool. Really, really cool."

"Oh. Okay. Well, call me . . . I mean, only if you need anything."

"Sure, but like I said, I'm fine." Then abruptly he said, "Gotta go. See ya!"

He clicked off the phone before he started laughing, then cupped his hands behind his head, leaned back on the sofa, and stretched his legs out onto the coffee table. This was exactly what he'd hoped for. He could hear it in Alexis's voice—she was good and hot. Pissed and confused. She had no idea what was going on.

At first, he hadn't been sure about working it this way. Alexis was too smart to fall for any tricks. But he knew that no matter what she said, he had her heart. And when someone steals your heart, sometimes they take your reason right along with it.

Not that he felt all that good about Alexis feeling bad. Every time he saw her, all he wanted to do was make love to her. When she'd walked in with all of that food on Saturday, he'd had to stuff his hands inside his pockets or else he would've jumped all over her. Not only did he love her, but there was nothing sexier than a woman who wanted to take care of her man.

But he'd stayed back, determined to make a new play. After

all, what else could he do? He'd chased and chased until his heart was tired of running. So he decided to stop, and his hope was that she would chase him.

He hadn't been sure, but as it turned out—he was brilliant! Alexis was trying to fight love, and there wasn't a soul on earth who could win that battle.

He jumped, startled when the phone rang again. Slowly, he lowered his feet, leaned forward to get a peek at the caller ID. Could Alexis be calling back already?

But it wasn't her number on the ID.

"Brian Lewis," he answered.

"Brian, this is Abel Perez, one of the producers at Crime Stoppers."

That made him sit straight up. "Mr. Perez, how are you?"

The two exchanged pleasantries, but only for a minute before Brian asked, "So, do you think you'll be able to do something for my daughter?"

Perez said, "That's why I'm calling. We want to do a short segment on tomorrow's show, then a more extensive interview with you and Jacqueline's mother on Sunday."

Filled with relief, Brian slumped back onto the couch. This was just what they needed. He said, "Thanks so much. You don't know how hard we've been working, trying to get the media involved."

"Well, it's tough. There are so many children missing, there are not enough television hours to cover all of them. Though I have to admit I'm a bit surprised that the media didn't jump all over this. Samuel Bush is such a prominent pastor, and his granddaughter has been kidnapped . . ."

"Yeah, well . . ." That was all Brian said. No need to go into the politics of Jacqueline's being a missing black kid. "So what do we have to do?" he asked, just wanting to move forward.

Abel Perez filled Brian in—on tomorrow's show, they'd use

stock photos and information from the police. Then on Sunday, they'd send a crew for a live feed. "You're in New York, right?" Perez asked.

Brian explained that although he wasn't, who they really should be interviewing were Jasmine and Hosea.

By the time Brian hung up, he had more hope than at any other time since he'd first found out about Jacqueline's abduction. This was huge, because once she was profiled, new leads would pour in. This was just the chance they needed.

See, Jasmine, he said in his head, *I promised you.*

That thought made him grab the phone. He dialed 212 and the first three digits of Jasmine's number, but then he hung up.

He waited for the dial tone again, and this time he called Hosea.

Sixty

ALL JASMINE COULD REMEMBER WAS HOSEA's voice. And the kaleidoscope of colors.

Now, as her eyelids flickered open, neither Hosea nor the colors were there. But in their place was a hangover.

At least that's what the jackhammer inside her head felt like—a back-in-the-day kind of hangover.

She squinted, then shielded her eyes as the sun pushed its way through the curtains. With the way the light shined on her pillow, she could tell it was about noon, though she had no idea what day it was.

Falling back onto the bed, she sighed. The way she felt, she wished she *had* been drinking. A trio of mojitos would have been so much better than having a headache from heartache.

She wondered how long she'd slept. There was little that she could recall from her darkness: the toy store, Dr. Howard, and the point at which she'd awakened and Hosea had held a cup while she sipped some soup. But she remembered nothing more.

The ache in her chest was ever present, a constant reminder that the devil had stolen her daughter.

Slowly, gently, she pushed herself up. The blood rush brought another memory—Brian. She closed her eyes and remembered their kiss. She groaned.

Her rest had brought her some clarity, and now she asked herself why had she done that. Maybe it was because he had been so kind, so caring, so understanding.

It was all of the above, but mostly it was his face. And the way he smiled. And the way he bunched his eyebrows. And the way he gestured with his hands.

The way he looked like Jacqueline.

Jasmine tossed aside thoughts of Brian as she flung away the duvet that covered her. She swung her legs over the side of the bed, then stayed still because she had no choice—she waited until she felt steady enough to move. As she shifted, her eyes focused on the photo of her daughter.

Her lips trembled, and she felt herself once again sinking into that cavernous hole of sorrow—a fissure so deep that she wondered if she would ever find her way out. Would she have to live in this darkness forever?

As long as Jacquie is gone.

With a final look at the picture, she stood and then took slow steps across her bedroom. She paused at the threshold and turned when she heard Zaya's giggles.

Moments later, when her son spotted her standing at the edge of the kitchen, he screamed, "Love Mama!" Kicking and waving, he was filled with the excitement that came from seeing his mother for the first time in days.

But when Jasmine turned to Mrs. Sloss, the nanny's face held more fear than enthusiasm.

"Ms. Jasmine, you're not supposed to be up." Her eyes were wide, as if she were looking at a walking ghost, and Jasmine wondered what Hosea had told her.

She swatted Mrs. Sloss's words away and picked up Zaya from his chair. "I'm fine, Mrs. Sloss," she said, though the unsteadiness of her legs made her return her son to his seat.

"But Mr. Hosea told me to make sure that you were resting comfortably." Mrs. Sloss's forehead was packed with creases. "I need to call him."

Before she could reach for the phone, Jasmine said, "Don't do that. I told you, I'm fine. Where's Hosea anyway? Did he go to work?"

"I don't think so." Mrs. Sloss shook her head. "He's been home with you every day."

Every day? How many days?

The nanny continued, "But this morning, he got a phone call. Then he dressed fast and left."

As Jasmine stroked Zaya's head, she asked, "Was the call . . . about Jacquie?" She wondered if Detective Cohen had dragged Hosea once again to the station. More questions about her, no doubt.

"I don't know. I don't think so, because all he said was to call him if anything happened to you."

The thought of Hosea once again with Detective Cohen made her weary, and all Jasmine wanted to do was crawl back into bed, return to the darkness, and sleep until . . .

She kissed her son's forehead and turned away. But before she got to the archway, Zaya called out to her.

"Bye-bye, Mama!" he shouted. "Bye-bye," he said over and over.

She glanced back at him, her little boy filled with glee, clapping, laughing; there were no cares in his world. When he saw her still standing there, he screamed, "Bye-bye, Mama," as if now he was dismissing her.

She remembered the days when he would cry when she left the room, but not anymore. After just a couple of weeks, he was so used to her being away that her presence in his life was no longer needed.

Her eyes teared with that thought—and she was filled with a new fear: she'd lost her daughter, was she losing her son now, too?

"Mrs. Sloss," she began, her voice raised a bit because Zaya was still shouting his demands for her to go away. "I'm going to go out for a little while."

"Ms. Jasmine, you can't! You have to rest . . . and eat."

But Jasmine was already halfway to her bedroom. She had no doubt that Mrs. Sloss would get right on the phone, call Hosea, and tell on her. She had to move quickly. She had to be gone by the time Hosea made his way home, before he rammed into their apartment and demanded that she return to bed and talk to the psychiatrist.

Well, she would rest, and she would talk to Dr. Howard . . . later. But right now, she had to do something more important. Right now, she had to save her life.

And there was only one person she knew who could help her with that.

Sixty-one

JASMINE ASKED THE DRIVER TO stop directly in front. She didn't want to take the chance of anyone seeing her through the side windows; her plan was to get in, get out, do this by herself.

Using her key, she opened the heavy double doors of City of Lights at Riverside Church. The three-thousand-seat sanctuary was without artificial light, brightened only by the sunbeams that pressed through the oversize, stained-glass windows.

Without the sounds of praise or the prayers of the congregants, her heels echoed against the stone floor of the grand room, then quieted as she stepped onto the carpeted section. Slowly, she walked forward toward the altar, feeling as if she should say some kind of prayer, as if she should ask God for permission to step to His throne.

This had not been her original plan. She'd come to the church to talk to Reverend Bush because he was the only one who always had the right answers for her. There had never been a time when her father-in-law had let her down, and she prayed that he could help her now.

But as she rode in the taxi, she had another idea. She'd also gone to God before. Maybe it was time to turn to Him again.

She paused at the front pew, then lowered herself onto the bench. She was sitting in her favorite place . . . the first seat in the first row. The seat of honor that had been reserved every Sunday for Lady Jasmine.

Without parishioners, the vast room was overwhelming, awe-inspiring, almost too much for one person to sit in alone. But she'd come to this space once before by herself. And on that day, she'd found the peace she was looking for. Today, though, she was seeking something else.

She'd heard Hosea say it. And her father-in-law and countless others . . . they all spoke about how God talked to them. Reverend Bush had even once said that prayer was not a monologue, but a dialogue, as if prayer was supposed to be some kind of conversation with a being you could not see.

Well, she'd done her share of praying, but not once had God ever taken the time to speak back.

So that's what she needed today, for Him to straight up talk to her. He needed to rain down His wisdom from heaven and tell her a few things. Like whether Jacqueline would come home. And He needed to tell her how to get herself together so that she wouldn't lose Zaya in this process. She had so many questions; she needed some holy answers.

She gazed upon the golden cross that hung behind the altar. She felt like she was in the center of silence, except for the faint hum of traffic as cars whizzed by on Riverside Drive.

Once she was ready, Jasmine closed her eyes and whispered, "Okay, Lord. Speak." And then, she sat and waited.

Minutes passed, and she waited some more.

Nothing.

More minutes.

More nothing.

Jasmine rose from the pew, walked slowly toward the altar. She wasn't really sure how to do this; maybe He wanted her to talk first.

She lowered herself onto the kneeling bench and looked up at the cross. Then she bowed her head and closed her eyes. "Lord, you have finally brought me to my knees."

She paused and wondered why she'd said that. Surely, she had been on her knees before—a lot! How many times had she prayed to God to get her out of one crisis or another?

But today felt different. Like this really was the first time that she was bowing down. She pondered that thought and then it came to her—today *was* different.

In the past, she'd knelt on her knees, even closed her eyes and lowered her head.

But today she was bowing her heart.

For the first time.

So she began again. "Lord, I come to you, truly on my knees, but I don't even know what to say. I'm just gonna talk to you real, 'cause my husband says that's how you like it. And I read someplace in the Bible where you said that anybody could just come boldly to you—so here I am, Lord. Scared. Hurt. So, so sad." She stopped because she thought this would be a good place for God to talk—to say something like He would take all her pain away. But when she didn't hear anything, she kept on. "I don't really know how to do this, so I'm just gonna start at the beginning." A breath. "I've done so many things wrong. First, I . . ." She stopped. Did she really have to give God a litany of her past sins? If she did that, she'd be on her knees for days, and surely, He knew it all. He probably had notes that could fill volumes. Her entire life had been riddled with schemes and lies. And truthfully, she hadn't done much better in her marriage.

But she and Hosea had made it through every single thing.

Until this.

Why this?

She waited and waited for God to answer that question. And then . . . it hit her.

Jasmine looked up at the cross that was blurred by her tears. "Lord, is that what this is about? Is this because of the dozens"—she paused and swallowed—"the thousands, maybe even millions, of sins I've committed? Please, Father, please don't make my daughter pay. Please don't let this be about the sins of the mother. Please forgive me for every single lie, every single manipulation, every infidelity, and all of that adultery. Lord, please, if a life has to be taken, let it be mine. I'm willing, but I don't want my daughter to suffer because of me."

She sobbed. "Please, God, talk to me," she whispered. "Am I the reason my daughter is gone?"

Even when she felt the cushion on the bench shift a little, she didn't open her eyes. She could feel another presence close, but if it wasn't God kneeling next to her, then she wasn't interested. She was going to keep her head bowed and stay right in that place until God talked to her.

Then, "You know," the deep voice began, "it's better to know God than to know answers."

She lifted her head—he wasn't the Lord, but he was the next best thing. She wiped her face dry as she turned to her father-in-law. She said, "But I need the answers. If He would just give them to me, then maybe I'd be able to go on."

Reverend Bush reached for her hand, pulled her up, and together they sat on the front pew. Together they stared at the golden cross.

"I'm glad to see you up," Reverend Bush said, his eyes still on the altar. "I've been quite concerned about you."

"I'm fine, really."

He nodded. "That's what I thought when Hosea called me on Sunday. But then I stopped by on Monday, and again yesterday . . . and you were still asleep." He shook his head. "I wasn't so sure anymore."

Inside, she counted. *Three days?* Had she really slept that long? She said, "I guess I was just tired." She leaned her head back and blinked rapidly, as if that would stop the fresh tears she felt coming to her eyes. "And sleep helps."

"I understand."

"But I don't want to sleep anymore, and so I need God to explain this to me. I need Him to tell me why He let this happen and why He hasn't brought Jacquie home. That's why I came here . . . so that He could talk to me."

Reverend Bush patted her hand like she was a child. "You could've stayed home for that, sweetheart. He was right there with you. You've got to know that He's always with you."

She shook her head. She loved her father-in-law, but sometimes he went into his Christian cliché mode, quoting phrases and scriptures that didn't have a thing to do with her life. Like what he just said—God couldn't have been with her all the time. If He'd been there, Jacqueline would never have been taken.

But then . . . maybe Reverend Bush was right. What if God was always there, with the ones He loved?

"Maybe God doesn't love me," Jasmine said, thinking of her history. After all those lies and schemes she could hardly love herself.

Without looking at her, Reverend Bush said, "Oh, He loves you. More than you know and more than you could ever understand. You can't even begin to count the ways, His ways."

Jasmine released a sigh. "That's what I've always wanted to believe, but I was just thinking about all the things I've done."

He nodded, just a little. "Well, you have been way out there, Jasmine."

Dang! That was not what she'd expected him to say. What did he mean by that?

Then he turned a little and looked at her, and she knew what he meant—he was referring to her life as a stripper.

This was something they'd never discussed—he had commissioned a report on her from a private investigator before she and Hosea had married. Until this moment, she'd never been sure whether he'd read the whole report. It had been mailed to Reverend Bush right before he had been shot, and then he had remained comatose for months.

Now she knew . . . he knew. As if everything else she was going through wasn't bad enough.

Glancing away from her, he said, "But you don't have to worry about your past because that's what grace and mercy are all about. There's not one of us walking this earth who can claim a sinless life. We're just blessed to be able to say that we have a forgiven life."

Forgiven. Her husband and his father had forgiven her for so much. But had God? "Maybe that's it—maybe He hasn't forgiven me."

"If you've asked Him to, He has. He's not even thinking about all those sins that *you're* still counting in your head." His eyes stayed on the cross. "I know you think that what you and Hosea and Jacquie"—he stopped and swallowed, as if her name was tough to say—"are going through has something to do with your past, but you've got to realize that pain is not always punishment, and suffering is not always because of sin." He paused again, as if he wanted Jasmine to soak in that understanding. "But both of them—pain and suffering—will drive you to a place that's beyond a superficial relationship with God. Both will drive you straight to His heart."

"His heart and your knees."

His chuckle was light. "That, too." A pause. "You've come a long way, Jasmine. Your faith has been stretched and strengthened."

"I'm not strong," she said, the memories of the last nineteen days were so fresh. There was not a single moment since Jacqueline had been abducted when she could claim that she'd been strong. She was much more the opposite.

Especially when it came to Brian.

Just thinking his name made her groan inside. She remembered the kiss and cringed with mortification.

After silent minutes, she turned her entire body to face the man she'd once hoped would be her lover but now was the man she loved so dearly as her father. "Do you think she'll come home?"

He waited a moment, then, "You want the truth?"

Her glance shifted back to the altar, then when she looked at him again, he smiled.

"All right," he said. After a breath, "I don't know. My fervent prayer is that my granddaughter comes home, but I just don't know." Now he turned so that the two were face-to-face. "But here's what I *do* know. I know God is God. He's beyond good. His grace is sufficient and His mercy . . ." Reverend Bush dipped his head a bit, held up his hand as if he was about to testify. "Thank Him for His grace, but thank Him even more for His mercy."

His words reminded her of the first sermon she'd ever heard him preach, when he'd taught the difference between grace and mercy. She hadn't truly understood then, but in the years that she'd been part of the Bush family, she'd gained an understanding. She'd been flooded in His grace, and she'd been given new mercies every single morning.

Until now.

She didn't even realize she was sobbing again until Reverend Bush took her hand.

"You've got to know that whatever God's plan is here, for this time, for this family, for you . . . His power is greater even than death."

She gasped; she never wanted to hear that word associated with Jacquie. She tried to pull away from his grasp, but he held on to her tighter.

He continued, "I know that whatever happens, God is gonna win. We may not see it that way, but He owns this game. Now, that doesn't mean that this is going to turn out exactly the way we want. It just means that it's going to turn out His way—the right way."

"How could this be right? For a child to be taken away from her family?"

He shrugged. "You know, God's thoughts, His ways, are so much bigger than ours. And though I don't always get it, I'm fine with that. 'Cause I'm not interested in serving a God who's as finite as I am."

Reverend Bush's words were soft and soothing . . . and they didn't give her a single answer. Inside, all Jasmine kept saying was, *Why, why?*

Reverend Bush said, "But not understanding doesn't have anything to do with holding on. We may not get God all the time, but we can keep on praying, and keep on working, and keep on doing everything we can. You've got to pray like it's up to God and work like it's up to you. When this is over—whichever way it turns out—you need to know that you did everything you could to bring Jacquie home. You need to know that you prayed it and worked it."

Jasmine nodded, but then she frowned. *Prayed it and worked it?* Had she really done everything she could?

He stood and looked down at her. "I think you need to go home; you need to rest."

She nodded, knowing any protest would be futile.

He said, "Give me ten minutes. I have to make a call, and then I'll ride home with you."

"You don't have to do that."

"I know I don't." He smiled as he bent over to kiss her cheek. "It's what I want. So give me ten, okay?"

She nodded.

"And while you're waiting," he said, turning toward the door that led to the offices, "look up something for me. A scripture. James five-sixteen. I think it'll help."

Then she was alone, in the quiet of the bright sanctuary.

James five-sixteen.

She reached for one of the Bibles stacked in the pew behind her, then paused.

When this is over—whichever way it turns out—you need to know that you did everything you could to bring Jacquie home. You need to know that you prayed it and worked it.

She couldn't stop thinking about Reverend Bush's words. Had she prayed it and worked it? Had she done everything that she could possibly do?

"Oh, my God," she whispered. She *hadn't* done *everything*. Her anger had blinded her and made her forget. Made her not do the one thing that could bring Jacquie home.

She snatched her coat, grabbed her purse, then ran toward the front doors. She'd call Reverend Bush later, as soon as she took care of this.

Outside, the wind whipped across the Hudson with a ferocity that would have driven anyone else back indoors. But Jasmine ran to the corner and held her hand up for the next available taxi. She stood there, determined and unmoving, oblivious to the wind digging its teeth into her skin. Her focus was on getting to where she needed to go, and doing what she needed to do.

"Please, God. Please, God," she whispered as her teeth chattered. "Please, don't let it be too late."

Sixty-two

JASMINE DIDN'T RING THE DOORBELL. She just knocked. Hard. As if she were the police.

But the woman on the other side of the door wasn't one who was ever intimidated. Jasmine heard her growling.

"Who is it? Banging on my door like you're some kind of crazy. I'm tellin' you . . ." The door swung open.

Jasmine didn't wait for Mae Frances to invite her inside. She barreled in, knocking the woman who used to be her friend back against the wall.

"Jasmine?" Mae Frances whispered, the fight totally gone from her voice. She closed her eyes slowly, then opened them the same way. As if she couldn't believe what she was seeing.

"Here's the thing," Jasmine began, not looking at her. She paced back and forth in front of the aqua-colored couch that she and Hosea had given Mae Frances right after they'd married. "I'm dying without Jacqueline."

"Oh, Jasmine," Mae Frances cried as she slammed the door shut. "You don't know how sorry—"

Jasmine cut her off; she wasn't here to listen to any more apologies. She continued, "And I have to do everything I can to find her."

"I know." Mae Frances nodded her head, though she stayed in place, not taking even a single step closer. "We've all been working so hard."

"See," Jasmine said, still pacing, still blocking out every word that came from Mae Frances's mouth, "if I want my daughter to come home, then I have to do everything I possibly can."

"Definitely. And that's why—"

"And I haven't done that." Jasmine stopped moving and, for the first time, looked up. Took in the woman whom—just three weeks ago—she loved as if she were her mother.

The woman standing in front of her, wringing her hands, made Jasmine pause. Since the day she'd met Mae Frances, the woman had dressed as if she had serious money in the bank, and today was no different. She wore a coral-colored sheath that was more appropriate for summer, but probably fit perfectly underneath the back-in-the-day mink that Mae Frances so loved.

Staring at Mae Frances made Jasmine remember just how close they'd been. Made her think about the number of times Mae Frances had come to her rescue with this plan or that scheme, using some shady connection, some unscrupulous person whom Jasmine had never heard of or met.

Well, that was all Jasmine wanted now. She wasn't here to rekindle good feelings. She wasn't interested in making up. All she wanted was one or ten or a hundred of Mae Frances's connections. However many it took to find Jacqueline.

Jasmine said, "So I have to do everything, and that's why I'm here." She inhaled, hating to say the next words, but willing to do anything. "I need your help."

Mae Frances smiled. Now she moved toward Jasmine with her arms open for an embrace.

But when Mae Frances took four steps forward, Jasmine took five steps back. She said, "You need to call your connections, everyone you know: Al Sharpton, Jeremiah Wright, Al Capone. I don't care who, call them all. And get them to help us find Jacquie."

Mae Frances frowned, confused by Jasmine's words. "But I thought you knew . . . of course I called." She gestured, her arms opened wide. "Everybody's been working since we left the mall when . . ." She stopped, as if she didn't want to remind Jasmine about what happened.

Jasmine dropped onto the couch; all during the cab ride over, she had played the video in her mind: how she was going to march into this apartment, demand Mae Frances's help (since she was the one who had screwed up in the first place), and then Mae Frances would hit her forehead with the heel of her hand like she couldn't believe that she hadn't thought of it herself. Then Mae Frances would grab the telephone, make a couple of calls, and within an hour Jacqueline would be home.

"So with everyone you know"—Jasmine began, her tone filled with disbelief—"no one has been able to find her?" She felt like crying all over again. If Mae Frances's people couldn't do it, then maybe it couldn't be done. Maybe Jacqueline *was* gone . . .

No! she shouted to herself. She wouldn't believe that; she would never believe that.

Mae Frances interrupted her thoughts. "No one has been able to find her *yet*, but Sonny's still working on it, and you know he's the best."

"Sonny who?" Jasmine asked, frowning.

Mae Frances leaned forward and lowered her voice, as if she was letting out the biggest secret. "I never knew his last name; everyone around the city just knows him as Sonny. But do you remember that big drug bust last year downtown?"

Jasmine didn't know what Mae Frances was talking about, but she nodded; if she didn't, Mae Frances would never get to the end of the story.

"Well, the police took down seven of the biggest dealers, but only six went to prison." Then she stood upright, pressed her shoulders back as if she was proud. "Sonny was the seventh one."

Jasmine's eyes were wide with astonishment.

Mae Frances continued, "Sonny will never go down 'cause he has so much on everyone—from the DA to the commissioner. No one messes with Sonny."

"So, Sonny . . . ?"

That was enough of a question for Mae Frances. "Sonny's been working on this with me."

All Jasmine could do was shake her head. Mae Frances had a drug dealer searching for her daughter? With a sigh, she thought, *I should've just stayed in church!*

It was the look on Jasmine's face that made Mae Frances say, "Jasmine, please don't give up. If anyone can find our baby, it's Sonny and his boys."

For a second, she believed Mae Frances. Her connections had come through every single time before. But then, she looked at the woman who was responsible for where they were now. And she remembered that she couldn't trust her.

Now Mae Frances took a few steps closer, and when Jasmine didn't bark, she sat down on the couch next to her. Her hand hung in the air a moment before she lowered her fingers to Jasmine's shoulders.

Jasmine flinched, but stayed.

"We're going to bring her home," Mae Frances said as if she was sure. "You know my people . . . they can do this."

But Jasmine shook her head. She'd gone to God and He hadn't said a word, but she'd left the church with such hope.

Now that hope was gone. It felt as if God was playing with her. And then, in the end, He'd let her down.

Why, God? Why?

The ringing of her cell phone interrupted her sadness. A millisecond later, Mae Frances's phone rang, too.

Jasmine slipped her cell from her purse as Mae Frances moved toward her desk.

Both picked up at the same time.

"Hello," they said together.

"Jasmine," Hosea called, sounding as if he was out of breath. "Where are you? They found our baby!"

"What!" she screamed, and shot up off the couch.

And then an echo. "What!" Mae Frances yelled.

"They found Jacquie," Hosea said. "She's alive."

"Oh, my God!" Jasmine said.

"Oh, my God!" Mae Frances said into her phone before it dropped from her hands.

For a second, they stared at each other. And then, with just three long strides, Jasmine fell into Mae Frances's arms.

"I told you," Mae Frances said, as she cried with Jasmine. "I told you!"

For just a couple of moments, they allowed themselves the pleasure of joyful tears. But then, right when Jasmine grabbed her purse, she heard the voice that she'd been waiting for.

It wasn't booming. It wasn't audible, at least not through her ears. But she heard it, loudly and clearly. It came straight from her heart.

It stopped her cold and made her listen.

I will never leave you. I will never forsake you. I am always here.

She wanted to drop to her knees right there, bow her head and her heart, and thank God. But she couldn't do that now.

She would thank Him and praise Him and magnify Him in the taxicab ride to the hospital, where Hosea told her they were waiting.

And though Jasmine had never before been sure what God really wanted from her, she knew at this moment that He didn't mind at all. He would take her praises in the taxi—that would be good enough for Him.

Sixty-three

JASMINE FELT AS IF SHE was running the one-hundred-yard dash when she sprinted out of the cab and through the revolving doors of Lenox Hill Hospital. What amazed her was that Mae Frances—who was at least two decades her senior—kept up with her, step for step.

"Hosea!" Jasmine screamed when her husband was finally in her sight.

He stood in the center of a circle—Reverend Bush, Malik, Detective Foxx, Mrs. Whittingham, Brother Hill, and a silver-haired man who wore a white lab coat. But Hosea broke past them all, pulled Jasmine into his arms, and hugged her so tightly, it was hard for her to breathe.

Jasmine pulled back. "Where is she?" she panted. Her eyes blinked rapidly as if she were trying to take a mental picture of every inch of the hallway where they stood. "Is my baby all right?"

Hosea nodded. Hugged her again. "She's alive," he breathed in a tone that revealed his disbelief. He gestured toward the silver-haired man. "Jacquie's been with Doctor Stewart, and he wants to talk to us first."

"Doctor," Jasmine said, turning to the man. "Is my daughter all right? I have to see her. Please."

His eyes were piercingly serious, and he didn't wear a smile. "In just a moment." He glanced at Detective Foxx, who gave him a small nod. "But first," the doctor said, "I need to talk to the two of you." His eyes moved from Jasmine to Hosea. He motioned for them to follow him down the hall.

Hosea moved, but Jasmine didn't. "No!" She stood in place, looking as if she was about to stomp her foot. "I need to see my daughter!" she demanded. She would tear this place apart—and Mae Frances would surely help her.

Reverend Bush slipped his arm around her waist and whispered in her ear, "Jasmine, talk to the doctor first. Jacquie is safe here. I promise."

The doctor said, "Just give me five minutes, and then I'll take you to her. Just five minutes."

Jasmine wasn't sure that she could do that—stay away another five minutes, after all the time that had passed? But the look on the doctor's face told her that she was wasting time.

And so, with a deep breath, she took Hosea's hand and followed the doctor who walked beside Detective Foxx.

Over his shoulder, Hosea said, "Pops, come with us."

Reverend Bush nodded, then gave a reassuring glance to the others, who stood in a semicircle holding hands as if they were about to pray.

In less than a minute, they were inside an office at the end of the hall.

"Please have a seat, Mrs. Bush." Jasmine folded her arms, shook her head. "I'm not trying to be rude," she said, hearing the trembling in her voice. "But I don't understand why this can't wait until after I see Jacquie."

"I understand your anxiety." The doctor nodded. "But I need to let you know what to expect."

Her hands fell to her sides. What did he mean by that?

"My daughter . . ."

The doctor held up his hands. "She's alive, but she's been . . ."

Jasmine inhaled a loud audible breath.

He said, "She has experienced trauma."

"What does that mean?" Hosea barked.

The sound of his voice scared Jasmine a bit. Made her forget about her own anxiety. She reached out for Hosea, but he would not take her hand. His fingers had curled into fists.

The doctor looked at Detective Foxx, and, with a nod to the doctor, Detective Foxx stepped in front of them.

He said, "For the most part, Jacquie is fine, but she was—"

"Molested," Jasmine whispered.

The detective took a breath. "She was raped," he said with a slight quiver in his voice. "Most likely, repeatedly."

Gasps filled the room, though it was Jasmine's cries that were the loudest. "My baby. She's not even five!"

This time, it was the doctor who spoke. "Unfortunately, we've seen this before . . . too many times. But she's being tested and treated—"

"For what?" Jasmine asked.

"Sexually transmitted diseases—"

"Oh, God!"

"AIDS."

Jasmine wanted to put her hands over her ears. There was no way she could listen to any more of this. But still, she asked, "Who would do this to my baby?"

"We have him in custody," the detective said. "I won't go into all the details now, but we got an anonymous call from someone who said that they had the building under surveillance and that if the police didn't come immediately, they were going in themselves to get Jacqueline."

"Who called?" Reverend Bush asked.

Detective Foxx shrugged; it was clear he didn't know. But Jasmine did—one of Mae Frances's connections. Probably Sonny, the dealer.

"We have the man in custody," the detective continued, "and he won't be going anywhere. Turns out he's a fugitive. There's a warrant for his arrest in Arizona. He's got a record . . . for this kind of thing. I don't know how he got away."

"Oh, my God," Jasmine cried while Hosea stood silent.

"But we think," the doctor quickly interjected, "that she's going to be fine . . . physically."

Jasmine spun around and away from the doctor. "I want to see my daughter," she yelled. She swung open the door and rushed into the hallway. If she had to, she would go from room to room and find her herself.

"Mrs. Bush, wait," the doctor called out. "I'll take you now."

She turned around and glared at him; a "you'd better" look was all over her face. Before she could protest more, the doctor was by her side.

His strides were long, but she kept up, her thoughts only on seeing Jacqueline. It didn't matter what had happened— her daughter was home. And she would take care of her. She would make sure that Jacquie was fine.

When the doctor stopped in front of the hospital room, Jasmine took a deep breath. With a quick glance over her shoulder, she reached for Hosea's hand. But he wasn't there.

She glanced to the left, then to the right. "Where's Hosea?" she asked her father-in-law.

He looked from side to side, too. Frowned. "I don't know. Maybe he went with Detective Foxx."

That didn't make sense. How could he want to talk to the police instead of seeing Jacqueline? Wasn't seeing his daughter more important than anything?

But she wasn't about to stand there, figuring this out. She wasn't about to stop and search for him—not when she was this close to Jacqueline.

So she reached for Reverend Bush's hand instead, and together they followed the doctor into the room.

Sixty-four

"Yeah, send her back." Brian dropped the phone into the cradle and grinned, wishing that he'd come up with this strategy sooner. All the money he'd spent on flowers, all the time he'd spent tracking his ex-wife down—it seemed like not a bit of that had been necessary.

Not that he regretted it—he would buy Alexis every flower in America if he could. It was just that that effort had done nothing.

But this—ignoring her—this had worked instantly. There had never been a time since their separation, then divorce, when Alexis had contacted him this much. First Saturday, then Monday, and now today. Sure, it was Wednesday, but all of their contact had been initiated by her—this was huge.

Laughing out loud, he adjusted the papers on his desk, making it look like he was in the middle of something serious, then placed a yellow pad right in front of him. When he heard the light knock on his door, he quickly slid on his reading glasses, grabbed a pen, and lowered his head.

"Come on in," he said, keeping his eyes down.

Alexis peeked into his office. "Brian?" She said his name as if she wasn't sure whether she should step inside.

He glanced up. "Oh," he said, like he hadn't been expecting her.

She frowned a bit. "I thought the receptionist told you that I was here."

"Yeah, yeah," he said, waving her inside, then looked down at the yellow pad in front of him. He slowly wrote his name, then just as slowly slipped off his glasses before he looked back up at her.

He was careful to keep his eyes on her eyes, but it wasn't easy. Even without letting his glance roam, he could see way too much of her in that belted coat that flaunted all her curves.

He shook his head. What he'd always loved about Alexis was that her mind was so sharp and her heart was so loving— those inner qualities far eclipsed her outer beauty. But that outer beauty? That was some good stuff that could not be denied.

"What's up?" he said, deciding not even to offer her a seat.

She stood in front of his desk, confusion suddenly all over her face. "I just . . . wanted to stop by and tell you that I saw Crime Stoppers last night."

You had to stop by for that? He said, "Yeah, they came through. They're gonna do something more extensive on Sunday. But last night was a great start."

"It was," she said, still standing, still looking as if she was waiting for an invitation to sit down. "Has anything happened yet? Any new leads?"

He shrugged. "I spoke to Hosea last night after he saw the show."

"What did they think?"

"He thought it was good." Brian left out the part about Jasmine, how Hosea had said that Jasmine hadn't seen the show. He'd thought that was beyond strange, but he wasn't about to ask the man any questions about his wife. Brian added, "I'm sure I'll hear something from him today. The phones should start ringing."

Alexis nodded. "I hope this helps. We've got to get that little girl back home."

"We?" He raised a single eyebrow to show her that he was surprised. To show her that he no longer considered her part of his inner circle.

"Yeah, we!" she exclaimed. She paused, and added, "I mean you. No, I mean we. I want to help, too, Brian. We're friends, so anything that I can do to help I want to do."

He had to fight to stop it—the smile that he felt rising from his lips. A smile wouldn't work right now, didn't go along with his new persona. So he paused until he was sure that he could hold it back. Then, "All right," he said with a sigh. "I'll keep you posted." He picked up his pen, looked down at the pad again as if what was on that paper was far more important than talking to her.

His glance away was for only a second, but when he looked at her again, Alexis's face had already changed. Her eyes were squinted. Her lips were pinched together. Her nose was scrunched like she smelled something nasty. She was a storm brewing.

Again, it was a battle to hold back his smile. "I'll see ya," he said.

"What is wrong with you, Brian!" she blew up.

He frowned. "What?"

"You're acting like I'm bothering you or something."

He stood, walked around the desk.

She continued, "I'm trying to be a friend, and you're treating me like—"

"I'm treating you like you've been treating me?"

Her mouth opened wide, but then shut tight.

"That's what you mean, right?" he asked, standing in front of her. "I'm treating you like I don't want to be bothered. Like I don't want you to be part of my life. Like being around you is so difficult." He crossed his arms. Leaned against the desk. "Yup, I'm treating you just like you treated me."

"I did not!" she said, her teeth clenched.

"Oh, yeah," he said coolly. "Think about it, Alexis. This is the way you've been treating me since we were divorced."

"So that's what this is? A game? You're getting back at me?"

He held up his hands. "Oh, no. Trust me, this is no game. I'm not playing. 'Cause," he said, now moving closer to her, "I don't play when it comes to you." As he moved, she did, too. Away from him. He said, "I'm very clear on what I want. And what I want is you."

She was still backing away. "No." But it was only a whisper. "I can't."

"Why not?"

"I told you—all I have inside of me is friendship, and that should be enough."

"I want more than that."

"This is not only about you, Brian!" Her fury was back. "This is about what I want, too. And I don't want to go backward."

"See, that's your problem." His words paused, but he kept moving, moving. "I never asked you to go backward." He waved his hand, as if he were wiping away all that was behind them. "I've only asked you to look to the future, and go forward . . . with me."

She was pinned against the wall now, barely an inch separated them. "Let's go forward," he whispered, his lips right in front of hers. "Together."

Her voice was as low as his. "No," she said. She swallowed. "I can't."

"You can."

"I'm scared."

"No need." With the tips of his fingers, he lifted her chin so that she had to look right at him. "I'll never hurt you again," he vowed.

She gazed at him, considering his words for a moment. "But there's no way either one of us can be sure that I won't be hurt again."

"You're right."

Her eyes widened, like that was not the response she had expected.

He continued, "I can't guarantee anything. But I can tell you the truth—and that is that I love you. And in all these years that we've been apart, all I've been thinking about, all I've been doing, is trying to make my way back to you."

Now he waited. Brian could see it in her eyes, the way she was calculating her emotions and adding up their past.

And as she counted the cost, he panicked. Maybe he'd revealed his plan too quickly. Maybe he should have just let her walk out of the office today—kept her off kilter, stewing, and wondering for another few days, maybe even another week.

Well, it was too late to second-guess. He was out there—he'd played his hand. And if Alexis decided not to join in now, it was over. For real this time. Because now she knew his trick, and she'd never be fooled again.

"I . . . ," she started, but stopped. Shook her head.

He could feel his heartbeat. *I blew it.* She wasn't ready to do the right thing, and now he was going to lose her. He leaned in closer. Looked into her eyes and saw all of her pain of their past. All of her fear of their future.

She was going to tell him no.

But he wasn't ready to lose. So he turned to what was left in his arsenal—their connection, their emotional umbilical cord. They were life for each other.

But Alexis didn't know that—she only felt it. So Brian knew that he had to show her.

He had to lean only a little—and aim his lips toward hers. He let them touch, just barely. This was going to be a slow seduction, one that she would never forget.

Now he moved his lips from side to side, grazing hers. And he kept his eyes on her eyes. But his hands were still at his sides.

Now, his tongue . . . and then the phone shrilled. It sounded like an alarm, startling both of them.

Inside, Brian cursed. If he backed away, Alexis would do the same. So he didn't move.

The phone rang again. And again.

And because the show had aired last night, he thought about Jacqueline.

But it was Alexis who was in front of him now. With her lips on his.

Another ring, and more thoughts of his daughter.

He cursed again and made a decision.

Backing away from Alexis, he dashed for the telephone. As he grabbed it, he glanced over his shoulder.

Alexis stood stiffly against the wall. But he saw it—the relief that washed over her.

That was when he knew that he'd lost—it was over.

He wanted to curse again. Damn whoever was on the other end. But he picked up and heard the scream.

"Brian! My baby." And then the sound of crackling air.

"Jasmine!" he shouted, as if that would help the cell phone signal.

"Jacquie is—"

More crackling. "Jasmine!" he yelled again.

"Home! Jacquie is home!"

And then, nothing.

He stared at the phone for a moment before he slowly turned toward Alexis. "She's home," he whispered. "They found her. My daughter is home."

Neither one moved. They just stared at each other. They stood as if they were in shock. And both thought about what that call meant. For both of them.

Then, as if their thoughts had registered at the same time, they smiled simultaneously, right before Alexis ran into Brian's arms.

Sixty-five

There was not a word in any language that could describe what was brewing.

Rage—that was not enough. Fury, wrath—they were not even close.

Nothing could describe the diametric emotions that were colliding inside of him. The joy—for the return of his daughter. The pain—for what Jacqueline had been through.

She was raped . . . Most likely, repeatedly.

Those words were grenades in his heart.

Hosea pressed his lips together, tried to keep the scream inside. But it exploded anyway, bursting through his lips, reverberating throughout the car, making even the windows quake. Gripping the steering wheel, he rounded the corner onto 119th, then inched down the street until he saw an open space in front of a fire hydrant. He turned off the ignition and, with military precision, scanned the area.

The day was growing older, and the afternoon sun cast long shadows against the gray brick of the police precinct house. In front, patrol cars were parked perpendicular to the curb, and people—civilians and officers—moved in and out and about.

Right in the center sat the van, and Hosea sighed with relief. This was the vehicle—the car that would transport Harvey Jonas from the station to Rikers.

Harvey Jonas. The lowlife scum. The suspect, as Detective Foxx had called him when they'd talked.

As Jasmine and his father had rushed behind Dr. Stewart, Hosea had turned the other way.

"Hosea," Detective Foxx had called after him as he marched down the hall.

He kept on, but the detective caught up, and matched him step for step. Silent seconds passed as they strode toward the front. It wasn't until they were outside of the hospital that Detective Foxx stopped him.

"Where are you going?" he asked, resting his hand on Hosea's shoulder. "I thought you would want to see Jacquie."

Hosea shook his head. "Not yet. I can't . . . see her yet."

It didn't take even a full moment for the detective to understand. "Hosea, come on. This isn't your fault."

"I didn't protect her, Fred," he said, calling his friend by his first name. "And I can't see her until I know she's safe."

Detective Foxx reached out to Hosea again. "She's safe, man," he reassured him. "We found him with her. He's in custody, and this time he's not going anywhere. Trust that. Trust me."

With a nod, Hosea looked back toward the hospital, trying to decide—should he go back in or not? "Who is he?" Hosea asked.

"The suspect? There's not a lot to tell. We found him at his mother's apartment on the Lower East Side," Detective Foxx said. "She takes in foster kids, and that's where he was with Jacquie. He was kinda hiding . . . in plain sight."

With his forefinger, Hosea pressed the spot at the top of his nose, right between his eyes. But that did nothing to ease the throbbing. "Jacquie was that close? All of this time, she was just a couple of miles away?"

Detective Foxx nodded. "It happens that way. I'm sure he never let her leave the house."

"So," Hosea began, "he took my daughter to his mother's."

"Seems like it." Detective Foxx sighed. "I've seen this too many times—a mother who knows what her child is doing and looks the other way. We're not sure if that's what went down, if his mother knew, but we'll find out her role in this soon."

Hosea opened his mouth, made a wide O, stretched his jaw. But that didn't do it either—nothing stopped the throbbing. The throbbing.

Detective Foxx said, "But here's the thing, man, more than his mother, it was us. The system blew it this time; we were the ones who let Harvey Jonas get away."

Harvey Jonas.

The detective's hand was back on Hosea's shoulder when he said, "But we got him now. And he's not getting away this time. I'm headed over to the precinct; Jonas is being processed, and we're taking him by special van over to Rikers. We're not even going to hold him for another group; we're taking him by himself. I'm riding him, so you don't have to worry." He patted him on the back. "It's over."

Hosea shook his head, his eyes once again on the hospital's revolving doors. "It's not over." He sniffed back tears, held back rage. "My little girl . . . what she went through." He faced the detective. "What's going to happen to her?"

Detective Foxx exhaled. "I'm not sayin' it's going to be easy. But she has you and Jasmine and a whole bunch of other people who love her . . . we'll all help her through. The thing to remember—what's most important—is that she's home." And then, as if he needed to reassure Hosea, he added, "She's safe." Another pause. "Go back in there, Hosea. You know Jacquie wants to see her daddy. You take care of your baby, and I'll take care of the rest."

Hosea had nodded, turned, and pushed through the hospital's revolving doors. But the moment Detective Foxx was out of his sight, Hosea swung through the doors again and went right back onto the street.

Now he sat in front of the precinct house.

With his eyes still on the building, he reached under the seat. His fingertips searched until he felt the box. He lifted it up, rested it in his lap.

His eyes scoped the perimeter of his car. But even though people passed by, no one was close enough to see through the tint of the windows.

Carefully, he unhinged the box, then fingered the eight inches of stainless steel.

She was raped!

Then Jasmine's howl, *"But she's not even five!"*

It was Jasmine's cries that made him cry. It was Jasmine's cries that made him secure the scope on top of the weapon. Click it in place, then reach for the shopping bag he'd folded on the passenger seat. Gently, he placed the gun inside the bag, then he slid out of the car.

As he closed his overcoat and locked the car, he glanced around, but no one seemed to notice him. He was in Harlem. And here he was nothing but an average black man, next to an average SUV, carrying an average shopping bag, probably filled with Christmas gifts.

On the passenger side, he leaned against his car and glanced at his watch, as if he were an ordinary New Yorker, waiting to do an ordinary thing. He didn't have to linger long.

He first saw the activity through the side-view mirror. No one else seemed to notice the way two officers trotted down the steps, their hands on their holsters, looking around the whole time.

Then Hosea saw Detective Foxx peek out before he stepped back inside then exited again, this time flanking a man, about five feet seven, dressed in jeans and a leather bomber jacket. The man's wrists were bound by metal handcuffs attached to a long chain that led to the shackles at his feet.

Harvey Jonas.

The man shuffled along, clearly off balance. The shackles made him move slowly.

Perfect.

With the shopping bag at his side, Hosea moved down one car, never taking his eyes away from Harvey Jonas.

It surprised him, the look of the man. His quick assessment was that Jonas was well over fifty—his gray hair visible even at this distance. He was slight, probably weighed no more than 160, 165 pounds.

One hundred and twenty pounds more than Jacquie.

The sun and the shadows gave Hosea the advantage—his view of the enemy was clear. He crouched down, placed his hand into his bag.

Detective Foxx and Harvey Jonas moved down the first step.

Hosea counted: *One, two.*

The pervert and his protector moved to the second step.

Three, four.

They were within range.

When they reached the bottom, Hosea snatched the gun

from the bag, jumped in between the two parked cars. He knew he had three seconds, tops.

He bent his knees.

He focused.

He kept his gaze steady through the scope.

He aimed.

He fired!

The shot exploded through the air.

Screams! Screeching cars! Cries for the Lord!

Pandemonium!

He heard, "He's got a gun!"

Hosea didn't wait to see if he'd hit his target—he hit the ground, scraping his chin as he made contact with the asphalt. He tossed his gun aside, underneath the car. Then he lay still, spread-eagle, palms up.

Just three seconds—that's all it took for the officers to tower over him, guns drawn.

He heard his friend's cry, "Hosea!"

But he didn't look up. He didn't make a move. He was a black man in New York City who'd just fired a gun—he knew the drill.

"Oh, God! It's Pastor Bush," one of the officers above said.

Hosea grimaced as another shoved his knee into his back, cuffed his hands. Then two policemen pulled him from the ground.

There was still mayhem all around. More police running out to assist. More people screaming, pointing. The officers lugged Hosea from the street onto the sidewalk.

That was when he passed his friend. Their eyes locked.

Detective Foxx looked like he was going to cry. "Why didn't you just go back to Jacquie?"

Hosea's eyes were clear as he tore his glance away, stared down at Harvey Jonas, who was already being attended to by medics. The man who'd stolen and violated his daughter lay facedown at the front of the van, blood seeping from beneath him and spreading across the pavement.

When Hosea looked back at Detective Foxx, all he did was shake his head. He'd simply done what he had to do.

Now he could see his daughter.

Sixty-six

"The verdict's in."

Jasmine didn't even say good-bye before she hung up. She knew Dale would certainly understand.

It took a moment for her to steady herself, and then another before she was able to take the few steps to the sofa.

Her heart was blasting.

Though that was nothing new. For the last seven months, on the regular, Jasmine's heart had beaten like it was trying to escape.

It had started on that day—a day that had been filled with the best of her dreams and the worst of her nightmares.

The best hadn't started out so wonderfully. Even though it was beyond a blessing that Jacqueline had been found, it had still been so difficult.

When she and Reverend Bush had barged into that room,

Jasmine's eyes had locked right in on her daughter. And her eyes had filled instantly with tears.

Jacqueline was lying on a broad bed, although she wasn't taking up much space. Her tiny body was pressed against the wall, as if she was trying to disappear into it. But her eyes were wide and aware, focused on a red-haired, bun-wearing, plump woman in a black suit whom Dr. Stewart said was the child psychologist.

The woman sat at the edge of the bed whispering words that Jasmine could not hear. Not that it mattered, because every one of Jasmine's senses was trained on Jacqueline.

"My baby," Jasmine had cried softly.

At that sound, the girl bolted up, her eyes darting around the room. She slipped back even farther, cowering in the corner. Her eyes moved from here to there, searching, searching, as if she was trying to find a place to hide.

Jasmine didn't even try to stifle her cries as she took in the sight of her gregarious child trying to curl herself into a ball. She ran to her daughter with open arms, and even though Jacqueline screamed, terrified, Jasmine pulled her close and tight.

"Oh, baby. My baby," she cried.

Jacqueline cringed inside her mother's embrace, and after a while Jasmine pulled back. "Jacquie, baby," she said, trying to look deep into her child's eyes. "It's me . . . it's Mama."

Though Jacqueline's eyes were clear, there was not a single sign of recognition—as if the horror of nineteen days had expunged her memory.

"Oh, baby!" She kissed the top of her daughter's head, where the girl's long, dark brown curls had been chopped off and traded for a style that was dyed deep black and spiked so stiff that it had to have been set with a heavy gel. "You're home, baby; you're home," Jasmine whispered as she cradled her daughter.

Still, Jacqueline trembled.

"You may want to give her some space," the psychologist had whispered.

Jasmine looked at the woman with wide, wild eyes. Some space? Her daughter had been missing for almost three weeks. She had no plans ever to let her go.

"Hey, precious."

It was then that Jasmine remembered that she was not alone. Not taking her glance away from Jacqueline, she said, "Jacquie, Papa's here."

But all Jacqueline did was fight to break free from her mother.

Then Reverend Bush started singing, "He's got the whole world in His hands . . ."

As if those words were magic, Jacqueline's whimpering began to subside.

Still softly, still gently, he kept on, "He's got me and Jacquie, in His hands . . ."

Jasmine watched as her daughter calmed. Her eyes were downcast, but now she sat like stone and listened to her grandfather sing. It took twenty-three stanzas before Jacqueline slowly raised her head. And then she raised her eyes. And then she raised her arms, the signal that she wanted to be lifted.

When Reverend Bush held her, she cried. And he cried. And Jasmine cried.

That was when Jasmine knew that the bad part of the good dream had come to an end.

But that was when the nightmare began.

For long minutes, Jasmine and Reverend Bush had sat quietly on the bed with Jacqueline between them; their arms were wrapped around her and each other.

Until Brother Hill busted into the room. He stared, for a

moment, at the sight of the trio before he made his way toward them, his arms open, welcoming the girl home.

But then, as suddenly as he'd come in, he abruptly stopped. Cleared his throat and spoke. "Ah . . . Jasmine, can I talk to you?"

She shook her head. Did he really think that she was going to part from her daughter? Nothing, no one, could make her step away from Jacqueline.

So Brother Hill summoned Reverend Bush instead. As Jasmine cradled her daughter, she watched the two men huddle. She saw their frowns, heard their gasps. Then she watched as her father-in-law turned back to her with astonished eyes.

She held Jacqueline tighter. "What's wrong?"

"I have to go to the police station." His voice was low. "Hosea," was all he said.

It was hard for her to take her hands off Jacqueline, but she handed her daughter to her father-in-law and led Brother Hill into the far corner. And in fewer than twenty words, he explained that Hosea had been arrested for attempted murder.

She would have fainted right there if Jacqueline hadn't spoken her first word.

"Mama!"

The decision was made. Reverend Bush would be the one to leave. And she would follow her plan—never, ever to leave her daughter again . . .

"Jasmine?"

Her eyes were glazed from those memories when she looked up.

Hosea said, "I heard the phone."

She'd been so deep in her thoughts that she'd almost forgotten the call. But now that he reminded her, fear returned to her heart. Thumping. Throbbing. She had to swallow before she nodded. "It was Dale. The verdict's in. We have to be at the courthouse in two hours."

He moved slowly, then lowered himself next to her on the sofa. She knew his thoughts were her thoughts: *Would this be the last time he'd be in their home? Would these be the last hours that he would spend with her and their children?* As she asked herself those questions, as she sat next to him, shoulder to shoulder, her fear dissipated and her anger returned . . .

She had been fighting mad, at first. As she had sat in that hospital room with Jacqueline, along with Mae Frances and Mrs. Whittingham, who had taken the place of Reverend Bush, Jasmine had tried to figure out what was going on. It didn't make sense . . . Hosea and attempted murder in the same sentence? This was some kind of big mistake. Didn't the police know Hosea Bush? Didn't they know that he was a world-renowned gentle man, who loved and obeyed the Lord above all else? And a man who loved God the way Hosea did would never do anything that came close to attempted murder.

Those were the thoughts in her head.

In her heart, though, was the truth. She knew exactly what had happened. From the moment Dr. Stewart had explained Jacqueline's condition, Hosea's rage had been palpable, filling the air with a suffocating stench.

And then he'd disappeared.

Somehow, he had found a gun . . . found that man . . . and made him pay for what he'd done to their daughter.

That was her theory as she carried Jacqueline home after Dr. Stewart had finally released her, with orders for the family to visit the child psychologist three times weekly. But although Malik had called and kept her posted on what was happening with Hosea through the night, she didn't have any real answers.

As the clocked ticked and the hours went by, Mae Frances

and Mrs. Whittingham had slept in the children's rooms, while Jasmine had held a vigil for Hosea in their room, with their daughter and son in the bed with her. She hadn't closed her eyes—all she could do was stare at Jacqueline. And when she blinked, all she could do was think about Hosea.

It was midmorning when the half-million-dollar bail had been set and posted and Hosea finally had trudged into their still-quiet apartment. Jasmine had met him at the threshold of their bedroom.

"I am so mad at you," she'd hissed. "How could you do that? How could you risk our family this way?" And then she'd thrown her arms around him and held him as if she never wanted to let go.

Still, she had questions, and she planned to ask him every one. Until she noticed that Hosea wasn't holding her back. She followed his gaze and realized that his eyes and his thoughts were beyond her. He was focused on Jacqueline.

Of course, she thought. He had left the hospital to go murder a man; he hadn't seen their daughter.

She released him from the embrace and watched with tear-filled eyes as he took slow steps to their king-size bed. He sat on the edge, on the side where Jacqueline slept, and reached toward her, his arm pausing in midair before he touched her. Then he just sat and watched her sleep. Jasmine wasn't sure how much time passed before his head began to shake and his shoulders shuddered. She crouched in front of him and rested her head on his lap.

He wept. And she cried with him. She cried . . . and had no more questions for her husband. Because now she understood.

Those were their last quiet hours.

Right after noon, the concierge called up to their apartment. "Mrs. Bush," he had whispered into the telephone, "there's a bunch of press here asking all kinds of questions."

"What?" Jasmine had exclaimed. "Questions about what?"

"Mostly about Mr. Bush. I didn't say a thing, but they're questioning everyone who comes in or walks out of the building."

She'd thanked the doorman, then told Hosea.

"Dale told me to expect this."

Expect it? Press was the last thing she'd expected. After all, there hadn't been much coverage for Jacqueline. Why were they interested in the Bushes now?

Then Dale and Reverend Bush had arrived, carrying coffee and newspapers with front-page stories about the Bushes.

The *New York Post* had the most controversial headline: "Uptown Preacher Packs a Pistol."

Inside the study, away from their children, who played under the watchful eyes of Mrs. Sloss, Mrs. Whittingham, and Mae Frances, Dale explained that this was going to be their lives for the next few months.

"It's a sensational story," Dale said. "The press is going to stay all over this."

"Why?" Jasmine asked. "Why now?"

Reverend Bush answered, "Because this is an attempted murder case," and he glanced at his son as if he still couldn't believe what he'd done. "At least that man didn't die," the reverend whispered.

"Yeah, that's the good thing. And actually, the charges have already been reduced," Dale said to them as he and Jasmine sat across from Reverend Bush. Hosea stood at the window, separate from them. As if he wasn't part of the conversation.

"Reduced? That's good news, right?" Jasmine had asked with hope in her voice. Since Hosea had come home, she hadn't allowed herself to think about the implications of his arrest.

"It is good news," Dale had said. "It's no longer attempted murder."

For the first time, Hosea spoke. "I wasn't trying to kill him," he said, without turning around.

Dale nodded. "The police kind of figured that out, and the DA wants a conviction, so he's going along with it."

Jasmine and her father-in-law wore matching frowns. Reverend Bush asked, "What did they figure out?"

Dale looked at Hosea, waiting for him to explain. But when he kept his back to the three, Dale said, "It seems your son knows how to handle a gun."

"Yeah," Reverend Bush said, looking between Hosea and Dale. "He was an expert marksman in the Marines."

Dale said, "So, if he'd wanted to, Hosea could have hit him in his head or his chest." He spoke as if Hosea was not in the room. "He could have killed him . . . but he didn't."

"I told you, I wasn't trying to kill him."

Jasmine looked up at Hosea. "So . . . you were just trying to hurt him?" Her confusion was apparent.

Dale answered, "Hosea shot the man right between his legs. He castrated him with a gun."

"Oh, my God!" she exclaimed, appalled at first.

"That's all I wanted to do," Hosea said, still not facing them.

Jasmine wasn't sure if it was the image or the pressure that made her giggle.

He castrated him with a gun!

And then she laughed. It became a full-out guffaw. She would have been rolling on the floor if she'd had enough room.

A couple of minutes passed before she noticed that she was the only one laughing, and that two pairs of male eyes were staring her down. Hosea still gazed out the window.

"Jasmine," Dale said, in a tone that told her he found nothing funny, "that man bled so much he could have died."

"I'm sorry," she said, waving her hand and trying to control herself. But she wasn't sorry about a thing. After what that man did to their daughter—that memory wiped any residual laughter right away. "So what happens now?" she asked, suddenly sober.

Dale glared at her, as if he'd taken her laughter personally. "Like I said, the charges have been reduced, but they're still serious. Assault with a deadly weapon and reckless endangerment. Hosea could still go away for a long time." Dale looked straight at Jasmine. "Twenty years."

That was the first time that her heart had pounded like it was trying to get away.

"Twenty years? Oh, my God!" She couldn't imagine a life where her children would see their father only through vertical bars or panes of bulletproof glass. "He can't go to jail, Dale. You have to do something. That man, he took our daughter. And the things he did to her . . ." She stopped when she heard Hosea moan. When she saw his fingers curl, she shut her mouth. She didn't want to say anything that might send Hosea after that man again.

"That's why we're here," Dale said. "To talk this out and make sure Hosea doesn't go to jail. I was thinking about an insanity plea . . . temporary insanity. Especially since his *intent* was not murder. And there's not a father in America who wouldn't be able to identify with this."

"That's good." Jasmine nodded. "Temporary insanity." She glanced at her husband, still standing at the window. Still not looking at them. It was clear, he wasn't yet in his right mind.

"The thing we have going for us," Dale continued, "is that this happened in New York."

Reverend Bush nodded. "Because of the city's history."

"Yup . . . vigilante justice. Start with Bernard Goetz and come forward. New Yorkers are hardened, sometimes heartless, civilians who have been tired of the city's crime for a long time, and they believe that there are moments when you've got to do what you've got to do. We put one of those people on the jury and, best case, an acquittal."

"And worst case?" Jasmine asked.

Dale shrugged. "Worst case is that he goes to prison for twenty years."

Jasmine groaned.

Dale stood and snapped shut his briefcase. "But I'm here to make sure that doesn't happen. Nicholas Abrams is going to be the lead chair, and we'll be here tomorrow to talk serious strategy." He glanced at Hosea. "Get some rest," he said to Hosea's back. "Enjoy the children. Because it's going to get rough from here on out."

Reverend Bush stood. "I'll walk you out," he said, leaving Hosea and Jasmine alone.

When the reverend closed the door behind him, Hosea sank into the oversize chair. Jasmine settled on the floor at his feet and waited for him to talk, knowing that he would.

It took some time, but then, "When I look back on yesterday," he began softly, "I feel like I was a bit insane."

Jasmine said nothing, just listened.

"Jacquie had been gone for so, so long."

She knew what he meant, but still she said, "Almost three weeks."

"A lifetime."

She nodded. She understood.

"I already had to live with the fact that I hadn't protected her."

"But she wasn't even with you, she was with me."

"Doesn't matter. I'm her father. And after Doctor Stewart told us . . ." He shook his head as if he didn't want to remember the doctor's words. "I started thinking about what she'd been through, and everything that's ahead. What is this year going to be like for her? And next year? And ten or fifteen years from now?" His head was still shaking. "I did what I had to do. I had to take him out."

"Take him out?" She frowned. "I thought you said you weren't trying to kill him."

He looked straight into her eyes. "If he had bled to death . . ." A pause and a shrug. "Oh, well," he said in his ordinary, gentle manner. Then he kissed Jasmine's forehead before he stood and walked out of the room. Leaving her alone to think about quiet storms and about how grateful she was that she would never have to testify against her husband.

After that day, they became the center of the circus. The case was fodder for the news channels—the Left, the Right, and those who saw themselves as independents—everyone wanted to tell it like they saw it.

Daily, *Eyewitness News* polled random men and women on the street.

"That was a little five-year-old girl," a thirtysomething man said. "If that had been my child, I would of done the same thing. Only I wouldn't of used a gun. I would of used my bare hands."

But there was the other side, too. The *Amsterdam News* printed reader letters in their opinion column. A woman who sent in a picture of herself clutching a Bible wrote: "Hosea Bush is supposed to be a Christian man. What kind of Christian would do something like that? The Bible says thou shalt not kill. That also means thou shalt not try to kill."

The city was evenly split. Half of New York wanted Hosea to walk: "Hey, at least that pervert didn't die!"

And the remainder of New Yorkers wanted Hosea to pay the price: "He's a pastor; what kind of example is he setting?"

The intensity of the arguments gave Jasmine a new fear

every day. But it wasn't the debate alone that had her shivering—it was the assistant district attorney as well.

The government had found the right one to try the case: A forty-six-year-old woman, with a seven-year-old daughter. A woman who had been in the district attorney's office for twenty years and was on the verge of being nominated to run for the top spot. A woman who, if she won the election, would be the first female district attorney in New York's history.

People v. Hosea Bush was just the case she needed, and that made Gloria Gallagher relentless and unyielding in her pursuit.

"I have a young daughter of my own." Gallagher made sure the jury knew this during her opening statement, the first day in the packed-to-capacity courtroom. "And so I truly understand how the Bush family felt." The petite woman with the powerful voice placed her hand over her heart. "I prayed for them every night. But what happened to Jacqueline Bush has nothing to do with what her father did. The two cases are not and should not be connected." She went on, "We cannot allow New York to become a lawless society. No one has the right to shoot anyone!" Her voice began to rise. "Especially not a man who was already in custody, already handcuffed, already in shackles, already being transported to prison, and, therefore, not a threat or a danger to anyone. Especially not a man who hadn't yet been convicted of any crime." She shook her head. "Anyone who shoots someone like that, an unarmed man, is not a hero to be celebrated." She faced Hosea, who sat between his two attorneys. She looked him dead in the eyes when she said, "A man who would do something like that is a coward." Then she growled like a cougar, "And we cannot allow a man like that to continue to walk on our streets!"

Jasmine's heart had pounded so hard then, she had leaned over to take deep breaths to keep the pain away.

But her chest pains continued. Not only because she had to sit in the courtroom every day and listen to a woman who was determined to send her husband to prison, but because she had to leave Jacqueline and Zaya at home.

That had not been her choice. But the attorneys had told her and Reverend Bush that it was important for the jury to see both of them standing by Hosea.

So Jasmine was there, doing what she had to do as the wife. But the moment the gavel dropped every afternoon, she became the mother and, with Hosea, rushed home to be with their children. Mondays, Wednesdays, and Fridays were especially busy days because they went home and had just enough time to gather Jacqueline and Zaya and rush to the psychologist's last appointment. The doctor tried desperately to get Jacqueline to talk about her three weeks away from home.

But Jacqueline never said a word. No matter how the psychologist posed the question, every session she sat mute and still for the entire hour.

After the first week, the psychologist said, "I want to try something else," and then she asked Jacqueline to draw.

Jacqueline smiled when the doctor gave her a crayon. Her parents held their breath as she slowly sketched a picture—four stick figures: two with hair, two large enough to be adults, two the size of children. But only one child wore a smile. She drew tears on the face of the girl figure.

Watching her child draw, looking at that picture—that was when Jasmine finally knew what it felt like to have her heart broken.

The psychologist said, "She just may not have the words to express what happened. She may not understand."

"Then why do we keep coming here?" Jasmine had asked. "Isn't it good that she doesn't want to . . . or can't talk about this?"

The doctor had shaken her head. "No, because as the picture shows, she remembers something, whether she can express it or not. It's in her memory. We don't want her to repress this. Repressed memories can lead to dangerous behavior later in life."

The woman had spoken as if she expected Jacqueline to grow up to be a murderer.

To Jasmine, that was ironic, since Jacqueline's father was being accused of something close to that. According to the district attorney, Hosea Bush had attempted murder (even though those charges had been reduced), and she was going to prove premeditation. She was going to convince twelve people (and two alternates) that Hosea was not society worthy—at least not for the next twenty years.

Gloria Gallagher paraded witness after witness to support her position. First, officers testified that Hosea Bush had planned this assault from the beginning—when he had lain in wait for the prisoner to come from the building straight through to the end when he dropped to the ground before anyone could shoot him.

"To me," one of the officers said, "it was clearly planned. A good plan, though."

Detective Cohen said, "I saw no signs of violence from Hosea Bush. He was just a father who snapped."

Gallagher had said, "But he *did* snap, and that makes him dangerous, wouldn't you agree?"

The detective never had a chance to respond once Dale had objected and the assistant district attorney withdrew the question.

After the police, Gloria Gallagher brought in the victim's family. Harvey Jonas's aunt said that he'd had a rough childhood—that's why he had kidnapped and raped a five-year-old. Next, his sister, who stated that Harvey was the most loving brother, but that their father had abused them so much, there was nothing else that her brother could do except kidnap and rape a five-year-old. Then, there was his niece, a practicing psychiatrist who said that even while Harvey had held Jacqueline in captivity, he had been trying to get help.

"He wanted to be well," she testified. "He didn't *want* to do any of those horrible things." That was her professional opinion.

Hosea's defense had their own witnesses: members of City of Lights, including Brother Hill and Mrs. Whittingham; staff from his television show; and the big surprise—at least for Jasmine—Brian Lewis.

Jasmine had been shocked the day Brian and Alexis had walked into the courthouse. She hadn't spoken to Brian since she'd called him with the news about Jacqueline, though she knew that he often spoke with Hosea about their daughter's progress.

Standing in the middle of the hallway, right outside of the courtroom, she had exchanged pleasantries, and then stared at Brian for an extra moment, just to see if she felt anything. But there was nothing there, not a bit of care—certainly nothing that came close to lust or love. She couldn't believe it—then, just shrugged it off. She'd been sick out of her mind—that's why she'd turned to Brian. And when Jacqueline had come home, so had her good sense.

"Dale called me to testify," Brian explained to Jasmine. "And I can't wait to do it."

"Wow, you flew all the way here to do this for us. Wow," she said, looking at Alexis who stood next to Brian, hanging on to his arm and glowing like she'd just won the lottery or something. "So are you headed right back afterward?"

Brian had shaken his head and took Alexis's hand. "No, we won't be back in L.A. for a while. We're going . . . on our honeymoon. We're on our way to Venice."

Jasmine figured they weren't talking about the area in Los Angeles.

Alexis said, "Yup, we got married . . . again," as if she thought that was something Jasmine would want to know.

The way Alexis giggled like a schoolgirl made Jasmine want to slap her out of it.

But she'd grown so much in the Lord, she just smiled, congratulated the pair, and thanked them for coming. And truth—when Brian got on the stand, he did a bang-up job. Not only did he talk about Hosea's character, since this was the man to whom he'd surrendered his parental responsibilities for Jacqueline, but in one of the most dramatic moments of the trial, Brian declared, "If I had been in New York, Hosea would have had some competition, because I would have done the same thing."

The judge, the Honorable Lynn Harris, had had to bang his gavel three times to stop the murmurs that swelled through the courtroom.

But Brian had continued, "God help me, but when I think about the things that man did to my . . . his daughter . . ." He hadn't been able to finish his statement. And the prosecutor let him walk off the stand without a cross-examination.

But the assistant DA did get her big moment when she faced off with Hosea. His attorneys had told Hosea that he didn't need to take the stand, but he'd insisted.

"I have a story to tell," he'd said. "People need to hear what I have to say."

"That could be dangerous, Hosea," Nicholas had warned. "You don't need to speak at all. Remember, they have to prove that you're guilty; we don't have to prove that you're innocent."

But Hosea had shaken his head. "I'm going to testify. And if that means that I have to go to jail, so be it."

Jasmine had wanted to slap some sense into him. Had Hosea forgotten that he had a family? But the truth—he *was* considering his family. He always did, and that's why they were all in this courtroom in the first place.

So on the stand, Hosea told the story of how he'd been sick with grief when his little girl had been abducted, how that had escalated through the weeks, and climaxed when he'd been told that Jacqueline had been raped.

"And not only had she been raped, but she'd been raped repeatedly." Hosea sniffed. "She's only five, and I'm her father. Her protector. I was thinking about Jacqueline and the other little girls that man may have gotten his hands on. I wanted to make sure that he never hurt a child again."

His attorney's final question was, "So Pastor Bush, were you trying to kill him?"

"No, not at all," Hosea had said calmly. "I could have, if I'd wanted to. But his death is not in my hands—that's up to God. All I wanted to do was protect the children. All I did was take away the weapon that man used to hurt little girls."

There was nothing but silence when Hosea's attorney sat down. It even took a moment for Gloria Gallagher to raise her head and stand.

"Mr. Bush," she began, refusing to address Hosea as a pastor, "how long did you drive around before you decided to take the law into your own hands?"

Then the district attorney didn't even let Hosea answer the question before she flung another one at him.

"Let's back it up," she said, looking down at her notes. "When did you purchase the gun that you used to take the law into your own hands?"

"Objection!" Hosea's attorney shouted.

"I'll rephrase, Your Honor," Gallagher said before the judge spoke. She asked, "When did you purchase the gun?"

"A couple of years ago."

"For what purpose?"

"To protect my family. After my father was shot."

"Oh!" she said, as if she was surprised. "So, you *planned* to hurt anyone who came after your family?"

Hosea shook his head. "I *planned* to protect my family. I have the gun legally."

"I see." The way the assistant district attorney smiled made Jasmine grimace. Hosea didn't know how to handle a conniving, underhanded woman. He was going to drown in Gloria Gallagher's hands.

The ADA asked, "Are you a trained marksman?"

"Yes."

"I see," she said, glancing at the jury. "So you knew exactly what you were doing when you aimed that gun at Mr. Jonas?"

Jasmine had wanted to stand up and shout her own objection. How could that woman refer to the man who had kidnapped and raped her daughter as Mr.? He didn't deserve any kind of credibility or respect—especially since, a week after he had been caught, he had pled guilty and was sentenced to a term that would make him 135 years old before he was set free.

"Yes," Hosea responded. "I knew exactly what I was doing. That's why he's not dead."

Jasmine moaned. She didn't have to be an attorney to know that wasn't the right answer. Why couldn't Hosea just do what she would have done if she was on the stand? Why couldn't he just lie?

"So I will ask again—when did you decide to take the law into your own hands, *Mr.* Bush?"

Gloria Gallagher continued to shoot question after question at Hosea, snarling at him like a pit bull, dragging him with her teeth into her trap.

"Isn't it true that you wanted Mr. Jonas dead?" she asked, her voice raised.

"I already told you, but I'll answer again—no," he said, not at all intimidated.

"Oh, come on, Mr. Bush. You can't tell me that you didn't want the man who kidnapped and raped your daughter to die."

"Objection! That is not a question."

Hosea raised his hand. "I know what she means, and I'll answer that." He looked at the jury. "It would not bother me one bit if Mr. Jonas was to die. But it was not my intent to take his life, nor was it my intent to harm anyone else. I simply wanted to prevent him from hurting another child, because the fact is, he's done this before—"

"Your Honor!" Gloria Gallagher shouted, wanting to stop Hosea from talking any more about Harvey Jonas's past.

But Hosea kept right on, "And Harvey Jonas ran away from his punishment. I just wanted to make sure that if he got away again, he wouldn't be able to hurt another child."

Jasmine had wanted to stand up and give her husband an ovation, though when she glanced at the jurors, they sat stone-faced, totally unimpressed.

But with Hosea's testimony, the defense rested. And then the futures of Hosea and Jasmine and Jacqueline and Zaya were in the hands of twelve people they did not know.

Right after the case had been handed over to the jury, they all gathered at the church to send up passionate prayers. There, Reverend Bush had asked Dale about their chances.

He'd shrugged and said, "The only charge that concerns me—as it did from the beginning—is reckless endangerment. Even if everyone on that jury hates Jonas, Hosea did shoot into a crowd and jeopardize others. But that won't carry too much time."

Too. Much. Time.

Jasmine hadn't been able to think about anything else since Dale had said those words.

Now, after two days, just twelve hours of deliberation, she was going to find out how much time her family would receive, because surely, any time that Hosea got was their punishment also.

Hosea took Jasmine's hand and lifted her from the couch. He hugged her when they stood, and then together they walked into their bedroom. It was time to face their fate.

Sixty-seven

JASMINE WAS SUFFOCATING.

From the people—every inch of the courtroom's perimeter was packed with news reporters and photographers wanting to be the first to deliver the breaking news. From the heat—the bodies generated enough warmth to set New York City on fire. From the pressure—she was choking on the waiting. It was excruciating.

Part of her agony came from the images in her mind. She could already see it—how the jury would declare that her husband was guilty beyond any kind of doubt. And then, they would glare at Hosea—and at her. Especially the five men on the jury, who probably felt sorry for Harvey Jonas. Who probably cried when they heard that a man had been castrated.

Hosea might have received more compassion if he had just killed the man.

"Are you all right?" Malik whispered as he took her hand.

She nodded yes, because what good would telling him the truth do?

She squirmed; it took too much effort to sit still. The bench felt much harder than it had on any other day. She should have been used to it; she'd been sitting here every day for the entire four-week trial. Sitting in the place that reminded her of where she sat on Sundays—the first row, first seat—the seat of honor. What she now knew was the seat of horror.

As they waited, the chatter in the courtroom was deafening, intense. She could feel the heat of probing eyes watching her, reporters waiting to get the money shot of the pastor's wife breaking down. But though she was on the verge, she wasn't going to give it to them. No matter what the outcome, she would be strong for Hosea and their children.

Their children. Today, for the first time, Jacqueline and Zaya were here at the courthouse. Under guard—with Mae Frances, Mrs. Whittingham, Brother Hill, and Detective Foxx. They never left the house anymore without an entourage. That was the only way that *she* felt safe.

She had to bring the children today, just in case.

That had been her thought.

It had taken some time, but Jasmine had talked Hosea into it. "Just in case," were the words that had finally got him to agree. But those words were also the ones that made her tremble when she looked into her husband's eyes.

From the moment this ordeal had begun, Jasmine had never seen even a flicker of fear from Hosea. But when she told him that she'd wanted to bring the children—just in case—he'd blinked. And a shadow had passed over his eyes. It was there for only for a second, but she had seen it—his doubt that he would be coming home with his family today.

At that moment, Jasmine had rushed into the bathroom and cried, which was exactly what she wanted to do now. But the reporters—they were watching, ready to pounce on any outward display of the terror she felt inside.

So she just waited and calculated the odds. But like Dale had told them almost every day, there was no way to determine what any jury would do. Hadn't O.J. gotten off? Hadn't Heidi Fleiss been convicted?

"All rise!"

It took a moment for Jasmine to realize that the Honorable Lynn Harris was coming into the room; she was the last one to stand on unsteady legs.

Then Judge Harris boomed, "Bring in the jury."

Jasmine's heart started that breakout thing again as she watched the men and women stride in, two lines, one after the other. She squinted and searched their faces, sure that she would be able to tell their decision before they spoke it aloud. But not one of them looked her way.

Jasmine didn't have to worry about her heart punching through her chest. Not anymore. Because now it stopped beating.

They won't look at me!

She'd seen enough *Law & Order* episodes to know that if the jury acquitted, someone always gave a signal—a slight smile, a small nod. They always made eye contact.

But today, these people walked in and sat down and gave her nothing.

She wanted to scream. It was over. Hosea was going to prison, and she was going to die.

She bowed her head and her heart when the judge asked Hosea to stand. Hosea did as he was told, buttoning the top button of his jacket as he rose. Dale and Nicholas stood with him.

"Has the jury reached a verdict?"

"We have, Your Honor."

"In the matter of the *People v. Hosea Bush,* on the first count—assault with a deadly weapon—how do you find?"

The room was more than silent; it was still.

Then, "We find the defendant, Hosea S. Bush . . . not guilty."

The room erupted, not so much with cheers but with chatter.

Jasmine breathed, but she still kept her head down. There was still another count—the one that Dale was worried about.

Too. Much. Time.

The judge banged his gavel for order. Then, "In the matter of the *People v. Hosea Bush* on the second count—reckless endangerment—how do you find?"

Again, that still silence.

"We find the defendant, Hosea S. Bush . . . guilty."

This time, the eruption was louder, but still, Jasmine's cries rang out. Hosea turned, reached over the divider that separated him from his wife.

"It's going to be all right," he whispered, without a tinge of fear.

But it was fine that he was fearless; she had enough fear for both of them. She couldn't hear, couldn't see, couldn't think—about anything except that her husband was going to jail. Would he even be given the chance to say good-bye to their children before he was dragged away?

"Order! Order!" the judge bellowed.

It took a while before the room was quiet again.

The heavy-cheeked judge faced Hosea. Looked down at him over the rims of his silver glasses. His expression was stern; his eyes were piercing.

His expression alone made Jasmine want to faint.

But she couldn't. Because of the children. She was all that they had now.

The judge said, "Hosea S. Bush, having been found guilty of the charge of reckless endangerment, is there anything you want to say to the court before your sentencing?"

"Yes, Your Honor," Hosea responded, his voice as loud and as clear as the judge's. He paused, then, "I am very sorry for the time and money that my case has cost the city and this court. I am sorry for the suffering of Harvey Jonas's friends and family. And I am certainly sorry for anyone who felt that they were in danger because of my actions. That was not my intent. I am trained; I knew that no one else would be hurt.

"As I said before, Your Honor, I am nothing more than a man who loves the Lord, a husband, and a father who, on that day, saw only one solution. It is in my heart, it's part of me, to protect my children, and that is all that I was doing. Thank you."

That's it?

Her heart was back, pumping wildly. Now she wished that she had written his speech for him; they should have practiced it together. Because if he had spoken her words, he would have begged for mercy. He would have cried, maybe even apologized to Harvey Jonas.

But that was a dream because Hosea would never do that. And that was the reason he was going to jail.

The Honorable Lynn Harris did not seem impressed as he gazed upon Hosea. "Pastor Bush, you have been found guilty of the charge of reckless endangerment, which in the state of New York can carry a maximum sentence of ten years . . ."

Jasmine cried out.

"Depending on the offense," the judge finished before he took a peek at Jasmine. After a pause, "As judge for the state of New York, Second District, I hereby sentence you to one year."

He had to bang his gavel again . . . and again. But that didn't stop Jasmine—inside Malik's arms, she cried and cried.

"It's only a year," Malik whispered.

It's only one year. She sniffed as she repeated those words in her mind.

She could survive this. She could—and she would—for the sake of their children. It wasn't too bad; Jacquie would be not yet seven and Zaya wouldn't even be three when Hosea got out.

Jasmine trembled as she waited for the court officers to drag Hosea away, but then, through her fog, she realized that the judge was still speaking.

He said, "However, using my judicial discretion, I am suspending your sentence."

This time, no words, no gavel was able to restore order for minutes.

Jasmine was not understanding and hardly breathing when the judge was finally able to continue. "I am suspending your sentence," he repeated to Hosea, "because of what I believe are extenuating circumstances. Our prisons are designed to keep dangerous people off the streets. And it is not my belief, Pastor Bush, that you are a dangerous man. I do believe, however, that you can use this situation. There is much that you can do, many things that you can accomplish for the good of the community if you are out speaking about what has happened to you and your family. I will ask that you think about the ways you can help other families, even come up with solutions . . . that do not include carrying a gun." He paused. "So as I said, your sentence is suspended." Then he knocked his gavel one final time. "Court adjourned."

Jasmine jumped from her seat and grabbed her husband. And even though the divider still separated them, he lifted her off her feet.

"Thank God," she whispered, over and over in his ear.

She held him, even as people clamored around them. She held him, even as photographers blinded them with flashing cameras. She held him, even as reporters assaulted them with questions over questions.

It was Dale who broke them apart. "Let's get out of here," he said. He nodded to one of the court officers, and though shouts and camera flashes followed them through the pandemonium, they were led through a side door.

As they rushed down the hall, Jasmine held Hosea's hand. She couldn't wait to get to their children. All she wanted to do was take Jacqueline and Zaya into her arms, then go home where they could move forward with their lives.

But then she stopped. Stopped moving, stopped thinking about the future. There was only one thing on her mind.

"What's wrong?" Hosea asked, his tone filled with worry.

Jasmine stared into her husband's eyes before she turned to Reverend Bush, Malik, and Dale. "I just think"—she paused for a second—"that we need to pray."

She couldn't tell which of them looked more shocked, though she couldn't figure out why. In these last weeks, if she hadn't learned anything else, she had certainly learned to pray.

Reverend Bush was the only one who didn't seem stuck in a stupor, and he stepped toward her first. "That's a great idea, sweetheart." He reached out his hand and, with his other, clasped his fingers around his son's.

Malik and Dale followed, and in the middle of that hallway, in the middle of the courthouse, in the middle of New York City, they bowed their heads and their hearts and gave praise to God. They thanked Him for His grace and His mercy, and they gave Him praise for the outcome—all of it—from Jacqueline to the verdict. This ending wasn't perfect, but it was faithful.

Never had Jasmine been through something that was so life changing. No longer was she going to think of the former things, the old parts and ways of her life. Tragedy had truly turned her to Christ. And all she wanted to do now was love Him, love Hosea, and love her children.

As Reverend Bush continued their prayer, Jasmine thought of the scripture that he'd given her at church the day Jacqueline had been found. It had taken her a couple of days to look up that verse, but once she had, she had stood on those words daily.

James 5:16 was the truth—the effective, fervent prayer of the righteous man *did* avail much! Look at what prayer had availed for her.

When Reverend Bush finished with "Amen," they all said the same.

She squeezed Hosea's hand, then glanced back at the closed door that led to the courtroom. This horrible part of their lives—from Jacqueline's abduction to the court case—was over.

The end!

But then, with just a little tug, Hosea made her look forward. Made her look at him. Made her smile and think not about endings, but what was surely their tremendous new beginning.

Sins of the Mother

After years of lying, cheating, scheming, and stealing, Jasmine Larson Bush has finally settled into a drama-free life as the first lady of one of the largest churches in New York City. She and her husband Hosea have been blessed with the best of everything and have two beautiful and happy children. But just when Jasmine thinks her troubles are over forever, her daughter Jacqueline is kidnapped at a mall in broad daylight. The police and the church community join in a frantic search to find the four-year-old, but as the days pass with no sign of her daughter, Jasmine begins to crack under the pressure. In her despair she turns to Brian Lewis, Jacqueline's biological father, for solace. As her nerves and her marriage are stretched to the limit, Jasmine wonders if she is being punished for her past sins. Will she and her family pay the ultimate price?

For Discussion

1. Reverend Bush tells Hosea: "Son, I told you before not to judge Jasmine and her grief. Maybe I should have reminded you not to judge yours either. You're more action oriented—you take charge and do something. Jasmine is more introspective. She's probably trying to figure out what's happening to Jacquie every moment of every day. Neither of you is wrong; neither of you is right." How are Jasmine's and Hosea's reactions to their tragedy each valuable? How might these reactions also be destructive?

2. How can loss create rifts between people? Consider some of the issues that Jasmine and Hosea may have had before that reappear as a result of Jacquie's disappearance.

3. After Brian's last visit to his therapist he decides not to return and tells Alexis he is "cured." Do you think there is actually a cure for his problem? Why does he decide not to go back? His therapist warns him, "Be careful. I told you before, don't make Alexis your new addiction." Do you think Brian makes Alexis his new addiction, or is he simply expressing his love for her?

4. How would you describe Brian and Alexis's relationship? Why does she forgive Brian after all he has put her through? Do you think she can really trust him again?

5. In Hosea's first sermon after Jacqueline's kidnapping, he discusses the issue of why bad things happen to good people.

This is an issue that many people grapple with. How are you able to come to terms with bad things happening to good people and good things happening to bad people? How does Hosea's faith help him through the situation?

6. How does Jacqueline's kidnapping bring Brian closer to Alexis? How does it change them both?

7. Consider how Jasmine treated Mae Frances after the kidnapping. Do you think her behavior was justified? Was she too hard on Mae Frances?

8. When Jasmine visits City of Lights at Riverside Church she gets down on her knees to pray. "In the past, she'd knelt on her knees, even closed her eyes and lowered her head. But today she was bowing her heart. For the first time." What does this passage mean? How is this a transformative experience for Jasmine?

9. Reverend Bush tells Jasmine, "'Thank Him for His grace, but thank Him even more for His mercy.' His words reminded her of the first sermon she'd ever heard him preach, when he'd taught the difference between grace and mercy. She hadn't truly understood then, but in the years that she'd been part of the Bush family, she'd gained an understanding." What does this passage mean? What is the difference between grace and mercy?

10. Do you agree with Hosea's decision to take the law into his own hands? Do you agree with the sentence he received? How might his behavior have been justified? Or was it inexcusable? How does his behavior in court help his case?

11. When Jasmine sees Brian in the courthouse, "there was nothing there, not a bit of care—certainly nothing that came close to lust or love. She couldn't believe it—then, just shrugged it off. She'd been sick out of her mind—that's why she'd turned to Brian. And when Jacqueline had come home, so had her good sense." Based on her history with Brian, do you think her feelings were really simply a matter of losing her senses? Why else might Jasmine have developed feelings for Brian again?

12. Do you think that the relationship Brian and Alexis end up in is a healthy one, particularly after his struggle with addiction? Where do you see their relationship going?

13. What do you think lies ahead for the Bush family, considering the horrific circumstances of Jacquie's kidnapping? At the end of the novel Jasmine is thinking "not about endings, but what was surely their tremendous new beginning." What are some of the positive and negative aspects of the new beginning the Bush family is about to face?

14. What are the main themes of this novel? Did you find relevance to your own life in these themes?

15. Share some of your favorite scenes and dialogue from the novel.

16. If you've read previous books featuring Jasmine, were you able to sympathize with her less or more in this book? How has she changed? What do you like and dislike most about her?

A Conversation with Victoria Christopher Murray

Kidnapping and child abuse can be difficult to read about. Was this a difficult book to write, particularly the parts about what happened to Jacqueline? Did anything in particular inspire you to explore this topic?

This was a tough, tough book to write, but it's a subject that has intrigued me for a long time. I lived in New York in the late seventies or early eighties when a young boy by the name of Etan Patz disappeared. It was the first time any of us had heard about a child disappearing. (Unfortunately, it's all too common now.) I remember praying for days and weeks for this young boy, and especially for his family. I couldn't imagine how his mother put her head down every night. And since he was never found, I couldn't imagine how she was able to move forward with her life. It was a subject that I wanted to explore.

After writing a number of books about Jasmine, she must be very close to your heart. How did you come up with this character? Is she based on anyone you know? Do you take any of your characters from real life?

Interestingly enough, Jasmine is not at all close to my heart. I never wanted to write even a second book about her, and definitely not a third or fourth. As she does for most readers, Jasmine got on my nerves—a lot! She's not based on anyone I know, but as I continued her story through my novels, people told me that they often saw themselves in her. That's a hard thing to admit, but I do believe there are parts (small parts) of

Jasmine in all of us—a woman who is just trying to do good, but is always dragged back (by her own behavior) to what's familiar. And no, I don't take characters from real life. Are you kidding me? My imagination is so much more interesting than my friends. ☺

What are you working on now? Are more Jasmine books in the works?

I thought I made it perfectly clear at the end of *Sins of the Mother* that there will be no more Jasmine books! She is over. At least in her own stand-alone books. I am thinking about doing collaborations with a couple of other authors, and Jasmine may show up in those books. But she will never be the major character in my books again. I am so glad to be working on and discovering new characters. My next book, *The Cougar*, introduces the readers to characters they've never met before. And that's all I'm going to say.

What do you like to do in your free time? Is there anything that particularly inspires your creativity?

Free time? What's that? Writing one book a year doesn't leave much free time. But I do make time for working out—I used to run marathons, but when I had my hip replaced last year, my surgeon told me my running days are over. I love, love, love to read. I'm one of those writers who's blessed to be able to read while writing—reading doesn't affect my writing at all. Besides that, I enjoy spending time with family and friends . . . sounds boring, huh?

How do you balance your writing career and your personal life?

That's a great question! I was just telling a friend today that I don't do a good job of balancing my career and my personal life. Unfortunately for me, I haven't been able to support myself on writing my novels alone. So, I have to do many other things. Hence . . . no free time and very little personal life. I'm hoping one day this will change. Maybe when I'm sixty or seventy . . . or ninety . . .

Do you hash out your entire plot before writing your novels, or do you just start writing and see what happens?

I used to just start writing, but because I'm trying to write more than one novel a year, I now work from an outline. With an outline, most of the plot is hashed out, but most times, the characters will surprise me and change course. I always let the characters do their thing. For example, the ending of *Sins of the Mother* is totally different from what I'd planned—the characters took over and I let them.

What are some of your favorite books? Your favorite authors?

My all-time favorite author is Richard Wright. Some of my favorite contemporary books are: *Child of God* by Lolita Files, *Freshwater Road* by Denise Nicholas, and *Abraham's Well* by Sharon Ewell Foster—just to name a few. I love books that entertain and teach me something at the same time.

What are you reading now? Do you have any recommendations?

I'm reading *Mistress of the Game*—the last Sidney Sheldon book. Last year was a great reading year for me—*The Devil Is a Lie*, by ReShonda Tate Billingsley, *Be Careful What You Pray For* by Kimberla Lawson Roby (she let me read the manuscript!), *What Doesn't Kill You* by Virginia DeBerry and Donna Grant, *The Warmest December* by Bernice McFadden, *After* by Marita Golden, *Sins of the Father* by Angela Benson, *Orange Mint and Honey* by Carleen Brice, and *Gather Together in My Name* by Tracy Price-Thompson. Those are just a few of the best. (I told you that I love to read!)

You do a lot of touring and motivational speaking. What do you enjoy most about these engagements? Do you connect with your readers? Do you have any favorite moments from your tours?

I really, really, really love touring. I love the chance to talk to readers about my stories. I love the fact that I have to tell readers over and over that the characters and stories aren't real! LOL! I enjoy speaking as much as I enjoy writing.

Who among your contemporaries do you admire?

I really admire Eric Dickey because he takes the craft of writing to a new level with every book he writes. I read his books to be entertained, but I also read his books to learn. No one teaches me and inspires me with their words the way Eric does. I also admire Kimberla Lawson Roby because she connects better with her readers than any writer I know. She's balanced her career fabulously—the right amount of creativity with business. Truly left brain/right brain, and because of that she has built an outstanding career. Her skills at writing and business puts the MBA I earned from a top twenty school to shame!

Do you have a favorite of your own books?

Nope! Okay, well, maybe *Joy* . . .

You write YA fiction and adult fiction. Do you approach the two types of writing differently? Do you enjoy one more than the other?

Yes, I approach the writing differently. I write all of my teen books from a first-person point of view. That allows me to get into the head of teenagers, to actually become the teenager. My adult books have all been written in third person—at least until this point. And I don't enjoy writing one more than the other—not at all. Writing for teens and writing for adults allows me the opportunity to satisfy my desire to write for everyone. There are other genres I'd love to write in—I'd love to write a nonfiction book about surviving my husband's death, and even a children's book, but I'm not able to do that yet because of contractual obligations. Hopefully one day I will be able to write all the books inside of me.

What is the single most important thing you hope that readers take from *Sins of the Mother*?

Wow! You know, I never sit down and say, What is the message I want people to take away? I truly just write the story and then the message shows up. And what's great is that the message is different for each reader. I guess what I want readers to get from all of my novels is that in every situation, God will carry you through.

Enhance Your Book Club

1. Visit the National Center for Missing & Exploited Children at www.missingkids.com. Organize a volunteer outing at a call center, or collect funds for a donation to the center. The Web site includes information on how to donate.

2. Check out Murray's other Jasmine novels, *Lady Jasmine, Too Little, Too Late,* and *A Sin and a Shame.* If you love Murray's work, pick up books by her contemporaries ReShonda Tate Billingsley and Kimberla Lawson Roby.

3. Visit the author's Web site at www.victoriachristopher-murray.com. The site contains fascinating biographical information on Murray and includes dates of her upcoming tours and speaking engagements.

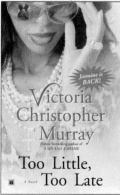
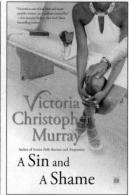
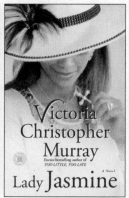
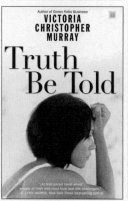
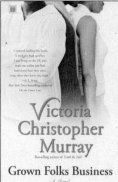
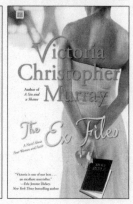